A Child of the Blood

A Blood Dancers Novel

Jo Reed

A Wild Wolf Publication

Published by Wild Wolf Publishing in 2010

Copyright © 2010 Jo Reed

First print

ISBN: 978-1-907954-00-9

www.wildwolfpublishing.com

Other Novels in the Blood Dancers Series

The Tyranny of the Blood

Malim's Legacy (coming soon)

Acknowledgements

My heartfelt thanks go to my test readers and editors, and especially to the long suffering Jill and Kat, to whom I owe consignments of red pens. Many thanks also to my cover artist, Ian Harrison, for all his patient hard work.

For Beth and Ru

The Line of Rendail

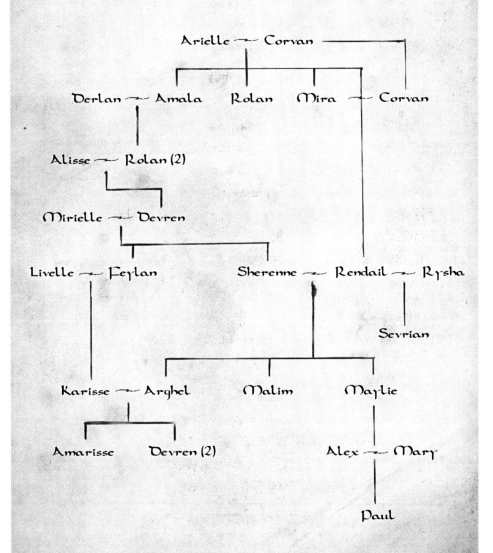

INTRODUCTION

When Corvan, the Dancer, isolated his family in the wilderness of the Scottish Highlands, his overriding ambition was to conquer the barrier of time. A chance mutation had, in the distant past, given the Dancers long lives, physical and mental abilities far superior to those of normal humans. He believed this could be manipulated. Through careful breeding to purify the blood, Corvan reasoned, the gifts of longevity and superhuman power would be enhanced.

But Corvan was insane, and his obsessive pursuit of his goal over the centuries led to madness and deformity among those born into the Family. Isolated from the outside world, Corvan's tyranny stripped the Family of its humanity. The blood was all that mattered, all actions governed by the Rule, the set of complex rituals by which each member lived, mated and died. The unfit were slaughtered, the women seen only as breeding stock. For those who survived, the blood bestowed unheard of power, but it was a power that was rapidly becoming uncontrollable.

At last, Corvan caught a glimpse of his dream. One of his daughters, Amala, broke the barrier and used her mind to leap forward into the future. But she escaped the Family and fled to the far south where she was given sanctuary by Derlan, a Dancer of another tribe. The Family pursued her, but Derlan kept her hidden and they had a son. So, the precious blood of the Family mingled with that of Derlan's tribe, and as the years passed Derlan's descendants became as powerful as Corvan's people.

On Corvan's death, he was succeeded by his youngest son, Rendail. At first, Rendail shared his father's ambition. The quest for knowledge of the future consumed the whole Family, believing it contained the key to control of the present. When Derlan's line produced Sherenne, a female of Amala's blood, she was, to the Family, beyond price, and so Rendail stole her from her people and claimed her as his own. But he had growing doubts. He understood that the elusive gift might not make the Family unassailable, but rather destroy them, given the seed of Corvan's madness running through the blood.

Sherenne grew to adulthood, and Rendail committed the greatest crime possible against the Rule – he fell in love with her. He confided his fears to her, and together they set out to alter, as much as they could, the dangerous path that Corvan had laid out for the Family. They could do little but contain the threat, through careful, secret manipulation of the blood. But disaster struck with their first son, Malim. Malim developed the gift all had been waiting for, but which Rendail dreaded. He could cross the Great Emptiness into the future. Malim was also dangerously insane.

Unable to kill his son without setting in motion a bloody conflict within the Family, Rendail did the only thing possible. He sired a second son, Arghel, a child who could grow to challenge and defeat his brother. To protect Arghel, Rendail forced him away, pretending hatred and contempt for his young son so that Malim would not perceive the threat. At Sherenne's urging, Arghel fled, as Amala had done, to his mother's people. Safe from Malim's corrosive jealousy, Arghel grew to hate his father and brother and all they stood for – just as Rendail planned. What happened next is the subject of this book.

CHAPTER 1

Arvan started down the narrow stone spiral, breathing slow, moving on the balls of his feet. He wasn't supposed to be there, but he couldn't resist one final check. With him he had a comb, a flask of water and a small vial of fragrant nut oil. As he neared the foot of the staircase the glow from the torches in the great chamber beyond bathed the steps red-gold. He made the last turn to the archway and froze.

The naked body of a man was laid out on a granite slab in the centre of the chamber as though for burial, arms crossed over the chest, eyes closed. The long blonde hair was combed back, away from the pale face, and Arvan could just see the rise and fall of the fingertips with each shallow breath.

It was not the corpse-like form that frightened him. The tall, dark figure of the head of the Family, Lord Rendail, stood with his back to the stairway, gazing down at the slab. Arvan knew that Rendail must be aware of his presence, yet the latter made no sign. Caught between fear and fascination, he watched as Rendail drew a long, curved dagger and held it up, tested its sharpness with his thumb. A thin stream of blood, glittering in the torchlight, welled from the cut and dripped onto the furs.

At the sight of it Arvan took in a breath. Rendail didn't turn round, but sheathed the knife and beckoned.

"It's all right, Arvan. Come here."

Arvan did as he was told, but stopped a few feet behind his Lord. He sensed that he was in no immediate danger of chastisement for his intrusion. It was never wise, however, to take Rendail's mood for granted. He waited until an impatient gesture brought him forward and the two were standing side by side.

"How long this time?" Rendail's voice was soft as a breath.

"Over a year," Arvan replied, risking a glance sideways. Rendail was staring at the body, blood still dripping from his hand. "Since the frosts began, the winter before last. Don't you remember, Lord?"

"Yes, I remember. It is four hundred and twelve days. And on each of those days, you have bathed him, combed his hair, rubbed oil into his skin. Do you think Malim knows that, Arvan? Do you think, when he wakes in some far future, his first thought is for his faithful friend and servant, who keeps his body warm and waits for his return – who risks my anger so easily for his sake?"

Rendail turned, then, and looked him in the eye. Arvan flushed, but didn't look away.

"I do my duty to the blood, Lord. That is all."

"It is not all." Rendail's tone hardened. "The more you come here, the greater the risk that you are followed. You know of this place because my son could not keep it from you. I know Malim well enough to understand that he needs you with him, even when he is not aware of it. Therefore I allow it. But if you were careless – if Thalis should discover the maze ..."

"Lord Thalis knows nothing," Arvan broke in. "I am always careful, Lord, I swear it."

Rendail nodded. "I know. But I should still have you flogged." He sighed. "Once every seven days, I will call you to attend me. Then, you may come to him, when I know it is safe. If I find you here at any other time ..."

Arvan bowed, taking in the meaningful look. "Thank you, Lord. You honour me."

"I'm sure I do," Rendail replied. "And in the meantime, you can be assured, my son has my attention always."

Arvan couldn't help but let his eyes stray to the knife. Rendail gave a grim smile. "Yes, I have thought of it, often. When he was no more than eight days old I put my knife to his throat. I couldn't do it then and, to my shame, I can't do it now. We both know he is a monster, but much as I wish to, I cannot harm him. He has seen enough of the future to know that – and enough to know where the real threat lies. Even so, he denies it to himself. He has not the wit to see the danger. Tell me, Arvan, what do you think he is doing in that far time?"

Arvan shook his head. "I don't know, Lord. When he returns he never speaks of it."

"It's just as well. If you knew, perhaps you would not be so eager to tend him with such love. He goes there because it is the one place I cannot follow. There is no one to restrain him, and so he does precisely as he wishes. For the moment."

Rendail turned to leave and, on an impulse, Arvan reached out and touched his arm. He felt the other stiffen at the discourtesy and stepped back.

"Forgive me, Lord – your hand …"

Rendail looked down, and raised an eyebrow as if only now aware of the neat cut along the ball of his thumb, which was still oozing blood. He smiled.

"You are right, Arvan. It looks most untidy. Perhaps you would be kind enough to see to it before I leave."

"Of course, Lord." Arvan ran a finger lightly over the cut, the torn edges of the skin closing at his touch, then damped a cloth and cleaned away the blood. Rendail gave a curt nod and strode to the foot of the stairway. There he paused and said, over his shoulder, "It will not be long, I think, before Malim returns. When he does, pacify him, but if he gives a command, do nothing until you have spoken to me." Arvan had no time to reply before his lord ducked under the arch and disappeared.

* * *

The road snaked round the foot of another granite outcrop, and David tightened his grip on a wheel already slick with sweat. The heater in his old Nissan juddered, then cut out, and he almost veered off the road in an attempt to wipe the windscreen clear. He cursed as he wound down the window and was slapped by an inrush of freezing air. The clock on the dash showed one-thirty a.m. The road was deserted, save for the tail lights of Malim's Range Rover up ahead. He accelerated slightly, not wanting to lose the other car when it turned off the road. It wasn't far now and he felt his numbed hands tremble, bile rise in his throat.

15

David wasn't a coward. Somewhere, beneath the roiling mass of terror that made his limbs quake and his bowels churn, he knew that. He'd been a lot of things in his youth, but coward wasn't one of them. He shook his head, trying to force away the memories.

* * *

As soon as David was old enough to take a swing at the old man, he knocked the bastard flat with the same brass topped cane that had given him more scars than he could count. Then he walked out, and never went back. He remembered that year, out on the streets of Edinburgh. It was cold and wet most of the time. He learned to hide, from the law and the pimps, learned to hover by the ATMs and lift credit cards. He lived well enough for a twelve year old with no home.

One night he took a wallet from a guy coming out of a jazz club – a rich looking guy with long dark hair and a cashmere coat. He did his usual thing, tripped in front of the mark and picked the pocket on the way up. But the man's hand closed over his wrist and he found himself back against the wall with nowhere to run.

"What's your name?" The man was smiling, as if it was a joke.

"Piss off – Like I'd tell you!"

"Fair enough." The man had the wallet back in his pocket and shrugged, still smiling.

"I'm Alex. Are you hungry?" He held out a hand, and that meant only one thing. Still, there was something about the smile, the eyes.

"I don't go nowhere with shirt lifters. Don't do that stuff."

"Just as well I'm not a shirt lifter, then. There's a café just over there. Lots of lights, lots of people. Are you interested or not?"

In that one night, David's life changed. He still wasn't sure how or why, whether he had picked Alex MacIntyre, or Alex had picked him. There were other people in Alex's house – a

16

rambling place north of Ullapool – old, young, passing through, staying put. There were a couple of boys around his age, one training to be a gardener, another washing and polishing cars. There was a teacher, too, making them learn to read, write and all the rest. It was like Alex didn't trust them to go to school. He was right about that.

The first couple of years were tough. He ran away once, but there was nowhere to go except the street, or a children's home. So he went back, and got a whale of a thrashing, not for running away, but for stuffing his pockets on the way out. Then Alex gave him a grand in cash, and said, "Take it and go, or open a bank account and stay. Either way, it's yours."

He stayed – first, because there was no reason to go – later, because he found reasons to stay. Alex was one, but there were more. The old lady, Mary, who lived in the kitchen, had made him toast and got him to talk. She'd rocked him to sleep and wiped his nose more than once, and not told anyone that he'd howled like a baby at the age of thirteen. And then there was Paul, Mary's son, a good deal older than him, who went round the council estates in the cities, teaching kids to dance. David tried too, and liked it, so after the college thing was done he stuck around, first helping out, then getting paid, and doing odd stuff for Alex now and then.

One time he was asked to post a big envelope full of cash through the door of a flat in Aberdeen. On another, he was sent potholing, told to take pictures of a rock formation way underground. Several times, Alex asked him to follow people. It was something he was good at. He was someone who didn't stand out – average height, average build, an average twenty-three year old dark haired native Scot; the sort who can walk into a pub, sit all night and never be noticed.

This time, though, something was different. When he walked into the library Alex was tense, leaning back in his chair with a hand on his brow, as if he'd been arguing with Paul, who was perched on the edge of the big oak desk. When Alex saw David he sat up straight. Paul patted David's shoulder as he left, but didn't smile. David wondered what he'd done wrong until Alex said there was a job for him, and then he was relieved.

"Sure, Alex. Anything – you know that."

Alex gave him a brand new digital Nikon and showed him an ink sketch that had been shaded in with colour here and there. The sketch made David do a double take.

"I know," Alex said, without smiling. "He looks like Paul, but that's as far as it goes." There was an address, too, a street in Inverness. "Follow him, David, see where he goes. Take photos if you can, but keep your distance. Stay in crowded places and for God's sake don't let him see you. If you think it's too dangerous, back off. Call me at once, understand? Don't take risks. I don't want to be impressed – I want you alive. Got it?"

"Sure, Alex. No problem. I'll see you in a month, right? Who is he anyway?"

He'd never seen Alex so serious. "I'd rather you didn't know his name. You don't want to know him, and you'd better pray he doesn't get to know you. Listen to me, David. This man isn't like other men. He makes your idea of dangerous look like a day at the fairground. He can sense people, and if he senses you, the first you'll know is when it's too late to run. He'll be inside your head, and believe me, you don't want that to happen. You're good, David, but even so – trust me on this. Don't try to be clever."

* * *

The tail lights of the Range Rover winked out as it turned off the road, headed to towards the small jetty on the other side of the crag. As David drew close to the track, he wondered what would happen if he didn't follow – if he just hammered it, got the hell out of there, caught the bastard off balance. His foot twitched on the accelerator, and for one long, glorious second he remembered what it had been like to be free. "Fuck you!"

Hard on the words came the pain – a gut wrenching lance searing through his right arm. His foot jerked and the car swerved. He forced back vomit and made himself look. His right

18

index finger was already starting to swell, the break clean, between knuckle and joint, snapped like a twig.

"Malim, you bastard!" He forced the words through clenched teeth. He had to work the gears and steering wheel with his left hand, his right hunched up to his chest, useless, oozing agony at every jolt over the rough ground. As he turned the car onto the track a soft laugh echoed in his head, and Alex's voice beneath it.

Believe me, you don't want that to happen.

The girl had been dragged out of the Range Rover. She was still alive – as David turned off the engine he heard her mewling through the open window of the Nissan. She had long since stopped struggling, had no strength left to scream. She was on her back now, spread-eagled on a rock, the flesh of her thighs white in the beam of the headlights. Malim stretched, let out a long grunt of satisfaction as his eyes roamed over her broken body. A sharp sleet shower had sent the air plummeting to near freezing. The girl's teeth were clacking, monstrously loud it seemed to David, shredding his already tattered nerves.

Malim seemed oblivious to the cold. His skin glistened, the moisture rising into steam. He shook himself like a dog, spattering the girl's body, hot sweat mingling with the blood and other, less savoury fluids dripping from her face, running down between her legs.

David hunched in his seat, his good hand still gripping the steering wheel, and prayed that he would be allowed to stay there. He knew it was a vain hope. Nevertheless, as he heard Malim's measured tread across the shingled turf, he shrank down further, screwed his eyes tight shut. The door was wrenched open, and before he had a chance to look up he was dragged out and flung onto his knees in front of the car. He put out his hands instinctively, screamed as his right hand landed flat on the stones, tried, unsuccessfully, to keep hold of the contents of his stomach. At least he'd been spared up to now. Most of Malim's pleasure had been taken in Inverness, where he'd been instructed to wait outside.

He kept himself still, tried to slow his ragged breathing. The girl gave an inhuman gurgle. He saw Malim's fist rise and fall, heard the crunch of knuckle against teeth, then of skull against stone. The body emptied its lungs in a long, bubbling hiss and went limp.

Malim stretched and strolled over to the Range Rover, where he towelled himself down and retrieved his neatly folded clothes. David huddled into his overcoat, clutching his injured hand to his chest. Malim dressed slowly, checking the creases in his trousers, twisting the diamond stud cufflinks to ensure the stones would catch the light. Then he turned to David, raised his arm and crooked a finger, accompanying the gesture with a perfect predator's smile. David didn't move. Malim turned away, and at the same time David felt his throat constrict, an iron band that hauled him, choking, to his feet, dragged him, stumbling, to the crumpled abomination lying on the rock.

"Please …" David's head was forced down, and his stomach heaved. He remembered the girl's face as he delivered her to Malim's door in Inverness. She hadn't been good looking to start with. Now, she was barely recognisable as human. He heard a familiar rhythmic soughing as Malim brushed out his hair in front of one of the wing mirrors. The fastidious grooming that followed was always the most chilling thing of all. David would have closed his eyes if he had been able. He shuddered, and muttered, "Oh, God."

The brushing stopped. Footsteps followed and a low, contemptuous laugh, close enough to move the air past his left ear. An arm fell heavily across his shoulders and a finger caressed his cheek. He was paralysed, his muscles rigid, eyes locked on the mangled corpse in front of him.

"You and your Gods!" Malim's voice was no more than a mocking whisper. "How many times must I tell you? There is only one God here. Tell me, David, who is God?"

One hand crept down towards his crotch. The other remained firmly on his shoulder.

"You are!" David's words came out in an anguished rush as the fingers between his legs grabbed and twisted. The pressure

20

lessened, and he felt the fingers creep up a little way, stroking, teasing, threatening. The pain of his broken finger was almost unendurable and his bladder was close to giving way.

"We have something to discuss, you and I." Malim's voice was satin in his ear. David said nothing, the sweat starting to freeze on his face. "You're pathetic. You can't even bring me a decent girl. Three times and she's broken! One of our women would have lasted for days. Next time, get me one worth having. Or would *you* like to be my whore, David?"

David felt the ripple of hard muscle even through the thickness of his coat.

"Fuck you," Malim whispered. "Isn't that what you said? You think you can run from me? Oh, I'll fuck you. I guarantee it." David was suddenly released, and fell back to his knees. As he hit the ground he felt warm dampness spreading, trickling down his leg, and gave a sob of mingled terror, pain and shame. Malim laughed. "But not now. Now, I want you to get rid of that. Then go and do whatever you pathetic creatures do. I'll find you – when it's time. Oh – before I go – give me your hand. Don't want you to drop her, do we?"

Before David had a chance to respond, he felt his hand grabbed tight and the severed bone grate as the two ends came together, the fierce burn as they melded back into one. He almost fainted.

David waited until the sound of the Range Rover was lost on the other side of the towering crag before crawling back to the Nissan. It was pitch dark and completely silent. The nearest croft was more than ten miles away on the other side of the loch. That was why it was Malim's favourite place. Resigned, he stripped and flicked the headlights back on. When he got back to the rock he vomited again, then hoisted what was left of the girl onto his shoulder and struggled to the water's edge. He dumped his burden unceremoniously into the small boat Malim kept there for the purpose, and rowed out far enough to pitch it safely over the side. That done, he set about hauling buckets of water to wash off the surface of the rock.

Once back in the driver's seat he wrapped himself in a blanket, turned the engine on and reached down between the seats. His hands were still trembling as he unscrewed the cap and took a generous slug of Jack Daniels. If he'd had any reserves left, he would have driven – anywhere, just as far away as he could get. He didn't. All he had was the bottle, and he wanted to get drunk. When he was through half of it he reached across and grabbed the camera that had been left on the passenger seat. His first instinct was to smash it, hurl it into the loch. But he couldn't.

He felt sick again, and took another swallow. Alex had trusted him – still trusted him. Weeping quietly, he flicked the switch on the expensive Nikon and stared at the photos he had taken three weeks ago. The first dozen shots were all rear or profile views, taken in the crowded streets of Inverness. It wasn't as if his target made any attempt to make himself inconspicuous. The man was over six feet tall, fit and broad shouldered, lightly tanned, with thick blonde hair tied in a pony tail. He dressed expensively, his height emphasised by the cut of his silk suits. Wherever he went he attracted stares from passers by. One more ogler in the crowd made no difference. David paused to take another drink before scrolling to the next shot – the one that had destroyed him. He squeezed his eyes shut as the memory overtook him.

* * *

The rail trip from Inverness to Nairn had been a short one – less than half an hour. In the morning, the train was crowded, easy enough to squeeze unnoticed into a corner at the other end of the carriage from his quarry. It was a smallish place, and the man spent the whole day wandering, along the beaches, in and out of the tourist shops, before getting back onto the train to make the return journey. Without thinking, David did the same. That was his mistake. He was so busy imagining how pleased Alex would be with the pictures that he forgot the warning. Keep your distance. Stay in crowded places. Don't let him see you.

The carriage was empty. Throughout the twenty minute ride he sat a few seats away, his back to the other man, staring determinedly out of the window. He wasn't worried. He was only another passenger, after all. People caught trains – even empty ones. His quarry alighted at Inverness, striding purposefully out of the station and into the deserted car park. David followed, leaving some two hundred yards between them. There was still enough light to take a good shot without a flash, and all the while he was thinking how pleased Alex would be to get a picture, not only of the man, but of his car, a fancy red Jaguar. The man hadn't looked back and was about to open the car door. David lined up the shot just in time to see the subject turn and look straight at him, a chilling smile forming on the face in the centre of the frame.

David knew it was over before he turned to run. He tried to lower the camera but his arms wouldn't move. As if someone had grabbed hold of his hand, his finger slowly lowered onto the trigger. He heard the click, was still looking through the lens when he heard footsteps, felt a hand take him firmly by the back of the neck and push him towards the car. That's when he tried to run. But all that happened was that his feet moved in the opposite direction, his captor walking casually behind him, laughing quietly.

The drive was a short one, during which neither man spoke. David clutched the camera, kept his eyes on the road, waiting for an opportunity to jump – a traffic light perhaps, or a pedestrian crossing. It was dark now, but there were plenty of people about, and he was quick enough to lose himself in the side streets. It never happened. The driver seemed to know the town well enough to take the back roads and after fifteen minutes or so the car drew up in front of a garage behind a fairly big house in a well off part of town.

As soon as the car stopped David lunged for the door. At least, that was his intention. When his limbs stayed motionless, he heard a low chuckle beside him. That's when he felt the first real tug of fear. The man pressed a button, the garage door opened and the chance was gone – if there had ever been one. Then, David heard him speak – smooth, mocking, patronising.

"Get out."

David reached for the car door, found he was able to move, and did as he as told. He went in front, up the stairs, into a large room furnished with antique style leather sofas, polished boards and Persian silk rugs. The door closed behind him and he heard a key turning in the lock. It wasn't until the man came up behind him, reached round and took the camera, that David realised he'd still been holding it. The atmosphere in the room was thick, oppressive. David felt his mouth go dry. When he spoke his voice sounded harsh; a kind of hoarse croak.

"Who are you?"

The man didn't answer, but sat comfortably on one of the sofas and started to flick through the shots on the camera. After a while he looked up and said, "Why are you taking pictures of me?"

David decided to try bravado, knowing that it probably wasn't the best move, but he couldn't think of anything else.

"You're a good looking bloke. Maybe I just liked the look of you."

The other responded with a raised eyebrow, before placing the camera carefully on a small occasional table and standing up.

"You liked the look of me? Is that so?" Slowly, purposefully, he took off his jacket and laid it neatly across the back of the sofa. Without taking his eyes off David he unfastened the gold, diamond studded cufflinks and put them on the table beside the camera. As he shrugged off his shirt he took a pace forward and drew in a deep breath, rolling his shoulders, muscles rippling like a hunting cat. The eyes were black, burning hot, a look that David knew from those days before the streets, magnified a hundred times. He tried to take a step back but was frozen, his knees trembling, seven years old and the front door closing, the shadow on the stairs.

"You liked the look of me?" The man was close up now, sliding off David's overcoat, the strong fingers underneath his shirt, tongue flicking, probing, leaving wet trails across his throat. *He gets inside your head.* "Who sent you, David?"

There was a sensation, strange against his forehead, a vagueness. *How do you know my name?*

"No one," David said aloud. No one sent him. In his mind he believed it. Then pain, as if a hand had reached inside his skull and scooped his brain out. When the pain stopped, David was on the floor, naked, curled, foetus like, on the silk rug.

"No one sent you. I believe you." The man nodded. "My name is Malim. I'm delighted to meet you, David."

He held out a hand and David shrank away. "Don't touch me!"

Malim threw back his head and laughed. "Don't touch you?" The laughter was suddenly gone. "Believe me, David. That's the least of your worries. I'm inside you. I don't have to touch you."

Malim stepped back, padded over to another table and poured himself whisky from a crystal decanter. As he raised his glass a wave of agony shot through both David's ankles. David heard himself screaming, a surreal sound that bounced off the walls of the genteel parlour. Through misted vision he saw Malim crouch in front of him.

"You see, David? I can do anything I like to you. It doesn't matter how far you go, what you do – you're mine. From this moment. Always." Malim stopped, musing, then grinned. When he spoke again his manner was businesslike. "Tomorrow, I think you can find me a girl – a boy, if you can't find a decent one. But for now ..." The grin grew wider. "Well, it's not as if you can go anywhere, is it?" Malim gestured towards David's useless legs. "So we might as well enjoy ourselves. Just like old times for you, yes? Not everyone gets to relive their childhood. And I suppose it's only fair to show you what will happen if you don't do exactly as I tell you. Don't you think?"

Later, through a haze of pain and terror, David saw Malim pick up the camera, heard the sound of soft laughter in his head.

That was three weeks ago. Every time he heard that laugh now, it turned his insides to mush. He took a last swallow before moving on to the next shots. There were six. In all of them, he was screaming. He tentatively pressed the 'delete' button on the first of the final six. It worked. One by one, he brought up the rest and did the same thing. Then he crawled onto the back seat, curled up under the blanket and tried to put the future out of his mind.

CHAPTER 2

By ten in the morning the wind had dropped, the snow petering out to occasional flurries as the clouds began to break. Malim strolled across the fields towards a nearby plantation of Scots pine. His light footfalls left shallow indentations in the snow, the quiet crunching of his fur lined boots echoing dully across the silent landscape. He was smiling.

He stopped to admire the view of the woodland and the high purple crags beyond, almost invisible in the grey, snow laden air. Looking down, he saw that his hands were streaked with dried blood and he licked it off, eyes half closed, savouring the taste. "David," he whispered, and heaved a deep sigh of satisfaction, then continued on to the cover of the trees.

The horse, a powerful, shaggy coated Clydesdale, stamped as he approached, pulling at its tether. The roof of its temporary shelter had held, despite the weight of snow, and Malim allowed himself another smile as he ducked beneath the tightly woven branches. The old skills, he thought, were still useful, now and then.

The horse whickered at his approach and thudded a hind hoof into the nearest tree trunk, dislodging a compacted lump of snow onto its master's head. Malim swore under his breath. Animals hated him, probably more than people did. He yanked viciously at the tether and pulled the reluctant beast into the open. It showed the whites of its eyes as he mounted, to which he responded by using his gift to send a spiteful jolt across its withers. He gave it a sharp jab with his heels for good measure and it trembled, but nevertheless started forward at a good pace across the deserted countryside, heading north.

It was getting on towards midnight when Malim reached his destination at the foot of a bare crag that had remained, miraculously, in the lee of the recent storm. He dismounted and dismissed the exhausted horse with a kick. Despite its fatigue, the

27

animal set off at a brisk trot across the barren country and was soon lost in the darkness, the sound of its hooves muffled by the fallen snow.

The cold was becoming uncomfortable, but Malim still hesitated before lowering himself into a narrow opening at the base of the crag. His enjoyment of pain was firmly restricted to watching the effect it had on others. The knowledge that he was about to experience it himself – a lot of it – made his legs weak, and he stumbled as he began to descend the ancient stone stairway that wound down and away from the crag.

Negotiating the worn, in places perilous spiral took a little under an hour and much cursing before he finally emerged into a large chamber, the walls of which were broken by a number of arched exits. In the centre stood a large stone table surrounded by thick dust. Its surface, however, was polished clean, the granite sparkling in the beam of his Maglite. He stopped again, torn between terror and desire. His father had lectured him often on the subject of ambition and sacrifice. He had never grasped the connection. His only thought was that it wasn't fair.

Resigned, he pulled himself up onto the table and lay flat, whimpering with fear. To take his mind off it he tried to immerse himself in the pleasure that the previous night had brought him, together with visions of the reason why he was going back. The woman was more than a child by now. His father could no longer refuse him – it was his right. He would take her, and she would suffer, just as he was about to suffer. She would bear his heir, and Malim would prove himself a worthy successor. It would all be worth it in the end. He opened his mind to the Great Emptiness – the blackness, the desolation that stretched beyond the boundaries of time. He felt the wave of darkness burn him, tearing flesh from crumbling bone, and he screamed.

* * *

Arvan felt the shift, even from the fields beyond the boundary of the settlement. A second later his mind received the summons, an incoherent cry, but one he understood only too well. He let out a single, shrill whistle, and the sea eagle left off its task and swooped down, coming to rest on his outstretched arm. He let his gift soothe the bird and fed it a sliver of raw meat from a pouch at his belt, then turned, ran up the slope and through the south gate, the bird still clinging to his wrist. On the way, he stopped briefly at his own house, grabbed a small packet of brittle honeyed nuts, then raced along the pavement and into Lord Rendail's house, breathing hard and trying to adopt an attitude of calm.

Arvan arrived in the underground chamber to find Malim writhing on the floor, sobbing and cursing by turns. Despite being used to such spectacles, Arvan flushed and averted his gaze, announcing his presence with a tentative cough. The bird, disturbed by the noise, shrieked and flew up to a ledge near the chamber roof, ruffling its feathers.

"Arvan! Arvan, where are you? I can't see! Come here, useless son of a rat! I'll take your eyes out, then you'll know what it's like, I swear. Where are you?"

Arvan knelt with a sigh and grasped hold of his master's wriggling shoulder.

"Here, Lord. I'm here." He shook one of the nuts out of the bag and pressed it to Malim's lips. The latter bit and swallowed hard, then sat up and opened his eyes.

"It hurts!" he whispered, collapsing against his servant, breathing heavily and sniffing.

"I know, Lord." Arvan shifted to a more comfortable position, and stroked the sweat soaked brow. "I know. It won't last long, Lord. Here – I have a whole bag full this time. You can have them all. That's better," he said, as Malim reached out to grab the bag and stuffed a handful of the sweet nuts into his mouth. "You see? Almost gone now – yes?"

Malim nodded and finished off the nuts, his head resting on Arvan's shoulder. By the time he got to the bottom of the bag his breathing had almost returned to normal.

"It's not fair," he protested, throwing the empty bag on the floor. "Why does it have to hurt so much?"

Arvan shrugged diplomatically. "I don't know, Lord."

"It's her fault. I wouldn't have to come back here if it wasn't for her. Just wait 'til she has to do it. When I make her go across the divide, then she'll know …"

Malim shook himself and stood up, revived by the thought. Arvan followed suit, taking a respectful pace backwards and making his expression as bland as possible. He held up an arm and the bird responded at once, settling itself back on his wrist, and together they followed their lord as he swept imperiously through an archway and down one of the underground corridors, heading for his own rooms.

An hour later, Malim emerged from his bath. Arvan waited patiently with warmed, scented oils and a tray of bread and wine. Malim submitted himself to a full massage, sipping his wine and nibbling as Arvan's practiced fingers kneaded the tension from his shoulders.

"Well?" he asked, pushing away the tray and lowering his head to allow his neck to be rubbed.

Arvan maintained the rhythm as he answered, "Reports say that her gift is strong for one of her age, Lord. Whether it is strong enough, it's hard to tell. She is still young, and her family keeps her close. Our watchers rarely see her alone."

Malim said nothing until Arvan had finished with his scalp and moved on to his feet, then went on, "And does she have a name yet, the future mother of my children? Or do they still call her 'It', as they did the last time I asked?"

Arvan risked a quiet laugh. "She is eighteen years old now, Lord. Of course she has a name. It is Karisse."

"Eighteen?" Malim brushed his servant off and sat up. "Eighteen? Has it been that long?" He pouted and cast around for a blanket to wrap himself in, which Arvan deftly provided. "That's ridiculous. I wanted her younger, Arvan. Fourteen would have been good. Eighteen is practically ancient – a woman can get very ugly after that. She won't be any fun if she's ugly!"

"But eighteen is still very young, my Lord." Arvan poured the last of the wine and held out the cup. "And they say that she is beautiful. Her hair is black, and straight, no curls at all, and I am told she has the most magnificent green eyes. Besides, as women get older they become more stubborn, it is said. She will be a challenge for you, and you will like that much better. And," he carried on, seeing the danger of a tantrum receding from his master's eyes, "your brother still intends to have her. He wouldn't do that if she was ugly."

For a moment he wondered whether this last statement might have been a mistake, as Malim's eyes sparked with fury.

"My brother? Arghel will have her over my dead body!" Suddenly he started to laugh. "Old or not, ugly or not, she is mine, and if he tries to get in my way it will be my pleasure to bury him, one little piece at a time!" He drained the cup and slammed it onto the low table. "Arvan, she must be tested. I must know how strong she is, and how well defended. You will go and see her and make sure she is ready for me."

"Me, Lord?"

"That's what I said, isn't it? You will go at dawn tomorrow, and take your bird with you. Don't come back until you have judged the strength of her gift. There's no point in my taking her if she can't survive the crossing, and if she is too weak we will simply kill her. At least then my brother will be disappointed as well."

Arvan felt apprehension settle into a tight knot in his stomach. "But, Lord – if I go, I may be away for a season. It's a long time …"

"For me to be left alone?" Malim sneered. "What's the matter? You think I can't manage by myself? That I'll be lost without you?"

Won't you? Arvan thought, but wisely kept his mouth shut and his eyes respectfully lowered.

"You have no need to fear," Malim ended, with a sweet smile. "I will be with you. My mind will be with yours every moment of the day. What you see, I will see. What you think, I will hear. We will never be parted, you and I. Now, does that make you feel better?"

"Of course, Lord," Arvan replied, and with a deep bow made his exit, rolling his eyes in exasperation as he hurried to his own rooms to start to pack.

31

Two hours later, Arvan sat in Rendail's private reception room waiting for the head of the Family to reach a decision. Although it made him uncomfortable, he was secretly grateful to share the responsibility for the consequences of his master's decisions. It had always been so – since they were children, and it had become plain that Malim would never gain control over his baser instincts. The two had grown up together, and in the early years Malim had relied on him completely – he still did, perhaps more now than in the beginning. When Malim raged, Arvan fed him honey, distracted him with soothing words, wiped his tears and rocked him to sleep. The only other who could exercise any control over the heir was Rendail himself, who did so, for the most part, by sheer brute strength when all else failed.

Rendail finally looked up and nodded. "At least my son seems to have shown some sense this time," he remarked, taking a wine jug and pouring generous measures for both of them. "You must go. If I refuse it he will want to go himself, and that would be a disaster. He has the right to claim her and to deny him would lead to unrest among his followers. I am not ready to confront them, at least not yet. To open the way to the future is the central tenet of the Rule, and I can't openly go against it. The girl's blood is valuable – but too valuable for Malim. You will go, Arvan, and satisfy his curiosity. But that is all."

Arvan drained his cup, got up and bowed. "As you wish, Lord." He made to leave, but Rendail held up a hand.

"Wait. Arghel is near her, always. It will be dangerous for you if he senses your presence – which he will, have no doubt about that. If he knows his brother has sent you, you may find yourself breathing your last before you have even been introduced. Be very careful."

"He is that strong, Lord?"

"Oh, yes. He is my son, perhaps more so than Malim. Whatever rumours of weakness you have heard, you would do well to disregard them. If he does give you time to talk, I would not be surprised to learn of your change of allegiance, and of your refusal to return here. Do you understand, Arvan?"

"My Lord?" Arvan's stomach lurched as the implications of Rendail's words hit home and the world as he understood it suddenly dissolved into chaos. It was well known that Arghel, Rendail's younger son, had been judged tainted, inferior, from birth. He had fled the settlement just days after his mother's death and no one, his father in particular, seemed in the least concerned at the loss. Malim, of course, had been delighted at his brother's escape, which left him indisputable heir to the leadership of the Family. Arvan looked up to see Rendail smiling at his puzzlement.

"I think we understand each other. And before you ask, Malim will be quite safe here with me. Now go, and speak to no one as you leave, not even your father. And take care, Arvan. You have served us both well. I hope to hear, in time, that you are still alive."

CHAPTER 3

It was close to dawn when David swung into the drive of the old mansion house. He turned the engine off and coasted the final stretch down to the garage block, hoping no one would hear the noise of tyres on gravel. Glancing up, he saw the glow of a reading lamp from Alex's upstairs sitting room and swore under his breath. He couldn't face the questions – not yet. He needed to gather his thoughts, think what he was going to say.

It was a week since his last sight of Malim. He remembered his tormentor's parting words … "I have to go, and so I have come to say goodbye. You will miss me, I know you will, but don't worry, David, I won't leave you alone for long. I thought, tonight, we would do something special – something for you to remember until I return …"

At some point, David had fainted. When he came to, Malim was gone. For six days he huddled in a hotel room, mostly locked in the bathroom, as if that might keep him safe. But Malim didn't come back and at last he found the courage to call Alex, tell him he was coming home.

He tried to close the car door quietly and crept round the back of the house, to the veranda that led to the kitchen. The kitchen door was always open. Old Mary was asleep in the big rocking chair by the range, head back, snoring lightly, a book still open on her lap. David took off his shoes and tiptoed past. He made it to the door out into the hall, but no further.

"There's coffee on the stove, and bacon pie if you're hungry. I saved it, just in case."

He fixed a smile in place before he turned round.

"Doesn't anyone ever get past you, Mary?"

"Never. You should know that by now. Come and sit down. You look famished."

She was on her feet, busying herself at the range, pulling a plate from the rack, pouring him coffee, setting a place at the big oak table. He started to panic.

"It's all right, Mary, really – I'm not hungry."

"Yes, you are."

The tone of her voice told him there was no escape without an argument. He sat, eyes down, and pushed the food around his plate, vainly hoping she would leave him be. He didn't hear Alex come in. It was only when the shadow passed across his vision as Alex drew up a chair that he jumped, and would have leapt up from the table if Mary hadn't placed a restraining hand on his shoulder.

"Hello, David." Alex's voice was gentle. David forced himself to meet his mentor's eye and smiled a greeting. His hands were shaking. "You look tired," Alex went on, his gaze unwavering. "You didn't have any problems, I hope?"

David shook his head, trying to calm himself, unable to look away. "No – no, everything's fine. Just tired, that's all. It's been a tough few weeks. The camera's in the car if you want it right away …"

Alex shook his head. "Tomorrow is fine. As you said, you need to get some sleep. I'll leave you to finish your breakfast. Just one thing, though, before I go …"

"Yes?"

"Tell me what he did."

The words took a moment to sink in, but when they did, David felt the blood drain from his face. Alex was still watching him, the dark eyes reflecting nothing but calm. Calm – and understanding. Alex knew. He knew everything. On that last night, Malim had dressed for the occasion; an expensive suit, a silk shirt with the diamond cufflinks he always wore and a set of false nails, fashioned out of stainless steel in the shape of cat's claws. The deep, scalpel-like incisions that ran down David's back were barely half healed. The last thing he remembered was having his mouth forced open, being made to lick the weapons clean of his own blood.

He shot to his feet and staggered back from the table, then found himself on his knees, his legs no longer able to hold him up. At a gesture from Alex, Mary stepped away. He saw Alex rise, come towards him, and he wrapped his arms tightly around

35

himself as if to ward off an attack. His vision blurred and he realised he was sobbing.

"It's all right, David." Alex knelt beside him. "It's all right. He's gone. He can't hurt you now."

"He said if I told anyone … He said he would … When he finds out …"

"He won't find out. I'll make sure of that. As long as you're with me he can't find you. You're safe now, with me, and I won't leave you."

David felt Alex's arms around him and he clung on, crying like a child, pressing himself into the warmth of Alex's body, saying he was sorry, over and over again. He felt himself lifted, carried out and up to his own room, where someone else was waiting – Paul, he thought, although his head was swimming too much for him to be sure. He tried to struggle as they undressed him, but he felt a cool hand on his forehead, then nothing until he woke, what seemed a long time later, to pale winter sunlight through the frosted window.

* * *

There was a full length mirror in one of the wardrobes. David stood in front of it, gawping in disbelief at the faint scars that had been livid, weeping gashes when he'd last looked. The only other evidence of his ordeal was the bruising that mottled his body, fading to yellow as the swelling subsided. He shook his head, not comprehending and, in a daze, reached for some clean clothes. He pulled on a pair of jeans and a T-shirt, but then faltered, unable to take a step towards the door. Awake and dressed, there was nothing now that prevented him from having to face Alex, be confronted with the consequences of his failure. The thought of having to explain his encounters with Malim turned his legs back to jelly and he flopped down on the edge of the bed, his head in his hands.

A knock at the door brought his head up. Without waiting for an answer it opened and a pretty redhead around his own age came in, smiling. Jenni was another of Alex's permanent house guests, picked up from the street as a youngster just as he had been. The two had been to college together and now Jenni worked as Alex's receptionist, in a big office at the top of the house. David had always felt closer to Jenni than to any of the others – as children they had confided in each other and he saw her as the sister he never had. Nevertheless, he tensed as she sat on the bed beside him, knowing why she had come.

"Alex says to come to his sitting room, when you're ready. If you want to eat first or have a bath, that's fine."

David shook his head. "I can't."

Jenni smiled and squeezed his hand. "You can't put it off. He's not angry, David. And he's not going to ask you anything awkward. He asked me to tell you that, in case you were worried." He turned to look at her, and she smiled. "It's going to be all right. Really."

"How much do you know?" He felt a sudden fear that everyone in the house would know – know what he'd done, what Malim had forced him to do.

"About what's happened? Nothing. But I do know that Alex has been with you for the last three days. He and Paul have been taking it in turns to watch you. All he's told us is that you were doing a job for him and you had an accident. That's all. It's good to see you up – we were all worried."

"Three days?" He ran a hand across his forehead, wondering how he could possibly have slept that long. And even after three days, the wounds and bruises shouldn't have healed as well as they had. He pressed his feet to the floor. His legs seemed able to hold him. He would have to see Alex sometime – it might as well be now. He pushed himself up and let Jenni take his arm. She supported him through the long corridors to the other side of the house. When they reached Alex's rooms she kissed his cheek, gave his hand a final squeeze, and left him without another word. He took a deep breath, turned the door handle, and went inside.

Alex was already on his feet. Before David could speak, he found himself in a gentle embrace.

"Forgive me, David."

Alex led him to an armchair by the fire and he sat, blinking in confusion. Paul was there, seated opposite, and as David glanced at him he gave a sympathetic smile. David took a proffered cup of tea and sipped nervously, his eyes flitting from one to the other. Alex hovered for a moment, then leaned back against the mantle and spoke again.

"There is one thing I want to make clear to you, David." The voice was soft, almost hesitant. "Whatever you may have done, whatever may have been done to you – you must understand that none of it is your fault. I should never have sent you. It was too dangerous. I should have known that. I'm sorry."

There was a silence as David, his hands tight around the cup, tried to absorb the words.

"I'm not going to ask you anything. I know enough, and the rest I can guess. But if you want to talk – later – I'm here. You can come to see me anytime, day or night, okay?"

David felt himself relax slightly and nodded, then looked up at Paul.

"You know as well? Alex told you?"

Paul took in a breath. "He didn't need to. I saw for myself. But only we two – and Mary. No one else."

"I wanted to see you as soon as possible," Alex went on, "because I want you to know you are safe. And the only way to convince you is with the truth. We owe you that, at least. It's not much recompense, but it's all I have, for the moment. Paul will go and arrange to have some food brought up if you like. It's quite a while since you last ate."

David said nothing, but nodded, grateful for Alex's ploy to allow them to speak alone. Paul got up at once, giving David's shoulder a squeeze on the way past.

"I'll tell Mary to make something light. Call when you're ready," he said, and was gone, leaving David with a sudden knot of dread at what was going to happen next.

Alex took the vacated chair and poured more tea. "You were lucky," he remarked. "There are very few who encounter Malim and survive. Even if I'd known, there was nothing I could have done without putting your life in more danger. I hope you can believe that."

"If you say so," David muttered, not wanting to remember, his anxiety becoming tinged with anger. He looked up suddenly and went on, "So who the hell was he anyway? And why did you send me to take pictures of him if you knew him already? I mean, what was the point, if you knew he was that dangerous? Or did you just send me because I was expendable – because I didn't matter? Maybe that's why you pick kids like me off the street. A ready made bunch of idiots who hang on your every word, who can disappear and no questions asked, is that it?"

He stopped, exhausted, hearing the bitterness in his voice. For a while Alex made no response, and then he said, "Is that what you believe, David?"

"I don't know. I don't know what to believe any more."

He started in surprise as Alex gave a grim laugh. "Perhaps there is a little truth in what you say, but only a little. I can't deny that I took a risk, and with your life, not mine. But there is more at stake here, David, than one life. Even with the little you know you must realise that. Unfortunately, you have had the misfortune to become intimately acquainted with Malim. Tell me your impression. Describe him to me."

David shuddered. "He's a total psychopath. What else is there to say?"

"That is true. And?"

"And … and he's not … I can't …"

"You can't say because it might make you sound as insane as he is, right? Okay, I'll help. He can control you, even when he's miles away. He can break every bone in your body without touching you, and put them back together in minutes, as if it had never happened. Yes?"

"Yes." David's voice was a hoarse whisper. "He's not human. So what the fuck is he?"

"Oh, he's human." Alex sat back in his chair. "Just a different kind of human. He is outside his time and place. He shouldn't be here – and neither should I."

For a moment, David just blinked stupidly. Then, as he looked into Alex's face, something slotted into place inside him, a key fitting a lock, the answer to a question he had never thought to ask. He could see, now, the faint resemblance between the two men – in the shape of the face, the long, elegant fingers, the graceful, cat-like movements, but most of all in the eyes, that seemed to look right into him, see his every thought. His mind drifted to the wounds that had miraculously healed during his long, unnatural sleep. He pushed down a stirring of panic and said, "You're one of them – like him. You can do everything he does. Right?"

"Yes, that's right. We are of the same family, the same time. But there is one difference between us. He is insane. I am not. Malim has stepped forward more than fifteen hundred years because he thinks there are none of our kind left in the world to oppose him. In his mind he believes he can subjugate you all, live out his twisted ambition in a place where no one can threaten him. He is mad, but he is also quite capable of succeeding unless he is stopped. And I intend to stop him, David. That is why I am here."

CHAPTER 4

The eagle shifted its weight on Arvan's shoulder, restless from the hours of enforced inactivity. A powerful talon dug into his flesh and he let out a sharp hiss. The great bird responded to the rebuke by stretching a wing, the splayed feathers of the tip brushing a sodden branch, releasing a shower of icy droplets that trickled down the back of Arvan's neck.

"Hush, now," he whispered, preening the creature's breast with a fingernail. "You have less patience than Lord Malim – if such a thing is possible."

He sighed and pulled his cloak tight around his tall, spare frame. Dusk was still several hours away, yet the damp chill of autumn that had been hanging in the air since dawn seeped through the thick fabric, making his bones ache. The small knot of trees under which he had concealed himself gave no shelter from the dew laden air. The constant dripping irritated him almost beyond endurance, and he sensed that his bird suffered the same misery. He cursed the Cambrian weather and longed for his own hearth in the remote highland settlement, where the damp would have turned to brittle snow a month since. He forced calm back into his mind, not wanting to further disquiet the bird. On the hilltop there was no other shelter and he did not dare stand in the open while it was still daylight.

From his vantage point he had a clear view of the village below, not yet shrouded in evening mist. The main street ran wide down the centre, stone houses densely packed along its length. Larger, more opulent dwellings fanned out around it, reached by networks of small tracks that reminded him of the intricate veins of a leaf. Beyond the houses the land had been hedged and fenced to provide plots for both grazing and cereal crops. He saw all this in the periphery of his vision. His sharp gaze was fixed on a single dwelling, one of the richer, two storey houses that backed onto the fields, its own private grounds bordered by a low stone boundary wall.

His brow furrowed in distaste. It was not the way of his people to associate themselves with those not of the gift. The short lived ones were too undisciplined in their thoughts, their clamouring an unwanted irritation that, for the more sensitive of his kind, occasionally led to pain, even madness. How anyone could make a conscious decision to immerse himself in such unbearable noise was beyond his understanding. But he had no choice, and so he must endure. He closed his mind to all but his task and focused his attention on the house. His position afforded him a clear view both of the grass terrace and the rear entrance door, and when the door finally opened he took in a breath, then let it out slowly, his lips curling in a smile of anticipation.

"At last!" he whispered, half to himself, half to the bird. "Ah, but she is beautiful. Truly, she is perfect." The smile faded as he added, "But such a waste. He will not see that beauty. If he is allowed to have it, he will destroy it, as he destroys all that he touches." He sighed. "But whatever our thoughts on that, they must remain our thoughts. I have my master, as you have yours. Be ready, my friend, it is almost time."

Man and bird watched together as the woman walked across the lawn to the wall and sat, looking out across the fields. She was dressed in a simple leaf green gown, finely woven, but dense against the chill weather. The fabric seemed to swamp her small, delicate form, and the long dark hair that spilled loose down her back accentuated the creamy smoothness of her skin. He saw all this with the eyes of his eagle, even down to the full redness of her lips, the eyes that matched the colour of the gown. The eagle started at a sudden movement far below. An unwary young hare had loped into the middle of the grass and reared up, seeking a route to better shelter. With the force of his will, Arvan stilled the bird. The woman had seen the little animal too, and was staring at it in rapt concentration.

Arvan held his breath, his body tensing as he readied himself. A second later he drew in an exultant breath. "She has my gift! She wishes to know what it is to see through the eyes of the creature. This is a better test than I could have hoped for!"

42

He lifted his restraint on the bird and at once it launched itself out of the cover of the trees and up, becoming no more than a distant speck against the grey sky. It hovered for an instant, then plummeted, its hunger driving it almost faster than his eye could follow, talons flexing in anticipation of the kill. The strike was breathtaking in its elegance. A single plunge, a beat of the great wings and the eagle was racing towards him, the hare struggling hopelessly against the tearing grip, the deadly claws locked in the flesh of its belly, squeezing the breath from its throat. But Arvan wasn't looking at the bird. The agonized scream of the young woman in the garden far below drifted up to him on the wind and he saw her fall, one hand to her throat, the other clutching at her stomach. Then she lay still, and the only sound was the rush of air as the eagle landed at his feet and offered him the still twitching prey.

He ignored the bird, his focus remaining on the figure sprawled on the grass. The door of the house opened and a man rushed out. Arvan recognised him at once from images he had received from Rendail's mind. It was the girl's father, Feylan. He fell on his knees beside the woman, at the same time peering wildly about, seeking the source of the threat. Long minutes passed and then, at last, she moved, brushing her father aside and pushing herself up onto her knees. Arvan let out his breath in a sigh of relief, but his satisfaction faded a moment later as, without hesitation, she turned her gaze in his direction, her expression betraying both pain and fury. He cursed quietly and withdrew further into the shadows of the trees. Then, turning, he made his way to the other side of the knoll and mounted the horse that was tethered there. A soft whistle brought the eagle to its perch behind his saddle, the hare still clutched tightly in its claws.

"So," he commented as he set his mount to a lazy canter down towards the cart track, "her gift is as great as her beauty. She will be hard to tame – much harder even than you. She would be a challenge for my master, without any doubt, and perhaps even for Lord Rendail. It would have been interesting ... But I have been instructed, and it is my duty to obey." He reached down and took a small loaf from his pack, while the eagle tore

43

single mindedly at the hare's carcase. He chewed thoughtfully for a while and then added, "At least, it is for the moment."

* * *

Karisse knew instinctively that now was not the time to reveal to her father what she had sensed. He was more unsettled than she ever remembered seeing him and it was making him short tempered. He had all but dragged her inside, bolting all the doors and insisting on checking the windows as well. He had then made up an infusion of calming herbs and they sat now, facing each other across the hearth, the cups and a stony silence between them. He knew, or suspected something, she decided, but her attempts to find the thread of his thought only resulted in a burst of anger.

"Do not do that again," Feylan said, his tone so threatening that she shrank back. "If you wish to know what I am thinking, you may ask me. Otherwise, wait until you are invited." He paused before adding, a little more quietly, "Never believe I am unaware of your gift, and, more importantly, never believe that others are unaware of it."

She took up her cup without replying, consoling herself with the notion that it was fear, more than anything she may have done, that was causing his mood. She unconsciously rubbed her arm, feeling the swelling bruise where he had grabbed her to pull her inside. At once his expression melted into concern and he moved across to her.

"Forgive me," he whispered. "I am a foolish man. Please, let me see." His voice was suddenly unsteady and Karisse realised, with a shock, that he was on the verge of tears.

"What is it, Father?" She tried to take his hand, but he snatched it away as though ashamed of showing weakness in front of her. He fumbled for her arm, and let his gift smooth away the bruising. When he finally spoke it was in a gruff whisper that barely disguised his emotion.

"I thought I had lost you. I thought … I almost failed your mother. I gave her my word …"

This time, when she took his hand he didn't pull away.

"How can you say such a thing, Father? It wasn't your fault." She hesitated, then added, "You can't prevent all accidents. No one can do that. Mother would have understood."

He met her eye for a second, the lie falling between them like a stone. He may not have sensed the presence on the hill as she had, but he knew full well that no sea eagles had territories outside their home ranges in the far north. He got up awkwardly and turned away from her.

"I can no longer keep you safe. If your mother was still alive, she would not have let this happen. She would have found someone … someone strong, who would …" He faltered and shook his head. She could see his hands form themselves into fists at his sides as he willed himself to go on. Suddenly he wheeled to face her, his tone once more sharp, his expression frozen with determination. "She would have found you a mate. She is not here to do it, so I must. You will join, and then you will have another to protect you." He ignored her look of horror and forged on. "You will join, and until it is done you will stay here. Inside. You will never leave this house alone. I forbid it!" He shouted the last words, and Karisse flew to her feet, her shock congealing into cold rage.

"What are you telling me? You will make me a prisoner here while you find me a man? Have you gone mad, Father? What is so dangerous that I can't go outside my own door? What do you know that I don't? Why should I need a man to protect me? My own gift is strong enough, and I can look after myself. After all," she added, unfairly, "I have been doing it for most of my life. You have no right to make such an imposition."

Her father visibly flinched. The tears stood clear in his eyes now, but he refused to let them fall. Instead, he drew himself up and almost spat the words, his hands still knotted into tight fists.

"You are *not* strong enough. Not by a long way. You have no idea what you face, and if you did you would see that what I do is for the best."

"Then tell me!" she shouted, frustration adding to her fury. "No, Father, I will not join, and you will not keep me here. I am only eighteen – too young to mate in any case. I am not ready and I will not have this forced upon me. I will choose for myself who I will take, and I will do it when I wish to choose, not before."

She got up and, striding to the back door, reached up to pull back the bolts. Her fingers had hardly touched the first one before Feylan pulled her round to face him.

"Leave me alone!" she shouted, and at once felt the sting of his hand across her cheek. For a long moment they both stood, staring at each other in disbelief. Tears were running freely now down her father's cheeks, his unspoken apology mingling with the pain in his eyes. He looked away, at the same time thrusting her gently from him.

"Go to your room now. Tomorrow. We will talk tomorrow."

"Father?"

"Please!" His voice was thick with desperation. "Please go. Tomorrow …"

She nodded without looking up, and slowly backed away to the staircase.

"Tomorrow," she whispered, and fled to her room.

CHAPTER 5

"So why not just kill him? If that's what you're here for, you could have done it by now, if you have the same powers that he does. Why aren't you out there looking for him, instead of hiding here as if you're scared of him?"

David sat back, feeling a lot calmer after the light breakfast of scrambled eggs and toast that Mary sent up to him. Alex joined him, and not just out of politeness. David realised, then, that most likely neither of them had eaten for at least three days.

Alex set his plate aside and sighed. "I am scared of him, David. I'd be stupid not to be. He may be mad, but he's also clever. And he's strong. You of all people should know that. At this moment he's much stronger than I am. There's only one shot at it, and if I fail, there's no fallback. But there is another reason why I've done nothing before now. If I were to kill Malim, all that would happen is that his consciousness would be blasted from this time back into his own. He wouldn't die – he would just die here, at this particular 'now'. So what would stop him coming forward again, to a hundred years ago, or two hundred? You should understand that this has never been done before. As far as I know, Malim and I are the only males of our kind ever to possess this gift. None of us have any idea what the consequences would be."

David shook his head, trying to fit the information into a world that had, in a few short weeks, been turned on its head. He would have thought Alex's words to be the ramblings of a madman, except for one thing – his first hand knowledge of what Malim could do made the whole thing, unwilling as he was to accept it, believable, at least as far as he could judge. His first instinct was to say that if Alex himself was so afraid of Malim, how come he'd been so quick to risk someone else? But he didn't want to face the answer to that. Not yet. And there were other questions, so many it was hard to pick out where to start. He was aware of Alex, waiting patiently for him to speak. At last he decided and said, "You say you're human. So what kind of human? Where from – and when?"

Alex smiled. "Where from? Not far from here. A little way north of Braemar, in fact. I was born around 300 A.D. if that's any help. As for what kind of human I am, that will take a little more explaining – more than we have time for, I'm afraid. But I'll try to make it simple. Two thousand years ago there were quite a few of us around. I don't know how many exactly, but not counting my family a few hundred, dotted about the country. I suppose we all must have stemmed from the same root at some time or other. We are what you would describe as a genetic mutation. We live longer, and have certain abilities that other men don't have, but in all other respects there is no difference between us."

David snorted at this, but said nothing. Alex's smile faded as he went on, "I said, not counting my family. Unfortunately, they are a little different. For my great-grandfather, those abilities weren't enough. He wanted our lives to be even longer, our power greater than any the world had ever seen. What he wanted more than anything else was to gain control over time. He thought that through knowledge of the future, he could manipulate the present to his advantage. It was a reasonable enough idea I suppose. So he took his family away to the most isolated place he could find, and began to experiment with what he called 'the furtherance of the blood'. Nowadays you would call it a program of eugenics.

"Now, you've studied biology. You should know what happens when there is too much inbreeding – deformity, insanity, hereditary disease. Madness ran in the blood, and that, coupled with our near invincibility, made us a great danger, to ourselves and to others. He got what he wanted, in the end, although he didn't live to see it. The blood gave us one who could step from present to future. Unfortunately, it gave us Malim. Malim is riddled with the family curse. He has the most powerful gift, and the weakest mind. Here, where there is no one to stand up to him, he is violent megalomaniac – a school bully with the world as his

48

playground. But like all bullies he will back down when faced with the risk of getting hurt. At home he's terrified of his father. Quite rightly – I don't know anyone who isn't. Faced with Lord Rendail, Malim is no more than a child, hiding behind his servants and hangers on."

"So why doesn't Rendail do something – stop Malim from coming here, if he's that powerful? And how do I know you're not completely insane, if you're a member of this family as well? If they were all so invincible, where are they now? Why don't you just round up the rest of them and go for him? Surely he wouldn't be able to beat a whole gang of you?"

Alex frowned. "Your first question is one I've often asked myself. I think perhaps Rendail doesn't want to destroy the gift that his father dreamed of for so long. He is every bit as obsessed with the power that visions of the future might bring. What Malim does while he is here is probably of no concern to him at all. As for me, my mother was lucky enough to get away from the Family – she was smuggled out of the settlement when she was a baby. I've never set foot inside the place, and never want to. Maybe I am insane, who knows? But I think you've seen enough of Malim to know I'm not delusional about that. He's my uncle, you know – my mother was – is – his sister. None of them know anything about me, and that's the way I want it to stay.

"The last question is harder to answer. Why aren't there descendants of the Family here? I don't know. I expected to find them and do exactly as you suggested. But I've been here for eighty years, and I haven't found a single one. I don't know what happened, but at some time in our history there must have been a great disaster. Maybe Malim had something to do with it, or maybe the madness destroyed them all. So here I am, alone, or almost alone. Perhaps that's a good thing. If there were any others here, they might just as easily want to destroy me as help me. But it's useless to speculate. I'm here, and so I have to try to do something, even if there is very little chance of success. If I fail, there's not much point going back."

He stopped, seeing the look on David's face.

"You've been here … how long?" David stuttered, feeling at the end of his ability to stretch his imagination any further. He wiped a hand across his brow, taking in Alex's smooth, lightly tanned skin, the long, dark hair, neatly tied back, the youthful, well muscled frame. It struck him, then, that Alex had changed little, if at all, in the thirteen years since their first acquaintance.

Alex grinned, clearly flattered, his eyes twinkling as he answered, "I told you. We have longer lives. Added to that, we don't age, at least not in the same way. I am one hundred and twenty years old or thereabouts, and I'll look like this until the day I die, which won't be for a while yet, I hope. I was forty when I came here. Malim is a few decades older, although you wouldn't think it from the way he behaves. That's the madness in him. Can you imagine it? Nearly two hundred years old, with all that intellect, and the emotional development of a child." He held up his hands. "Sorry – you don't have to imagine it. Anyway, that's the story in a nutshell. Here we are, me and Paul, and Paul isn't even fully developed yet …"

"Paul?" David sat up, shaking his head. "What the hell's Paul got to do with it? I thought you said there weren't any others like you here – and anyway, he's Mary's son, isn't he? Or is that another lie?"

Alex sighed, and reached out a hand to touch David's shoulder, but David pulled away, nearing the limit of his ability to cope with the assaults on his perceptions.

"Paul *is* Mary's son," Alex said, getting up and moving to the window. "Mary's, and mine. Mary is my wife." He paused a moment to let David absorb the new shock, then went on, "We met fifty years ago. Paul was born ten years later, and it was inevitable that he would be one of my kind. You see, though, why that isn't common knowledge? Mary is almost seventy, while my son and I don't appear to age. It would look – odd. It was Mary's choice, not mine. Now you understand why Paul and Malim look so alike. They are of the same blood, the same Family. Paul is still young, according to our measures. He hasn't yet reached his full strength and, apart from that, he has no experience of others of the Family. If Malim sensed him, it's likely he could destroy him in a second."

"So you sent me after him instead of your precious son. Now I understand." David couldn't help but let the bitterness creep into his voice. Alex turned to him, and to his amazement he saw his mentor brush away a tear.

"No, David. You don't understand. If Paul had gone, Malim would have recognised him for what he was. He would have learned he was not alone and, inevitably, he would have learned I was here. If that were to ever happen, everything we have worked towards would come to nothing. I was able to mask my presence in your mind in a way I could not with my son, so that even when Malim was close to you, he sensed nothing, and I remained invisible to him."

David shuddered, remembering that first probing, when he had been asked who sent him. He nodded, acknowledging the truth behind Alex's words. At last, he was ready to ask the question.

"So why did you send me to watch him, if you knew how dangerous it was?"

Alex sat down again, his shoulders still tense.

"I'm sorry, David. It was important that I knew precisely where he was, and there was no one else I could send. Paul and I needed to try to find someone, and we had to be sure Malim was as far away as possible. You see, he might have been looking for her too, and the last thing I wanted was to bump into him by accident."

"Her? There is a woman involved in this? Who? And what does she have to do with it?"

"Oh, yes, there is a woman – and it is vitally important that we get to her first, if, indeed, she is here. Malim wants to start a dynasty, and he can't do that unless he breeds. He and I are the only two males with the gift to cross into future times, but there is another – a female – and it is Malim's plan to lure her here. He would attempt to take her in his own time, but he has a slight problem. Karisse is destined for his brother. Arghel watches over

51

her day and night, and he is someone that even Malim dare not tangle with.

"Like you, she is an innocent pawn in this game, and she is the one who will determine all our futures. Rendail refuses to act, therefore Arghel is the only one capable of destroying Malim in his own time. When Malim succeeds in pulling Karisse across the divide, Arghel will be spurred into action. But the timing must be exact. When Arghel realises his brother is responsible, he will attempt to break into his father's stronghold, find and destroy Malim's body. The plan is that we find Karisse and use her to draw Malim into a trap. His mind will be so preoccupied with her that Paul and I will be able to take him unawares, before he has a chance to react. When all is in place, my mother will go to Arghel. He must find a way to be present at the exact moment we force Malim's consciousness back to its own time. For a very short period, Malim will be weakened, disorientated. That is when Arghel must strike. It is the only way to be sure of success. He must die in his own place and time, and while his mind and body are together. Otherwise, we have no idea what the consequences might be."

"And this woman – you think she is here, now, in this time?"

"I thought there was a possibility," Alex replied, his forehead creasing in a frown. "I thought I felt … something. But Paul and I found no sign of her when we searched. Perhaps it is not time, or perhaps something has gone wrong. I don't know. But for now, all any of us can do is wait."

CHAPTER 6

Karisse's fear and confusion gradually gave way to curiosity. She curled herself on the wide oak window sill of her small room and gazed out across the lawn. It was past sunset, but she could still make out the grey outline of the hill, the knot of trees on its summit that had sheltered the eagle and its owner. The garden birds had gone to roost, and in the peaceful silence all seemed once more safe and familiar.

She had never before sensed such fury in her father, nor seen him in such distress. He had answers, but Karisse knew that his defences were too strong for her thoughts to penetrate. Instead, she turned her attention to the presence that had revealed itself in the garden. The structure of the mind had been complex and powerful. Although not coherent to her at the time, she recalled snatches of excitement, triumph and, oddly, regret. Hoping that Feylan was too distracted to be paying attention, she allowed her gift to probe outward.

Within moments, she had locked on to the essence of the mind she sought. It was still close, yet no longer close enough to pose a threat. Her task was made easier by the fact that it was not just the man she sensed but the bird also, its primitive consciousness bonded to the other's gift. She closed her eyes and focused.

The man sat in a small clearing, back against a broad oak, feet stretched towards a small fire. Like all Dancers, he was clean shaven, his long dark hair neatly tied back, cloak flung to one side. The eagle perched on the horse's saddle, wings folded, head curled in sleep. Its master wasn't sleeping. He stared unblinking into the flames, his mind filled with images that were alien to her, of barren crags towering over wide pavements enclosed by stone buildings three or four storeys high. It was snowing, the heavy flakes settling on the stones.

Someone appeared on one of the pavements, and she realised the visions were not his memories, but the linking of his own gift to somewhere an unimaginable distance away. The figure came into focus – a man, bare footed, bare chested, bronzed skin glistening in the light of torches along the path, blonde hair whipping behind him in the breeze. He stretched, oblivious of the cold, a long, languid movement sending ripples through the hard muscles of his chest. Karisse felt her heart beat faster, her mouth go dry as an unfamiliar thrill spread through her body. The exhibition, somehow, was for her, and her alone.

The figure began to dance, each graceful movement bringing him closer through the swirling snow, his footfalls forming intricate patterns on the white covering of the pavement. The urge to respond became irresistible, thc fire that was rising in her unbearable as he became the locus of her vision. The pulse of her desire matched each rhythmic step, and she imagined that his hands stroked her body as they traced the air, igniting more passion with each delicate, yet demanding touch. In a daze, she reached out, eager to close the vast distance between them, desperate for the feel of his solid flesh against hers.

The dance stopped. His body, glistening with sweat, radiated steam into the cold night air. Very slowly, he raised his head and looked straight at her. He mouthed a single, silent word; "Karisse." Then he bared his teeth in a chilling grin, and let his tongue run over his lips in a bestial gesture that turned her stomach to ice. She opened her mouth to scream, but no sound came, her throat constricting as though the long, elegant fingers had reached around her neck, squeezing, crushing until all she could see was the glitter of lust in his heavy lidded eyes.

A sudden darkness swept across Karisse's vision, her gift blinded by a sharp force cutting through the fragile weave of the Dance. In a flash of panic she struggled against oblivion, unable even to sense the presence of her own body. Then, as quickly as it had come the veil lifted, the bleak stone landscape was gone and the clearing came back into focus. Still trembling, she registered another surge of fear as the man leapt to his feet, the eagle's warning screams splitting the night air. She tried to pull her gift away but was trapped, helpless, watching the scene with mounting horror.

Two men entered the glade, their faces clear in the light of the fire. She recoiled as she recognised one of them. Even though she had not seen him since childhood, the tall, blonde figure of her father's uncle, Vail, was unmistakeable. The other was a stranger, slightly taller, broad shouldered, with a head of dark curls falling almost to his waist. His face, half in shadow, was expressionless, yet there was a fire in his eyes that sent a chill down Karisse's back.

For a brief moment all three stood motionless, and then several things happened at once. Vail took a step forward and crumpled as though he had been struck by a rock, his limbs twisting in grotesque angles as he fell. Karisse uttered an anguished cry as she realised that Vail wouldn't rise again. As the stranger turned, the eagle launched itself at him with a high pitched scream. He shot up an arm to deflect it, and gasped as the bird's talons closed around his wrist. His free hand snaked out, the fingers closing around the eagle's neck. The bird shrieked, the powerful wings pummelling the man's body, the talons letting go of his arm, raking towards his face. He held his grip and squeezed. Karisse heard the snap of the bird's neck. He flung it to the ground and whipped round to face its master. His eyes met empty air, the faint movement of the leaves the only evidence that his adversary had been there at all.

In the silence that followed Karisse was assailed by two emotions, both so violent that her chest tightened, her stomach knotted in pain. The first came from the owner of the bird – an inward shudder, not of anger, but of grief at the loss of a valued and much loved pet. His tremor, however, was drowned by a sudden outpouring of hatred, the source of which had a horrible familiarity. For an instant she saw a different mind, one a great distance away, heedless in its rage, the full brunt of its fury aimed at the stranger, who remained alone in the clearing rubbing his injured wrist. He was turned away from her now, but she knew he had detected that wave of anger, and felt his smile. Then he stiffened. There was a moment of growing awareness in him, a tendril of his thought coming towards her and then, with a suddenness that made her stomach heave, the thread that joined her to the vision was forcibly snapped, hurling her back into the isolation of her own mind.

She sat for several minutes, breathing hard, trembling with both fear and anger – fear at the fact that the stranger had been able to detect her presence, anger at the perfunctory manner of her dismissal; batted away like an irritating fly. She knotted her fingers together to stop her hands shaking. The image of Vail, a lifeless mess of twisted limbs on the grass of the clearing, the screech of the eagle as the stranger twisted it neck, clung to her senses. She curled into a tight ball on the bed and wept.

* * *

Lord Thalis, second advisor to the head of the Family, former tutor, now bed partner to Lord Malim, and possibly the most cowardly, obsequious creature within the settlement, tried not to cringe as Malim reached out to stroke his thigh. It was the fifth time in as many hours, and would probably not be the last. As he rolled over on the sleeping rugs to accommodate his master's silent demand, his main thought was that he would likely start to doze off in front of Lord Rendail in the morning. He expected no sympathy from that quarter. It had happened just once before, following a night of Malim's embraces, and he had been lucky to keep the skin on his back. As it was, he had been forced to endure the jibes and sniggers of the whole settlement for more than a week afterwards, even, to his humiliation, from some of the women. He was tired past caring, and ached abominably in places that he had, during Malim's long absence, forgotten existed.

He pressed his face into the rugs, stifling a grunt of pain as Malim bore down with his full weight, knocking the breath out of him, grabbed his wrist and wrenched his arm.

"You are not paying attention, Thalis. Am I being too gentle for you? Or perhaps you are thinking of someone else. Tell me, did you take another lover when I was away? Some fresh faced lad from the stables, maybe? Or one of Karim's house boys? They say he has a good collection, and has them attend him

56

three at a time. I would envy him, if it weren't for the fact he is so ugly. "

"Of course not!" Thalis did his best to sound shocked. "A few women, that's all. You must forgive me, but you have been gone so long that I am not used to your ... your stamina, my Lord. You have exhausted me."

Malim rolled onto his back and laughed. "What a delightful servant you are, Thalis. You are lying, naturally, but I forgive you. I will leave you to your rest and go to the compound. Perhaps I can exhaust a girl or two as well before morning."

Thalis waited until the door had closed before heaving a sigh of relief. He had hardly begun to doze, however, before a sharp summons jerked him back into wakefulness. It was as though the head of the Family had been waiting for Malim to leave. It was still more than an hour before dawn. Between father and son, Thalis thought, it would be a wonder if he ever slept again. He cursed, and reached for his clothes.

* * *

When the door to her room opened Karisse stayed huddled in the fur blanket, feigning sleep. Still in shock, she couldn't bear the thought of her father's recriminations if he learned that she had deliberately sought out the man who had sent the eagle to attack her. As for Vail's death, she still hardly believed it herself. She felt him lower himself onto her bed. He sat in silence for what seemed an age, then she felt the light touch of his hand on her hair, his lips on her cheek. She heard his quiet footsteps padding away, the click of the latch. He had known she wasn't sleeping. Just a little of his gift had been in the touch, enough to take away care, if not memory. The images still swam before her eyes, but the pain of them, for the moment, was blunted. How much, she wondered as she drifted into sleep, did her father really know?

* * *

57

The knowing half smile that played about Rendail's lips as he greeted his advisor was insufferable.

"I trust, Thalis, that I did not disturb your rest."

Thalis gritted his teeth and stifled a yawn. "No, Lord. I am ready to serve you, as always."

"Good. Then tell me what Malim has learned so far. He is still in contact with Arvan, I take it?"

Thalis noted he had not been invited to sit. "Yes, Lord. Arvan found the girl yesterday, just before sunset. She is reported to be strong in the gift, and unusual, in that she is able to reach the minds of other creatures, as Arvan can. He also believes that she made contact with him briefly, but he blocked her and she was unable to sustain it."

"And the other gift?" Rendail's gaze was steady, but his eyes sparked with interest.

"No sign yet, Lord. If she is indeed able to cross the Great Emptiness, she has not made any attempt to do so, and is possibly not aware of the existence of the skill. Arvan did not press the enquiry, for fear of discovery, I think."

Rendail nodded, apparently satisfied. His expression as he asked the next question was unreadable.

"And Arghel? Is there any sign of his presence near the girl? Has Arvan had any word of his doings?"

Thalis blinked, surprised. "The traitor, Lord? No, no word, as far as I know. I think Lord Malim would have mentioned it. But surely, he would not venture close to one of us? He is too much of a coward to challenge us openly. If he is stupid enough to try to defend the girl, he will not live long enough to realise it, that is certain."

The hint of a smile once more crossed Rendail's face. "Thank you, Thalis. You may go." Thalis bowed gratefully and made his way to the door. As he reached it, Rendail spoke again. "How do you find my son? It must be difficult, since Arvan left."

Thalis turned, trying to hide his frustration.

"It is ... difficult, Lord, as you say. I think he misses his servant more than he will admit. Lately, he has been a little restless, and he has always had a wild temper, as you know."

For a moment it looked as if Rendail was going to say something else, but after a long pause he merely waved a hand. Thalis wasted no time in obeying the gesture, and hurried back down the corridor, hoping that Malim was still engaged in taking his pleasure elsewhere.

CHAPTER 7

When, after three days, her father had said nothing concerning Vail's fate, nor shown any sign of unease beyond his protectiveness of her, Karisse began to doubt the truth of what she had witnessed within the Dance. He would have felt the death of one so close, she was sure of it. She wondered whether her sight had given her a false image. It was something she had never heard of, but that did not make it impossible. She found some comfort in the idea, and as his general agitation seemed, for the moment, to have abated, she said nothing in case it might disturb the fragile harmony between them. On the third evening, however, the peace was shattered once again.

The wave of Feylan's grief hit her as she made her way up to her room. He was outside, walking the boundary as he had done every night since the incident with the eagle. The force of his emotion left her gripping the stair rail for support, and an instant later the full import of it struck her. Vail was dead. It had not been an illusion. She steadied herself, then rushed downstairs and out into the garden. She came to a halt at the end of the path and took a sharp breath, her mouth falling open in surprise. Her father was not alone.

The stranger was the same man she had seen with Vail in her vision three nights before. He and her father were standing by the boundary wall, talking urgently, their voices low. She couldn't catch the words, but realised they were arguing. Feylan suddenly became aware of her and turned, his face pale in the moonlight. He took a step towards her, but the other man touched his arm, and Karisse saw his slight shake of the head. Feylan nodded, then came over to her and, placing an arm round her shoulder, tried to guide her back to the house.

She shrugged her father off, however, and took several paces towards the stranger. He turned, then, and she saw his face fully for the first time. His expression was the same as in her vision, blank, unreadable. The eyes, though, as they locked onto hers, flashed with a passion more ice than fire, and she felt the same chill as on the first encounter. Through the mounting fear, magnified by his physical presence, she realised he was trying to force her away from him, block her gift. Her mouth was dry, her body trembling with the effort, but she stood her ground, returned the stare, and said, "When?"

She heard her father shift towards her, but the man gestured for him to stop.

"Tonight," he said. "Just after moonrise." The voice was low, barely above a whisper, the tone matter of fact.

Karisse glanced back at her father. "No! That's not true. He's lying. Liar!" she hissed, swinging round to face him again. "Liar! It was three days ago – I saw it. I saw you! You were hurt – the bird attacked you ..." She lunged forward and grabbed the man's wrist, pulled back the sleeve of his shirt. He grimaced, but made no attempt to stop her. His wrist bore three deep slashes, fresh, still bleeding. She took a step back and clapped a hand to her mouth to stifle a scream. Feylan had come up behind her and she fell against him, suddenly dizzy. He took her in his arms, but when he spoke, it was to the stranger.

"You should have told me you were hurt."

The other shook his head. "It is nothing. It will wait. Take her inside. When she is calmer, send her out to me."

To her amazement, her father simply bowed his head and guided her towards the house. Too shocked to protest, she let him lead her. At the door she glanced over her shoulder. The stranger was staring at her, but as their eyes met he turned his back and drew his cloak about him, his gaze on some distant point beyond the fields.

Once inside, Karisse felt her legs give under her. Feylan pressed a cup of water into her hands and stroked her hair as she drank. At last she managed to steady herself enough to say, "Is it true?"

Feylan didn't answer, but drew up a chair and sat, taking both her hands in his. She looked up at a face drawn with grief and worry.

"I saw him die," she whispered. "It was after dark, on the same day the eagle came. I was going to tell you, but ..."

She pulled away and got up, moved over to the window. The moon was just past full, its light spilling over the fields. She could see the outline of the low boundary wall, and of the loathsome stranger, waiting, still as the stone, gazing out towards the hills. She was trapped, not even able to seek refuge within her own mind. Even there, hidden in the shadows of her gift, there was no solace, only terror. She was shaking again, tears streaming down her cheeks as she whipped round to face her father and shouted, panic rising, "It isn't possible!"

In the next breath her father was with her and she was a child again, cradled in his arms, sobbing with fear and exhaustion. He said nothing, but held her until she quieted, then led her back to the couch. They sat down and she pressed into him, arms round her knees.

When she was able to speak again she wiped her eyes on her sleeve and said, "Well?"

She sensed him struggle, but after a while he answered, "It is rare – very rare, Karisse, but it is possible. The gift runs in our blood. I suppose I hoped that you would never find it, that you would not be the one to possess it. Perhaps I should have warned you, told you more of our history, of the danger ..."

"What danger?" She fought to stay calm. "You mean it will happen again? I will see people die, and not be able to do anything about it? Or maybe the fact that I see it makes it happen. Is that it?"

"No, of course not!" Feylan hugged her close. "It will happen again, surely. It is a part of your gift. But you will recognise it, learn to use it. That is not the danger. There are those who know about this gift, who would do anything to gain control of it. They are powerful people, Karisse, and if they try to take you from me, I won't be able to stop them. You need protection – more protection than I can give."

"The one with the eagle," she whispered. "He was one of them. Vail went after him, and that's why he died." The thought made her feel a little sick. "I saw where they come from. I saw

…" The thought of the blonde man, his dance, the smile of triumph as she reached for him, made her shudder, but before she could go on Feylan spoke, his voice filled with horror.

"You communicated with him? You probed his mind? Oh, Karisse, you have no idea what you have done. The threat is not from him, but from the ones who sent him. Even if he was not aware of you, they will have detected your presence. They will know of your gift. And now that they know, they will come. You must leave here, go with Arghel as soon as possible. He is the only one with the power to protect you now."

"Arghel?" Her mind flew to the still figure in the garden and she took in a sharp breath. "You mean that insufferable creature outside? I tell you now, Father, I would not go as far as the next house with that – that *thing*! He's not even human!" She pushed herself away and swept a hand across her forehead. "I don't know how you can even suggest it." When her father didn't respond, she went on, "You're frightened of him. I can see it in your face. He terrifies you. Who is he, and why is he here? And why, if he is so powerful, did he let Vail die?

"Or maybe," she added, lowering her voice, "he was responsible for Vail's death, and not the other one. Maybe the eagle attacked him to try to save Vail's life." She stood up and tossed her hair out of her eyes. "I'm not going anywhere with him. I'm staying with you, so you might as well tell him to go back to wherever he came from – if you dare, that is."

She sat down and folded her arms, glowering. Feylan's mouth curled into a half smile.

"You are right. Arghel does frighten me, often. He is a very dangerous man. I certainly would not dare to tell him any such thing, but even if I did, I would not. Neither will you, if you have any sense. You would do well to tread carefully – you have already called him a liar, and I doubt he took kindly to that. Still, for my sake, will you at least talk to him? If, after that, you want him to leave, I will tell him so, although I should warn you that what I say probably won't make any difference to what he does."

He paused, and she let out her breath in a sigh of angry frustration.

"Give me one good reason why I should. I don't like him. Being near him makes me shudder. And I don't like the way he orders you about – it isn't right."

Feylan shook his head, and met her eye. "Unfortunately, what you do or don't like is not an issue now, Karisse. There are many reasons why you should talk to him, but for the present I can only give you two. Firstly, because I ask it of you, but secondly, because it might save your life, and that is by far more important. Without his permission, I can say no more."

"His permission? Since when did you need permission to speak? It's preposterous! Just who does he think he is?"

Feylan gave another weary smile. "I think, perhaps, you should go and ask him."

She stepped out into the garden, hoping that the stranger would not be there, that she would be able to go back in to her father and report that Arghel had left, taking any threat away with him. But looking out across the lawn she saw his tall figure, still with his back to her, unmoving, by the stone wall. There was no indication, even to her inmost sense, that he was aware of her presence at all. Nothing emanated from him, not even the weak surface ripples that characterised those not of the gift. That, in itself, was unsettling, and she cautiously sent out her gift, probing for some hint of his thoughts.

The space taken up by his body was a pool of darkness, impenetrable. Trying to focus on it disoriented her completely, the ground shifting under her feet like quicksand. Quickly she pulled her thoughts away, putting out a hand to steady herself against the wall until the giddiness receded and the ground was solid beneath her. At the same time a vision came to her, the images forced into her mind from elsewhere. It was as though her whole being was being sucked into a deep well of emptiness. She was both blind and deaf, lost, imprisoned in some cold and lonely place far from home. For a moment she was totally immersed in this new terror but, realising that she was sinking under the weight of the vision, managed, with an effort, to pull back.

Gradually the world settled itself and, gathering her courage, she began to walk decisively forward. She found she had to concentrate hard to keep her mind from focusing directly on the figure of Arghel, who remained exactly where he was, giving no sign he even knew she was there despite the sound of her footfalls on the frosted grass. Her heart was pounding, her breath coming shorter the closer she got.

She stopped some six paces from him. Still he did not turn round. She opened her mouth, intending to offer some kind of apology for her earlier accusation. However, no sooner had she formulated the words than her fear transformed itself into a sudden and intense wave of anger at his silence, at the fact that he would not even turn to look at her and, most of all, frustration that she could not read him, that not even the slightest trace of his consciousness was there to guide her words. She could feel her father's anxiety as he waited inside the house and it fuelled her anger further to think that the creature in front of her must feel it too, yet made no effort to lay it to rest. In that case, she decided, as he showed her no courtesy, she in her turn owed him none.

Finding her voice she said loudly, and with as much authority as she could muster, "You may do as you wish with me, but I forbid you to harm my father."

There was no answer, not even the smallest movement from the figure on the grass. Infuriated, she went on, "You might at least have the good manners to look at me when I am speaking to you!"

Again, there was no response, and as the seconds dragged by her courage started to fail her. She began to tremble again, so much that she could hardly move, but with an effort took two or three steps backwards, intending to turn and run back to the house as fast as she could as soon as she had put sufficient distance between them. But before she could send the signal from her mind to her feet, he finally spoke. Still with his back to her, she heard his voice, soft, but clear.

"We have a bargain, then?"

She stopped in her tracks, stunned, unable to grasp his meaning.

"A bargain?" All the strength was gone from her voice.

"I may do with you as I wish, and in return I will not harm your father."

Words failed her. Her only thought was that whatever he was going to do, he should do it, and go somewhere far away. But he did not do anything. He just stood, exactly as before, waiting for her to answer. Gradually, fear gave way to dull resignation and, unable to bear the silence any longer, she answered blankly, "Yes, we have a bargain."

"Then," he said, turning finally to face her, "it is my wish that you should join with me." When she did not respond, he continued smoothly, "After all, didn't you say to your father that you would not join with any man that you had not chosen yourself? You appear to have made the choice."

She struggled to find her voice, then finally said, "You are being unfair. You have forced me to make a choice. Now you are playing with me, and I wish you would stop." Realising how childish this sounded, she added, "Whatever it is you mean to do, please do it, or go away."

He ignored her remarks and went on, "Am I not appealing to you?" When she continued to stare at the grass he said, "Come, you may look at me. After all, if we are to join it might be a little awkward otherwise."

Reluctantly she lifted her head and looked at him. She still could not sense anything other than what she could see and hear. His mind was completely closed to her. However, despite her initial dislike she found herself studying him closely. He was plainly dressed in travel worn deerskin trousers and a coarse cotton shirt. His boots were so mud stained it was hard to say what colour they had originally been. He had removed his thick woollen cloak and draped it over the wall, despite the chill of the night. He carried no weapons that she could see, not even a hunting knife. His long black curls were tied back with a simple leather thread, save for one or two that fell haphazardly about his face.

There was something oddly familiar about him, although she couldn't quite place it. The lightly tanned skin was smooth, and glistened in the moonlight; the mouth, curved and sensitive below a straight, softly angled nose, made him look younger than she had first thought. There were faint lines on his forehead, betraying worry or fatigue, she couldn't tell which. She met his eyes, large and framed by long curving lashes, and was trapped there, unable to look away. For a moment she felt the dizziness again, but steeled herself against it, forcing herself to return his stare. Behind the mask of silence with which he shrouded himself she thought she caught just a hint of sadness, well hidden, but there nonetheless, deep in the blackness of his eyes.

Abruptly he released her from his gaze and said, "Well? Now that you have seen me, tell me whether or not you find my appearance acceptable."

In truth she found him physically mesmerising. However, when she replied it was to say, "I can't deny that I find you quite acceptable to look at." She paused, then took a breath and went on, "But I also find you cruel, and ill mannered, and ..." She searched for another insult, "... and a coward!"

Unable to think of anything else to say, she folded her arms and glared at him. The ink black eyes widened a little, and for several seconds he stared back at her in apparent disbelief. Then he started to move towards her, and she could not help but think that this was to be the end, whatever 'the end' might be. But rather than retreat, she stayed quite still, her arms folded firmly across her chest, and simply closed her eyes and waited.

From the warmth of his body she judged that he stopped no more than a pace from her. He didn't touch her, but said quietly, "I don't think I have ever been insulted so many times in a single sentence." After a pause, in which she tensed, but did not open her eyes, he continued, "Or deserved so many insults all at once."

She looked at him in surprise, and saw in his handsome face a shadow of regret, and something else which she took at first to be amusement, but then realised with a little shock was actually relief. He took his cloak from the wall and laid it on the damp grass, then gestured for her to sit. She obeyed, and he sat next to her, crossing his long legs comfortably on the grass, careful not to look at her.

"I treated you very cruelly just now," he said, "and I ask for your forgiveness. It must also seem very ill mannered to so treat a young woman, as you have rightly pointed out, and I ask your forgiveness for that also." She opened her mouth, but he held up his hand to silence her. "However, I don't understand precisely what it is that makes me a coward. Perhaps you would explain?"

She shrugged. "Only a coward would veil his thoughts so completely. You have not shown me even the smallest part of you, and I can think of no reason for you to hide yourself from me, except that you might be afraid of what I might see."

He appeared to think about this, then nodded slowly, and turned to her with a smile. It was the first time she had seen him smile, and she tried to ignore the little rush of pleasure it gave her.

"You are quite right," he said. "I am afraid of what you might see, and so, by your definition, yes, I am a coward too." He hesitated, then went on, "but my fear is only for you. I will not cause you any harm. Your father knows this, or he would not have allowed you to be alone with me."

"Allowed? You mean he actually had a choice in the matter?"

He smiled again. "I suppose he didn't." He held out a hand and she took it as if the gesture had been a command. "Karisse, I would no more harm your father than I would deliberately cause any hurt to you. Come, ask me anything you wish, and I will answer if I can."

She thought for a moment, then said, "If you don't want to hurt anybody, why do you make people so afraid of you? Is it true, what he says, that you are dangerous?"

"I would prefer that you only ask me one question at a time," he replied with another smile. "But in answer to the first, people make their own fear. It is true that I do very little to dissuade them, and sometimes I forget that it isn't necessary to be intimidating all the time. It is a bad habit. As for the second, yes, I am very dangerous, although not, I hope, at this precise moment."

She nodded. After a brief silence, she said, "What are you doing here?"

"You should know that, in part at least," he answered. "After all, you were a witness to Vail's death." She tried to speak, but he silenced her with a gesture. "Before you ask," he went on, "Vail was perhaps my closest friend. We had known each other since I was a boy. I grieve for him, and I will avenge his death, you can be certain of that."

She drew herself up and wrapped her arms round her knees. "I know, now, that you were telling the truth about when he died." She raised her eyes to find him studying her. "Why does my gift see the future? Do you know that?"

He looked away, as if considering his answer. At length he turned back to her and said, "Karisse, you must have seen how the gift within your family differs from that of most others in very important ways. Surely you know that those differences, both in your mother and father, have been passed to you, but in much greater measure?"

Until now, it hadn't occurred to her.

"I know that Mother and I could see things differently. But I don't understand how being able to see with the eye of a fox or a sparrow is in any way important. It is just a game we used to play, no more, no less."

He searched her face as if unsure whether or not she really believed what she had said.

"It is more than a game," he replied, his tone serious. "You are one of very few in the world to possess that gift. Your mother was another. A third is the master of the eagle. That is how you were able to seek out his mind so easily. Now, you have discovered a gift that is even more rare. In time, you will be able to cross the Great Emptiness at will, and act in the future as you do in the present. There are some who would go to any lengths to possess control of that gift, use you to manipulate the path of time. At all costs, that must be prevented."

Karisse felt suddenly cold. "You mean I can change what is going to happen? That if I hadn't seen you and Vail …"

"Vail would still be dead," he said, without hesitation. "There is nothing you could have done, and seeing or not seeing would have made no difference." Then, seeing a sudden panic sweep across her he added, "What you saw when you came outside just now was an altogether different thing, one of many possibilities, an event that is not yet fixed. At this moment you are in no danger, I assure you, at least not from what you have seen."

She relaxed a little, but then found herself becoming angry with him again, and said, "But if they were not true visions, why did you make me see such terrible things. Did you simply wish to frighten me for your own amusement?"

"I would never willingly frighten you, and I did not make you see them," he said, a touch of irritation creeping into his voice. "However, I will tell you that this meeting was inevitable, although I had hoped you might be a little older. A gift of such magnitude requires some maturity. "

She flushed and made to get up, but he held her hand fast and gently pulled her back down.

Infuriated, she turned on him, shouted, "Let me go!" and at the same time struck him across the face as hard as she could with her free hand. For a moment there was no reaction, not even the blink of an eye. Then he turned his head away, and she could hear amusement in his tone when he said, "There is one more thing you have to ask me, is there not?"

His response, or lack of it, to the blow wrong footed her completely. She answered without thinking, in the same conversational tone. "And the bargain you forced me to make. It was just a lie, a game you were playing?"

"No," he answered simply. "It was no lie. You made a pact with me and I will never release you from it, except under one condition."

"Which is?"

"There is someone I wish you to speak to – someone who will tell you everything you need to know. If he judges against me, then I will abide by that decision. If not …"

70

"Who? And how do I know I can trust what this person says, any more than I can trust you?"

He laughed. "You will know. But perhaps, in the meantime, you might consider the terms of our bargain. After all, despite my cruelty, my ill manners and my cowardice, you do find me quite acceptable to look at." He turned back to her, smiling. "Stay here," he said, "and do as I have asked. Whatever happens, don't be afraid. I promise that you will be in no danger, not from me, nor from anyone you see tonight. Tomorrow at first light I will come back, and you must tell me what has been decided."

He got up, pulled her to her feet, and without another word wrapped his cloak around him and disappeared into the darkness.

CHAPTER 8

Malim landed in a sprawling heap on the floor of his father's reception room. He pushed himself onto his knees, snivelling. To be thrashed by servants was bad enough, but for his father to have them do it at the scene of his supposed crime, in front of the women's compound, was an unendurable humiliation. He felt a trickle of blood run down his back and risked a nervous glance at Nyran, who stood behind him stone faced, the five tailed lash hanging loose in his right hand. Nyran was one of Rendail's favourites, his principal bed partner, and for that reason alone Malim hated him. He returned his gaze to the mat in front of him as he heard soft footsteps, and found himself staring at his father's boots.

"Well?" There was only one person in the world who could apply so much menace to a single word.

"I didn't do anything wrong," Malim muttered through his teeth. "You said I wasn't to go near her. You said …"

"I think, Nyran," Rendail interrupted, sounding a little bored, "that my son still fails to grasp the issue. Your opinion?"

"I must agree, my Lord." There was a measure of satisfaction in Nyran's tone. "Perhaps the fault is mine. Clearly, I failed to give Lord Malim sufficient instruction."

Malim kept his eyes down.

"Perhaps," Rendail agreed. "In that case I suggest you take him back outside and instruct him further."

"No!" Malim jerked his head up, desperate. "No, please, Father. I'm sorry. I won't do it again, whatever it is, I promise, I won't – *please*!"

There followed an interminable silence, during which Malim bit his lip until he tasted blood and prayed for deliverance. It came, finally, as Rendail let out a long sigh.

"Wait outside, Nyran. Be ready in case I need you again."

To his relief, Malim heard the door close. He bowed as deeply as he could, considering that he was on his knees.

"Thank you, Father."

Rendail sniffed. "You may thank me for not breaking every bone in your body. And stop making such an exhibition of yourself over a few scratches. Are you my son, or a kitchen boy?"

Malim forced himself back on his heels, biting back a whimper.

"Yes, Father. I mean no – I'm sorry, Father."

"So you keep saying. One day, perhaps, your remorse will translate itself into obedience. Now, would you like to explain to me precisely what you thought were doing?"

"It was *him*!" Malim spat the word, jabbed a finger at the floor, winced and tried to compose himself. "I felt him. He's close to her, I know he is. She's mine, Father. He can't have her. I couldn't help it. I had to see her, surely you can't blame me for that?"

"By 'him', I assume you mean your brother?" Rendail turned his back and stared out of the window. "No," he said after a pause, "I can't blame you for wanting to see her." He whipped round and treated Malim to an icy glare. "But I can blame you for letting *her* see *you*. What do you think it achieved? Sometimes, Malim, you try my patience too far. Were you thinking at all? Somehow, I doubt it."

"I couldn't help it," Malim muttered. "What was I supposed to do? That's why Arvan went there – to see her, make sure she was ready for me. If you didn't want him to go, why didn't you stop him? I don't understand."

"It is painfully obvious that you don't understand," Rendail replied, but this time without impatience. He sighed again and sat down. When Malim looked up, he saw a softer look in his father's eyes. "What else has happened, Malim? Tell me. I don't want to find out from anyone else. If you talk to me now, I will consider Nyran's presence unnecessary, at least for tonight, and send him to his bed. That would be easier for all of us, don't you think?"

Malim resisted an impulse to ask whose bed Nyran would be going to and nodded.

"Three days after I saw her, Arvan was attacked. *He* did it. I watched. There was someone else with him, an even weaker one. Arvan killed him." Malim grinned inwardly at the memory. "But then *he* killed Arvan's bird. The coward didn't dare fight Arvan. He couldn't stand against one of us. He …"

Rendail held up a hand. "And do you know why he was there, Malim? How did he get there? tell me that."

Malim shrugged. "I don't know. Because he's watching *her* I suppose."

"No." Rendail shook his head. "He was there, Malim, because you invited him. You revealed yourself, and in doing so you revealed Arvan. Now Arghel knows you have seen Karisse. Did you think he would ignore that? Did you think he would not try to find Arvan, get rid of him? You have put your emissary in danger. You, and no one else. Now do you understand?"

"But Arvan can defend himself, Father. He's strong and he's clever. He won't let anything happen. He'll come back, I know it."

"And if he doesn't, Malim?" Rendail's tone was gentle. "What will you do if he doesn't come back?"

The pain of the flogging was suddenly forgotten as Malim stared at his father in horror. He tried to think of something to say, but words failed him. The idea of a world without the ministrations of his constant companion since childhood was simply beyond his ability to contemplate.

Rendail smiled. "Go to bed, Malim. I'm sure Thalis will apply a salve to your back if you ask him sweetly enough. But he is not to use his healing gift at least until dusk tomorrow. I want you to think on what I have said, and a little pain will often concentrate the mind."

Malim struggled to his feet and bowed, still too dumfounded to speak. When he reached the door, however, he found his voice, and without turning back, muttered, "Arvan will come back, Father. He *will* come back."

***

"He is gone, then? You are sure?"

Alex stretched, and carefully laid aside his well thumbed copy of the Financial Times. He didn't answer straight away. When, he thought with some amusement, would Paul learn not to ask a question until he was ready to give his attention to the answer? He looked on as his son divested himself of boots and bike leathers, then helped himself to hot coffee before joining his father at the kitchen table. It was still early, the sharp ground frost just starting to melt in the thin rays of the morning sun.

"Was she worth it?" Alex asked as Paul grasped the mug in both hands, letting the heat seep into his chilled fingers. The quick 'mind your own business' look was followed by a wry grin.

"Put it this way – I didn't leave my phone number."

Alex returned the smile and shrugged sympathetically. It was a long ride from Inverness, and tricky on a motor bike in a greasy frost. He admitted to himself that he had been worried, and also that he needn't have been. Paul was probably possessed of more common sense than he had himself. He returned to the original question.

"Yes, I'm sure. The girl's gift has matured. He was bound to make an attempt on her while she is still vulnerable. If he succeeds now it will save him a lot of trouble later."

Paul downed his coffee and refilled his mug.

"Surely he knows that isn't possible?" he commented, rooting in the biscuit tin for something edible. "History is history. He must realise his brother will defeat him if he tries anything now."

Alex shrugged again. "How can anyone know what is and is not possible? I am here, now. That should not be possible. You, dear boy, should not be possible. Yet you exist." He sighed. "If he does do the impossible, I may have come a very long way for nothing. I refuse to accept that. Besides, Arghel is there. Malim will not confront him directly. Rendail won't let him, for one thing. Neither is Feylan a fool. He will not let his daughter walk into danger."

He paused and rubbed a hand across his eyes, then realised he was allowing his frustration to show.

"Then what's worrying you?" Paul asked, trying to sound offhand. "She has enough protectors for the moment, at least. Or is it that you wish to go back? I know it must be hard for you, sometimes. It is a tiring thing – waiting."

Alex gave a wry laugh. "Go back?" His voice softened into sadness. "Go back, to empty country, with several days in the saddle to go from one place to the next? Go back to hunting for meat and hoping there are no wolves to drive me from my kill? Oh, Paul – there are times when I would give anything to be back in my own place, my own time."

His gaze had drifted back to the table in front of him, but sensing his son's disquiet he looked up to meet Paul's eyes.

"Well, almost anything. But not you. I could never leave you, nor your mother. Besides," he went on with a grin, "there are things about this time that attract me. Life is so much easier, in so many ways. Were it not for the task that faces us I think I might be content. If I survive I will stay here, although my mother, no doubt, would have something to say about that. Perhaps, at times, it is a good thing I can't hear her."

Paul nodded. "I think I would rather I couldn't hear my mother sometimes. I swear she still thinks I'm ten years old, and not forty!"

Alex laughed. "Be thankful," he replied, "that your mother is short lived. To mine I am still a child, and I am past a hundred! But I miss her. Her mind reaches across time to me, and I feel how lonely she is without me." He sighed. "If my gift were greater I could perhaps see my own world again through her eyes, as she sees you through mine." He gave a rueful smile. "But there is no point in wishing for the impossible. I must make the best of what I have, and assume that of which I have no direct knowledge."

They sat for a while, enjoying the warmth of hot coffee and the gentle heat from the big range that took up an entire wall of the old Victorian kitchen. Paul finally broke the silence.

"So, if Malim does succeed in doing the impossible, what then?"

Alex sighed. "I think he will still try to force her to cross the Great Emptiness. Karisse is too young to be completely aware of her gift. She may not yet be aware that she possesses the skill to cross time. Feylan has kept her close – perhaps too close, too sheltered from the truth. Nevertheless, she has a strong will, and Malim may find it more difficult than he imagines to accomplish his plan. Certainly he will be thwarted if his brother gets there first. There is nothing for us to do now but wait. One way or the other, Malim will return, and if he reaches Karisse before we do, then I fear our battle may be a futile one."

He paused, then reached across and laid his hand on Paul's.

"Promise me," he said, his voice low and earnest, "if it comes to that, you will take your mother and go. I must face him. It is my duty to my people. But if he takes the girl, he takes our only weapon, and this is not your mother's fight. You will be her only protection and your duty is to her, not to me."

Paul snatched his hand away, aghast.

"What are you saying? You know we will have no chance against him unless we act together. Are you asking me to let you go alone, knowing that you will die? I can't do it, Father. I won't do it. And if you asked Mother, she would say the same thing. I wouldn't be such a coward, and neither would she."

"Enough!" Alex accompanied the word with a sharp reminder of the power of his gift that made Paul wince. "That is enough," Alex repeated in a softer tone. "You are my son, and you will do as I ask. Whether you like it or not."

The two men stared at each other, Paul breathing hard through his nose. His father appeared outwardly calm, but the warning stood clear in the unblinking gaze. It was Paul who finally acquiesced, bowing his head in acknowledgement.

"It may not come to that," Alex repeated. "But if it does, I need your promise. Not just for your sake, or your mother's, but for the sake of the blood. You may be the only one of us left when this is over, and if that is so, you must use your blood to sire young who can defeat him. I hope that we fight together, my son, but together or alone, be assured, we will both fight."

The long silence that followed was broken only by the occasional spark from the wood burning in the range. At last Paul raised his head to meet his father's steady gaze and, reaching across the table, grasped Alex's hand.

"I promise," he whispered.

CHAPTER 9

Thalis made his way swiftly down the pavement towards the central compound, thankful to be about his duties as overseer of access to the women's quarters. He didn't have Arvan's skill in quelling Malim's rages, and once or twice during the last hours he had been in fear of his life. Even the threat of calling out Rendail in the middle of the night had been largely ineffective, mainly because Malim doubted that anyone would dare disturb the head of the Family simply because his son was having a fit of temper. In that, Thalis reflected, Malim was right.

Thalis made a quick round of the women's rooms, although he was certain before he entered the compound that he would find no untoward liaisons. The aftermath of the clash between Rendail and his heir hung like a pall over the settlement, and as a result both pavement and courtyard were deserted. The clouds had parted, leaving the air bone-cold, the light covering of snow hard and treacherous underfoot. A wind was rising in the north, bitter against his skin as he emerged from the shelter of the great compound building and made his way down to the south gate. Judging by the moisture it carried, morning would bring fresh snowfalls. It was going to be a hard winter.

As he rounded the corner his sense caught a faint summons, no more than a whisper, as if the sender had waited for him to come close before daring to communicate. He turned at once and made for a door a few paces back on the other side of the south gate. It opened as he approached, and he took the stairs two at a time up to a small but comfortable sitting room and the pleasant sight of a well fed log fire.

"Karim." He stepped forward and grasped the arm of the ascetic figure that stood waiting to greet him. Karim responded, inclining his head and gesturing for Thalis to take a seat close to the fire. His hollow cheeks looked more cadaverous than usual, the hook nose even more prominent in the shadows of the dimly lit room. By the Family's standards, Karim was an unbecoming specimen. His bloodline had not let him down completely, however. His less than pleasant appearance was balanced by a powerful gift, sharp intelligence and a cunning Thalis could only admire – that, and a capacity for cruelty unmatched since the days of the first head of the Family, the tyrant Corvan himself.

His other main attribute was ambition. Over the centuries, Karim had gathered a strong band of followers, some close to Rendail's inner circle. Thalis was his oldest and most ardent admirer. Every day, Thalis saw the coveted gift, to cross the Great Emptiness to the future, firmly in the hands of the man he hated most. That Rendail should have been the one to sire a son possessed of that rare gift enraged him. It had been inevitable, of course. The head of the Family was the only one with access to the bloodlines that made it possible. He had taken the only woman capable of bearing such a child, and luck had been with him. Now, the woman was dead and control of the future was in Rendail's hands, out of reach of those who would use it for the benefit of the Family as a whole. But, Thalis thought as he settled himself and accepted a cup of warm wine, a chance may have presented itself. The unthinkable might have happened – Rendail might have made a mistake.

"I take it Lord Malim is still a little temperamental this evening?" Karim leaned his back against the wall and crossed his feet on the low table between them.

"More insufferable than usual," Thalis admitted, hunching in front of the fire to warm his chilled fingers. "With Arvan gone he is impossible. I'm still not sure what the argument was about. It's unlike Rendail to be so unrestrained. He had the heir publicly whipped – it's extraordinary."

Karim chuckled. "I know. I was watching. It was delightful!"

"But why? What's going on that we don't know about? Malim won't say a word, and that's even more odd. Obviously his father has scared him into silence. I tried to broach the subject when he came back to his room, and nearly got both arms broken. Then he just raved about Arvan, and about his brother. I couldn't make any sense of it."

80

"His brother?" Karim sat forward, his eyes glittering with interest. "I wonder …"

"What?"

"My dear Thalis, sometimes your lack of insight astounds me." Karim grinned, an unsettling expression in the half light. "We know Arghel is in the south, yes? He ran away to the spawn of the traitor, Derlan, his mother's tribe."

Thalis nodded his agreement.

"And we know that some months ago Malim sent Arvan south. Now why would he do that, Thalis? More to the point, why would Rendail let him go? Don't you think that's strange?"

Thalis shrugged. "I assumed Malim sent Arvan to get rid of Arghel. After all, it's about time. He's both a traitor and an embarrassment to all of us. Rendail should have strangled him at birth, like any other deformed child. You have another idea?"

Karim shook his head, laughing. "Oh, Thalis, I often wonder what mix of blood left you with so little intelligence. Life would be dull without you, it's true, but I do tire of having to explain everything. You could at least make an effort!"

Thalis felt himself colour, but said nothing. Sometimes Karim could be as wearing as Lord Rendail.

Karim sighed, and poured more wine. "Apart from Lord Malim, who else has shown this long awaited ability to transfer themselves to a future time?"

"Just one. We all know that."

"And who was that 'just one'? Think, Thalis – it's not that difficult."

"Amala, of course. The sister of Rendail's mother, the one who ran away and was stolen by Derlan …" Thalis stopped, catching up with Karim's reasoning. "And you think his tribe has spawned another? They have one who can cross the Great Emptiness? And Arvan went to find out, and bring him here?"

"Her, Thalis. *Her*. It's a woman, I'm sure of it. When Rendail stole back one of their young, he took a female, didn't he? And he mated with her. He got what he wanted – the result was Malim. But now there is another, and Malim wants to do the same thing. They both want to keep the gift within their own line.

It stands to reason. He who holds that gift rules this Family. They want to keep it within their own blood. They will keep it secret until the woman is beyond anyone's reach and they have the ultimate power. I know how Rendail's mind works. Imagine – if he controls the future he can shape history as he wishes. He can stop anyone from getting in his way. So, my guess is that Malim sent Arvan to get confirmation of the existence of the gift. But like always, he overstepped the mark and his father didn't take kindly to it. If he put the prize at risk I'm not surprised Rendail had him flogged. I probably would have done much worse."

Karim sat back with a satisfied look as the implications of it all began to dawn on Thalis. If Karim's deductions proved true, the grip of Rendail's line on the Family could only be strengthened, and any faint hope that he and Karim might have of seizing power would be lost.

"So, what do we do?" Thalis asked. "If they have already found this woman, our chances of reaching her are virtually none."

Karim grinned. "They *are* virtually none," he agreed. "But Corvan's brood have, I think, finally made an error. Arvan was indispensable to the heir – the only man that Malim ever trusted completely, yes?"

Thalis assented with a wave of the hand.

"And now Arvan is gone," Karim went on. "That is fortunate for us, as I would have had to get rid of him anyway, eventually. They have done it for us. Malim is alone, and without his confidant he is vulnerable. In a short time he will need someone to take Arvan's place. You, Thalis, are perfectly placed to be that man. Cultivate him. Give him pillow talk, advise him. You know he will listen to you if he has no other ear, after all, you were his tutor once. If we have the heir, we have his brood mare as well, and what Rendail does becomes irrelevant, as long as he doesn't find out of course. The power is in Malim. If we have Malim, we own the future. You understand?"

Thalis wiped his brow, his mind suddenly full of possibilities.

"It will not be easy," he commented, although he was smiling as he turned his gaze from his cup to Karim. "Arvan was more skilled at controlling Malim's moods. And the heir would never knowingly betray his father, that much I know. It is not just fear, either. It may not seem like it a lot of the time, but they are like that, the two of them." He held up his hands, index fingers linked together. "They are father and son, and that bond is impossible to break."

"You won't have to break it," Karim said with a shrug. "You only have to get close enough to know what Malim intends, and make yourself indispensable to him. I have a feeling that when he stakes his claim to a future empire, he will start to see his father as more of a hindrance than a help. Rendail can't go on forever – he has already lived longer than is natural. If Malim sees us as allies, then when the time comes …"

He spread his arms wide and lifted an eyebrow at Thalis, who nodded his understanding.

"When the time comes," Thalis said, "we will take the blood from Corvan's line and spawn ourselves power over the Great Emptiness." He laughed. "You never know, when Malim gets the woman he will probably tire of her within days, just as he tires of all of them. He may even give her to us – if she is still alive, that is."

* * *

Karisse shivered, and wandered across to the low wall, where Arghel had been standing a little while before. She looked out across the fields, rubbing her hands on her arms and wishing she had thought to bring a cloak. There were perhaps two or three hours until dawn; the moon was sinking low, casting lengthening shadows across the landscape. She turned her mind to the latest encounter – the one that had done more than anything else over the last few days to shake her certainty in her own judgement.

When she thought of the early part of the exchange with Arghel, of how he had played on her fear, she hated him, wanted him gone. Later, he had been altogether different. Even when she had struck him he showed no anger. It was as if he understood her distress and allowed for it. Worst of all, when he smiled he seemed to become a different person, one that might even laugh given the right circumstances. But it was the nature of his gift that confused her most. It hovered around him like something that could be touched, as though he was unable to contain it. She had thought her own gift stronger than most, but this kind of power was completely unknown to her. Furthermore, the encounter had revealed almost nothing about him. He had deliberately hidden his inner self from her in a way no Dancer should, indeed would, find possible. She cursed herself for being stupid enough to agree to his unthinkable bargain. At least, she thought, if she could persuade whoever it was she was supposed to be waiting for of the folly of the situation, her promise would become void and Arghel would disappear, taking her turmoil with him.

"He came that way. I remember it clearly. He was younger than you are now, and so afraid as he walked alone across the fields to greet us."

Karisse gasped, and stumbled back against the wall as she turned. She had been so deep in her own thoughts that she hadn't heard the newcomer come up behind her. She recognised him at once. Although she had never seen him in life, she knew his image from her father's thoughts. She should have screamed, but there was nothing left in her but a dull acceptance of the string of impossibilities that kept on presenting themselves to her exhausted mind.

"Grandfather?"

He smiled. "Don't be afraid, Karisse. You and I share a gift. Arghel asked me to come. He thought you might accept my word, better than you might accept his."

"Arghel?" She blinked, not comprehending. "He talks to the dead, now?"

"Aren't you?"

She could think of no answer to that. She suddenly felt very cold, and shivered. At once he unfastened his cloak and wrapped it round her.

"Come and sit down," he said, guiding her round the side of the house to a long stone bench beneath a pergola draped with climbing plants. "It has been a struggle for you, these last few days," he went on. "You are strong, though, I feel that. And beautiful, too, just as I knew you would be."

She blushed at the compliment and he laughed, then put an arm round her shoulders.

"But you are still so young," he sighed. "It will be difficult now. You can't go back to what you were, you know that."

It was a statement, not a question. She didn't answer, still trying to make sense of the fact that she was sitting next to Devren, her father's father, who had died many years before she was born. He was no ghost; she could feel his solid warmth through the thick folds of the cloak. She could even perceive his gift, gentle, reassuring, reaching out to envelop her, make her feel safe. She remembered listening, as a child, to Feylan's reminiscences of his father. She had heard tales of Devren's gift, of his skill in calming the most troubled mind, man or animal. According to her father, he had spent a good part of his life among those who had lost loved ones, particularly if those lost were children. Despite her anxiety, she couldn't help but nestle against him, feeling some measure of calm for the first time since she had seen the eagle swoop down onto the lawn.

"How does Arghel talk to you? And why? What does he have to do with us?"

"He has what is called the 'gift of memory'," Devren answered. "Just as you and I can use our gift to place us in a future time, so he can travel into the past. When he needs me, he can seek me out."

"When he needs you? Grandfather, who is he?" The idea that the man who was causing her so much turmoil could act as though he were a part of her family was unsettling.

"Ah, but he is," Devren said, reading her thought. "You are not my only grandchild, Karisse. Arghel is my grandson."

The feeling of warmth suddenly drained from her and she sat up, startled.

"That's impossible!" Even as she said it, however, she realised what it was about Arghel that had seemed so familiar. Before, she had only seen her grandfather through the eyes of her father's memory. Now, staring at Devren, his solid form beside her, she saw the likeness, in the curve of the mouth, the set of the forehead and, most of all, in the long, dark curls that were common to all the descendants of Derlan. She shook her head.

"How? If that's true, why haven't I seen him before? Where does he come from?"

As though this latest revelation was just one crack too many in the crumbling stability that had been her life up to now, she began to feel light headed and a little sick. Devren, his arm still round her shoulder, gently pulled her back and laid his free hand on hers, which were tightly knotted in her lap.

"Hush, now," he whispered, and she felt him intensify the flow of his gift just a little, willing her to be calm. She succumbed to it and relaxed back into him. "There is no need to be afraid," he went on, "not while I am here. There is a story to be told, and I have always been the one to tell it, at the right time. Now is the time, if you are ready to hear it."

She looked up at him and nodded. "I'm ready."

CHAPTER 10

A short silence followed, in which Karisse realised that her neither her father nor anyone else had ever mentioned the existence of another child born to her grandparents, Devren and Mirielle. She wondered what tragedy must have taken place before her birth, to make them so tight lipped about a whole branch of her family. Clearly the child had not died, at least not until the birth of Arghel.

"You are right." Again, her grandfather responded directly to her thought. "There was a tragedy, and the child did not die. Perhaps it might have been better if she had, although when I see Arghel I can't bring myself to think it."

He paused, sighed, then said, "It began a long time ago, in the lifetime of my grandfather, Derlan. It has always been known that the gift changes from generation to generation. It grows, reveals new abilities, becomes stronger if the blood that carries it remains pure as it is passed from joining to joining. Even before Derlan was born ours was among the strongest lines, our lifespan and the skills within the gift fuelled by the blood.

"By the time Derlan was a young man a family of very ancient blood, headed by a powerful Dancer named Corvan, had isolated itself in the far north and forbidden any joinings outside its circle. In an attempt to create ever more powerful facets of the gift, brother mated with sister, mother with son, and it is known now that many of these matings were enforced, and not by choice. For many years our only information was rumour and speculation.

"We heard tales of men of supernatural power, who could kill from a great distance with just a single thought. Every so often a group of them would appear in the forests on the borders of their land, hunting. They allowed no intruders near their settlement. They traded in horses with the nearest towns, but never mixed with or spoke to the people there. Apart from that they stayed within the enclave they had chosen for themselves and turned their backs on the world outside. So, they were all but forgotten.

"It was not until Derlan was reaching the end of his life that we learned the full horror of existence under Corvan's rule. In those days, many of our clan lived much closer to the sea, and a group of them, including my grandfather, were returning from a fishing expedition when one of the young ones rushed up to say he had seen a dead woman under the water. Derlan followed him and found a young girl, one of our kind, no more than eighteen years old, washed up on the water's edge. She was not dead, although close to it, and had several broken bones.

"He took her home, healed her injuries and nursed her back to health. But despite recovering completely from her physical wounds, she refused to communicate with anyone, even the other women in the house. She let no one near her except Derlan, and even then she sat hunched in a corner as though she were afraid of him, keeping her eyes closed or looking at the floor. He was a skilled healer, though, and patient, and after several weeks, during which he sat with her every day for hours at a time, she began to trust him. When she finally did speak, the story she told filled my grandfather, and every other Dancer who heard it, with dread.

"The girl's name was Amala. She was one of Corvan's many daughters. By the time she was born, the settlement was already quite large. It had been founded by Corvan and his two brothers, together with two women, the brothers' mates, and four children, all of the same bloodline. All of them were persuaded by Corvan that by careful manipulation of the blood they would be rewarded with gifts beyond their imaginings. In the beginning I'm sure they really didn't think where it would lead. Corvan knew, of course. He had complete power over his brothers, and would go to any lengths to achieve his ambitions. He had but two. The first was to rule his own empire. The second was to gain control over time. In his twisted imagination he believed that it would bring him immortality. The only thing he feared was death.

"His first act as leader of the new clan was to forbid the joining of men and women as a permanent state. The right mixing of the blood was all that mattered, and he laid out what later became known as the Rule, the process by which men were chosen to sire young by women selected for the enhancement of the gift. As the settlement grew, the Rule became more complex. Corvan's sons were given relative freedom to mate with any women they chose, but others were severely restricted, and those whose gift was not considered worthy were denied the right to mate altogether. Women, of course, had no choice at all, and they resisted the Rule as much as they could. The birth of a child became a time of fear rather than joy, because any born deformed or without the seed of a gift deemed useful by Lord Corvan were put to death. Finally, when one woman, Amala's grandmother, tried to escape the settlement, they were all herded together into a great central compound and imprisoned there."

Devren paused, and Karisse shook her head in disbelief.

"They murdered their children?" The picture her grandfather was painting was so far removed from her imagination that it hardly made sense to her. He held her closer, and stroked the hair out of her eyes.

"That, and worse," he said, his voice calm, although she sensed a burning anger close to the surface of his thoughts. "As time went on, the Family, as they called themselves, grew in strength. As Corvan predicted, their lives were lengthened, the gift grew more powerful with every passing generation. Finally, some of the women began to show signs of the gift he sought. One of his daughters developed the ability to take her mind back in time, and speak with members of her distant kin, long dead. Corvan took her for himself, and forced her to bear him four children. The eldest was a boy, Rolan, and the next was Amala.

"Both had strange gifts. Corvan never knew it, but Rolan could hide his thoughts from others of our kind, a skill that probably saved his life, because he hated his father and all the Family stood for. In Amala, two things happened. First, the gift came to her when she was still a very young child. That was unheard of. Until then, the coming of the gift had always been signalled by the change to adulthood. Corvan never realised it, simply because he did not expect it, and so never looked for it.

89

Second, and more important to Corvan, she fulfilled his dream. She could travel forward into the future.

"She didn't know it herself until she grew up and was taken before her father so that he could examine her for any changes in the gift. She was so terrified as he approached her that her mind took her forward and she saw a vision of herself, lying on a cloth pallet, in terrible pain and hardly able to breathe. It was only for a moment, but Corvan saw what she had done. She realised then that he would want her, make her bear his children, and in a panic she ran.

"When she reached the edge of the settlement, two of Corvan's servants sent out their gift and snapped the bones in her legs and chest. They took her back and locked her in a room, laid on a cloth pallet to wait until Corvan came for her. But when the door opened it wasn't her father, it was her brother, Rolan. He bound her broken bones, hid her under his gift of silence and carried her out to the edge of the fields. There, he put her on a horse and commanded it to ride. It was next morning before anyone discovered her escape and by then she was far away.

"Derlan calculated that she must have ridden for at least ten days and nights to reach the beach where she was found, exhausted and close to death. When he learned the truth about the Family and its insane ruler, he realised that Corvan would stop at nothing to get Amala back. The gift that was in her blood was too valuable to lose. He also understood that he and his clan were no match for the unnaturally powerful riders who would come for her. He took her away that night, and told no one where they would go. For many years they travelled around the country, never staying more than a short while in one place. Always, searchers from the Family were close behind them, but they were never discovered.

"Derlan, of course, had fallen in love with her. She was a beautiful woman – a tiny waif of a thing with blonde hair and blue eyes. But he never tried to touch her. He was so much older, and he felt that to tell her would be a betrayal of her trust in him. He didn't want her to come to him out of obligation. Then, for only the second time in her life, Amala crossed the great

Emptiness and saw Derlan lying in the grass, his head against a rock. She knew he wasn't asleep, but his face, in death, was peaceful – she was seeing the end of his natural life.

"That night she took him a small box, the only thing she had taken with her from her former home. Rolan had fastened it to the horse's saddle before she rode away. In it was a token, a clasp of joining, and she fastened it in Derlan's hair, then made love to him, and almost every night afterwards until their son was born. They named him Rolan in memory of her brother. Three nights after the birth she went outside to find Derlan, just as she had seen in her vision, lying in the grass, peaceful in death.

"She brought the child here, to this house, and gave him to a couple who had once befriended them, asking them to care for him until she returned. Then, she rode back to the place where Derlan had found her, and let the sea take her at last."

There was a silence in which Karisse could hear her own rapid heartbeats, and then she whispered, "Rolan was your father – and they didn't find him?"

She heard Devren give a low laugh.

"No. They didn't find him. At least, he thought himself safe. His guardians adopted him as their son, and gave him this house when he joined with Alisse, my mother. They owned another across the way, and once he was settled they wanted to have children of their own. They told him of his true origins and he was always wary, but never saw any sign of the Family. The union of Derlan and Amala had produced a Dancer of extraordinary power. Like his namesake, Rolan was able to guard his thoughts, keep himself hidden from others of our kind. Perhaps that was one reason why they never came. It is impossible to know. I remember only that my childhood was happy, that he was a gentle man, graceful and quietly spoken, who had great skill in healing.

"When I grew to adulthood it was clear that my gift was also enhanced by Amala's blood. I had no gift of silence, but once or twice saw visions of the future, as she had. I tried to keep it hidden from my father, but he could always see my thoughts easily. He made me swear to tell no one, nor ever to use the gift. I

91

obeyed him, right up until tonight. Whether or not my violation is discovered, I suppose I will only know when I return. But somehow I think that if I don't stay too long it will be overlooked. Even the Family can't keep their eyes everywhere at every moment. It is worth the risk if it keeps you safe.

"Around that time a rumour came to us that Corvan had died and his place taken by one of his many sons, Rendail. The news was no comfort to us. It was said that Rendail was every bit as obsessed as his father with the furthering of the blood, but with many times the gift and therefore far more dangerous. Nevertheless, the news of Corvan's death brought some hope that the search for Amala and her children had ended.

"I paid little heed at the time. I was in love with Mirielle, the young daughter of Rolan's foster parents. She was the most beautiful thing I had ever seen, blonde haired, blue eyed, just like my mother. We had been inseparable since childhood, and once of age there was no question but that we would join. For several years we were completely taken up with each other. The rest of the world might not have existed. Mirielle loved children, and we both had a skill with young ones, so we spent most of our time caring for those who had no one else to look after them. There has never been a shortage of abandoned offspring, especially among the short lived, not then and, I suspect, not now.

"Eventually, our thoughts turned to having a family of our own. I think that when Mirielle announced she was to have a child it was the happiest moment of my life up until then. When the time came for her to give birth we came back here, so that my father would be close enough to help if need be. I was too anxious to be any use at all. My first sight of my daughter was a moment I will never forget. She was the tiniest, most beautiful thing I had ever seen, and looked exactly like her mother. We named her Sherenne, and the weeks that followed were filled with such contentment they seem like a dream to me now. And then …"

"And then?" Karisse looked up, and to her surprise saw tears flowing freely down Devren's cheeks. "And then, Grandfather?"

"And then," he said, "Our dream became the worst of nightmares, and our lives were destroyed forever."

CHAPTER 11

"It was a hot, still night in mid summer. There had been no rain for several weeks, and the lawns behind the houses were as brown as the dusty streets. Little Sherenne was almost four months old. She had a tooth coming and that, combined with the sultry weather, had set her off crying non stop, so that one or other of us had to constantly go to her in the night to try to rock her back to sleep. I was tempted several times to use my gift to calm her, but Mirielle would not allow it. Such interference with little ones is always frowned on as overprotective, but I remember thinking on that occasion that I was more in need of protection than Sherenne – an ironic thought, looking back.

Both Mirielle and I were exhausted, and when Sherenne began to wail it was all I could do to lift my head off the pillow. So I was grateful when my mother whispered through the door that I was not to concern myself, that she would take the poor mite outside and stroll with her round the garden where the air was a little cooler, as the heat was making her as restless as the baby. I drifted back to sleep, but it wasn't long before something woke me – not a noise, but more a feeling of vague apprehension, of the sort people have when they remember something that they should have done, but can't quite work out what it might be.

"I struggled with myself for a little while, but the feeling wouldn't go away, and tired as I was my mind was wide awake, so I slipped out of bed, taking care not to wake Mirielle, thinking to join my mother and Sherenne in the garden. It seems I was not the only restless one, as I met my father in the upstairs corridor, his puzzled expression a match for my own. We stood together at the top of the stairs, wondering what the cause of our anxiety could be.

"The air around us seemed unnaturally still and the silence was oppressive – I don't think I could even hear the creak of a grasshopper, even though the house was normally overrun by them at that time of the year. A feeling of foreboding was slowly creeping over me, and I could see that my father's face reflected my uneasiness. We started down the stairs together, and at that moment I caught a sensation, the presence of someone, close by, coming towards the house. This was followed by another, and yet another.

"A sudden chill of realisation swept though me and, glancing at my father, I realised he had felt it too. At the same time we heard a scream, followed by Sherenne's frantic cries, coming from the archway to the side of the house. For a fraction of a second we stood frozen in horror, then both of us dashed down the stairs and out into the garden in time to see three men making away across the field beyond our lawn to where a group of horsemen were waiting. One of them was clutching the wriggling, crying bundle that was my daughter.

"In a haze of desperation I bore down on them, letting loose every particle of strength that was in my mind with a rage I did not know I possessed. I heard my father call for me to stop, that it was too late, but I didn't heed him. I just kept running, using my gift to try to snare the one who carried my child. I saw the one next to him fall and not get up, then the other, but he reached the group and was astride his mount before I was half way across the field. He and all but four of the others turned tail and rode, faster than the wind, into the night. I heard little Sherenne's cries grow fainter and fainter, until at last they disappeared into the distance.

"The remaining horsemen stood their ground between me and their fleeing comrades, and although I was outmatched I still dashed madly forward in the vain hope that I could perhaps unhorse one of them and set off in pursuit. However, I don't think I had gone more than two paces when I felt a sudden jolt run through my body, as though I had been struck by a bolt of lightening, or run head first into a solid wall. I remember being tossed into the air and falling backwards, then nothing but blindness and pain for a long time. When I woke I found myself back in the house, lying on my back, with my father and Mirielle on either side of me, their tear-stained faces telling me that it had not been just some terrible dream.

95

"It was only then that I learned the full horror of the events of that night. As I lay, unable to move, Mirielle clutching my hand with both of hers, my father related the story in a voice that he could barely control, such was his anger and grief. He had been behind me as the horsemen struck out with their thought and had seen me fall into a heap on the ground. They had galloped away to join their comrades, and in just a few moments it was as though they had never been there at all, but for the dust thrown up by the hooves of the horses. They had thought to kill me but by some instinct, even in my distracted state, I had somehow drawn my gift around me to afford me some protection.

"Nevertheless, when he reached my side I was barely conscious and my back was broken in three places. I might still have died, or been unable to walk for the rest of my life, had he not been so prodigious a healer and so close at hand. Even so, it took every ounce of his skill to mend the bones and the nerves beneath them, so that I could be safely moved back into the house.

"By this time Mirielle had woken and rushed out to us. When she realised what had happened she was distraught, shouting hysterically for her baby. Then she saw me lying so still upon the ground and, thinking me lost as well, ran back into the house to fetch a knife, then to the stable for a horse, crying that she would get back her child and avenge herself on the Family for my death. My father was forced to restrain her and took away the knife, finally making her understand that I was not dead and that what she proposed was complete madness. He picked me up and made her go with him back inside, then left her to tend to me while he went to find Alisse.

"My mother had been with Sherenne, sitting in her favourite place underneath the side arch – just where we are sitting now – and my father knew what he would find there. No one can say with any certainty, but I think that if she had not tried to fight them they would not have harmed her and our tragedy might have been lessened. But it's no use wondering what might have happened. My father found my mother lying on the path beneath the arch. Her attackers had not used their minds – one of them had taken a knife and stabbed her in the chest, but not an instantly mortal wound, so that all the time my father was with me, giving me back my life, she had lain dying on the other side of the house.

"How terrible it must have been for Rolan, faced with such a choice. I don't believe he did not know that he must sacrifice either his beloved Alisse, or his son. The bond between them had always been complete, so that they could see each other's minds even when he chose to make his silent. Perhaps she made the decision for him – he did not speak of it, neither then nor later, and I have never asked. There was nothing for him to do but carry her body back to the house, where it lay that night, and the next morning he made her a final resting place, close to the archway where she had so loved to sit. Then he came back to my bedside to sit with Mirielle, and they waited three days for me to come back to life and open my eyes.

"I was not fully myself for several weeks after I first woke. I slept a great deal, and although I was aware of either my father or Mirielle close by, I would not speak to them, nor eat any of the food they brought to me. Occasionally I accepted some water, but that was all. I could feel my back becoming stronger, and knew that I should get up and walk about to speed the healing process, but I couldn't bring myself to move. After a while, I didn't want them near me. Every time I looked at them I saw my own guilt reflected in their eyes. Mirielle cried constantly for her lost baby and, when I saw her tears, I thought that I was responsible for them. I took no thought for the fact that she needed me to comfort her.

"As for my father, it was I who had allowed Alisse to go out with Sherenne, a thing I should have done myself, and which might have prevented the whole series of events from ever happening. Later, I had forced him to choose between us, or at least that was the way I saw it. Whichever way I looked at things, the only conclusion was that I had been the cause of everyone's misery and my mother's death, and finding the burden unbearable, I simply added to their grief by my indifference to them.

"Rolan knew the cause of my unreasonableness but let it pass, hoping I would come to myself. But when I didn't, he decided that things had gone far enough, and came to speak to me. At first I wouldn't look at him, but I had to listen, and what he said made me realise how much we had underestimated the Family, and what their purpose had been all along. At least twenty of them came that night. They surrounded the house, and if my mother and Sherenne had not been outside they would undoubtedly have come inside and taken the baby from her cradle. In such force we could never have prevented them.

"What he found incredible was that I had somehow succeeded in dispatching three of them before I was finally stopped. But, more importantly, we now knew why we had thought ourselves safe for all this time. When Amala hid Rolan to keep him from being taken, the Family knew it. They could have come for him at any time, and even with all of Derlan's clan watching over him, they would have succeeded. They had seen my birth, and only my father's wariness had prevented them from learning of my gift. Still, they had done nothing but watch, and wait. Now we knew what they had been waiting for. They had taken no interest in us because we were males. Those they had in abundance, and most with gifts far exceeding our own. They had been waiting for one of us to have a daughter, a girl child who might have the gifts of Amala. Finally we had given them their desire, me and Mirielle, and they had come to claim their blood right from us. There was nothing I could have done to stop it; it had been inevitable that they would come and take my little Sherenne, for the precious gift that might be in her.

"As I listened to my father explain all this, my feelings started to reawaken; grief for my darling child and for my mother, sorrow for my father and for Mirielle, who had grieved all this time alone; anger that the Family should come so coolly out of the night and destroy our lives beyond all hope of future peace. I started to cry then, and Mirielle, hearing me, came running into the room. We all held each other and cried together.

"Thanks to my father, my body recovered completely in time, save for a pain in my back every now and then. But the pain in my heart could not be mended, and it was the same for all of us. I think it would have been better if we had learned that our Sherenne was dead. We all knew the fate of women within the Family. But we heard nothing, and not a day passed that our minds were not full of memories of her, her blue eyes, her yellow curls and that pretty little smile. I would go out each night and stand in the garden, staring off to where the horsemen had ridden away, as if by some miracle my child would come riding back to me. Mirielle quietly went about blocking off the path at the side of the house that led to the archway, so that no one could approach the place without first going through the house.

"The years turned into decades, and then into almost two centuries of unbroken silence, with no news of our precious child. Our lives continued, but a part of us was frozen, as though we were living part in, part outside what went on around us. My father went about the towns and villages much as he had always done, rendering aid to any who were in need. Mirielle and I took on our former roles, helping orphaned young ones come to terms with themselves and preparing them for adulthood.

"Then, something happened that gave our lives back to us. Mirielle announced that she was once again with child. At first I was filled with dread at the thought of it, but when the time came and she gave birth to a boy I knew he would be safe, just as my father and I had been. He grew, and joined with your mother, Livelle, and for a while our lives were almost as carefree as they had been before Sherenne's birth.

"Then came a night, as hot and sultry as that one so long ago, when someone came riding across the fields once more, and we finally learned what became of our daughter. It was very late, and Mirielle had long since retired to bed. Feylan was away, newly joined and travelling with Livelle. My father and I were standing together as we often did, lost in our own thoughts, both dreaming of those far off days when we had all been so happy together, my mother still alive and my first child peacefully asleep in her cradle.

"We heard it first, the sound of a horse's hooves, faint but clear in the stillness of the night, coming across the field, getting closer with each passing minute. Slowly a shadow appeared, still quite far away, of a rider making his way directly toward us. As he drew nearer we could see quite plainly that this was a Dancer, tall, long hair streaming out behind him, and with the confident air of one who knows the gift.

My first thought was that there might be others behind him, that the Family had returned to wreak some other havoc upon our lives. I reached out with my mind but could perceive nothing, not even a hint of his presence beyond what I could see. It was clear that this man had the gift of silence, just as my father did, and that could mean only one thing – that he was of the Family, as no one outside their blood was known to possess it. If anything, his gift was greater than my father's, for every attempt I made to seek him out found what I can only describe as a blank space, as if a hole had opened up in the world and swallowed him.

"I started forward, anger rising in me at the thought of what they had already done to us. I heard my father's breathing quicken and knew that he was beside me, ready to defend our lives. But as we strode towards the horseman, I heard his silent voice in my head assuring us that he meant us no harm and, looking at my father, I saw that he had heard it too.

"We stopped halfway across the field, unsure, suspecting some trick, thinking that the stranger was perhaps acting as a distraction while others broke into the house. He stopped too, a little way from us, and dismounted. Leaving his horse he came forward on foot, as calmly as if he were out for a gentle evening stroll. As he came nearer, we realised that he was actually no more than a boy – a youth of about twenty or so, but with a power so great that it could be felt on the air even at some distance, and the degree of control he seemed to have far outstripped his age.

"He stopped just a pace or two away from us and stood still, so that we were able to see him perfectly in the moonlight. There was something familiar about him, but I could not quite determine what it was. My father and I both stood in silence, waiting for him to make the next move. He looked from one to the other of us, then he turned to me and spoke.

"I am Arghel," he said, "son of Sherenne and Rendail. I am your grandson."

CHAPTER 12

"Nobody moved. He simply stood there, waiting for us to respond. My eyes absorbed every inch of the newcomer, and all that seemed familiar began to crystallise in my mind. There was still no inner sense of him. Although my ability to penetrate the minds of others was formidable, the shield he wrapped around himself was stronger. But I did not need the gift to see the long black curls that so closely matched my own, and the echo of his grandmother in the delicate curve of his mouth. I knew he had spoken the truth, just as I knew he meant us no harm. I was still wary, for even if he were innocent, no one of the Family would be permitted to leave the settlement alone, and certainly not unwatched, especially one as young as this boy seemed to be.

"And that was the most startling thing about him. The eyes of a Dancer are the mirrors of his age, and it could have been the tale of centuries that looked out at me from the face of this youth. Once again I heard his voice in my mind, and realised that through the veil with which he covered himself he had been reading my every thought, which up to now I had believed impossible. The voice said, 'I am alone,' meaning that he had not been followed, but beneath the message lay a deeper significance, a feeling that swept straight to my heart, of a child's loneliness and longing for love.

"As I watched I saw a single tear roll down his cheek and, unable to be still any longer, I reached out a hand. As he took it a tiny thrill ran through me, as though the power of his gift were spilling onto the surface of his skin. A picture formed immediately in my mind of a woman, with long golden hair and deep blue eyes, the image of Mirielle – it was clearly the boy's mother as he held her in his memory. I pulled him to me and we embraced, and then my father, who up to now had stood silent beside me, did the same. Without another word we took Arghel with us back into the house.

"We called for Mirielle to come down, and the moment she saw Arghel she gave a little cry, needing no sense other than her eyes to see her blood in him. He stood quietly while she smothered him with kisses and let her lead him to a chair, whereupon she sat beside him, holding his hand so tightly I thought she might never let go of it. We got him food and drink, and settled down to hear what he would tell us.

"First, he answered the question we dared not ask. Our daughter was dead, and had been these past four years. It was a grievous blow, even though in some way we had expected it, and we sat in silence for a while, filled with grief for the child we would never know except, perhaps, through the eyes of her son. What her life must have been in that place is hard to imagine, but as Arghel told us what he knew of it we formed a picture in our minds of a woman of great courage and resourcefulness, very like her great-grandmother, Amala.

"Like Amala, the gift had come to her in childhood and, just as Amala had done, she kept it secret. It also became clear early on that she had both the gift of memory and the gift of silence. So, although our child had been lost to us, we learned that we had always been with her, that she had known and loved us through the remnant of her childhood memories. She had even spoken with Derlan, and with her grandmother Alisse. This news brought us both joy and sorrow – joy that she had known us, and held on to her own history, and sorrow that we had never seen her. It is not possible for one with that gift to contact those still living, and she had been too far away for our thoughts to touch.

"She didn't use her gift of silence to try to escape. She learned quickly that the Family did not yet know of it. They had never divined its presence in Rolan, the only other within that place who possessed it. Since Amala, no Dancer had crossed the Great Emptiness, even a little way, but even though Sherenne had not the skill it was in her blood and so she was a precious prize. In one way that blood was her salvation, as Rendail ordered that no man should touch her, even when she came of age, in case she was harmed and rendered useless to him. In another way it was her curse, as Rendail took her for himself, and his nature is truly evil, a reflection of his father's madness, but with many times the power.

"She bore him three children. The first was a daughter, Maylie. From the moment the child was born, Sherenne set to plotting how she could get her daughter away from the Family. Using her gift, she searched all the towns and villages within a night's journey of the settlement. There were two within reach, and after several days of patient searching with her mind she found what she was looking for. That night, as soon as it was dark, she took the baby and left the settlement under cover of her gift, just as Rolan had done with Amala. It was late spring and the horses had been left out to graze, so she was able to lead one away and, once out of sight under the trees, she rode like the wind to where an ailing child lay dying in its cradle, deep in the warren of houses in the centre of the larger town.

"Infant deaths are not uncommon among those without the gift but, even so, to find a girl child just a week old, with dark hair and blue eyes matching her daughter's, was a thing she could hardly have hoped for. She stood outside the door, and with her silent voice commanded that the parents inside should go to sleep. Then she entered, took the dying baby from its cradle and replaced it with her own. By the time she got back to the settlement, just before dawn the next day, the baby in her arms was dead.

"Fortunately, the men of the family take little interest in their young until they reach an age where they can be of use, so when Sherenne showed the body to Rendail and told him his daughter was dead, there was no way for him to know the difference. He went into a fury, but she had expected that, and I think he might have killed her had his desire for her offspring not been so great. He searched her mind for the cause of the child's death, but she pulled the gift of silence across that part of her knowledge, and so he believed she knew nothing of how it had happened.

"As time passed, it became clear that her plan contained an advantage that she had not considered. Rendail, concerned that any future children should be healthy left her alone and even, in

104

his way, made efforts to ensure that she lacked for nothing, except of course her freedom. Sherenne's second child was a boy, Malim, and from the beginning he was his father's son. He had his mother's fair hair and blue eyes, but that is where all resemblance ended.

"From the moment he could talk he had nothing but contempt for his mother, and indeed for all women. Nothing Sherenne did made any impression on him, and his hatred of her was so great that when he was only six years old he struck her on the head with a heavy pot while she slept, claiming his father would be proud to learn that he had rid the world of such an inconsequential creature. But Rendail was not as impressed as his son had hoped, not that he cared much about the injury that had been caused to Sherenne, but only about the risk that she might have been unable to provide him with future offspring. To prevent further incidents Rendail took Malim away from his mother, and from that moment on she didn't see him again until he was a man. Later, she heard that father and son had become inseparable, and that as her son grew he became more and more the image of his father's soul.

"Some years after the birth of Malim, she bore Rendail his third child, a second son, Arghel. The gift came to Arghel when he was only four years old, and became the focus for all that the women of the Family had dreaded. A male child cannot hide the changing of his eyes, and Arghel's turned in a single night from blue to the black that signals the gift. So, the existence of the childhood gift was finally discovered. But a mother's vision is sharper than any, and Sherenne knew long before it could be seen that her son was possessed of the gifts of both memory and silence. She showed him how to use them, and gave him all her knowledge of our family, so that by the time his father saw what was happening to his son Arghel knew his entire history through his own eyes as well as those of his mother.

"Of course, when Rendail saw the transformation taking place in his child he took him away, and so Sherenne thought all her children lost to her. But Arghel was not so easily parted from his mother. His heart belonged to her completely, and with the early gift had come an adult intellect which he used to find her both in mind and body, both of them using the ability that they shared to make their minds invisible to all but each other.

"As time went on it became clear that Malim's hatred of Arghel was shared by Rendail. He was constantly in danger from Malim and Sherenne, helpless inside the women's compound, feared for his life. Rendail did nothing to protect him. He was a child in a man's world, rejected by his father, despised by every man in the settlement.

"The one thing that was certain in Arghel's mind was his desire not only to escape the Family, but also to oppose them in any way he could. However, as long as his mother lived he would not leave her. Rendail was vicious and unforgiving, and it was no secret that his heir, Malim, harboured a murderous hatred of Sherenne, considering her the descendant of a traitor who had almost robbed the family of its greatest gifts. That Derlan's blood also ran in his veins, thus making him guilty of the same offence, did not appear to have occurred to him. Nevertheless, it was only by the will of his father and the vigilance of Arghel that Sherenne remained alive.

"Time passed, and Arghel entered his sixteenth year possessed of a strength that was matched only by his father and brother. Sherenne knew he was no longer safe despite his power. His anger kindled too quickly, and he made no secret of his rejection of the Rule. When he saw one of Rendail's cousins mistreating a woman on the far edge of the compound one night, he let loose his gift in a flash of temper and knocked the man dead. Luckily he wasn't seen. His mother, however, saw the danger at once, and begged Arghel to leave before another upsurge of anger betrayed him. He in his turn begged her to come with him, but she refused, knowing that while it was a certainty that Rendail would pursue Arghel, his chance of survival would be far greater without her.

"She tried every argument she could think of to persuade him, but still he refused to leave her. Therefore, my daughter resolved to release her son in the only way she knew how, through her own death. Closing her mind to him, she crushed the leaves and berries of the nightshade plant and drank the juice. When her breathing came short and she knew that even he would no longer be able to flush out the poison, she called out to him. He was too late, as she knew he would be, and she died in his arms. When Rendail came to take the body, Arghel locked the door against him and stayed there alone with his grief for more than three days, neither eating nor sleeping. Finally, Rendail came back with Malim and his servants, they broke down the door and took Sherenne's body and burned it.

"When they had gone and Arghel was alone, he used the gift of memory to find her. They spoke together for a long time, and she told him of his sister Maylie, a thing she had kept secret all the time she was living. She also told him again of her fears concerning the Family and the blood and asked him to find us, and help to keep us safe. As soon as it was dark, he cloaked his mind and rode away from the settlement. Of course, Rendail sent men out, not to bring him back, but to destroy him. He killed them all before they ever knew he had seen them.

"When he left the Family he was sixteen years old, but he didn't come to us until four years later. In the intervening time he searched for his sister, but couldn't find her. He kept himself apart from others and told no one anything of his history. During those years, both his body and his mind continued to grow in strength, until he finally deemed it safe to come to us and I was able to see my grandson at last.

"Shortly after that first visit my father Rolan died. I think he had been waiting to learn what had happened to Sherenne, and having seen Arghel he was content to let go of his life, knowing we would be as safe and strong as we could be, with our grandson at our side. We laid him with Alisse, here, by the arch, and although I have tried to find him with my gift I cannot, so perhaps for two people to meet in history, the gift of memory must be there in both, I don't know.

"Arghel stayed with us for several years, and then went his own way, although I know he kept us in his mind, ready to return if the Family should threaten us. He wanted to make his own place in the world, I think. Finally, after years of wandering, he came upon an old deserted fortress, probably built by the Romans at the time of their invasion. It was a strong place, set on the top of a hill, and its North wall faced directly towards the road that led back, over many miles, to his father's hated fiefdom.

"He would have been content to stay there alone I think, but before long people began to come to him, some from the town, some from the countryside, knowing that as long as he was there they would be protected. Some of our kind also came, mainly out of curiosity, having heard of his origins in the mysterious northern clan. Many stayed, so that a community began to flourish and Arghel, without ever having sought it, became its head.

"Of course, the Family soon heard of it, as he made no attempt to hide himself from them any longer, and several times they sent out riders to kill him. None succeeded, and I think Arghel secretly hoped that either his father or his brother would come, so that he might have the chance to avenge himself for all that he had suffered at their hands, and for the death of his mother. It is as well that they stayed away, for even Arghel, now an adult and many times stronger than he had been on the night he first came to us, might not have prevailed against them.

"Arghel has watched over our family just as he promised his mother he would. When you were born he left his home, and has watched over you ever since. It is sad that Vail is gone, as he and Arghel were very close. Their friendship, I think, was based on a shared reticence with words. He comes to me often and we have talked together of all manner of things, but particularly, I have to say, we have talked about you. But there – I have perhaps said more than I ought, and in a short while the sun will rise, and Arghel will be waiting for you."

Devren fell silent, and Karisse could hear the birds beginning to wake, the chirruping of sparrows above her head announcing the coming of the dawn. Far from learning the answers that she needed, her head was filled only with more questions. Most importantly, she needed an answer to take back to Arghel, and time was getting short.

"I know," said her grandfather. "Now that you have heard the story, at least the main part of it, ask, and I will answer if I can."

"Why did I know nothing of what you told me? Why has my father has never spoken of it, not of Amala, nor Sherenne, nor even of Arghel, until now?"

Devren sighed and stroked her hair gently. "And what good would it have done, for you to know all this, and live in fear that they might come for you? Karisse, you are only the second daughter born to us, and you can cross the Great Emptiness. After what you have heard, you must understand what that means."

"Then," she replied, "If I am so important, why have they not tried to take me? Why have I never seen, nor heard anything of them in eighteen years? Perhaps they no longer need us, and have decided to leave us be."

"Why they have not come until now, I don't know," Devren said. "But they are here now. You are in great danger, because they will not stop until they have you, or either you or they are dead."

It seemed the world was tumbling around her, yet at the same time many things began to fall into place. Her father's behaviour since the eagle made perfect sense to her now.

"So," she said flatly, "Arghel wasn't telling me the truth when he said I was not responsible for Vail's death."

When her grandfather answered, it was in a voice sharp with anger.

"The Family, and they alone were responsible for Vail's death. Arghel and Vail found their emissary, but not before the message had been passed." He paused for a moment to calm himself, then went on in a softer voice, "My dear Karisse, you don't know yet just how great the gift has grown in you. You have the gift of silence, which you have used without realising it, to guard your secrets. You can follow the form of any creature, and you can cross the Great Emptiness, possibly, in time, a greater distance than Amala ever could. The power you have is such that you were able to break through Arghel's silence without even knowing it. What you saw when you went outside and first

109

looked at him was the fear he felt for you, and it was only by a great effort that he was able to turn your mind away.

"But the Family also has its fears, and its weaknesses. What they, and Malim in particular, fear most is that you and Arghel will join, as your offspring would be the most powerful ever known, there is no doubt of it, and your descendants could well destroy them. On the other hand, should you fall into their hands, your blood would make them unassailable for all time, and there is no doubt that Malim would take you for his own. As things stand, your greatest hope of safety lies with Arghel, as he is the only one who can protect you from his father and his brother."

"Then what you are saying," Karisse said slowly, "is that I have no choice. Both Arghel and his brother want me for my blood, and not for myself. So, Arghel will force me to join with him in order to keep me away from Malim. Grandfather, can't you help me? Arghel has said that he will abide by your decision in this, and so far he has given me no reason to suppose that he has any feelings for me beyond his desire for my gift."

"Are you sure of that?" Devren asked, with a smile. "In the first place, I don't believe Arghel would force you to do anything against your will. In the second, he would never abandon you to the Family, and not just because of what you carry within you. Remember, he knows what would await you there, and would give his life to prevent it. However, there is no time left to debate the matter, and I must give you a message to take back to my grandson. Firstly, it is my decision that you should only join with Arghel if it is your own true wish. Secondly, I have to tell you that in one respect he was not entirely honest. You must tell him that before you decide, he must tell you why he hid his thoughts from you so completely. If he does that, and shows you what he kept from you, I think you will know what to do."

He took her in his arms and kissed her cheek, then got up and walked away under the arch. When he reached the end of the path he turned, and said, "I have left something for you. If you choose in Arghel's favour, go to the large oak at the south end of

110

the wall. Count three stones to the right, and two down. Remove the stone. That is where you will find it."

The next moment, he was gone. She felt exhausted. She got up, stretched her tired limbs back into life and walked out from under the arch to the lawn at the back of the house, where the tall figure of Arghel was waiting for her.

CHAPTER 13

Karisse didn't go straight out onto the grass, but leaned against the corner of the house, watching as Arghel crossed to the wall on the far side of the lawn and sat on it, the rays of the rising sun highlighting the pale golden shade of his skin. She knew that he was aware of her but he made no sign, his mind still completely unfathomable, although she fancied she caught a faint sadness in him as he sat, gazing across the field through which he had ridden all those years ago to meet his grandfather for the first time.

As she stood looking out at Arghel, all her grandfather had told her began to take shape in her mind. It seemed suddenly that her whole life up to this moment had been a falsehood, the truth kept from her by everyone she had known, trusted and loved. This man had watched her, followed her since the day she was born, and she had not set eyes on him until now.

She wondered what his thoughts had been as he had seen her grow in foolish, untroubled ignorance, while he and those around her took on the burden that should have been hers. What had he felt as he watched her great-uncle, his friend, Vail, die because of her? It was natural that he should only have contempt for her, despise her utterly when he compared the comfort of her childhood with the horror that must have been his own.

Why, then, would he wish to join with her, if not for her blood? After all, he was of the Family, and men of the Family were taught from their earliest years that all women were to be taken and mated as a man desired without any thought of love or companionship, but only of what offspring he could sire. But her grandfather had said that Arghel would not force her to do anything against her will, and that she should only join with him if it was her own choice. It was clear that her grandfather both loved and trusted him, and that the feeling was shared by her father. Her final thought, as she set off across the lawn to meet him, was that things would be much simpler if she did not find him the most attractive creature she had ever seen.

She felt his eyes on her as she walked across to the wall, but didn't look up. She sat down beside him and waited for him to speak first. But when time passed and he said nothing, the urge to see his face became irresistible and she looked up at him. As their eyes met she saw again the shadow of sadness pass across him, and realised with a little start that he had known all along what her grandfather was going to tell her.

"Yes," he said, "I knew, and yes, that the time had come for our history to be given to you made me sad. I would not have you live in fear, knowing what the Family will try to do."

Once again she felt frustrated by him, and angry that he should think he had the right to keep things from her.

"Then tell me, son of Rendail," she retorted, "if you don't wish me to be afraid, why you would have me fear you, as you did last night? Your father is the one that has caused all this misery. How can I know that you and he are not more alike than you wish me to believe?"

In answer, her mind was filled with an image, of two men walking across a large courtyard, laughing and talking together. One, the taller of the two, was without doubt closely related to Arghel, having the same delicate bones and golden skin, and she knew immediately that it was Rendail. However, although the hair was the same glossy black as his son's, it hung straight almost to his waist, with not a solitary curl to match those that tumbled around Arghel's face. She recognised the other at once. She had watched the lithe, blonde figure dance in the snow, entranced by his beauty until he had shown her his knowing, terrible smile. She realised that this must be Malim.

In the vision they were coming towards her. When they were some twenty paces away Rendail took Malim's arm and they stopped, looking straight at her. She suddenly had the feeling they could see her, and as she gazed into Rendail's eyes she felt a hatred so intense that it stopped her breath. Certain now that they were watching her, she tried to pull back from the vision but remained trapped, unable to look away, her heart pounding in her chest, the blood turning to ice in her veins, pure panic rising in her throat. Rendail smiled then, an expression that served only to

113

increase her terror, and the message it gave was one of cold satisfaction, pleasure at another's fear.

The vision disappeared abruptly, and she found she was shaking, her body cold despite the warmth of the sun. She realised she had discarded her cloak on the stone bench under the arch. Arghel took off his shirt and wrapped it gently round her shoulders.

"Don't be afraid," he said quietly. "He couldn't see you. It was a memory, nothing more."

She wasn't sure she believed him, but decided to change the subject.

"The man with the bird, he was one of them? They sent him?"

He nodded. "His name is Arvan. Malim sent him. He used his eagle to test the strength of your gift. He wished to know if you had the power to resist the hare's death. He got his answer and the message was sent back to Malim. Now, Malim knows you are here, and that is very dangerous."

She shivered and drew the shirt closer around her shoulders. Arghel spoke again.

"Now that you have seen my father, do you think we are alike?"

She examined his face, comparing every tiny detail of it with the man she had seen in her vision. At first she could hardly distinguish between them, but as she familiarised herself with the one seated beside her, she saw that the structure of his bones was softer, the skin smoother and more radiant, the curve of the mouth altogether different. Whereas the night before she had thought his eyes unfathomable, without reflection, she now saw a warmth and a depth in them that was matched only by the icy darkness that lay in those of the other.

But most of all what made them different was the mass of long unruly curls, just like her grandfather's. They were the mark of his line, seemingly a direct challenge to the smooth, well tended, but no less striking locks that Rendail bore. Tentatively she reached out and caught a silky twisting strand in her hand and ran her fingers through it. Then, on an impulse, she reached back

114

and untied the thread that held the rest, letting the long, sable tresses tumble freely down his back.

She sat back to observe the result and saw that he was smiling. At first she thought perhaps he was laughing at her, but then realised that behind the smile lay a pain so sharp that at once she wanted to scoop him up into her arms as though he were a child, and hold him until it went away.

"You see," he said, "how easily you use your gift, as though it were the very air you breathe. You draw from me things I would keep hidden, and you don't even realise it."

It took a moment for the meaning of his words to become clear, but then she understood. He had not given her the vision of his father and brother. Rather, she had reached in and plucked from his mind a memory that, by choice, he would not have had her see. Likewise, when she released the tie that held his hair in place, it was in response to another memory, but one much deeper, so that she felt only the echoes of feeling around it, rather than its substance.

"It was what he hated most," he said in response to her unspoken question. "He would beat me for my curls, on all the days he couldn't find another reason."

She nodded. "Then the vision I saw was through your eyes, and the fear I felt, that was yours too?"

"Yes." He turned slightly, so that she could see a long, fine scar, faint, and only visible when caught in the rays of the sun, that ran from his left shoulder blade almost to his waist, curling round and ending just below the ribcage. "It was the day of my seventh birthday, and this was my father's and my brother's gift to me. Malim heated a poker in the fire, and used it to give me this scar, while my father looked on. I think that is the only time I ever cried in front of him – not because of what they did, but because they would not let me go back to my mother afterwards."

He spoke in such a calm, accepting tone that at first the meaning of the words were lost. Not knowing what else to say, she took his hand, and whispered, "No, I don't think you and your father are alike at all." Then, finding such a thing impossible to imagine, she said, "Why did your father hate you so much?"

He gave a small shrug.

"That is something I never understood. Perhaps because he knew that my heart was with my mother's people. Perhaps because, no matter what he did, I would not yield to him."

She felt a second ripple of sadness pass through him, as though a gust of wind had disturbed the still surface of a pond, but in a breath it was gone, as though he would not have her touched by it.

"I'm sorry," she said. "I shouldn't ask you such questions."

"There is no question that you shouldn't ask," he replied, "and there are none that I won't answer." He smiled again. "Don't be concerned for me. It was long ago. But can you understand why it was that, rightly or wrongly, we didn't wish you to know of such things while you were still a child?"

"Yes," she replied. "Yes, I do understand, now that I have seen for myself, and have felt the evil in them." She hesitated, and then said, "I should tell you what my grandfather said in respect of our joining. After all, it was the reason that you asked me to speak with him. Unless, of course, all that you said to me last night was just a trick, so that I would go and hear the other things that he would tell me."

He ignored this last statement, much to her annoyance, simply saying, "So what did Devren decide in respect of our joining?"

"That my greatest hope of safety lay with you, but that I should not join with you unless it was by my own choice."

She waited for a response, and when he said nothing she found herself becoming frustrated by his silence, and wondering again if he was really laughing at her. There was more than a little irritation in her voice as she went on, "My grandfather also said that you have not been honest with me. That I can believe, as I can't think of any reason why you should wish to join with me unless it be solely for my blood, despite what I have seen. He says that you must tell me the truth, show me what you have kept hidden, and then I shall know what I should do."

116

This time, the response was wholly unexpected. She saw his eyes widen in surprise, and he gave a little laugh under his breath.

"Our grandfather is a very clever man," he said, "and also a perceptive one. He is right, there is something that I have kept from you, that perhaps I should not have done. And he is also right that I have not been entirely honest. Last night, you asked me why I kept myself so completely hidden from you, and I told you that it was because of my fear for you. That was not a lie, but neither was it the whole truth."

He paused, and this time it was she who remained silent, giving him no help, watching with some satisfaction as he lowered his eyes, struggled for the right words. Finally, he seemed to make up his mind, and turning back to her, took both her hands in his.

"Can you really see no other reason why I would wish to join with you?" He sighed, and then laughed, as though he had just seen the answer to a riddle that had puzzled him. A pure pleasure shone in his eyes, which served to confuse her completely, yet at the same time made her want to laugh, if only at the sudden lightening of his mood. "Of course you don't see," he went on. "If you did, you would not be who you are, and I couldn't love you as I do. You asked yourself the same question, over by the arch. You asked, how could I not have contempt for one so ignorant, so foolish, and so stupid – is that not so?"

"Yes," she said uncertainly, embarrassed that he had been following her thought.

"And do you think me any of those things?"

"No, of course not. How could I think so, after what my grandfather told me?"

"Then," he said, "your reasoning is flawed, because I must be equally foolish and contemptible. What you call ignorance is rather innocence, a thing that I have never known, or at least I can't remember it. How can it be foolish to spend a childhood loved and protected by all around you? Again, it is a thing I didn't know, or at least I didn't until I watched you grow, sharing your joy in life, and wanting to protect you from all that was evil

117

in the world. You said last night that you found me acceptable to look at. I tell you now, I find you the most beautiful thing I have ever seen, and I have discovered something else – that you are the bravest. Despite your ignorance and foolishness, you would have given yourself to me against your will, because you thought I might harm your family. What Devren saw so clearly, and has asked me to tell you, is that I kept all these things hidden from you because of my own fear, and not entirely on account of yours. I would say all this to you with my silent voice, if I thought that you would trust me."

Karisse searched his face for any sign of insincerity, but found none. Rather, she saw an apprehension now behind his eyes, as though he waited to see what judgement she would pass on him. She reached out and once more caught a handful of his jet black curls, letting them run through her fingers like slivers of silk. Her hand came to rest on his cheek, and she followed the lines of his face as though the sense of touch would tell her more than her sight. At last she let her arm fall, and took his hand again.

"Our grandfather said that you should show me what was hidden. I trust you. Come to me with your silent voice."

At first there were no words. She felt the essence of him wrapping itself slowly around her own thoughts, tentative, as though he wished to give her the chance to change her mind and shut him out. Neither did he show her any vision of himself, but only sensation, as though she were lifted up on a warm current of air, swaying with a gentle rhythm, and she knew he was mimicking a gliding bird. It was a simple representation of his desire, not an imposition, but a question. She lost herself in the sensation, and realised that she had shifted her body. His arms were around her, holding her close to him, her head resting against his chest so that she could hear the slow and measured beating of his heart.

It seemed natural that his mind should be a part of hers, and suddenly she couldn't imagine existing without it, as if, up to now, she had never been whole. The idea that she might soon be flung back into the isolation of her own thoughts made her panic, but the thought had no more than brushed her consciousness than she heard his voice inside her, saying, "I am here, and unless you wish it I will never leave."

She slipped her arms around his waist and held him, at which she felt the thrill of his own pleasure rippling through her, making her want to laugh. As she moved her hand across his skin, her fingers found the tiny indentation of his scar, and she traced it back to its beginning, just below his shoulder. With a great effort, she found her silent voice.

"Will you take away your thought, if I ask you to do it?"

"As I said, if you wish it, I will leave."

"I wish it."

The wave of his disappointment shot through her, but he obeyed, and she felt the sensations receding like rivulets of tide water running round a rock, until she was alone. Immediately she felt an unbearable emptiness, a yearning for him so strong that she almost changed her mind, but she remained firm, and instead clung to him even more tightly so that she could still surround herself with the feel, the scent and the warmth of his body.

"What is it?" he said, and from the concern in his voice she knew that he had deferred completely to her request, was no longer reading her thoughts. He asked again, "Karisse, what is it? What's wrong?"

She drew back from him a little, so that she could look at him.

"Nothing," she said, taking his face in her hands and brushing the curls back from his forehead. "Nothing is wrong. I wanted to be certain that the things I say are the words of my own mind and my own heart, and not a reflection that you have placed there."

He nodded, and said, "I understand. Tell me what you want to say."

"Is it true that when two of our kind join, a part of each is in the other always, whether they want it or not?"

"Yes, it is true. Once joined, a link is made that cannot be broken, and one can never be free of the other, even if they wish it."

She nodded and got up, then walked over to the oak tree at the far end of the lawn. With trembling fingers she counted three stones to the right, and two down. At once she saw that the stone was more regular in shape than the rest, and designed to be removed without disturbing the ones above or on either side. She tried to pull it out, but it was held fast by years of grit and dirt, compacted by the rain. She looked back to see that Arghel hadn't moved, but was watching her, a look of puzzlement on his face. She beckoned and at once he came up beside her.

"Can you move this?"

He shrugged, and with a confused smile produced a blade from inside his boot. She held out her hand for it, but he shook his head.

"What are you hoping to find?"

"I suppose I'll know that when I've found it."

"In that case," he said, "I suggest you proceed with caution. If you will allow me?"

She nodded reluctantly, and watched as he set about scraping away the accumulated dirt from around the stone. After what seemed an age he knelt back on his heels and said, "I think you will be able to remove it now." He wiped his blade on the grass, returned it to his boot and went back to sit on the wall, leaving her alone.

She slid her fingers into the gaps he had made and pulled. To her surprise, the stone was no deeper than the width of three fingers. It had been sawn off, leaving a cavity behind. She reached in and her hand touched something hard. Holding her breath, she drew out a grey metal box, some two hand spans wide by one deep. She blew off the dust and took it back to where Arghel was waiting, a mystified expression on his face.

She took her time, a part of her enjoying the novel situation of being in possession of knowledge that Arghel didn't have. She was too impatient, however, to see what was inside the box to stay silent for long.

"Our grandfather told me where to find it," she said, sitting next to him, unable to keep the excitement out of her voice. "He said that if I decided in your favour, I should take it."

Arghel's eyes widened. "Are you saying, then, that you have decided in my favour?"

She blushed and looked down. "It looks like it, doesn't it?"

She felt a tremor run through him, but he didn't touch her. There was a short silence, then he said, "What is it?"

"I don't know. Grandfather didn't say."

He laughed, breaking the tension.

"Perhaps, before you make any more rash decisions, you should open it and find out?"

She carefully wiped away the rest of the dust with her sleeve. Despite its long sojourn in the wall the box showed no signs of rust or discolouration. It was a dull grey, of no metal she recognised. It was unmarked, with a plain square catch. She placed it on the wall between them and slipped a fingernail under the catch. It was stiff, but workable, and she pulled it back and opened the lid.

They both took in their breath together. Inside was a large, polished silver hair clasp. At least, it looked like silver, but was completely untarnished. It was oval in shape, almost the size of her hand, and unadorned except for a set of finely engraved symbols that ran across its surface. She glanced at Arghel. He was staring at it in disbelief.

"Do you know what this is?" he asked, his voice barely a whisper.

"A token," she said, running a finger along the fine script on its surface. "It is a token of joining, but I've never seen one as large or as beautifully made as this." She tipped the box and took it out, then handed it to him. The back was as finely polished as the front, with a strong toothed hasp, hinged at one end, the other slipping over a small ring moulded into the metal. A long, curved pin, attached to the ring by a fine chain, slipped through once the hasp was closed to hold it shut. The strength and delicate workmanship were like nothing she had ever seen before.

He turned it over in his fingers, then laid it flat on his palm. "It is a token. But not *any* token. This is Amala's token, the one she carried from the Family and gave to Derlan. Devren must have hidden it, when …"

"When your mother was taken," she finished for him. She looked up to see the trace of a tear on his cheek. He wiped it away with the back of his hand and nodded.

"It was to have been hers, passed to her by her father to offer to the man she loved." He carefully placed the token back in the box. "He never had the chance to give it to her, and she never had a choice. You are the next female born of this line. Now, he has given it to you. Think carefully, Karisse. This is yours to offer, to any man you choose. The letters that run across it mean 'for eternity'. I will not hold you to a blind bargain. That would make me no better than my father. Whatever you decide, I give you my word, I will not let you suffer the same fate as my mother, not as long as I am alive."

Looking him in the eye, she said, "I have just one question."

"What is that?"

"Do you love me?"

"Yes." He started to say more, but she touched a finger to his lips.

"That is all I needed to know." She took the token back out of the box and placed it in his hands.

For a moment he seemed lost for words Then, he bent forward, and kissed first her forehead, then her cheek, and finally, carefully, her lips.

"You are sure?"

She nodded. He gathered up the long curls at the back of his neck and snapped the clasp shut around them. They sat for a long time, unmoving, letting their minds run together, absorbed in the simple pleasure of silent communication. Finally she heard his voice in her mind say, "Don't you think that perhaps we should go inside and tell your father?"

CHAPTER 14

Sevrian, personal advisor to Lord Rendail, leaned on the rail that separated the pasture from the training fields. The weather was glorious, the first clear sky for days, the scents of pine and fresh grass rising in the still damp morning air. The sun was already warm, and it promised to be a good summer. The enclosures were bulging with spring foals. As soon as they were weaned most of the mares would be turned out into the valley to graze free until the first snows drove them back to the hay barns.

He rolled up his sleeves to let his skin feel the sun and watched with a half smile as his master put a young mare through its paces. She was a powerful beast, a good eighteen spans and not well disposed to the imposition of a rider. The head of the Family, though, was the greatest horseman the settlement had ever seen, and the creature was no match for his skill. The animal had tried every trick, rearing, bucking and wheeling to try to dislodge its unwelcome load, but now it was cantering steadily in a wide circle while Rendail, riding bareback and without a bridle, steered it by the lightest of touches with his bare heels.

Sevrian waited for the session to end and his Lord to dismount before ducking under the rail and joining him in the middle of the field.

"Come slowly, Sevrian," Rendail cautioned as he drew near. "She's still a little skittish, and likely to kick."

The light sheen of sweat on Rendail's forehead was the only evidence of two hours of severe exertion. The horse was still flighty, and Sevrian was relieved when Orlim, the master of horse, came across to hand over a towel and lead the mare off to the stables.

"She is a good animal," Rendail remarked as they walked up the hill towards the stable yard and, Sevrian hoped, breakfast. "Not for the faint hearted though. She would make good breeding

123

stock too, but I think I'll wait until autumn to decide. Meanwhile, I like a challenge."

Sevrian grinned. "It seems you have more than your share of those, Lord," he replied as they passed through the gate of the stable yard.

"True, but at least a horse only makes my muscles ache, and not my mind." Rendail stopped and turned to his second in command. "There is something you wish to discuss?"

Sevrian hesitated. The subject of the heir had become more of a knotty one lately than usual. Rendail sighed, and rubbed his forehead.

"All right, Sevrian. I suppose a day spent not thinking about my son was a little too much to hope for." He signalled to a couple of the stable hands, who quickly packed hot bread and wine into a basket and brought it over to them. Sevrian took it and followed Rendail on a long hike across the pasture, under the eaves of the pine forest beyond.

"At least," Rendail said as they finally came to a halt in a small clearing well away from the boundary fence, "if I have to give my attention to unpleasant subjects, I can make sure I am in pleasant surroundings while I am doing it." He poured them both wine and chewed on some bread for while, then sat back and motioned for Sevrian to speak.

"Lord Malim's relationship with Thalis concerns me," Sevrian said, without preamble. "Arvan has been gone five years now, and I'm sure Thalis has taken advantage of his absence to worm his way closer into the heir's confidence. The current situation doesn't help either. Forgive me, Lord, but your son fails to understand why you have not given him leave to pursue the girl. What little patience he has is fast running out, and with Thalis whispering encouragement at every opportunity, he is likely to go against your command very soon and cross the Great Emptiness, try to reach her from some future time. He is not the only one to question your lack of action. There are some who believe you should have sent riders out at the first sign of her gift. Thanks to Thalis there are others now who know that the girl exists, and suspect the value of her blood."

124

Rendail sniffed, and poured himself more wine.

"By 'others', Sevrian, you mean Karim, and by 'situation', you are referring to the fact that Arghel has her under his protection, yes?"

Sevrian nodded. "Quite so, Lord."

"Karim is blinded by his own ambition." Rendail sat back and half closed his eyes, his expression one of mild distaste. "I won't say that he isn't dangerous. We both know he is, and far more intelligent than Thalis." He laughed. "I sometimes pity Thalis. It was bad enough for him when he served just two masters. It must give him quite a headache to try to accommodate three. After all, none of us are easy to satisfy, Malim least of all. But I take your point, Sevrian. Something must be done, or I will put myself at a disadvantage. I think I will give Malim leave to go. The time is right, and it will dispel any notion that I am not in control of his behaviour."

The response was unexpected, and Sevrian shook his head, puzzled. "But if you let him go, Lord, he will be out of your reach, unless you decide to kill his body while his mind is elsewhere. What if he succeeds in drawing the girl to him? Then you will have lost her as well, and your control over the gift. It is a great risk, especially in the light of Karim's growing strength. I must advise you against it."

Rendail sat up, his expression serious now.

"Sevrian, my friend, the whole of life is a great risk. My life in particular. We both know that this gift is an abomination. It will see the end of all of us if it is not contained. I can't kill Malim while his essence is elsewhere – the consequences are too uncertain, but if I allow him to fall too much under Karim's influence it will lead to conflict, and that, at this point, would be a disaster. No one is ready to see the truth, that sight of the future is the route to death, not to power. Karim believes that if he can manipulate Malim's activities in the future it will give him the leadership of the present. I think he may be disappointed. If I let Malim go before he is pushed, so to speak, I will have gained an advantage simply by doing nothing. I remain the wise guardian of the gift, and Malim will be as much out of Karim's reach as of mine."

"And the girl?" Sevrian murmured. "If he takes the girl, will she survive? And if she doesn't, are you ready for what Arghel will do?"

A look of profound sadness crossed Rendail's face, but was replaced almost instantly by an unreadable mask.

"Am I ready? Not for Arghel, no. Perhaps I never will be. For this to be settled, Malim must take the girl. Nothing can change that. Whether or not she survives is something none of us can see. I hope, for Arghel's sake – and for mine – that she does."

* * *

The voice was there again, calling to her, pleading with her, its silky tone twisting itself down into her dreams, filling her with its desolation, its loneliness.

"Karisse, you must come. It is so dark, and I am lost. Only you are strong enough to find the way. Help me Karisse, come and bring me home."

And so the voice went on, crying like a lost child, until she woke to feel Arghel's arms around her, soothing her gently, his concerned look telling her she had cried out in her sleep. He couldn't hear the voice, but the part of him that rested inside her thoughts caught the essence of its presence, and he would always wake before her dream ended. What he sensed was not at all as she described it.

"It's so sad," she told him, "like a baby alone in the dark wanting its mother, and in my dream I try to find it, but always, when I call out to it, I wake up and it's gone."

But the thing he felt was neither lonely nor lost, and when he reached out with his mind to find it, its echo had a sharp coldness that disturbed him, although its identity eluded him. As if on cue, a little snuffling rose out of the dark. He reached down and lifted up his baby daughter, settling her comfortably between them so that, for the moment, they were both distracted by another pressing puzzle; whether or not the wispy dark locks on Amarisse's head were beginning to curl.

The first shaft of early light from the high window in the southern tower fell on Karisse's face as she lay peacefully asleep, Amarisse snuggled in the crook of her arm. Arghel rose quietly, careful not to wake them. He watched as the baby wriggled closer to her mother's breast, stretching an arm and waving the tiny fingers as if in farewell. However many times he saw the two of them together, the surge of feeling that rose unbidden still unnerved him. Love, protectiveness, fear – he knew they were all natural, the right things for a man to feel, gazing at the two most precious parts of his existence. But the emotions stirred something else in him, resurrected the echo of a memory he couldn't place, a sensation that refused to fully identify itself.

It always caught him unawares, a sharp twist as painful as a blade plunging deep in his belly, causing tears to prick behind his eyes. For an instant he was a child no older than Amarisse, held high off the ground in a warm embrace, a man's embrace, strong but gentle, the musky male scent all around him. His mother was there, watching, his precocious gift picking up her feelings of contentment, her joy in the scene; the same joy he felt when he watched Karisse with his daughter. But he couldn't visualise his mother, any more than he could see the face of the man holding him. The gift that gave him the ability to recognise events far beyond the capacity of normal memory denied him the luxury of sight. He shook himself, forcing the feeling away from his consciousness, and walked out to face the day.

The fortress was dominated by a square, fortified building of grey stone. Wide, shallow steps led up to the only entrance, a set of heavy oak doors leading into a large windowless reception hall. Torches burned along the walls day and night, but even so, sections of the great hall were in perpetual darkness. Behind the hall another room acted as a meeting chamber, where problems were aired, disputes settled, matters of stocks and provisioning discussed. The centre of the building was just one story high, flat roofed, with a parapet designed to protect archers. The roof was

127

only accessible from the inside, from staircases that ran through each of four tall towers, one at each corner, two emerging in the meeting room, the others in the reception hall.

Each tower had windows facing one of the cardinal compass points. Arghel had chosen the south tower as his family's living space. it was warmest, got most sun in summer, and had views over the rolling countryside that led back to Karisse's home, a good ten days ride to the south. For decades he had slept wrapped in a single fur on the stone floor of the highest room in the north tower. Comfort was something he had seldom considered. He remembered the day, five years ago now, trembling with fear at what his new matc might say as she came over the rise, saw the dark, forbidding stone rampart surrounding the entire site, the gloomy towers reaching up behind the wall, stark against the winter sky. As they rode through the only narrow gate in the wall, the other two hundred or so short lived inhabitants of the settlement had welcomed them in an unexpected show of affection for their leader, calling him 'Lord', greeting Karisse as though they were at a wedding celebration. Five years on, he had just about come to terms with the title, and the whole place was different. Everywhere, there were cushions, flowers, soft pallets and rugs, low tables to eat off, woven matting on the floors of the living rooms. At the foot of the stairs he stooped to pick up a discarded leather loop threaded with painted wooden beads and smiled; one of Amarisse's playthings, the handiwork of the blacksmith's wife.

He emerged into the reception hall and out onto the front steps, then called to two of his serving men, instructing them to keep a watch outside Karisse's door. There had been no sign of any of the Family, not since the events that had brought him and Karisse together, but he hadn't relaxed his guard. If anything, now that there was a new female of the blood under his protection, he was even more vigilant. They never spoke of it, but he knew Karisse shared his concern. He closed his eyes for a moment and let his thoughts drift to that part of her he held in his mind, the irrevocable sharing that was part of their joining. Even in sleep, she responded to the mental touch, a pulse of warmth that brushed against him like a kiss. Reassured, he set out, through the jumble of dwellings that surrounded the central keep to the stables just inside the gate.

Although he didn't like to acknowledge the fact, Arghel had inherited his father's rare affinity with horses. His mount, a magnificent seven year old grey gelding, was snorting with impatience the moment it caught his scent. As he came up to the stall it stretched its head to greet him and he rubbed its neck before leading it out into the yard. He waved away a young groom and made the animal ready himself, then set off down the ridge towards the river that ran through the wooded valley floor.

The river was fast flowing, even in summer, with a stony bed that here and there gave way to pockets of deeper water lined with fine shingle. He left the horse to graze and stripped, then plunged into water still icy from the hill springs, not yet warmed by the rising sun. There were carp and trout in the still water of the pool, enough to smoke and keep for winter if his hand and eye were fast enough. It was a good time of day to hunt, while the fish were still sluggish. He absorbed himself in the task, a skill learned in childhood in the biting waters of the northern mountain rivers. He was under water, diving low to flush the game from beneath the rocks when he felt it, a warning tingle in his senses, the presence of another of his kind, coming closer through the trees.

He thrust his body upwards and broke surface facing the direction of the intruder's thought. Someone was standing on the bank, holding two sets of reins, one belonging to a handsome, well muscled bay, the other to his own grey. His horse whinnied as he pulled himself out of the water. At the same time he heard a voice in his head.

"I am within your beast. If I die, so does he."

For a moment he hesitated, then sent back a wordless acquiescence. The figure nodded, but didn't move. Arghel dressed slowly, pinned back his wet hair and collected the stock of fish he had caught, dropping them with deliberation into a woven sack. He walked towards the man, stopping some five paces away.

"Arvan."

"Lord Arghel." Arvan gave a shallow bow, and let go the reins of the grey. "He is a fine animal. I have no wish to harm him. Nor you. You know it is not in my nature to kill. I do not think it is in yours either, if it can be avoided. I wish to talk. Will you listen?"

"Do I need to listen? The death of one close to me speaks for you, Arvan. I think you may have to shout very loud to be heard over the memory of his last cry."

"As the call of my eagle is still in my ears, Lord. We were companions for many years, and I grieve for him. I regret both deaths, but then was not the time for talk. I had no choice but to defend myself. Had your friend been of our blood he would not have died. It was an error on my part, for which I am truly sorry. I need to speak with you, for the sake of your mate. As a token of faith I will release the horse. If, after you have heard me, you wish to take a life for a life, I will not resist you. Will you stay your hand, at least until after you hear what I have to say?"

A thrill of fear ran through Arghel at the mention of Karisse. He forced it down and made his expression a blank mask.

"The loss of a horse would be a small sacrifice in return for your death. Say what you have to. I can wait. But as my brother is no doubt listening, I have this to say to him. Karisse is mine. If Malim turns his thought on her again, I *will* kill him, even if I have to drag him from behind our father's robes. If he doubts me, let him try. I will be waiting."

Arvan nodded. "I understand, Lord Arghel. However, Lord Malim no longer sees through my eyes. Your father forbade it after that night. He also commanded me not to return to the Family. I am exiled from my home, unable to take a mate, to further the blood. My life is therefore of no value. Except for one thing. I can tell you what I know. Just after the last full moon, your brother crossed the Great Emptiness. He aims to lure your woman there by any means he can. He is out of everyone's reach now. If he persuades her to follow, you will be helpless to prevent

130

it. Not even Lord Rendail can act. You must warn her, and guard her well – he may attempt to take her at any time."

Arghel tried to quell his rising panic.

"You have been Malim's keeper since before I was born. You want me to believe that you would betray him now? As for the rest, it is a lie. One of the blood does not 'leave' the Family. Rendail would never permit it. Unless …" His mind struggled for an explanation, "unless my father understood that I would hunt you down, make sure that your precious blood reached no further than the soil on which you stand. If that is so, then for the first time in my life I am happy to do his bidding."

"I have been Lord Malim's servant, yes," Arvan replied. "After all, I have much skill with animals, even those who appear in the guise of men. I am the only one to fully understand his weaknesses, and I believe that over the years my knowledge has saved many lives – yours, more than once, when you were a child. My task is finished. I have no master now, and I have chosen to try to prevent another death. Search my mind if you wish. I can hide nothing from a gift such as yours. Otherwise, finish it. I have nothing more to say."

Arghel blinked as sudden surge of memory overtook him, of his childhood terror, Malim's murderous rages, and a blurred image of Arvan, turning his master aside, soothing him with words and sweet nuts. He hesitated as Arvan bowed, mounted his horse and began to ride, keeping the animal to a slow walk. He watched until the figure was no more than a speck in the distance, following the course of the river to the north. He sighed, drew a hand across his eyes and took up the reins of the gelding.

Then it came, a sudden void that made his ears ring, his vision tilt. He almost fell. The fish were left forgotten on the grass as he kicked the horse into a frantic gallop, flat against its neck as it plunged through the dense woodland between the river and the fortress.

As soon as he was through the gate he leapt from his mount and ran in a blind panic, thrusting aside anyone in his path. At the top of the south tower he let the full force of his gift loose at the closed door without breaking his stride. The door exploded into fragments, sending one of the door wardens flying backwards. The unfortunate guard hit the ground and slid, neck snapping as he ploughed into the wall at the top of the stairs. The other crumpled and lay still, foot flopping at a grotesque angle, too terrified even to cry out in pain. Arghel ignored them, his attention focused on the still figure lying where he had left her, curled on the soft pallets in the centre of the room. She seemed asleep, every contour of her face relaxed, her chest rising and falling gently. The baby was missing from her side.

For a moment he just stared. Then, in a fury he shouted, cursed, grabbed the limp body and shook it hard. Finally he stepped back, reached into his shirt and pulled out a jewelled stiletto. His hand trembled as he plunged the weapon through the palm of her hand. There was no response. A trickle of warm blood spilled through the motionless fingers onto the blanket and at the same moment, behind him, the shrill cry of a baby cut into the silence.

He snapped his attention to the doorway, where Sasha, Amarisse's nurse, leaned against the door frame looking on in horror, desperately trying to quiet the squalling child. Arghel leapt towards her, knocked her aside and ripped the bundle from her arms as she stumbled backwards. He held his crying daughter at arms length, his mind unable to comprehend the fact that she was still with him. Then, he clutched her to him and began to rock gently, calling out Karisse's name, over and over again, the loudness of his voice frightening the child, making her cry even more.

It may have been hours that passed, his calls fading to no more than a hoarse whisper. The baby was quiet now, lulled by the steady motion of his rocking. Every so often he sighed and clutched Amarisse closer to his chest, aware of nothing but the emptiness in his mind, the desolation of a mate lost, the sudden ending of the consciousness inside him that was Karisse. The agony of bereavement overwhelmed him, the shock of isolation unbearable, eating at his reason. But Karisse was not dead. The shell that had contained her remained, breathing, nurtured and preserved by the gift, unchanging across the expanse of the Great

Emptiness, reclaimed in some far time beyond his reach. Beyond his reach – but not Malim's.

He slowly became aware of a voice, tentative, trembling with fear.

"My Lord?"

His eyes started to focus.

"Please, Lord, the baby … let me take her. It's been a long time. She needs to eat."

He shook his head, struggling against the pain, and realised that his chin was resting heavily on Amarisse's head. A hand touched his arm and he flinched, then turned to see Sasha's terrified face. The nurse took a step back.

"The baby, Lord. Please, let me take the child … she …"

Sasha faltered, and he realised he was staring at her, frightening her. He swallowed and looked down at Amarisse. He nodded, gently adjusted the baby's wraps and stroked the tiny cheek with the edge of his finger. The child turned her head, fastened her mouth on the finger and began to suck contentedly, wriggling deeper into the crook of his arm. He bent his head and kissed her other cheek, then took a step towards the nurse and held his daughter out to her.

"It's all right, Sasha. All right now." He couldn't speak above an unsteady whisper. "Take care of her. She needs you now." He kissed the child again and stroked her head.

Sasha nodded, took his daughter from him and left the room. A groan brought him to himself and he turned, becoming aware for the first time of the worst consequences of his grief. The youth with the broken ankle was drifting in and out of consciousness, so he worked quickly, using his gift to mend the bones and plunge the boy into a deep sleep, long enough for them to knit. That done, he turned to the dead servant, reached down and laid a finger on the cold forehead, remembering.

After a few moments he opened them and let out a long sigh. Not married, no children, mother and father both dead. The boy had been totally alone, not even a pretty girl to cry for him. There had been no time for shock or confusion. Death had come before the youth had realised the danger. He sighed in gratitude for that small mercy and, because there was no one else, he wept for the boy, embraced him and closed the sightless eyes.

* * *

At the same time, many miles to the north, the lone figure of a woman, dark haired, clothed in the doeskin trousers and coarse linen shirt of a man, lay flat on a ridge, her gaze fixed on the bleak outline of the Family's settlement, far below. From her vantage point she could see men coming and going through the East Gate, the main route into the central complex. There were no women, of course. They were hidden away, locked in the inner compound, a fate that would have been hers had it not been for her mother's foresight. Smuggled out of the settlement as a newborn, no one, not even her father, knew of her existence. It was dangerous to venture so close to the sphere of her father's influence, but she was confident of her gift. Like her brother, Arghel, she had the ability to read the minds of others while keeping her own hidden. No one could take her by surprise and, to the eyes of the Family, she was invisible.

She tensed as a rider came into view, rounding the boundary fence from the southern side of the settlement. His mount was young, not fully trained. She could tell by its skittish movements, the way it tossed its head, fighting the rein. It was a battle doomed to failure. The man on its back was possessed of infinite patience and determination, and his strength would far outlast that of the horse.

"Good morning, Father," she whispered, as Rendail turned the mare, urging it towards the bank of the wide river that flowed through the valley. In places, it was shallow enough to ford during the summer months, and she heard a whinny of protest as he guided his mount down into the fast flowing stream, kept it to a steady walk as they crossed, the horse wading in water well above its hocks. Once on the bank, on her side of the river, he set it to a light canter along the valley floor, coming in her direction.

Despite her hatred she couldn't help a stirring of admiration, a desire to reach out, make contact with the man who had sired her, whose presence constantly brushed against her senses no matter how far she travelled from his seat of power. He dismounted almost directly beneath her to adjust the animal's bridle. She was too far above him to see his expression, but his movements as he calmed the nervous beast were patient, gentle. It was a pity, she thought, that a man who treated other creatures with such apparent affection could not have found it within himself to spare a little compassion for his own mate and children. But within the Family a woman, like a horse, was valued only for her bloodline, and a male child only by the strength of his gift. Love, by her father's own edict, was forbidden.

"What would you think, Father," she murmured, "if you knew I still lived? That I plan to help destroy your heir, take from you everything you have fought to possess?" She smiled to herself. "What will you do when Arghel comes? He *will* come, Father. And when he has painted the walls of your chambers with Malim's blood, I hope he will have the sense mingle it with yours."

As if in response the figure below straightened and, to her horror, turned and looked up. She knew she was well hidden, that he could not detect her thoughts, but nevertheless pressed herself flat against the stone of the crag, her heart racing. For a long moment Rendail remained still, seemingly staring straight at her, then he returned his attention to the mare, gave the bridle a final check and remounted, turning it back the way it had come. She let out her breath in a sigh of relief and made her way down the other side of the ridge, to the protection of the thick woodland beyond.

Part Two

CHAPTER 15

"Fascinating," the tall thin one repeated. "There are many similar cases, but none quite like this. Let me see those notes again. Seven years? That is really remarkable." He lowered the clipboard and stared at her again. "She eats well, you say? And will move if someone helps her?"

"That's quite right Dr. Morgan." The red faced fat one, whose name was Flynn, looked delighted at the other man's interest. "The point is, she will perform all basic functions – eat, walk, see to… well…other bodily needs – but never of her own volition. It's extraordinary." To demonstrate he bent forward and grasped her just beneath her armpits. "Come on, Queenie, show the doctor here what you can do."

He pushed upwards with his hands, his face close enough to hers for her to smell him. Terrible bad breath. As he did so she rose until she was standing, taking the weight on her feet. He moved his hands to her shoulders and with another gentle push turned her round to face Dr. Morgan. Then, carefully, he stood back leaving her standing unaided and grinned at his colleague, giving a little grunt as though proud of his own performance. Morgan responded by raising one eyebrow and renewing his visual inspection, tapping his chin with his knuckle.

"Yes – most extraordinary," the latter agreed. "And apart from this, there appears to be no awareness at all. And yet…hmm." He reached into his pocket and fished out a small, pencil like torch. "Do you mind, Dr. Flynn?"

Morgan walked her up and down slowly, leading her by the hand, watching the movements with rapt attention. She responded to every light push on the shoulder or tug on the arm. As soon as he withdrew the pressure, however, she stopped dead, eyes staring straight ahead, making no acknowledgement of the presence of anyone at all. Morgan nodded thoughtfully, then transferred his attention to her face. He examined her ears and nose with the thin torch, opened her mouth with a spatula and looked at her teeth. Finally he shone the strong light into each eye in turn. He jumped in surprise and dropped the torch. He bent down to retrieve it, forcing his expression back to scholarly interest. He switched off the torch and glanced quickly at Flynn, who was gazing out of the window.

"Thank you, Flynn," he said, his voice cheerful, polite. "I've seen enough for the moment. Perhaps if … Queenie you said? Perhaps if Queenie could go back to the ward now, we might discuss the case over a drink? Maybe even a meal? I didn't get the chance to eat anything on the plane."

* * *

The excitement was clear in Flynn's face as they made their way down the stairs and out into the hospital car park. Morgan could almost see the avarice flood over Flynn's features. He smiled inwardly. No one was more easily manipulated than a middle aged professional, hungry for success.

"I know the perfect place," Flynn said, clearly straining to keep his voice even. The oldest Inn in Bristol you know – the 'Llandoger Trow'. It's close to the harbour and has a very decent menu. I'm sure you'll find it relaxing."

"Yes, I'm sure I will," replied Morgan, smiling politely.

They strolled onto the waterfront, Flynn practically dancing round his guest, twice accidentally thumping him in his efforts to point out one famous landmark after another.

"…and just to your right is the Arnolfini Gallery, and oh, the SS Great Britain is just round the corner. You can't possibly leave without visiting … perhaps after dinner if you're free…" and on and on.

'Interminable,' thought Morgan as they climbed Park Street, heading for the Clifton suspension bridge. 'The idiot has an absolute genius for inane babble. And the woman. To have had her here for seven years before I found out about it – unforgivable! Unforgivable that I should not have been aware of it. Well, now I am aware …'

138

As the famous bridge came into view Morgan touched his companion on the shoulder. Flynn swayed slightly and blinked. Meekly, he allowed himself to be led to a bench, half hidden beneath the trees, some way from the well trodden paths. One hand still resting on Flynn's shoulder, Morgan raised the other to gently turn Flynn's head until their eyes met. A few minutes later Morgan rose and strolled back towards the centre of the city. He took a mobile phone from his pocket and dialled.

"Pick him up at eleven," he said. "You know where."

* * *

Alex pulled his Mercedes roadster into the long gravel driveway to the mansion house just after midnight. He stopped outside the front door, too tired to drive round to the garage block behind the house. He grabbed his overnight bag from the boot and walked round the side of the main building, through a large kitchen garden and up to the veranda that led into the kitchen. It was late spring, and the bite in the highland air contrasted sharply with the mild, almost balmy weather in the southwest of England. Nevertheless, the kitchen door was open. He smiled and went inside, closing it behind him.

"Well?" Mary didn't turn round, but kept her attention on a large pot simmering on the range. He came up behind her and slipped his arms around her waist, peering over her shoulder at the contents of the bubbling cauldron; a broth of meat and vegetables. He kissed her neck and rested his chin on her shoulder.

"I'm hungry."

"This is for tomorrow. You should've eaten on the plane. And you haven't answered my question."

He stroked the grey hair that had once been the colour of ripe wheat and whispered, "Feed me and I'll tell you everything."

She dropped the spoon and turned to him.

"Since when did you tell me everything?" She pushed him away and waved a hand at the table, then got out a bowl, ladled broth into it and sliced some bread. "Sit down. It's gone midnight, so there's not time for 'everything'. The last twenty-four hours will do. So? Did you make a convincing psychiatrist? Was it her?"

"Yes, and yes," he answered, between mouthfuls. "Mary, this is delicious. I love you."

"Don't change the subject. Tell me."

"It's her, I'm sure of it. What I don't know for sure is what went wrong. It's the wrong time, the wrong place, and she's catatonic. It doesn't make sense, unless…"

"Unless?"

"All right, I have a theory. She's very young, and she's never made the full crossing before. She might have allowed her mind to jump a little way, but fifteen hundred years – that's a big leap. If she wasn't expecting it or wasn't in control she may well be in shock, and without one of us to pull her out of it …" He shrugged. "But she should have had a link. That's what I don't understand. There is always a link, a mind that can keep contact, a thread to follow back to the starting point. In my case it is my mother, in Malim's, Rendail. Arghel should have been hers. Something went wrong, and I don't understand what or how. As for the timing, Malim has not yet returned. I would feel his presence if he had. I can only surmise that he called Karisse from some time even further into the future and she wasn't strong enough to go the whole way. She fell short by at least seven years, and because her mind is buried I didn't sense her."

He finished the last of the bread and pushed the bowl away, watching as Mary poured him coffee from a percolator on the hob. She brought it to him, sat next to him and took his hand.

"Will she be all right?"

"I don't know, Mary. Paul and David are going to get her out tonight. Until they get her here there's no point speculating. I'll do what I can – I just hope it's enough."

* * *

Just about the noisiest place to be in the middle of the night is inside an institution. Hillside Psychiatric Hospital was certainly

140

no exception. An ancient Victorian pseudo-gothic ruin of a building, the imposing exterior glowered down from its perch on Moordown Hill at the northern edge of the city, yellow windows glinting like the eyes of a giant black owl hunting rats. The interior was an equally uninviting maze of echoing corridors coated in blue vinyl leading to dormitories furnished with long rows of steel bedsteads, some twenty or so to a room, a dozen identical rooms per floor.

In these enlightened days of 'care in the community', only two floors were still in use, one for male patients, the other for women, all cases too severe to be cared for elsewhere. Even these were half empty, adding to the desolation of place. For the last year negotiations had been underway to sell the building, turn it into a modern conference centre cum health farm for company executives. The destination of the forty or so remaining patients had not, so far, been considered.

On the ground floor, which housed the patients' day room, staff offices and consulting rooms, some effort had been made to add a little appeal to the surroundings. The vinyl had been covered in buff coloured industrial carpeting. Prints of Constable, Turner and Monet were arranged haphazardly on the walls. There were even a couple of large pot plants in the reception area, of the kind that produce copious amounts of foliage on a teacup of water a month and grace the foyers of company offices the world over.

Up on the second floor however, there was no greenery and no carpet to stifle the clangs and echoes that travelled along the corridors all night long from one end of the building to the other. Up here the standard cure for enforced insomnia was 50mg of flurazepam, although for those nursing auxiliaries wanting to be sure of an easy shift, an unprescribed second dose was often administered to the more troublesome patients. Jim Marchant flopped into his chair at the night desk in the small staff room at the end of the corridor, grinning as he stuffed the illicit key to the drugs cabinet into his back pocket. He then settled to his nightly task of drinking Scotch and reading a crumpled copy of yesterday's issue of whatever tabloid had been left in the canteen.

He didn't see or hear a thing until it was too late. Reasonably drunk and trying hard to focus on the half naked celebrity on page six, the only warning was a small puff of air behind his left ear. A split second later he found himself flat on his back on the office table. It took several moments for the room to stop spinning and his stomach to decide it was going to hang onto its contents. At first his sluggish brain suggested that something had fallen from the ceiling and knocked him out of his seat – a light fitting perhaps, or a chunk of plaster. The place was neglected enough. Then, it slowly dawned that the weight bearing down on him was human – not only human, but devilishly strong.

He made a couple of feeble attempts to struggle back upright, without success. Whoever it was had him pinned down, immobile. He tried another tack, opening his mouth with the idea of raising the alarm, hoping that Brian, the attendant on the first floor, might just not have the TV going. The minute he tried to intake breath he felt an increasing pressure on his windpipe. It was not enough to stop him breathing altogether, but enough to cause him to snap his mouth shut.

Unable to move even his head, his eyes flitted to and fro, trying to work out exactly what was going on. First, the man who had him pinned to the table – tall, over six feet, slight build, blonde, blue eyes – one hell of a lot stronger than he looked. The man wasn't looking at him, but had his head turned slightly away towards a movement behind him. Someone else was there, by the drug cabinet in the corner. With an effort that made his eyes ache, Jim could just see that the cabinet was open and the second man was searching carefully through the contents. Now it made sense. Junkies after a fix and, moreover, very stupid ones, as no attempt had been made at any sort of disguise or concealment.

A comforting thought came to him. If they were planning to murder him, wouldn't they have done it by now? There were plenty of blunt instruments lying around the place, and the guy on top of him felt strong enough to have broken his neck without even having to exert himself. All he had to do was lie still, not that he could do much else, and wait for them to get what they wanted and leave. In fact, the situation could turn out to his advantage. His own forays into the drug cabinet would be put down to the burglary. He would create an impressive image helping the police with their enquiries and, best of all, he would be able to milk at least two months sick leave out of it, suffering from post traumatic stress. He just needed to stay quiet for the next couple of minutes. Perhaps he should shut his eyes, pretend to pass out. That would be even safer.

So it was that he didn't see anything more until his eyes jerked open at the prick of a needle in his arm, and the last thing he saw was a massive dose of flurazepam being slowly emptied into his alcohol ridden bloodstream.

* * *

She saw them coming, two shadows outlined in the dim light from the window, moving quietly down the ward towards her bed. When they reached her, a dark haired one emptied a small pack containing clothes for her – underwear, blue jeans, an oversized navy sweatshirt and a pair of white tennis shoes. Together the two men removed the white hospital smock and dressed her. The jeans were far too long, so taking a leg each they rolled them up to just above her ankles so that she wouldn't trip over them when she stood up. The other, a tall blonde, lifted her effortlessly and carried her down the corridor to the stairway, his companion going ahead, listening for any sign of staff moving on the floors below.

On the first floor any noise they might have made was drowned by the racket of an overloud television coming from the staff office, where an auxiliary sat engrossed in a late night chat show. On the ground floor there was no one. The dark haired one slid through the already open window and she felt herself lowered gently to the ground. The blonde followed, lifted her again, and they continued through the grounds some three quarters of a mile to the road. Throughout the whole proceeding neither man had spoken and their footfalls were almost noiseless on the soft grass. She was able to hear, for the first time in as long as she could remember, the sound of the breeze rustling the grass, the creak of

143

tree branches above her, the shuffling and occasional twittering of birds.

There were other, unfamiliar noises – muted roars that got louder the nearer they drew to the bottom of the hill, and seemed to coincide with gleams of light that shot past, momentarily illuminating the night sky. There was also a low buzzing that seemed to be everywhere and never stopped, but rose and fell on the wind, making a picture in her mind of vast numbers of insects all whirling together in one gigantic swarm.

The trio reached the road and once again she was set lightly on the ground. Facing the way they had come she was able to see, in the distance, the dark outline of the building from which she had been liberated, and which had been her only experience of the world. At least there was no memory of any other place, only a vague feeling that there must once have been other places, other memories. There was a soft metallic click just behind her and then the feel of the blonde man lifting her again, placing her inside what appeared to be a form of transport, one that was enclosed, warm, with soft leather seats.

He strapped her into the rear seat, then moved round to the other side and got in beside her. The dark one sat in front and turned a key, which resulted in a noise that momentarily made her heart beat faster, followed by an uncomfortable vibration, the source of which she couldn't quite place. The vehicle started to move, slowly at first, then accelerating to an enormous speed, lighting its own way in the dark by means of powerful lamps, like great eyes peering ahead over what seemed a vast distance. Similar lights were visible now and then through the windows, some going in the same direction, others appearing to be heading straight for them.

She knew that her companions were not in the least troubled either by the noise, which was now a comforting drone, or the speed. Her fellow passenger on the back seat rooted out two thick blankets, one of which he attentively tucked around her. The other he folded and placed behind his head. He now sat with folded arms, long legs stretched out, eyes closed, breathing deeply.

144

After several hours of travelling they stopped briefly to eat. The driver disappeared, to return some ten minutes later carrying packs of sandwiches and coffee, things that she recognised from her time in the hospital. While they were waiting the other lifted her out of the car, rubbed her legs and arms and walked her round on one of the grass verges. Back inside he fed her a few mouthfuls of one of the sandwiches followed by some of the coffee before they sped off again into the dawn. There were several more stops and it was late afternoon before they finally turned off the road onto a long driveway leading up to a huge, solitary Victorian house, three storeys high, hidden from the road by a forest of encircling pine trees.

There were several other buildings in the grounds, including a large stable block and a row of small cottages off to the right of the main house. The driver pulled up outside leaving the engine running, put something to his ear and spoke quietly, the first time she had heard either of them utter a word. Once again she was lifted out of the car, and carried up a set of wide steps to a black front door which opened as they approached. Once inside the blonde one exchanged a few quick words with another man, the one who had opened the door. Then he proceeded up two more flights of stairs, into a room, and set her down in an armchair. He stood back and studied her for a moment, then left, his fading footsteps dulled by the carpet in the hallway outside.

CHAPTER 16

The armchair was huge and soft, with a green and gold pattern like growing vine leaves. The plush carpet seemed like a continuation of the armchair, deep green like a forest floor, with pastel flowers and leaves sprouting all over it. It was difficult to see where the chair ended and the carpet began. The man had placed her carefully, making sure her legs were comfortable, supporting her sides and back with big tasselled gold cushions and setting her hands in her lap. The armchair had been placed facing the door, so that anyone entering the room would immediately come into her field of vision.

A fire crackled in a hearth somewhere to her left and the lighting was dimmed, so that the room was bathed in a comforting glow, the flames dancing prettily on the walls.

The firelight was just beginning to die down when the door opened. She recognised the tall man from the hospital, the one who had examined her some thirty-six or so hours before. In the consulting room he had worn large, thick spectacles and a white coat over a drab grey suit, giving him the appearance of a rather stuffy academic. Now, however, the spectacles were gone and she could see the jet black eyes shining even in the dim light. He was dressed casually in black jeans and loose sweater, his long dark hair tied behind with a black velvet bow. The whole effect was striking, but beyond that she felt a tiny rustle in her mind of familiarity, almost of recognition, not of this particular man but of men like him – men who were tall and dark and moved with the same easy grace as he walked, barefoot and almost cat-like, across to the fire.

He added several logs from a metal box beside the hearth and flames shot up at once, intensifying the light so that she was able to see him clearly. He moved up to her and, dropping onto one knee so that his face was level with her eyes, took her left hand in both of his and said softly, "My name is Alex MacIntyre. Welcome. You are safe now and welcome in my house."

He examined her swiftly, his deft hands feeling her pulse, checking the movements of her joints, lifting her chin to look into her eyes. He continued to speak in the same quiet tone.

"I know that you can hear and understand me. I also know that you can't answer, not yet. Don't worry, that will come. In a little while, you will be able to move and speak. It is just a question of time, now you are here. By the end of this evening you will speak to me. In a day or two you will walk in the garden with me. I promise you this. Don't be afraid, I know who you are. At least, I am fairly certain of it, but I can't tell you, as that much you need to discover for yourself. Know only that I am your friend and that you are among friends now."

The door opened behind him, and a young woman came in carrying a heavily laden tray. She set it down on a small table by the window and came over to join them.

"How is she, Alex?" she asked, squatting at his side. "Everyone has been asking since they got back. Paul won't say anything. He hasn't slept at all – he's just pacing up and down in the kitchen driving us all mad. He won't even eat. He wanted to bring the tray up himself but I wouldn't let him, so he made me promise to go straight back down and give him a report from the horse's mouth."

All this was spoken with hardly an intake of breath, all the time surveying the newcomer with unrestrained curiosity. Alex laughed softly.

"My dear Jenni, you can tell Paul that our guest is fine. At least, fine considering that she has been nowhere but an asylum for seven years. In fact her condition is remarkable. I think she may turn out to be stronger than any of us, and if all goes well she will be telling us all about it before tomorrow. Tell him to get a few hours sleep." He sighed. "And tell him that the other matter will wait until morning. Meanwhile, if you are not too tired, can you be on call if I need you?"

Jenni nodded and gave him a quick kiss on the cheek.

"Of course. I'll be here. Just call if you want me. And everyone will be delighted to get Paul out of the kitchen. We love him dearly, but … well, you know…" She rolled her eyes in

147

mock exasperation. At the door she turned, a shade of worry clouding her eyes. "The other matter – is something wrong?"

Alex went up to her and stroked her cheek.

"I don't know, Jen. I hope not. But one thing at a time, yes? I'll speak to Paul tomorrow, then we'll see. Right now I have other things to worry about." He gave a reassuring smile, and she returned it at once.

"You'll make it right," she said. "You always do."

* * *

Alex wandered over to the table. Jenni had provided tea and enough cake to feed the entire household. He picked up an iced bun and nibbled on it absently. After a while he turned and, drawing an armchair closer to the fire, added more logs and sat staring into the flames, his face grave. There was not much time. Even so, he was hesitant, unsure. Up to now, his sole concern had been to find the woman. Beyond that he had refused to think. Now, for the first time, he was confronted by the fact that he would be solely responsible for what happened next. There were two possibilities, and neither was attractive. The mind was a delicate thing, and while hers lay protected within a hard shell of shock and confusion, it was safe. To blast away that shell might destroy the fragile creature that lay within. That, or she would come to the full realisation of who she was, and of what might be lost to her across the unbridgeable darkness of time. Would she survive that knowledge? And if she did, what would happen when she learned the truth behind the reason for her presence here, the full horror of the task that lay before her?

He sat back and closed his eyes, brushed a hand across his forehead. When the door opened and closed again quietly, he didn't look round.

"I told you to get some sleep," he murmured, still lost in his own dilemma, not wanting to be confronted with another.

Paul came forward silently and crouched before the hearth, the deep orange glow illuminating a streak of wetness on his cheek. "I didn't think …"

"Well, what did you think?" Alex saw Paul flinch. "Did you think it would be easy? Did you think you would forget? That you would not have to carry it with you for the rest of your life? Tell me, Paul – what did you think?"

Paul's body seemed to shrink under the assault. He lowered himself into a sitting position, arms round his knees, head turned away.

"I thought it was right," he whispered finally into the strained silence. "I couldn't stop. I saw what he did to her – I saw …" He stopped, unable to keep his voice steady. Alex gave him no help, and after another tense pause he gathered himself. "Did you ever …"

"Kill someone?" Alex finished the question for him, then went on in a gentler tone, "Yes. When I had to. When I was threatened, or when those I loved were threatened. But never one that was not of our kind, and never out of anger. That is the difference. Yes, I have killed, when I had no choice." He paused and stretched before saying, with a bleak finality, "You had a choice."

Neither heard the faint rustle behind them. It was only when Alex noticed the movement of a shadow against the wood of the oak mantle that he jumped to his feet, startled, and turned round. Paul twisted to follow his gaze and both froze, momentarily dumbstruck. The effort of raising her arm was evident in the woman's expression, which was no longer blank, but strained with determination. There was desperation in the eyes, in the clenched teeth as she held the arm outstretched, fingers reaching, grasping the air. The arm was extended not towards Alex, but to Paul.

Alex gave a brief nod, as if afraid that any sound or movement would break the spell. Paul slowly rose.

"Father?" He used his silent voice, and Alex responded likewise.

"It is you she wants. Be careful. You have no experience of this. If she takes you into the Dance I can do nothing to help."

Paul nodded his understanding. It happened quickly. Alex saw the tremor that ran through his son's body as the fingers touched. He was unprepared, however, for the agonised cry that followed, and for the speed with which Paul's body crumpled into insensibility on the carpet at the feet of the silent figure in the chair. The woman's arm had fallen limply into her lap, and a faint smile played now about her lips. Paul's violent shivering contrasted sharply with the woman's stillness. Alex had witnessed the ravages of epilepsy in others, more than once, and his son's spasmodic jerks might easily have been mistaken for it. He hurriedly unbuckled the belt from his jeans, doubled it and forced it between Paul's teeth. Then he sat back, waiting. There was nothing more he could do.

* * *

Gerald Flynn was in a far from comfortable situation. He had, for the moment, been left alone in the bare, chilly police interview room, staring into the plastic cup of cold, watery coffee that a police constable had brought to him two hours before. A few minutes, the man had said, his voice full of polite apology.

"I'm very sorry, Sir," (at least he had called him 'Sir'). "I'm afraid something has come up. I won't keep you long, Sir, but I would be very grateful if you could bear with us for a few minutes."

No explanation – nothing. He was worth a little more consideration, he thought. After all, he was here of his own free will, helping the police with their enquiries as they put it. He was the one whose whole life had suddenly been turned upside down. One of his nursing auxiliaries dead, apparently from an overdose of drugs stolen from the drugs cabinet with an illegal key. One of the most important patients – no – *the* most important patient in the hospital missing. He should be in his office, setting the wheels in motion for a full security and health and safety inquiry. Instead, he was sitting in this wretched room, accounting for his movements over and over again as though he were the one who had stolen the drugs and abducted his own patient.

The whole thing was ridiculous. He had been there for over six hours now. First, he had been questioned by a young and rather pretty redhead who had introduced herself as Detective Constable Wroughton. Next to her had been a portly, dour faced man called Constable Blake. Detective Constable Wroughton had placed two tapes into a machine on the table and asked politely if he minded having his statement recorded on tape. She had emphasised that he was not under arrest, that it was perfectly normal procedure in a case like this, so if he had no objection...and of course, he had had no objection at all. He could account for all his movements, both during the day, and later that evening when Dr Morgan had dropped him off outside his executive detached residence in Frenchay at around 11.30pm. Morgan had even helped him to his door, on account of his being a little over the limit, so to speak.

He had gone through the events of the day several times already. First, the meeting with Dr Morgan in the morning and the examination of Queenie (patient 457, to be accurate). Next, a large and satisfying lunch at the Llandoger Trow, accompanied by a very passable bottle of Rioja and a couple of cognacs with the coffee. It had been a long lunch over which there had been much discussion of the case, including, he remembered particularly, a suggestion by Dr Morgan that he should draft a paper to be published by them jointly in the British Journal of Clinical Psychology.

After lunch, to Flynn's delight, Morgan had expressed a desire to view the Avon Gorge from the famous suspension bridge, and so the two had walked from the harbour the two miles or so through town up to Clifton. On the way, it being quite a warm afternoon, they had broken their journey at a wine bar in Park Street at around 4.30pm, where they had stayed, resuming their conversation about the Queenie case, until almost six o'clock. It had taken another half an hour to reach the gorge and walk out onto the bridge. Morgan had been quite overawed by the view and had insisted on staying until sunset, almost two hours later. They had toured the downs above the gorge and visited the site of the Camera Obscura before going once more out onto the bridge to watch the sun go down.

By this time it was almost 9pm and both were feeling a little peckish. As Flynn was affiliated to Bristol University and therefore entitled to dine in the staff restaurant at Senate House, they had then made their way to Tyndall Avenue, where they had availed themselves of a warm seafood salad accompanied by a bottle of Chablis, followed by Crème Brulee, coffee and more cognac. They had left Senate House at a quarter to eleven, Dr. Morgan insisting that he pay for a taxi, first to take Flynn home to Frenchay, then to go on to Bristol Airport. Thus, Flynn had arrived home very tired and a little merry at about 11.30pm and gone straight to bed. According to the police the events at the hospital had occurred not long after midnight. Even had he been sober and had not retired immediately, it would have been absolutely impossible for him to have made the journey back to the hospital in less than three quarters of an hour.

He had related his story twice now, not counting interruptions and reiterations, once to DC Wroughton, (she had done all the talking, with Blake simply sitting by her side looking bored and annoyed by turns), and once to another officer who had relieved DC Wroughton two hours ago. This man, Detective Inspector Taylor, had gone through his story with him again, stopping him every few minutes or so to ask for more details, such as 'What had they had for dessert at lunchtime?' or 'How many glasses of wine had each of them drunk?' or 'What exactly were they both wearing at the time?' until Flynn was practically bursting with exasperation.

Then, an hour ago now, DC Wroughton had stuck her head round the interview room door and asked apologetically for a 'quick word' with the inspector. Blake was still in the room, standing at the wall by the door, studiously ignoring Flynn. A couple of times Flynn had tried to engage the man in conversation, asking the time, or how long he thought the inspector might be. Blake had merely replied, "I really couldn't say, Sir," and, "He shouldn't be too long now Sir," and gone back to his intense visual examination of the ceiling.

Finally, the door opened and DI Taylor reappeared, DC Wroughton in tow. He seated himself opposite Flynn, Wroughton taking a chair beside her boss, a little to one side. Taylor studied the table for a moment, clearing his throat with an embarrassed sounding cough. Then, his soft brown eyes meeting and holding Flynn's, he began.

"I am really very sorry that you have been kept waiting, Sir. Most unforgivable. Oh dear, I see that your coffee has gone cold. Blake – one coffee please. And make it a proper cup will you, not the dishwater from that wretched machine?" Flynn opened his mouth to object. All he wanted to do was get on with it and go home. But the Inspector had already snatched up the paper cup and was waving it in Blake's direction. Blake truculently took the foul looking brew and sidled out, Taylor watching until he was sure that Blake had closed the door behind him. He turned back to Flynn, who was becoming more infuriated by the second, but with an effort was managing to hold onto his temper.

When Taylor spoke again, it was to enquire, "You do take sugar don't you, Sir? You see, I'm always having to remind Blake not to put it in mine. Excellent lad, Blake, but some things you just can't get into his head you see, like who takes sugar and…"

"Inspector, *please*!" Flynn almost shouted. Then, taking hold of himself, "Inspector, please, could we just get on with this. I have a hospital to run, and with all that's happened I really should be back at my desk, don't you think?"

"Of course, Sir. I do apologise. Been a long day you see. I'm sure we're all a bit the worse for wear." Taylor shifted in his chair, leaning forward very slightly. "Right. DC Wroughton, the tape if you please. You don't mind I'm sure, Sir. Just procedure."

Flynn shook his head impatiently and there was a click, then a high pitched beep as the tape whirred into action. Taylor went through the usual identifications of those present, then gave another uncomfortable little cough.

"You see Sir, there is a slight problem. Nothing serious I'm sure. Shouldn't take long to clear up. The thing is, well, we …" He paused, his face flushing slightly, and clasped his hands together on the table, leaning a little closer, eyes still locked on

153

Flynn. "The thing is Sir, we have made some enquiries about your colleague, Dr Morgan. You say you spent the whole day with him, is that correct?"

"Oh, for goodness sake, Inspector," cried Flynn. "How many times do I have to tell you. Look, all you have to do is call the British Psychological Society. He is an eminent neuropsychiatrist, a member of the Society. The man is unimpeachable – hundreds of publications. I'm sure they will give you his home number. All you have to do is ask him what he was doing yesterday."

"Well, that's just the thing Sir," said Taylor, looking even more uncomfortable. "We did just that, and you see … well … there is no such person as Dr Alex Morgan. He doesn't exist. We called the Psychological Society, the British Medical Association, we even had a librarian do a search for publications in that name. There aren't any. Never have been any. And there never has been anyone, psychiatrist or otherwise, in the records by the name of Alex Morgan."

Flynn's mouth was working up and down like a fish. He half got up, then sat down again, his face a mixture of confusion and rage. Finally he managed to splutter, "But…but that's nonsense! You must have the wrong name, wrong phone number – the Society must have the number! just because you bloody idiots can't remember a name I've just given you…"

He had risen from the chair and was glowering over DI Taylor, who hadn't moved, and was still staring calmly at Flynn. Gradually it dawned on Flynn that this was getting him nowhere and he slowly sat back down, breathing hard.

"Now then, Sir," continued Taylor. "Perhaps there has been an error. Yes, that must be it. I assure you that we will do our best to find out what's happened. Now if you will calm down …"

The door opened and Blake entered carrying coffee in a china mug. It was real coffee. Flynn could smell it, and decided that he actually could do with a shot of caffeine right at this moment. Blake set down the mug and shuffled out, closing the door behind him.

"There you are, Sir," Taylor said placatingly. "A nice cup of coffee. Just the job, eh?"

Flynn took a gulp and realised that it really was very good coffee, strong, the way he liked it, with just a scant spoon of sugar. He felt calmer. At least the police had admitted they might have made a mistake. That was something, anyway. Taylor waited until Flynn had drunk half the mug then continued in soft, even voice.

"I'm sorry Sir, but there are just another couple of things to clear up before we finish. I hope you don't mind. Best to have everything clear, makes our job easier."

Flynn nodded. He couldn't disagree with that.

"The thing is, Sir, this patient of yours, patient number 457, is that right? The one that you and Dr Morgan examined in the morning?" Flynn nodded again. "Well, unfortunately we don't seem able to find anyone who saw her leave. I know it's early days yet, but despite an extensive search of the area we haven't come up with a single lead. Now, assuming she was alone, on foot and probably disorientated, I would have thought she couldn't have gone very far. Unless, of course, someone helped her – spirited her away, so to speak."

Reality started to dawn on Flynn. "Surely you don't think …You're mad!" he whispered. "Completely crazy! Do you really think I would have anything to do with the abduction of my own patient? Why would I? She's been in my hospital for seven years, for God's sake. Look …" He felt his temper start to boil over. "I don't know what the hell is going on here, but I'm bloody well going to find out. You can't keep me here. I haven't been charged with anything, so if you don't mind …"

He stood up and tried to get round the table. Taylor and Wroughton also stood, completely barring his path.

"Now you really don't want to do that, Sir," began Taylor, but Flynn was suddenly beside himself. He flung himself at the inspector, roughly pushing the constable aside, trying to beat Taylor back towards the door. The next moment, the shrill wail of a siren started up and, a second after that, the sound of footsteps echoed in the corridor outside. The door burst open and two large

155

policemen dashed in, grabbed Flynn and forced him onto the floor, one of them holding him in a very efficient arm lock. He heard Taylor's voice through the hubbub.

"Now then Samson, I think that's quite enough. You can let him go now. Wroughton, get that alarm turned off would you?" Flynn felt himself lifted firmly but gently to his feet, and looked up to find Taylor guiding him back to his chair. "That will be all, Samson, Crawford, thank you. I don't think we will be needing you again. Will we, Sir?"

The alarm cut out and Flynn, dazed, shook his head and fell back into the chair. There was a moment of silence as Wroughton and Taylor settled back into their places opposite him. Then Wroughton explained the events of the last two minutes 'for the benefit of the tape'.

"Now, there is just one final thing, Sir," Taylor continued as if nothing had happened. "We have just had the forensic report back on the dead nursing auxiliary. You see, at first we thought he must have been filching drugs to feed his own habit. You know the sort of thing I'm sure. But when we got the report, well, the theory just doesn't add up. No one in their right mind, not even an addict, would give themselves a dose that big. Admittedly he was drunk – a whole bottle of whisky apparently. But even so … no, Sir. It just doesn't add up at all. There were bruises on his back and neck you see. Couldn't possibly have been self inflicted. Our theory now is that he was attacked by person or persons unknown, who then injected him with a dose of flurazepam they knew would be lethal, especially if mixed with all that alcohol."

Taylor paused for a minute. Flynn hunched in the chair staring at the table, his brain not believing what his ears were telling him.

"So," resumed Taylor, "If I can sum up, it seems that we have a non-existent doctor who comes from we don't know where, to visit a patient of yours that disappears for no good reason. You spend all day and most of the evening with this … er … person who, apparently, is the only individual who can corroborate your movements yesterday, especially yesterday

156

evening. This morning a dead man is found in your hospital, who it now appears has been murdered for a reason yet to be established. Your explanation, or rather lack of explanation of events would only make sense if your dinner companion actually existed. Which he doesn't. In view of these discrepancies," here, DI Taylor leaned forward again, suddenly no longer hesitant, and peered inquiringly at Flynn, "perhaps we could start again, and go through your movements between 9am and midnight yesterday, 14th May?"

CHAPTER 17

Everything was black. She was falling; falling at great speed. Her eyes were open, yet she could see nothing, just endless darkness and a rushing of wind, but wind that could only be heard, not felt. Some force had ripped her away, was pushing her down into an endless void. The blackness and the falling went on until she lost all sense of time, and so she didn't know how long it was before she realised that her eyes were closed, and the motion had stopped.

There was a warmth around her, holding her close, making her feel so comfortable she wished only to stay quite still, enveloped in the rich, sweet scented darkness, the ruffle of clean air on her cheek. She stretched her limbs and sighed, but as she settled back she caught a sudden sense of sadness inside her. She had been crying – crying bitterly for what seemed a long time. She had exhausted herself, and finally fallen asleep. She felt her body shifting slightly, as though she had settled in a tree branch caught in a puff of breeze. There was another shift, and she felt herself tilted slightly upwards. She blinked, and opened her eyes. A thrill of distant recognition ran through her. The walls, rough, washed white with a hint of gold from the morning sun; the scent of burned tallow mixed with fragrant oil; all had a vague familiarity she could not place.

It was a long way down. Too far down. There was another sudden swaying and she tried to whimper, fear rising in her throat.

"Mother? Don't worry, Mother, I am here."

"Mother?" Her head began to spin. "Who are you?" She tried to turn her head, but it was surprisingly difficult. Her muscles didn't work as they should, but seemed weak, uncontrollable. She tried to look up but her head felt leaden, the slightest movement only gained at huge effort. She heard a soft, tinkling laughter.

"Here, Mother. I can help. If we look up, then you will see." Her head moved, seemingly of its own accord, so that she was looking upwards. She was staring straight up at a man's face.

It was a face she knew. Every line, every small detail was familiar to her, as it was to the creature who called her 'Mother'. She could sense the warm familiarity between the man and the one who was sharing her mind. There was no fear, not of the height, not of the man. Her eyes passed over the smooth golden skin, the deep darkness of the eyes, the long black hair that she could now see in her mind's eye, tumbling away behind the shoulders, held back by a wide silver clasp engraved with an ancient symbol; 'For Eternity'. As the floodgates of memory opened, the being that was with her held her firm, giving her an anchor until the storm subsided, the flow of images stemmed.

She looked down again at her own body and saw the blood still flowing from the palm of her right hand where Arghel, in desperation, had plunged the knife. Then, turning her attention to the creature that shared her thoughts, she formed the question.

"Amarisse?"

The response came back to her as a wave of joy. "Mother. You remember."

"Yes, I remember. I remember everything now."

She felt her own grief and panic begin to well up inside her and tried to reach out to Arghel, touch his face, tell him of her presence inside the baby he held in his arms.

"Don't worry, Mother." Her daughter's small voice broke through the tide of longing. "The bond between you is not broken. You will come back to him, and until then, I will be with him. We will be very strong, Father and I. Nothing will hurt us while you are gone."

There was something unnerving in having a conversation with a child not yet old enough to speak or walk. Karisse wondered just how much her daughter understood, and how such a thing was possible at all, for the gift to be with one so young. There was a little ripple of laughter.

"It has always been with me, for as long as I can remember. I listened to you and Father talking before I was born.

159

Then, when I was outside, I could see you. I didn't understand at first, but then the words became pictures, and I could see the things that you and Father could see. Then someone came, and said to me that I should not talk to you, not yet, because you had to go away, and if you knew that the gift was in me you would not go. This other one said I was not to be sad, because you would come back, and there would be others to take care of you and help you."

Karisse was startled. "Who is this other one?"

"I don't know, Mother. The Other said you would come, and that I would see you. You came. I was here waiting. The Other wanted you to remember. I don't know how, but the Other knows where you are. When it is time, and I am older, the Other will come to Father, and together we will make everyone safe and you will come home. Those who are with you know too, and they will help, just as the Other that is here will help Father and me. The Other said that I should tell you all this, but I don't understand any more, only that the Other is good. When I listen, it makes me feel as I do when I listen to you, or Father. It's not like the voice that made you go away. I heard that too, and when I heard it I felt cold, like Father did."

Karisse tried to gather herself. She had always known that the coming together of her gift with that of Arghel might produce something extraordinary, but she had never imagined that the result might be a child born with the gift and, not only that, but with the knowledge of how to use it. It was clear that the 'Other' had shown Amarisse how to use the gift of silence to hide it, even from her and from Arghel. But her own instincts told her that Amarisse was right, that the 'Other' was good.

Her fear for her daughter subsided a little, although the yearning to be back with them was so strong she thought her heart would break. She watched as the flow of blood from the wound in her hand formed a little stain on the white blanket beneath, and recalled, with a sudden shock, the small pain that she felt whenever anything touched her right palm. He had hoped she would feel it, and that it would help her remember. She sent out the thought with all her strength.

160

"I love you."

There was a sudden movement that made Karisse feel dizzy.

"It's all right, Mother. Father won't let us fall."

Arghel had shifted the baby's weight, hoisting them a little higher on his arm. They both looked up at him and she saw that he was gazing at his daughter, eyes still full of tears. He reached down and stroked the baby's face, then put his finger to her lips. Amarisse's infant urge to suckle overwhelmed them both and Karisse joined in, grasping at the warm flesh, drawing it into her mouth, willing him to understand that she was there, with him, that he was not alone.

"You have to go soon." There was sadness in the soft, childlike voice. "Now that you remember, you have to go. But you will come back, when I am older, and he and I have seen the Other. We will wait for you then."

"How long must I wait?" It seemed such a small step, a leap of a few feet through the air and back into her own body. She knew she could do it, and the yearning began to overtake her.

"No, Mother! You must go. You must stop the voice, or we will die. And," Amarisse added in a whisper, "Father will die."

Karisse hesitated, but with each passing moment the longing to return to them increased until all other thoughts were blotted out, and she wished only to feel Arghel's presence, around her and within her, as it had been since their joining.

"Mother, no! You can't stay. You must understand – you will condemn us all."

Karisse felt the urgency, the desperation in her daughter's mind, and faltered for just a second. At the same moment Arghel moved away from the body, walked towards the nurse who stood quietly waiting on the other side of the room.

"You see," said Amarisse quietly, "Sasha will look after me, and I will look after Father, until you come again." They were cradled in the nurse's arms. Sasha turned to leave, and Karisse saw two men lying on the floor. She knew at once that one of them was dead.

161

"Father killed him," said Amarisse simply. "He was angry. I felt it. He is not angry any more, and he is sorry." After a pause Karisse heard her daughter's voice again. "There is another. He was angry too. But now he is very sad because of what he did. Just like Father."

"What other? Is there another of these creatures with you?"

"No, he is with you," Amarisse replied. "He came with you across the void."

"Then how do you know that he is sad, or what he did? Do you know who he is?"

"Yes – because you know. You know of his sadness, and you know his name."

"Paul." Karisse suddenly wondered how she could have not known it. The presence was there, weak, disorientated, but unmistakeable. She felt Amarisse's confirmation.

"Yes. He gave you his gift so that you could come here, so you would remember. He is young, Mother, and all alone. The Other loves him very much, and asks that you do not hurt him."

"The Other is here now?"

"Yes, listening to us, just like I listen to Father."

"Can you show me?"

"The Other doesn't want you to see, but says you must trust the ones who are with you. You must go back to them now, and together you will make the voice silent."

Again, Karisse asked, "How long must I wait?"

"For us," came the reply, "it will be a long time. But for you, no time at all."

Sasha turned in the doorway and Karisse, for what she painfully realised might be the last time, could see Arghel, waiting quietly for the nurse to depart. She felt the distance start to grow.

"We love you, Mother." Her daughter's voice seemed far away.

"Tell your father I was here." As her sight faded she reached out with all her strength and called his name, even though she knew that, for the moment anyway, he would not hear.

She woke lying flat, and for a brief moment of panic thought she might have been taken back to the hospital. A pale shaft of sunlight pooled on the pillow and she raised a hand to touch it, glorying in the simple movement. She laid her hand flat on the pillow and felt a slight twinge in the palm. She smiled and mouthed the word; "Arghel." Groggily, she raised herself up on one elbow. Every muscle in her body ached. She moved her head slowly, easing the stiffness in her neck, and looked round the room. A large bed, soft, with sheets and a thick eiderdown of gold silk. A thick pile carpet the colour of a wheat field, chests and cupboards of ancient oak. The window stretched from floor to ceiling directly opposite the bed, and led out onto a small balcony. It was a door, she decided, and sat for a moment marvelling at the smoothness of the glass. Beyond, she could see branches, green leaves and clear sky. She lay down again and wept.

A voice reached the other side of her closed door, a murmur too low for her to catch the words. She searched her memory – *My name is Alex. You are welcome in my house.* There was a reply from the corridor outside and she recognised Jenni's light tones. There was a trembling in the voice – Jenni had been crying. Then Alex again, soothing, comforting. The voices moved away and she let out a breath, unaware she had been holding it.

The bedroom had another door. Next to it, on a chest, was a pile of clothes. Rising was an effort and at first her legs refused to move, but at last she managed it and made her way to the chest. In the bathroom she stood for a long time, letting her fingers run over the smooth, shining metal of the taps, twisting the tops to make hot water gush out, splashing into the smooth porcelain bowl underneath. The water had a strange scent to it, unnatural, and she found herself wondering where it had come from, and where it went when she pulled out the stopper and heard it gurgling away down a tube to somewhere below the house. She opened all the bottles that were laid out on a counter next to the bowl. They had the same unnatural smell, like flowers, but not like any that grew in the ground. Her mind went back to the place that had imprisoned her before Paul had come and released her from it. The same smell there, but stronger.

She sat on the floor watching the steam rise from the running tap, and thought of all the other things. Roads that were wide, hard and grey, with fast cars that made frightening noises from outside, but were like rooms inside. No horses that she had seen. Floors that did not seem to be made of wood or stone but like the woven rugs she knew, only much bigger, much softer, in bright colours. They didn't smell of sheep, but of the non living smell that seemed to be in everything. Some floors were hard and slippery, and had patterns on them to make them look like stone, but they were made from a material she didn't recognise. And everywhere, the same faint scent, lying like a fog in the air, dulling everything that was real in the world.

Most remarkable of all, she had accepted all these things, knowing how to use them, being neither surprised nor frightened by them, just curious. In all the time that she had lain, bereft of volition, a part of her must have watched, absorbed the newness, the strangeness of what she now knew to be a future time, so that something in her recognised all the essential things, knew how to react to them.

She showered slowly, the hot water easing out the stiffness in her body, clearing the haze in her mind. When she had finished she dressed in a fresh pair of jeans that fitted her almost perfectly and an oversized plain white T-shirt. She was no less overwhelmed by the grief of loss, but it was buried now beneath a sense of purpose. The Great Emptiness was, for her at least, no longer unknown. She had crossed it, and had not died. As she left the bathroom she paused at the mirror. The face that looked back at her was the one she remembered. A little gaunt perhaps, and paler, but it was her own. The full power of the gift was stirring and she felt its strength increase with every stride as she walked purposefully out of the bedroom, down the corridor and towards the scent of food that was wafting up from somewhere on a floor below.

It was eight o'clock on Saturday morning and Detective Inspector Sam Taylor was not a happy man. He had given up any hope of getting back to sleep two hours before, and had finally slipped out of bed and crept down to the kitchen, careful not to wake his long suffering wife. She was not going to be happy, he thought miserably. He sat at the breakfast table in dressing gown and slippers, staring at his third cup of black coffee. Not for the first time, he wondered how it was that he had had the misfortune to inherit the contradictory qualities of intrinsic laziness and a meticulous mind.

He had spent the last month clearing his desk, ensuring there were no loose ends to impinge on his long anticipated week's leave. And he'd almost got away with it. Then, with just two days to go, the memo had arrived on his desk containing the dreaded words 'suspicious death'. Shortly afterwards he'd found himself in the interview room confronting the wretched Gerald Flynn and his ludicrous tales of invisible men and disappearing patients. Just an hour before the end of his shift, he had been forced to release the man through lack of evidence of anything except an impending nervous breakdown.

"Don't worry about it, Sam," his DCI had said soothingly. "Not your problem – you're on holiday, remember? Now just go home, forget all about it, and take Anne off to France in that van of yours. You know how much she's been looking forward to it."

He knew all right, only too well. However, he was saved from further contemplation by a loud knock at the door, which made him jump, mutter an oath under his breath and glance nervously at the staircase all at the same time. DC Michelle Wroughton was leaning on the door jamb, rubbing the sole of one of her Doc Martins on the leg of her jeans as he answered the door. It resulted in a noisier and more dramatic entrance than either had expected as she reeled into the hallway and crashed against a radiator. He caught her by the arm, desperately gesturing for her to keep the noise down – a vain hope where

Wroughton was concerned. There was a rumour in the canteen that the reason for Mickey Wroughton's accelerated progress through the force was that her voice had been classified as a deadly weapon. Indeed, many a petty crook, finding himself on the wrong side of an unstoppable tirade from the little redhead, delivered in her Newcastle accent, had begged to be taken into custody at once, or at least be granted the mercy of a set of earplugs.

Despite the brashness, however, Taylor had soon discovered that she was in fact a very bright girl, a graduate in Psychology who was able to apply her knowledge well to analyses of the criminal mind, and she certainly knew her interview technique better than anyone he had ever worked with. He had just completed his own degree in Psychology with the Open University and so, on her arrival at the station, he had thrown the odd academic comment her way in the hope of interesting conversation. To his great pleasure she proved to be as enthusiastic about the subject as he, and they had become regular canteen companions, discussing everything from group dynamics to the diagnosis of Asperger's Syndrome. Not long afterwards he'd become aware of just how good a copper she was, and had mounted a covert campaign to get her onto his team. He had finally succeeded, and 'Mickey the Mouth' as her colleagues affectionately christened her had, over the last six months, become a very welcome and indispensable member of his little band of detectives.

Wroughton lurched back upright in time to see the frantic wave of the arm, and tried to whisper, "Sorry, Sir," but the expression on her face told him it was too late. Anne Taylor stood glaring down at them from the head of the stairs, making Wroughton shuffle uncomfortably, while Taylor froze for a moment in indecision, weighing possible courses of action. He finally decided on his usual ploy, a helpless 'What could I do?' sort of half shrug. And as usual, it had the desired effect as his wife grimaced, then said, "Better get some more coffee on then," before sweeping into the bathroom, closing the door and clicking the lock with unnecessary firmness. Taylor sighed, and with an air of resignation nodded his protégé through into the kitchen, where he busied himself making a fresh pot of coffee.

"Sorry Sir," she repeated, then ventured, "Thought you might be up though."

"And so I was, Detective Constable, so I was." He brought the coffee pot over to the kitchen table, gesturing for her to take a seat. Seeing her nervous glance towards the staircase, he gave her a reassuring wink. "Don't worry. Whatever else my wife may think of me, she knows as well as I do that my days of chasing pretty young constables are well and truly over. No, I'm afraid the problem is far more serious than that Mickey – far more serious."

"Oh." She relaxed and smiled as he handed her a mug of coffee and slid the sugar bowl across the table. "You mean your trip to France, Sir?"

"Indeed I do, Mickey, indeed I do." His gaze drifted towards the window, sensing impending doom, emphasised by the fact that he had repeated himself three times in as many sentences, which he often caught himself doing, much to his irritation.

Wroughton was watching him carefully, and said, "You're thinking the same as me aren't you, Sir?"

"I'm afraid so, Mickey. I just can't leave it. You know what our esteemed colleagues are like – they don't have an inkling of what's happening. The DCI still suspects that idiot Flynn, you know."

"Yes. He told me that yesterday. They've got a twenty-four hour watch on him. But I don't think he's going anywhere, unless it's to check himself in as a voluntary patient." She helped herself to three heaped teaspoons of sugar, stirred noisily, then drank her coffee in one go, plonking the empty mug down on the table with a grunt of satisfaction. "You make great coffee, Sir." He refilled her mug. She went on, "There's no way he could have made all that up though. I mean, you saw him. He was as shocked as I've ever seen anyone when we told him about Morgan. The whole story was just too complicated. In the first place, he is far too stupid to have invented it, and in the second place, what motive would he have? I mean, given there was no need for him to abduct the patient in the first place, it doesn't make sense."

"Precisely, Mickey," he replied. "There obviously was someone called Morgan. And whatever else we think of Flynn, my guess is that he could tell a real Psychiatrist from a fake, especially if he was consulting with him on a case he knew well. And I can't see why anybody would want to hide a patient that hasn't spoken for seven years. It's not as if she could have spilled any beans. What I don't know is how they did it, or why. People, even brilliant criminals, can't just disappear into thin air without leaving any trail at all behind them. And what about witnesses? Morgan, or whoever he is, must have been seen by several people at the hospital in the morning, or the restaurants, or somewhere. But all the people we've interviewed can't remember either of them. Someone, Mickey, is playing a game, and I, for one, want to know who, and why."

She nodded, and was about to reply when they both heard the bathroom lock slide back.

"Look, Mickey – give me a couple of hours will you? When I've finished here I'll go over to that sandwich bar by the market cross. See you there around eleven?"

Wroughton nodded, and grinned as he let her out.

"Good luck, Sir," she mouthed, and disappeared round the corner, still smiling.

Anne Taylor knew her husband better than he knew himself. She had already made a call from the upstairs phone to confirm that daughter Alice was on her way to drop off her children with their Aunty Carolyn for a week on the farm, and another to Carolyn to remind Alice not to arrive until their father had been suitably briefed. Besides, having Alice as a stand in for Sam had advantages – more shopping trips for one thing. An eminently practical woman, she had ceased to be cross with her husband long before bedtime the previous night, but there was no reason, she thought, why she shouldn't put up a pretence, at least for an hour or so. In fact, there was every reason to do so, as he had been planning his line of approach at least since yesterday evening, which accounted for the tossing and turning most of the night. The last thing she wanted him to feel was that his discomfiture had been for nothing.

When it came to it she could only keep it up for some twenty minutes. There had been something in the way he had tried to explain the nature of the investigation, his reservations about handing it on to someone else, the theories he was trying to formulate to fit the known facts. As he talked, she had realised how important this was to him, not just as a policeman, but as a psychologist. It was his first opportunity to practise the skills he had mastered over hundreds of hours spent poring over texts at the end of his shifts, and was much more than simply an excuse not to have to spend his week's leave driving the length and breadth of Normandy.

Her way of letting him into the conspiracy was to present him with a list containing instructions for meals, washing and other household duties, all calculated with a military precision he couldn't help but admire, and which had obviously been drawn up the night before with the help of his daughters. He and Anne both knew that the planned dinner invitations would be gracefully declined, and that by mid week he would have run out of clean socks. As he kissed her a fond goodbye and stood, waving at the camper van until well after it had disappeared from the end of the drive, he thought her the most marvellous woman he had ever had the good fortune to meet.

He stayed in the doorway reflecting on his good fortune for several minutes, then sighed, made his way back inside and finished the remaining coffee. He was just thinking that perhaps it might have been nice to get away from it all for a few days when his eye caught sight of the kitchen clock – ten fifty-five. Throwing his mug into the sink, he grabbed his jacket from the hallstand and leaped into the car. He was halfway to the Market Cross Sandwich Bar when he realised that his door keys were still on the kitchen table.

CHAPTER 18

It was late on Saturday evening when the telephone finally rang. Sam Taylor was back in dressing gown and slippers, up in the guest bedroom putting the finishing touches to his latest home video, a grand production of his fifteen year old granddaughter's performance in a national gymnastics competition. For the last four hours he had tried to concentrate on the video images without success.

As so often, it was Anne who put him on the scent. Earlier in the day, as he and Mickey sat in the sandwich bar munching Danish pastries and desperately trying to come up with a new approach, the mobile in his pocket trilled. He pressed the button and Anne's voice, shouting above the hum of the camper van engine and signal static, arrived in his ear.

"What about the M32?"

"What?"

"The M32! Were there any cars, you know, on the hard shoulder, looking as though they had broken down?" He was silent for a minute. "Sam? Sam, you still there? What do you think?"

"Darling – I think you're a genius! Don't go to France. Come back – I need you!"

He heard laughter from the other end of the line.

"Too late now! You just solve the mystery and get a decent corkscrew ready for when I come back. Love you!"

The line went dead. He glanced up to see Mickey Wroughton looking at him eagerly.

"What?" she asked, seeing the smile begin to spread on his face. He told her what had been said. She slapped the table, setting the coffee cups rattling and attracting stares from the scattering of Saturday morning shoppers. "Of course! There isn't a slip road for miles, but the motorway runs right alongside the grounds. I can't believe nobody checked."

"No one checked," replied Taylor, "because everyone believes the abduction is a figment of Gerald Flynn's imagination. The DCI has fallen back on the drug addict/break in theory and is, as we speak, searching the inner city back streets for a sudden flood of tranquillizers onto the market." He took a last bite of his pastry and grabbed his jacket. "Come on, WDC Wroughton. We have work to do. And your first job is to help me break in to my own house."

Back in his kitchen, Taylor started making phone calls. Within minutes, he had something. At around one o'clock on Tuesday morning a passing motorist had seen a black S-type jaguar stopped on the hard shoulder of the M32 northbound carriageway just outside Bristol. The motorist had called the police as the car hadn't been showing any hazard lights, and he had been worried in case the occupant had taken ill at the wheel.

"Thank goodness for nosey parkers," Taylor said to himself, and taking a deep breath asked the duty constable if by any chance this Good Samaritan had noticed the number plate.

"Sorry, Sir," came the voice on the other end of the phone. "Only a partial I'm afraid. It started 'A1', but he didn't get the rest. I asked how he managed to see any of it at all if the car had no lights – the motorway has no lighting along that stretch you see – and he said he glimpsed the start of it in his headlights as he went past. He realised it was a personalised plate and tried to catch the rest of it in his rear view mirror, but it was too dark. Anyway, we asked the patrol car to take a look on his next pass, but by then the car was gone. We reckoned that whoever it was might have just stopped to relieve himself or something, so we didn't bother about it. I hope that's okay, Sir."

Taylor could hardly contain himself until he got off the phone. He turned triumphantly to Wroughton. "Right. Black Jaguar, S-type, with a personalised number plate beginning A1 something. Whoever it is isn't short of cash, that's for sure. The only question is, did they carry on up the M32, or did they turn round?"

Wroughton thought for a moment, then asked, "What about traffic monitoring, Sir? There are lots of road works and bridges in that area on both motorways. I seem to remember something about new cameras to look at traffic flow, assess congestion at the city exits. Worth asking, don't you think?"

"Right." He let his brain cells work on the idea for a minute, then jumped up. "Mickey, you get off up to the M32, northbound carriageway. While you're on the way I'll make a few calls, find out where the nearest cameras are, and hope they still have film of Monday night and Tuesday."

"Got it," said Mickey, halfway to the door, her eyes shining with excitement.

"When you get there we're looking for at least two people," he shouted after her, "one female, one driver, with possibly another passenger." Wroughton waved an acknowledgement, jumped into her car and sped off.

By lunchtime they had established that the Jaguar had continued up the northbound carriageway and joined the M5. Birmingham had been tricky, but luckily a camera was installed to provide information for proposals for a new relief motorway just off the M5/M6 interchange, and a computer analysis of the tape revealed a black Jaguar, registration A1 EX, with three occupants – a male driver, two passengers in the rear, coming onto the M6 at a little after three on Tuesday Morning. Just after eight a CCTV camera had spotted the car refuelling at services north of Manchester. Wroughton sounded tired when she called from the services at five pm, having verified the sighting.

"I'm going to stop for half an hour," she said. "If I don't, I might end up charged with dangerous driving. And," she added mischievously, "I was off duty two hours ago, Sir."

Taylor smiled. "Take it easy, Mickey – they've got four days start on us, so I don't think a few hours is going to make a difference. Look – I've just had a call from Glasgow saying they might have something for us. Do you think you're up to it?"

He could almost hear Wroughton bristle on the other end of the line.

172

"As long as you're up to my expenses claim," was the reply, then she hung up. A second later, the phone rang again, and Taylor snatched it up. As he listened, a look of exasperation spread across his normally genial face.

"Like I said," the duty constable was explaining, "We just didn't think it was important. It was a busy night and there had already been a couple of minor accidents further up near the M5, so we were a bit stretched. As far as we were concerned, nothing was untoward in that area, and we didn't even have the whole plate, so …"

There was a pause, into which Taylor interjected wearily, "So you didn't check it."

"No, Sir – sorry, Sir," was the sheepish reply. Taylor put the phone down without bothering to inform the young constable that he *had* checked, as soon as he had the full plate, and that no details had been forthcoming. It looked frustratingly as though the plate was a false one. Well, he mused, at least they, whoever they were, hadn't bothered to change the car between Bristol and possibly Glasgow, so they were still in with a chance.

* * *

Taylor threw the camcorder onto his desk and grabbed the phone before the second ring. Wroughton sounded excited.

"They're in Scotland, Sir, no doubt about it," she said triumphantly. "I confirmed the sighting in Glasgow and they let me phone through to Edinburgh and Inverness. No luck in Edinburgh. They had a camera but it was switched off on Tuesday. I thought that was the end of the trail, but then Inverness phoned back. They are testing a new traffic control system, and guess what? There are our friends in glorious monochrome at around midday on Tuesday, leaving Inverness heading West."

"Where are you now?" Taylor asked

"On the way to Inverness," she replied. "Our Super has already been in touch with them and they're expecting us. Once I've verified that they have our vehicle, I'll call you back."

"Don't bother." He was already in the main bedroom, phone jammed against his chin, rooting through the wardrobes for a change of clothes. "Just book into a decent hotel, then call and let me know where you are. I'll get the first flight I can to Inverness. With a bit of luck I might make it in time for breakfast."

"Right you are, Sir," said Wroughton, adding, "Would that be a champagne breakfast?"

"Only if you're paying." He rang off and rubbed his hands together. The addictive tickle of excitement had started somewhere in the pit of his stomach. He threw some clothes into an overnight bag, fished his mobile out of his pocket and dialled Anne's number.

"Scotland? And here I am stuck in Paris, away from all the fun. Don't do anything too dramatic, like arrest them before I get back. Oh," she added quickly," it's a bit chilly up there even at this time of year. I hope you've packed a couple of sweaters."

Next, he dialled the airport. Yes, there was a flight leaving for Inverness in two hours time, and he just had time to check in if he was quick. He grabbed the bag and made for the door, but stopped halfway down the stairs and dashed back to the bedroom. In the bottom of a big chest of drawers he found what he was looking for – an oversized Aran sweater with a designer label that his daughter in law, Kim, had given him last Christmas. He generally had no need of anything but a light jacket in the damp and warm West Country, and the sweater was still sitting in its polythene bag. "Thank you, Kim!" he declared to the chest of drawers and, stuffing the sweater into the overnight bag, he set off for the airport.

* * *

It was mid morning by the slant of the sun's rays, and pleasantly warm for late spring. After a good number of missed turns, staircases and dead ends, Karisse found herself on the threshold of the source of the enticing aromas that had beckoned from her room upstairs. At first she thought the huge kitchen deserted.

Piles of dirtied plates and mugs told of a number of hearty and well appreciated breakfasts, and the strong smell of fried meat was making her mouth water. She came to a stop just outside the open doorway. For what must have been the tenth time since leaving her room, she struggled to initiate movement. Once a little momentum had built up, walking was relatively easy, but the energy required to get going once she had come to a halt was starting to exhaust her.

She was still wrapped in the effort of making her feet move when a figure appeared from the other side of the door and almost bumped into her.

"Good Lord! Are you trying to give me a heart attack?" Her interrogator, an ageing, short lived woman, plump, grey haired and pinafored, peered at her for a moment with the narrowed eyes of a territorial hound. Almost at once, though, she stepped back and made a gruff noise in her throat. "What on earth is Alex thinking of?" she muttered, more to herself than to Karisse, then her expression softened and she held out a hand. "Poor thing. I expect you're starving."

Karisse took the hand gratefully and, released from the need to instigate her own movement, allowed herself to be led into the kitchen and to an armchair close to a big cooking range.

"I'm Mary," the woman went on companionably, grabbing a frying pan and bustling over to a large fridge in the corner, wedged in next to a set of crowded worktops and a metal sink. "I make sure everyone here is fed and watered three times a day – if they want it, that is." She gestured towards the piles of crockery on the table. "Pretty much a full time job, as you see. I take it you like bacon sandwiches?"

Karisse nodded, although not quite sure what had been offered, and thought that she should perhaps say something. Only then did it occur to her that she hadn't spoken a word aloud to another person for as long as she could remember. Mary squeezed in front of her and plopped the frying pan onto one of the hotplates, then turned to her and took her hand.

"It would be good if you would try, dear," she said encouragingly. Karisse drew her hand away, confused.

"Oh, I can hear you all right." Mary answered the unspoken question. "But I'm not one of you. Some of us can. Didn't you know that?"

Karisse shook her head, and automatically formed the shape of the word with her lips.

"No." The sound was little more than a whisper, but in making it she startled herself. Mary laughed and turned to tend to the pan.

"Alex won't like that," she said, her voice mischievous. "I think he was hoping to be the one to hear your first word. Never mind –he can't have everything! Not that he doesn't try. Now, do you want to stay there or sit at the table?"

It seemed the kitchen was never empty for very long. Karisse perched herself at the corner of the massive table, closest to the range and furthest from the door. As she savoured both the taste of the thick, dripping bacon sandwiches and her ability to eat unaided, several people came and went, some through a large set of French windows that led out onto a wooden veranda, and from there to the grounds at the back of the house. Mary hovered protectively close to her, keeping up a quiet commentary on who did what, where they came from and where they were going. In the course of the next two hours she was smiled or waved at by two gardeners, both of whom were called Jim, one old, one little more than a boy, a pretty blonde named Susan and a middle aged hawk faced woman, Grace. Mary explained that they worked as Alex's secretary and accountant, descriptions that made no sense at all to Karisse. They variously dropped off verbal messages, grabbed cups of coffee, sandwiches or buns, but none stayed more than the time it took to get what they wanted.

"It's like this day and night," Mary explained, pouring Karisse a cup of fresh coffee from the filter machine. "They know I'm always here, and there's no one who doesn't come in at some time of the day. I've suffered from insomnia since I was a child." She pointed to the large stack of books piled up by an old rocking chair next to the range. "I don't see the point of lying awake all night in a bed, so I stay here. I have my own room of course. I keep asking Alex to give it to someone else, but he won't hear of

176

it – in case I want my own space, he says. I said to him, this kitchen is my space. Well, he had to concede that, although he still hasn't let anyone else use the room."

Karisse was on her third mug of coffee and still coming to terms with its bitter, but not unpleasant taste, when a dark haired young man strode in, whom she recognised at once as the driver of the car that had transported her from the hospital. Mary introduced him as David and he gave her a nervous nod, but didn't meet her eye. She thanked him, her speech still a little halting, and he shrugged, but didn't reply. Instead, he spoke to Mary, taking her hands and kissing her on the cheek.

"Don't worry about me," he said. "It'll be a good break. I'll be back in a couple of weeks."

Karisse could see that there was a great deal of affection between them. Mary smiled and reached up to ruffle his hair.

"You mind you are," she said, pulling his head down so that she could return the kiss. "And don't get into any trouble. You know what those big cities are like."

He laughed, a little nervously, Karisse thought.

"I'm big enough to look after myself now, Mary. And if Alex thought there was a problem he would have said so. Somebody's got to take Paul's dance classes for the next few weeks. I'll call, I promise."

She snorted. "You'd better!" She hugged him close, and he disappeared out of the French windows onto the veranda.

"He's a good lad," Mary said, when David had gone. "You mustn't think he was being rude just now. It frightens him, you see – people like you, I mean. He's fine with Alex and Paul, but you're new, and he doesn't like the idea that you might read his thoughts. Alex thought it would be better for him if he went off for a while."

"Why does he think I would do that? I have no reason to."

Mary shook her head. "He had a bad experience, once. It was …" She stopped, catching herself. "Never mind. I'm sure Alex will tell you all about it when the time is right."

Sensing that asking more questions would get her nowhere, Karisse said nothing, but went back to her examination of the coffee, puzzling over the fact that despite its being hot and having an odd taste, it had an effect strangely like the sour wine she was used to at home.

The bustle continued until well after noon, and Karisse found being in the middle of it both exhilarating and exhausting. There had been no sign of Alex, nor of Paul, the one who had helped her to reach back to her memories. Neither had the red-haired girl, Jenni, appeared.

By mid-afternoon the kitchen was quiet, and for a while Mary and Karisse were alone. Mary offered her a seat on the veranda, which was starting to catch the late sunshine, and Karisse found herself starting to doze. Mary's voice went on, telling her about the miracles of dishwashers and washing machines against a chorus provided by the former, which was humming and whirring in a corner like a great contented cat. Karisse shook herself, not wanting to sleep, realising she was actually afraid that to do so might imprison her in her body again. It was strange, she thought, that waking and sleeping had not seemed very different in the hospital.

"You didn't know who you were then," Mary commented, coming to sit beside her to peel potatoes.

"And Alex?" Karisse asked, still only using her silent voice, finding it hard to keep focussed in the gentle heat, with the buzzing flies and the humming machine. "Who is he?"

Mary made a little 'harrumph' in her throat. "Most people here think that Alex is simply a very rich businessman who likes to spend his time and money rescuing people from some mess or other, giving them a leg up, so to speak. Not that he's a soft touch, not in the least. Some people want to stay on here, and he always finds a job for those that do. Others get qualified and take up a career somewhere, or just find their feet and move on. Nearly all stay in touch though, and people come back to visit, or when they are in trouble. There are no visitors here just now, except for you of course, and around eight who live here permanently, like Jenni, David and the Jims." She paused and turned her eyes to Karisse. "And me, of course."

Karisse couldn't help smiling, unable to think of Mary as someone who might ever have needed 'rescuing'. She noted, however, that Mary hadn't really answered her question. She felt herself becoming a little light headed with the effort of staying awake, and couldn't prevent a pang of anxiety from twisting her stomach. Mary sensed it at once and got up, returning a moment later with a mug.

"Just chamomile," she said reassuringly. Karisse lifted it and drank. Just before consciousness left her she thought she was aware of someone close to her, inside her mind. "Arghel," she whispered, the third word she had spoken aloud since her awakening. Then she fell down into a dreamless sleep.

When Karisse woke again she was back in her room. Someone had carried her there. She glanced up at the window and realised with a shock that it was morning again. A tentative stretch informed her that her body was working well – better than the day before. The stiffness was gone, and when she swung her feet to the carpet the movement was fluid, without effort. She laughed aloud, then spoke her own name, and that was easy too. She washed and dressed, then strode out onto the landing. She needed information, and there was one person who could provide it. She let her gift range the house and grounds but, to her surprise, found no sign of the one she sought. Another sweep brought her nothing and she sighed in frustration. Then she heard a soft voice in her mind.

"Here." A veil was lifted, just slightly, and a picture of the sitting room where she had been taken on her arrival formed itself in her mind. She followed the path that was being carefully laid out for her and reached a door on the same floor as her bedroom. Without hesitating she opened it and walked in.

"Alex." He was sitting in the armchair that she had occupied, his back to her, facing the hearth. He didn't turn at the sound of his name, but gave a slow nod.

"Karisse," he answered softly.

Paul was sitting on a couch on the other side of the fireplace. His face was pale, his hair, shining like burnt gold in the shafts of morning sunlight, falling loose and dishevelled around his shoulders. His height and features betrayed his nature, except that unlike any other male of the gift she had ever seen, his eyes were a deep cobalt blue, not the characteristic dark, almost black that set Dancers apart from ordinary men.

His eyes avoided hers, and as she came closer she saw his body start to tense. She understood at once. He was wholly unused to the intimacy of the Dance, and had revealed a part of himself he had not wanted her to see, that he would have hidden even from himself. He had hoped for some kind of comfort in the sharing, even absolution, but had found none – only a deeper horror of himself, a confirmation of his guilt. What was worse, unable to break free of her, he had been pulled back with her across the blackness and had felt, possibly even seen what had come after.

Distracted by the enormity of her own experience, she had been unaware of his presence at first, and thus had done nothing to shield his more fragile consciousness. The intense flood of her emotion had hit him like a tidal wave, tearing his mind away from the moorings of its own reality, and for a short time forcing him into hers. He had taken an enormous risk, acting as both her catalyst and her anchor. Alone, she could not have made the crossing, and without him she could not have returned. He had chanced all to give her back her life, and one with a lesser gift might have been destroyed by it. But here was one with no lesser gift. He had survived the encounter, and his suffering was in part exhaustion from the effort it had taken to regain control of his own mind. He had not slept or eaten, and the consequences of the enforced sharing lay heavily on him.

She moved past Alex, touching his shoulder briefly to signal that she understood, and took Paul's face in her hands, stroked his hair back gently. Then, she put her arms around him and held him. Slowly she felt his body relax, until with a sudden, fierce movement he came to life, throwing his arms about her and clasping her to him in a tight embrace. After a long moment, he pushed her away gently and looked at her, his eyes posing the question.

She smiled, and said softly, "What you did was right." Then, after a pause, "All of it. Except for one thing – you should not have taken such a risk for me."

"It was necessary," he said simply. His voice was low and soft, like silk, a Dancer's voice.

She turned to Alex. "He had no choice," she said firmly. "You were wrong to accuse him. To preserve the lives of others it is sometimes necessary to kill."

She raised her eyes in challenge and Alex sighed, then nodded his acknowledgement. With a shrug he reached for the coffee pot that was sitting on a small table near the hearth and poured them each a cup.

"We can discuss Paul's actions another time. For now, I am simply grateful that you are here and that you are well. There is a great deal I must tell you, and if I am correct we don't have much time. It is essential that you …"

There was an urgent knock on the door. Before Alex could say anything more it was flung open and Jenni rushed in, looking flustered.

"Alex, there are two policemen here – well, actually a policeman and a police woman. They say they want to see your car, and they have descriptions of two men and a woman they say they want to interview. They only have clear descriptions of one of the men. I'm sure it's Paul, and the woman is definitely …"

"Don't worry, Jenni," Alex said quickly. Paul and our guest are just leaving, and I have sent David into town. Go and tell our visitors I will come down to speak to them in a moment." Jenni scuttled out, and Alex turned to Paul. "Both of you need to leave now. You know the way. Take Karisse to the house in Durness and wait for me there. I should be with you before evening. And then," he turned to Karisse, "we will have a very long talk."

CHAPTER 19

Sam Taylor had seen the inside of a lot of houses in his time. In particular, he was an expert on hallways. In the little back streets of Easton and St Werburghs, there were grubby, narrow hallways, with threadbare carpets that smelled of cat and last night's takeaway, and mould from peeling wallpaper. There were equally threadbare hallways whose owners battled fiercely against the tide of poverty with liberal use of duster, hoover and cartons of carpet freshener. Up on the Downs, where the other half lived, one entered graciously past half-sized plaster-moulded ball finials. Once inside, the odour was of overpriced supermarket filter coffee, served in undersized china cups beneath prints of Caravaggio and Botticelli that hung incongruously against the backdrop of magnolia emulsioned woodchip.

This hallway, he thought, running his eye along the finely polished antique claymores that hung above the original stone fireplace opposite the front door, reeked not only of money, but of refinement and discernment. Whoever owned this house was a very intelligent and educated man. There was no other adornment on the walls and there was no need of any, for the eye was drawn to the shining blades, reflecting the light from the fire that burned beneath. A real fire. A fire that someone lit every morning, every day of the year, that was lovingly swept and laid with an attractive arrangement of pine logs that gave off a sweet scent. It said, 'Visitors are Welcome' with a warm crackle, which was not too warm, even in midsummer. There was no carpet here. Just a thick green rug in front of the fire, with leather sofas on either side of it. Each sofa had its own pair of little oak tables, one at each end, where passing guests might place their hats and gloves, or even, he thought wistfully, their drams of whisky on a cold morning.

The thought had no sooner crossed his mind than he heard light footsteps, and the cheerful young woman who had let them in a moment before came back carrying a large tray. With the manner of a receptionist in a country house hotel she beamed at them and said, "Mr. MacIntyre apologises for keeping you waiting. If you would care to take a seat, Sir," (Sir, not 'Inspector', Taylor noted), "he will join you as soon as he can. In the meantime, please make yourself comfortable, and Mr. Macintyre will be with you shortly." The woman beamed even more widely, and gestured towards one of the leather sofas, the tray expertly balanced in one hand.

She turned the smile on DC Wroughton, who was staring about her open mouthed, thinking that this was the sort of house that policemen visited in books like Poirot or Miss Marple, and that perhaps she should warn her superior that the chances were, the body was in the library.

"Madam?"

Wroughton realised that the woman was gesturing her towards the other sofa and, feeling suddenly self conscious, she perched herself at the end furthest from the fire, thankful she had not tripped on the rug or knocked over one of the little oak tables on the way. When they were both seated the woman set about distributing the contents of the tray. There were two individual cafetieres of fresh coffee (not the supermarket kind, but freshly ground with a deep chocolaty aroma), white china jugs of steaming milk and matching breakfast cups and saucers. The sugar came in brown rocky lumps, and instead of the ubiquitous highland shortbread on the biscuit plate there was an artistic arrangement of wafer-thin, caramel coloured fingers which gave off a scent as though they had been freshly baked.

The woman lifted a third table, positioning it carefully in the centre of the rug. On it she placed a crystal decanter, half full of what Taylor knew would be an expensive and tasteful single malt, together with three matching tumblers and a jug of water.

"Please," the woman said again, "make yourselves comfortable. I'm sure you won't be kept waiting long." With another smile she disappeared through a doorway to the right of the front door, leaving them alone.

It was at this point, Taylor thought, that an intelligent policeman would say to his sidekick, "I think someone ought to nip round the back and see if anything is going on." Somehow, though, it seemed inappropriate, even impolite, and the idea of his protégé being discreet among flowerbeds full of priceless exotic plants and carefully manicured shrubs did not appeal to him at all. Besides, it was the best smelling coffee he had come across in a very long time. With an inward shrug and an outward sigh, he reached forward, pushed down the silver plunger on the cafetiere, and poured himself a full cup of black coffee. Wroughton hadn't moved but sat, staring nervously at the little arrangement on her table.

"What's the matter, Mickey?" Taylor asked. "They might be rich, but they are only people you know. And you won't get coffee as good as this too often – at least not for free, so make the most of it."

"Oh, it's not that, Sir," said Wroughton, flushing with embarrassment. "It's just …well, I can't … it's those *things*. I've never been able to manage them. Either it shoots out over the top and I get it all over my face, or it tips up all over the floor. Why can't people put coffee in proper pots, like tea? I swear they make those things just to make me look stupid …oh!" She gave a squeak, and jumped in her seat as a long, delicate finger appeared out of nowhere and slowly pushed down the plunger on her cafetiere.

"To tell the truth," said a quiet voice just behind her ear, "I'm not too keen on them myself." A hand lifted the little pot and poured some of the coffee into her cup. "Milk and sugar?" asked the voice.

"Er…just milk thanks," she said, not daring to turn round, and watched the hand take up the milk jug and, with an elegant flourish, top up the cup with steaming milk. She felt a movement behind her and the owner of the voice stepped around the sofa into her field of vision. Taylor had risen to his feet, but for the moment stood ignored as Wroughton found herself held in the gaze of a man whose attributes did more than full justice to the superlatives that she and her best friend Melissa would use to describe, over a glass or two of wine, the best sightings of the week at the local clubs. As she had the thought she saw a little glitter of amusement in the dark eyes. One eyebrow raised just a little, so that she was suddenly certain she had spoken aloud, and felt vulgar, crude and, worst of all, as though she wasn't wearing any clothes.

She felt herself going as red as her hair, and in an attempt to break the spell muttered, "Thank you," in a voice that sounded, to her, like the harsh cawing of a crow.

The man bowed his head slightly and murmured, "My pleasure," in a voice that made her think of warm honey and turned her stomach into knots.

Mercifully, he turned his attention to her boss and said, in the same silky tone, "You really must forgive my rudeness. I simply can't bear to see a lady in distress. Alex MacIntyre, at your service, Sir. I apologise for keeping you waiting. A business call that could not be put off."

He shrugged ruefully and held out his hand. Taylor took it, and was invited with a graceful gesture to be seated. Taylor sat, and Wroughton realised, in a panic, that Macintyre intended to sit next to her. For the last minute or so, her body had been forcibly reminding her of what it had been like to be thirteen. Memories surfaced of sleepovers with Melissa, the two of them fantasising wildly over what it must be like to be one of the hapless heroines trapped in a gothic castle at the mercy of the deliciously overpowering Christopher Lee in one of the Hammer Horror midnight movies.

She could feel the blood rushing to her face and was quite sure that both of them could hear her heart thumping, as to her it sounded louder than an express train. She was gripping her cup so tightly that her knuckles were white and, as he sat down, respectably at the other end of the sofa, she didn't dare look, but found herself thinking irrationally, *God – don't let him touch me, I think I'll faint!*

As soon as she had the thought he stretched out an arm along the back of the sofa as if in deliberate provocation, bringing his long, slender fingers to rest just an inch or so from her shoulder. Her insides flipped over so rapidly it made her feel a little sick. She looked across at Taylor, and realised that he was completely unaware of her. He was politely complimenting their host on the coffee and expressing an interest in the claymores that hung above the fireplace. There followed a discussion on the history of the region and the finer points of armaments during the battles of Culloden and Bannockburn. This mostly passed her by completely, but at least neither of them seemed to be paying her any attention, so she was able to relax a little. Nevertheless, she didn't risk setting the coffee cup back on the table in case it caused Macintyre to look once more in her direction.

Taylor was also mesmerised, in his own way. The conversation had turned to the use of firearms in the Napoleonic wars, and the role of swordsmanship in modern warfare. The topic had fascinated him on and off for years and his host was a mine of information on the subject. There was a pause, in which Macintyre leaned forward and poured three generous glasses of whisky from the decanter. Taylor opened his mouth with the intention of uttering the stock phrase without which no respectable old British crime film would be complete; 'Sorry, Sir, I'm on duty.' But before he could say it, the vapour from the glass wafted to his nostrils, a rich earthy smell, like smoke from a peat fire. Beneath that, he detected something sharp and sweet that reminded him of one of the fragrant spring shrubs that Anne had planted outside the back door years ago – on their tenth anniversary, he thought. He took the proffered glass and breathed in deeply. Macintyre watched as he lifted it to his lips and took a small sip, rolling the liquid on his tongue. He swallowed and, without taking his eyes from the glass, exclaimed, "Good Lord!" Macintyre bowed slightly in acknowledgement. "I've tasted some single malts in my time," said Taylor admiringly, "but nothing quite like this. What is it?"

Instead of answering Taylor directly, MacIntyre picked up a second glass and, turning to Wroughton, fixed her once again with the gaze that made her feel entirely naked. Her body's reaction was immediate and ferocious, so that it was all she could do to stop herself from crying out loud. Her mind was filled once more with adolescent fantasy, deep in some dark and brooding castle in the grip of a lustful and, of course, delectable demon who was about to steal her soul, but not before he had stolen much else besides. She could feel every hair stand up on end and, for one mad moment, imagined he might actually do it. Then he glanced away and she realised he was simply holding out the glass, waiting for her to take it.

Which presented her with a problem – well, two problems. Firstly, she was still holding onto the coffee cup, so tightly she could no longer feel her fingers. Secondly, she had never been a whisky drinker, and avowed strongly to anyone who ever offered it to her that the very smell of it made her feel ill. Thankfully, he didn't look directly at her again, but with his free hand reached out for her to hand him the cup. When she didn't move he took it gently and, leaning across her, placed it on the little table. Then, once more, he held up the whisky glass.

"Strathisla," he said. "Try it. It's not like anything you might have had at home. Don't worry. If you don't like it I won't be offended."

Her fingers were aching and she worried that she might drop it, but she took the glass and, despite her misgivings, took a tiny sip. Immediately the fiery warmth shot through her and she felt calmer, more relaxed. She took another, larger swallow, and realised that she actually quite liked the taste. No – she liked the taste a lot. He was looking at her again, and although her body still wouldn't behave, the tension seemed to have gone. He smiled his dizzying little smile and said, "You see? You never know what you will like until you try it."

She tried to smile back and took another mouthful, which made her head go round, and she couldn't help musing that in the old Hammer Horror movies the demon would trick you into drinking blood, and then you would have to stay in the castle, being ravaged, nicely of course, forever.

But MacIntyre was speaking to Taylor again now, and although the tone was still light and pleasant, the conversation had taken a more serious turn. Taylor was explaining their presence at the house, asking whether 'Sir' owned an S-type

Jaguar, and if so, would he mind terribly if they took a look at it, just, he would understand, to eliminate his vehicle from their enquiries. No, of course MacIntyre wouldn't mind, and was always ready to lend assistance to the police. He would take them round to the garages on the way out, and would there be anything else?

Taylor had fished two stills from the Manchester CCTV camera out of his jacket pocket. Macintyre pored over the blurred black and white images for some time, one of a tall, good looking, long haired man, perhaps blonde, wearing jeans and a white T-shirt, leaning casually against the rear half of the Jaguar. The other contained the same man, this time helping a young woman out of the car. The woman was small and slim with long, straight, dark hair and her clothes, jeans and sweatshirt, appeared to be several sizes too big, as the jeans had clearly been rolled over several times at the bottom. Finally, Macintyre looked up and said, "I'm terribly sorry. I'm afraid I can't help you with either of these people. However, I can tell you without any doubt that it is not my car in the photographs."

"Really?" asked Taylor, a little surprised. "How can you tell that? After all, the pictures are blurred, as you say, and I would guess that one S type Jaguar is much like another. You have already pointed out that you don't drive it a great deal, and so might not be aware if someone 'borrowed' it for a few hours."

"Ah, I see," came the reply, and Taylor thought he caught a hint of amusement in the voice. "I think it is time we took a stroll down to see the car, don't you?"

MacIntyre rose from the sofa and waited for Taylor to drain his whisky glass. Wroughton, meanwhile, had been only partially following the interview, as she had finished her drink in three or four swallows and now definitely felt a little drowsy. She realised that both men had got up and it was time to leave, but when she tried to follow their example found that one of her legs had gone numb. She fell back down onto the sofa, frantically rubbing at her right calf to get some life back into it. Taylor's eyes hit the ceiling, and she heard his exasperated little cough.

"Sorry, Sir," she said, hoping he didn't think she was drunk, adding lamely, "pins and needles." She stopped rubbing and was about to make a second attempt when MacIntyre appeared in front of her, holding out a hand in a very gentlemanly fashion to help her up. She stared at it as if it was a snake, then muttered, "Thanks. I can manage." She pushed herself onto her feet while he neatly stepped aside to give her room.

When they got outside Taylor said, a little gruffly, "Wroughton, perhaps you wouldn't mind waiting in the car. I'm sure this won't take a minute."

She felt a little put out but didn't want to argue, so simply said, "Yes, Sir," and started to walk over to the hired Nissan Micra on the driveway.

"Allow me to escort you," said MacIntyre, catching up with her, letting Taylor wait by the front porch. When they reached the car he moved round and opened the passenger door for her.

"Thank you," she said, without looking up, not wishing to be hurled once again into a state of complete helplessness. But before she could get in he reached down, took her hand and kissed it, the effect of which was so devastating that her legs gave way and she fairly fell into the seat.

"See?" he said playfully as he closed the door. "No fangs!"

Taylor stared in disappointment at the bright sunshine yellow S-type Jaguar that sat gleaming in its own, custom built garage unit.

"I just got very tired of black," MacIntyre was explaining. "As you see, I favour black in my clothing, and it just seemed a little too much – black shirt, black tie, black car, if you know what I mean." Taylor wished he did. "So," MacIntyre went on, "I decided it was time for a change. I had the respray done two weeks ago. The proper authorities have been informed, and I am sure they can provide you with dates, as can the garage who did the job, over in Inverness. As your photographs were taken only a few days ago, they couldn't possibly have been of the same car.

Besides that, I'm afraid one of your colleagues at the licensing centre must have made a typing error. "

Taylor, staring at the number plate, A1 EXM, was starting to feel as though his hand had been called by an expert poker player. He thanked his host profusely for his help with their enquiries, particularly for the whisky, and apologised equally profusely for taking up the gentleman's time. Macintyre responded with exquisite politeness, saying he was sorry not to have been more help, that it had been his pleasure etc. etc. Taylor said not to trouble, he would see himself out, and Macintyre offered his hand. As Taylor took it, he said casually, "He had form you know."

"I'm sorry?"

"The dead man. He had form. Should never have been employed in a hospital like that – must have used false references and lied on the disclosure forms. It's illegal you know, for people with his type of record to work in that kind of establishment."

"Ah. You mean he had a criminal record. Anything serious?"

"I'm afraid so, yes. Two counts of rape. Served a total of seven years for those. And four counts of sexual assault, plus three for GBH." Taylor shook his head in disgust. "I reckon he had been assaulting the patients virtually all the time he was working there. It's my guess that someone found out about it, or maybe caught him in the act so to speak, and, well," he gave a little cough, "you know – killed the man in a fit of passion if you see what I mean."

"Yes, I think so," responded MacIntyre thoughtfully. "What a terrible thing, to have people like that near patients in a hospital, people who can't defend themselves."

"Yes, exactly. You know, I think I have a pretty good idea what happened."

"You do?"

"Oh yes, Sir. The more I think about it, the clearer it gets. Suppose someone was there, visiting a relative, or a friend. Suppose he didn't realise the time, or that visiting hours were finished, and he nipped down to get himself a coffee or some such from the canteen. Then, he came back up to say goodbye to whoever it was he was visiting and he came across the victim making a victim of somebody else, maybe even the person he was visiting – you see?"

"Oh yes, I see precisely." MacIntyre nodded, his eyes veiled, but alert. "The visitor would lose his head, be absolutely furious, and maybe do something that he might very much regret later, while – what's the phrase? While the balance of his mind was disturbed?"

"Exactly, Sir. While the balance of his mind was disturbed. Of course, any good solicitor would advise a plea of guilty to manslaughter under such circumstances, and I haven't met a judge or a jury yet who wouldn't be most sympathetic, especially if they knew about the victim's criminal record. I reckon that whoever did it, if he were to come forward voluntarily, would be damned unlucky to get anything more than a suspended sentence. It's a shame we can't find him, because I'm sure if he understood the way things are it would be a great weight off his mind, don't you think?"

"Yes. Yes indeed, I think you may well be right on that. Well, I'm afraid I must get back to work. It was very nice meeting you and, of course, your delightful constable. You are welcome to visit any time Inspector. I hope you have a pleasant journey back to Inverness."

Alex watched until the Micra had exited the grounds and was on its way back down the main road, then walked slowly back to the house, his features set in a thoughtful frown. He skirted past the main door, following the path round to the back, across the vegetable garden to the kitchen. He found Mary standing on the veranda, arms folded, eyeing him crossly.

"How could you?" she declared, delivering one of her most withering looks. "It was cruel, what you did to that poor girl, utterly cruel, and unforgivable, and you should know better." She emphasised her displeasure by folding her arms even tighter across her chest and letting out her breath in a little snort.

"Oh, Mary, don't be angry with me," replied Alex with a smile. "I was only having a little fun – really. Nothing serious. Tell me, you are not jealous? I think you are." He went to put an arm round her but she shrugged him off. He noticed, however, that her arms unfolded just a little.

"Tell it to that young girl," she replied. "Poor thing, you scared her to death I expect."

"Oh, I don't think so. And I do think you're jealous. Admit it."

"Not in the least," she said, still sharply, but the corners of her mouth were beginning to twitch. He took his chance, grabbing her firmly round the waist and planting a huge kiss on her lips, until she had to flick his ear to make him stop.

"Why don't you take the room I gave you?" he asked. They were arm in arm now, her point made. "It would be so much more comfortable than sitting in a chair all night, you know it would."

"And you know I prefer it here. I like to be where people are, Alex. I would be lost in there. It's too big and the bed is too soft, and it's time you realised it and gave it to someone else. It's far too good to waste."

He sighed, defeated. "All right," he said. "I will give the room to one of the others, but only on condition that you stop being cross with me, and let me hug you at least twice a day."

"Once," she said, and when he went to do it she stopped him, saying, "and that counts the one just now." They both laughed, and he managed to grab a quick peck on her cheek before she shook him off.

They drank tea in silence out on the veranda and, when he had finished his, he said quietly, "Mary?"

"Yes?"

"About Paul."

"Yes?"

"I don't think you need to worry any more. I think it's all going to be all right."

CHAPTER 20

Karisse was glad she was not alone. Without sun, moon or stars to guide her, she would have been completely lost within minutes, unable to retrace her steps back to the house. They had been walking in silence, hand in hand, for almost an hour in the pitch black, the light from Paul's powerful torch illuminating the ground for perhaps four feet in front of them, after which the dark swallowed the beam, making the path ahead totally invisible. But Paul never faltered, leading her forward with a confident stride. Every so often he would stop, and use the torch to warn her of a jagged spike of rock jutting out in their path, a sudden narrowing of the tunnel or a change in the level of the ground. At intervals he would turn off sharply into one of the many other tunnels that branched off to the left or to the right.

After Jenni's warning he had taken her down through the house using a steep, narrow staircase, skilfully carved between the inner and outer wall, plummeting straight from the top of the house right down into the cellar. Surefooted on the smooth, slippery stone, he had gone first to ensure she didn't fall. At the bottom he had moved aside an old chest in the corner of the cellar to reveal a trapdoor, beneath which the tunnels ran out in several directions under the foundations.

She was beginning to wonder how far the tunnels stretched and how long they had to keep walking when suddenly there was a change in the air – a sharp, sweet/sour smell that she recognised at once as salt water, and the movement of breeze on her face. Her heart began to beat faster. Of all the things she had ever seen in the world she loved the sea most and, although she had only seen it with her own eyes three times before, it was a favourite vision within the Dance. They walked on for a few more minutes, then Paul switched off the torch and she could see a shadowy light up ahead that grew brighter with each step. They emerged on a ledge some six feet above a small cove, its pebble beach cut off on three sides by a sheer rock face towering up above them, and on the fourth by the water, lapping gently on the stones.

"The sea!" she exclaimed, speaking for the first time since they had left Alex's rooms.

"Not yet." Paul jumped down from the ledge and held out his arms to catch her as she followed. "It's called a Loch. It has sea water in it though, and when we get to the other side we'll sail out of its mouth into the sea."

He pointed to a small boat moored to a buoy a few yards off shore. She was transported with delight at the idea of actually being on the water, the apparent urgency of the situation completely forgotten. Paul lifted her and carried her out to the boat. The water came up almost to his waist but he didn't seem to mind. In fact, as she watched him nimbly hoist himself in after her, she saw a soft light in his eyes and a smoothness in his brow that told her he was more at home here than anywhere else on earth. He let the boat loose from its mooring and went forward to a little panel, which contained some dials and buttons and a small wheel.

"There's going to be some noise," he warned, over his shoulder, "and we will go quite fast, but don't worry. Just hang on!"

He pushed a button and there was a huge roaring behind her as the motor sprang into life. Before she could catch her breath the boat was speeding across the Loch, the cove just a tiny speck behind, the shores on either side flashing past in a blur. It was not at all as she imagined and at first the experience was terrifying. But once she had become accustomed to the noise it became exhilarating, like riding a horse over uneven ground, only much faster and a lot less tiring.

As they drew nearer to the far end of the Loch she felt the nature of the water begin to change. The wind grew stronger and the waves grew higher, hitting the tiny boat with heavy thuds that caused it to shudder and lurch so violently she thought it might come to pieces beneath her feet. Paul reduced the power until the noise of the motor was no more than a soft puttering, and began to steer towards a much larger vessel that lay at anchor some way

194

out from the shore. He drew smoothly alongside underneath a metal ladder and, taking hold of it, he motioned her to climb up. As she neared the top a burly figure appeared, holding out an arm to help her up, and she found herself standing on a wide, polished wood deck that rocked gently under her feet, surrounded by metal rails that gleamed in the late morning sunshine.

She went to the side and watched Paul toss up a rope to a second man, then climb the ladder to join her. The man shimmied down into the speedboat and accelerated away with a cheerful wave. Meanwhile, the one who had helped her on board was joined by another from somewhere below the deck. She watched as Paul took them aside and spoke to them quickly and quietly. The men sprang into action with a lot of clanking and good natured shouting, followed by a deep throbbing somewhere under her feet, and they began to move.

She was fascinated by every tiny detail of the boat, the gentle swaying, so unlike the bumping, bouncing speedboat; the feeling, not of being on a horse, but on a moving house, one that seemed alive and had its own mesmerising heartbeat. It made her feel as though she were a part of it, her body vibrating in time with its gentle rhythm. She saw Paul coming towards her with a concerned look and realised suddenly that she was shivering with cold. Her T-shirt was soaked with spray from the speedboat and there was a keen, blustery wind, growing sharper as they headed out to the open sea.

"It's wonderful," she said, through chattering teeth, as he came up to her.

"Yes, it is," he replied, his eyes still bright with pure enjoyment, not seeming to notice that he too was thoroughly wet. "Alex gave her to me last year. She can handle any kind of sea, but generally I only use her when I need to get somewhere quickly. I much prefer the yacht – you know, one that has sails, and not a motor."

Karisse thought back to her old visions of the sea and remembered the wooden boats, with great sheets towering above, being blown across the water on the wind.

"Yes, I know the ones," she said. "I think I would like to be on a yacht too."

"Then I would be happy to show her to you. But you must get warm and change into dry things. We'll be sailing for another two hours, and the wind will get colder when we round the headland."

He pointed to the last outcrop of rock, coming up fast on the starboard side. He led her across the deck and down a central stairway. To her amazement there were rooms underneath the deck. They walked through a small kitchen area, past a kind of sitting room lined with luxurious velvet seats and cushions, and through a doorway into a bedroom, which he called a cabin, in which she found a wardrobe filled with clothes of all sorts, from plain jeans and sweaters to sophisticated ball gowns of silk and sequined lace. Left alone, she spent a while looking through the assortment and took out some of the ball gowns, intrigued by the sequins. They appeared to her like little jewels from a distance away, but when seen close up they took on the appearance of cheap, painted glass, of the sort the poorer short lived people used on celebration days at home. For the most part, Dancers took no interest in such things except for their intrinsic beauty, the women seldom adorning themselves with anything more than perhaps a fresh flower or spray of leaves, although the men quite often used ornately worked slides or combs for their hair.

She set the dresses aside and picked out a fresh pair of jeans that fit more or less, a T-shirt and a kind of sweater made from an odd material, like grey fur, but not from a living thing, and which smelt of the usual 'not real' smell that was everywhere, even on the boat. In a drawer under the little bed she found an assortment of shoes, including a number, in different sizes, that were very light and had soft, springy soles. They were designed, she deduced, especially for walking on boats. Finding a pair that fitted well, she completed the outfit and left the cabin to go in search of Paul.

She found him in the big living area, filling mugs with hot coffee. He had changed into dry clothes, and there was a pan of scrambled eggs on the stove, the scent of which made her realise she was hungry. He turned and gestured for her to sit on one of the velvety chairs, then brought her a plate of eggs and toast. He grabbed two of the mugs and, giving a loud whistle, set them down on the deck at the top of the stairway, then came to sit with her while she ate.

He was still pale, his face lined with exhaustion, and she noticed that although he seemed more relaxed he didn't look at her, but kept his brilliant blue eyes firmly on his coffee, his expression as closed and impassive as his mind. She wanted to ask him why they were on the boat, where they were going, and what it was that had caused their sudden flight from the house. However, when she spoke she said something entirely different.

"I have never seen a Dancer with blue eyes. Tell me, are there many of our kind like you in this time?"

He seemed shocked at her use of the word 'Dancer', as though he had never heard himself referred to by the name. He hesitated for a moment, then turned his head aside so that she couldn't see, lifting both hands to his face. A second later he turned back to her, his eyes as black and penetrating as those of any Dancer she had ever seen. She sat back with a gasp, almost dropping the mug that was halfway to her lips. He held out a hand and showed her two tiny circles in the palm.

"They are called contact lenses." He gave a tiny smile, the first she had seen on his serious, thoughtful face. "My mother likes me to wear them. She says it makes me look less different." He turned away again and slipped the little glass-like covers back over his eyes. For an instant she was mute with astonishment, both at the idea of changing one's eye colour so easily, and at the wish to do so.

"Why," she asked, "would your mother wish you to do such a thing?"

He didn't answer at once, seeming unsure whether or not to go on. She sensed an inward struggle and felt a desire to see his thoughts, but held back, knowing that the presence of another in his mind without warning might shatter his fragile defences.

Finally, he got up and said, "Would you like to go back up on deck with me?"

197

She nodded and followed him up the steps, back into the wind. The boat was moving fast, staying fairly close to the shore, but with a view of what seemed like an endless stretch of sea on the other side, the surface flashing and shimmering in the sunlight with the movement of the waves. He took her hand again and led her up onto a narrow walkway that ran by the deck rails to the boat's prow. She clung to him with one hand and to the deck rail with the other, and was quite glad when they reached the place where the walkway opened out again onto a short stretch of deck, just large enough for two people to sit. Although, while standing, she thought the position very precarious, once seated it was actually quite a beautiful place to be, watching the spray coming up from the prow and listening to the sound it made as it slashed through the water below them. Paul was still holding her hand and continued, as though there had been no break in the conversation.

"Because," he said, "There are no others of my kind here. I am the only one born in this time, and the short lived ones have forgotten us."

For a moment, Karisse was too horrified to reply. It just did not seem possible, for every Dancer to be gone, all memory of her people lost.

"But," she protested, "you are not the only one here. What about Alex? If he is here too, then surely there must be others that you have not seen?"

Paul shook his head. "Alex is not of this time. He came here from the past – what you call to 'cross the Great Emptiness'. He jumped across the darkness just as you did, and he came here to wait for you."

She held her breath, willing him to go on, but at that moment they were interrupted by an odd, high pitched, musical noise. Paul reached into the back pocket of his jeans and fished out a small, box-like instrument. He pressed something on its front and the noise stopped. Then he placed it to his ear, listened, said, "Thanks, Jenni," and put it away again. Seeing the look on her face he said, "It's called a mobile phone. It's the same as the telephones you have seen at the house, only smaller and without any wires. Jenni says the policemen have just left and Alex will join us soon after dark. He says that until then I should not say any more."

Karisse sighed in frustration, but decided against pressing him any further, knowing he would not go against Alex's wishes. By the end of the evening, she thought, she would know all she needed to know, and meanwhile there was no point in trying to force the issue. As for the idea of a mobile phone, it was too much to think about, so she pressed herself close to Paul to keep out the wind and concentrated on the vision of the sea, and the droplets of spray that leaped up into the air around her, sparkling like tiny jewels.

* * *

Mickey Wroughton was scared. For perhaps only the second time in her life she could feel her legs shaking as she sat, hunched in the passenger seat of the Micra, interpreting Taylor's stony silence as a clear and unambiguous condemnation. The only other time she had felt quite like this was when a drug pusher had grabbed her in the middle of a raid in a back street of St. Paul's and held a replica pistol to her head. The last two hours were a blur. She couldn't quite remember what she had said, or done. It was rather like knowing she had been drunk and done something terrible, but was unable to remember quite what it was.

The only thing she did know for certain was that every time she thought about MacIntyre her stomach went into such a tight knot that she felt sick. Somehow the man had gotten right into her head, drawn out her most private, intimate thoughts and held them in front of her, much as one would dangle a ball of string to attract a kitten. She saw herself sitting in some counsellor's office, earnestly explaining that this man, in the course of helping the police with their enquiries, had violated her using telepathy in the presence of a senior officer, who had apparently been quite oblivious to the attack, but had, however, observed her consume a large tumbler of strong alcohol just prior to the supposed event. What she did not want to admit, even to

199

herself, was that a part of her had wanted it to happen; that had they been alone she might have abandoned herself to the experience, allowed him to bring to life every fantasy she had ever had, the dreams that had been buried under the weight of bitter disappointment that the reality of adulthood had forced her to accept. That was what terrified her most, more even than the notion that there was such a thing as supernatural being, who had revealed himself to her in the knowledge that she would be helpless to betray him.

She suddenly became aware that the car had stopped. They had reached the pretty town of Ullapool, a natural stopping place, a fork in the road, leading in one direction to the North coast and in the other to the East, back to Inverness. Taylor had pulled in next to the low harbour wall, beyond which the working fishing boats bobbed up and down in the picturesque harbour, mingling with the dinghies, yachts and gin palaces of the more well to do holidaymakers touring the western highlands. Taylor glanced at his watch and, business like, said, "One o'clock. About time we stopped for lunch. They're bound to have a decent pub here I should think."

He unhitched his seat belt, got out and began to stride across the little street in what looked the most promising direction. It took Wroughton a full thirty seconds to haul her body into action and she had to run to catch up, almost losing him as he disappeared through the side door of a cosy looking establishment just off the main street.

Despite the good weather and the crowds of tourists milling about the harbour, the pub was fairly empty, and they managed to find a private little table in a corner next to a window at the far end of the lounge. He handed her a menu and went off to the bar, returning a moment later with a half of local bitter for himself and a large gin and tonic with ice and lemon, which he set down in front of her. He perused the menu intently for a minute or two, then asked, "Well, what do you fancy? Local fish looks good."

Just about the last thing she felt like doing was eating but, rather than say so, she mumbled, "Whatever you're having, Sir," which she knew sounded both feeble and a bit ridiculous, but she was too miserable to care. A waitress came over and took an order for two grilled Hake with new potatoes and fresh vegetables. Then, they were alone, and she waited for him to ask her what the hell she had thought she was doing back there, or something of the sort.

Instead, he set the menus aside and said, "Look – I'd feel a good deal better if you took a large slug of that." He pointed at her glass. She nodded, but couldn't get her hands to move. He reached over and patted her arm. "Now, come on, have a drink. Looks like you need one." He poured some of the tonic into the glass and pushed it towards her. Obediently, she took a large swallow. He smiled. "That's better." "Now, tell me, how long do you think we were in that house, being entertained by our Mr. MacIntyre?"

It was an odd question, and when she thought about it she couldn't answer it.

"I don't know," she said, puzzled. "Perhaps an hour, maybe a bit less. Why?"

"That's what I thought, about an hour," he replied. "But we arrived at nine thirty or thereabouts, wouldn't you say?" She agreed. It had been just after half past nine. She had looked at her watch just as they got out of the car to make a note later in her book. "Okay," he continued, "and we were let in, and waited, how long? No more than fifteen minutes before Mr. MacIntyre arrived, agreed?" She nodded. "Well, I looked at my watch while he was seeing you to the car and the time then was a quarter to twelve. That's more than two hours. Now, I've been a policeman for probably as many years as you've been alive, and one thing I know about is time. And I know that my brain tells me we weren't in that house for two hours, not by a long shot. That is," he paused uncertainly, and cleared his throat. "That is, unless something happened in there. Unless our Mr. MacIntyre did something."

Wroughton was staring at him, fearful of what he was going to say next. Then she realised that he had stopped because he was embarrassed he might say something that would make him sound a bit stupid. She decided to help him out.

"You mean like hypnotism or something, Sir?"

"Yes, exactly!" He grabbed the suggestion. "It was a strange thing. He was talking about something that is a particular interest of mine, and it was almost as though he was anticipating everything I was going to say, giving me just enough information to draw me further and further into the conversation. I couldn't resist it. It was all so fascinating. He knew things that I had always been asking myself and been wanting to know the answers to, and …"

He stopped, realising that across the table his DC had her hand over her mouth, the tears spilling down her cheeks. He reached across, took her free hand and said gently, "So something happened to you too. Now look, Mickey, I don't know what it was, but if it happened to both of us, either we're both insane, or there is something here that needs further investigation – maybe both. I'm pretty sure he was lying about that car."

At that moment, the waitress arrived with the Hake, which they had both completely forgotten about, and it seemed so incongruous that they both started to laugh.

"Well?" he asked. "What do you think? One thing I know for certain is that he knows who this blonde chap is, and the girl, and very probably where they are at this moment. They might even have been in the house when we arrived this morning and, whatever his little party trick was, the purpose of it was to delay us. I vote we stay here for a day or two and see what we can find out. It's a pretty little place. Dammit, I wish I'd remembered my camcorder. Come on, what do you say?"

"I say," said Wroughton, relief written all over her, "that I could murder this fish. And then we can ask at the bar about rooms if you like, Sir."

"Fine," he said, picking up his fork. "Just one other thing. Whatever this chap is up to, I get the impression it's not criminal – at least not in the sense we understand it. I know it's a strange thing to say, but I don't think he wants to break any laws if he can help it. It could be that whatever happened in the hospital was an accident, and now he is simply trying to protect someone who got caught up in it." He told Wroughton about the conversation at the garage. "I don't think they are villains, any of them," he concluded. "He seemed to think carefully about what I told him, and he might even help us if he thinks he can trust us."

"Can he trust us?" she asked, thinking that the question was more, could she trust herself if their paths ever crossed again.

"Oh, yes," her boss replied. "You know what they say, Mickey – an honest man never has anything to fear from the police." He winked, and helped himself to a generous portion of new potatoes.

Part Three

CHAPTER 21

Like her father, Amarisse had never really been a child. From the first moment of her life there had been things that she simply understood. She had understood warmth and cold, happiness, sorrow, and love. But while all children know these things as impressions, things that just are, which feel good or bad, and which appear and disappear from moment to moment, Amarisse knew them as abstracts, as constants that shaped the world, which were always present but not always felt. She even knew their names and how they were spoken. Lying in a warm cocoon of blankets, she would listen to her parents talking softly together, seeing the pictures in their minds that helped her to understand and store away the words. She saw the twining of their thoughts, the part of them that was one person, and she saw the part of each that was separate, different.

At first there was only her mother and her father, but before long there came the Other. She knew from the way the Other spoke that it loved her, just like her parents did, and that it watched over her parents, just as they watched over her. It showed her the nature of her gift, and told her what she would be able to do when she got older. It told her, before it happened, that her mother would have to go away, and that she should not be frightened, because it would not be forever. Then, her mother was gone and her father cried. She felt the sadness in him and sent out her thought angrily to the Other.

"I don't believe you," she said. "If you loved us, you would not let Father cry."

But the Other said she must trust it and say nothing, that it was important that what they knew stayed secret until it was time.

"Otherwise," it said, "Arghel will try to follow, and neither will return. Your mother will come to you, but you must not tell him, Amarisse, not even when you show him that you have the gift. It is because I love you all that I ask you this. Arghel must cry, and you must be silent."

Amarisse probed the Other and knew that it was telling her the truth. Then, her mother came to her in essence, just as it said she would, and so she kept silent.

She was eight years old when she finally let Arghel see her gift and, when she did, she felt a veil draw across a part of him, a part that he did not want her to see, that he had hidden, for the most part, even from her mother. But it was too late. She knew already what was there, although she vowed to herself she would never tell him so. The childhood gift, she reflected, could be a dangerous thing. It brought with it great knowledge and great power, but also an awareness of great ignorance, of what could not be known until the proper time and place. For the most part, the gift would answer any question that began with 'What', but it almost never satisfied the overwhelming need to know 'Why?' For that, one needed to grow, to experience, and to understand those things that come with age and not with knowledge.

A time came for Amarisse when she not only observed and accepted, but also began to wonder, to interpret and to question. In particular, she wondered about the centre of her world, the man who was her father. Even when he was busy and left her with Sasha she felt him close, his thoughts constantly with her, loving her, wanting to keep all bad things away from her. From the time she could walk she followed him everywhere, even when he said she could not come because the journey was too long or the business too urgent. Mindful of his every mood, she knew when she should cry, sulk, or stay silent and creep out after him, to be found, hours later, fast asleep outside the door – closer if she could manage it without being seen. Eventually, he accepted that she would do it and would come out to pick her up, so that when she woke it was nearly always curled up against his chest. He even took to carrying a little blanket around with him so that she should not get cold.

On the rare occasions that he did go somewhere without her she felt bereft. Her thoughts could follow him of course, but she missed his physical presence, the warmth and the smell of him, his voice, not in her mind but in the air, and the feel of his arms around her, cuddling and carrying and caressing her curly head. She missed him so much that she would cry endlessly, she couldn't help it, and drive everyone to distraction until he came home and the crying stopped.

Thereby lay the source of her question. Why? Her father missed her mother just as much as she missed him when he left her behind. There was a huge well inside him filled with a sadness greater than any she had ever known, and yet he never cried. She kept asking herself the question, but the gift told her that her understanding was not yet great enough. She asked the Other, and It said it was because her father was too sad, and that sometimes people can be so unhappy that to cry is not enough.

"Besides," said the Other, "he has you, and you make him happy. Then he forgets the sadness he carries with him."

But the Other's explanation did not satisfy Amarisse. She did not understand the notion of 'too sad', or of anything more sad than a thing that made you cry. She wanted to make him feel better, and her logic told her that if you cried then you would be comforted, and then you would be happy. She had seen him cry but once with her own eyes, on the day her mother went away. Almost seven years had passed, but still the grief lay in him and had not diminished. Why, then, she thought, does he not let himself be comforted, and let the sadness go away?

She could not answer the question. To do that she needed to know more, so carefully, so that he would not sense it, she began to probe his mind looking for other times that he might have been sad, to see if he had ever cried before. Almost at once she saw that right after her mother had gone he had wept for the man he had killed. But the feeling was of a different sort. It was not grief that he felt, but despair. He had been angry, and for some reason he was afraid of it. She heard his thought as he cradled the dead boy, repeating, "I am not like him," over and over, not sad, but horrified.

Now, there was a new question. She felt her way further, very carefully, moving back through his memory. She saw him care for her mother, watch over her, even when Karisse was small and knew nothing of him. She saw him kill, many times, but never with the same despair he had felt when he killed the boy.

207

She saw him sitting cross legged on a stone floor. A woman with golden hair was laid out beside him and he was holding her hand. It was his mother, her grandmother, and she was dead, gone, never to return, but he didn't cry over her. He simply sat with a calm expression, stroking the hand, and every now and then reaching out to smooth away a stray wisp of hair, blown by the breeze across the beautiful face.

Her probing brought resistance, even though she knew he was unaware of her questioning. It was like a fog that grew thicker the further in she reached, and seemed to grow more and more solid, like a wall, as she went forward. She realised suddenly that her mother had been here before her. She felt the trace of her, and knew that she had come in a little way. But her father had known of it and had allowed it, only for a moment, before he shut her out. But now, he was completely unaware of his daughter, wrapped in her gift of silence, her curiosity leading her back to the only other time in his life that he had cried.

At first she felt, rather than saw. She felt apprehension, uncertainty, and comforting arms around her father's tense body, stroking his head. She heard a voice, saying, "Hush, Arghel. You must be brave. Be patient. It won't go on forever." Then she felt fear, a terror that grew and grew until the whole world was filled with it, but when her father spoke it was in a voice that was calm, resigned.

"He's coming, Mother."

She heard a noise, a bang as loud as a thunderclap, and felt her father's heart thumping so hard she thought it might jump right out of his chest. She heard the woman's voice again.

"Please, don't take him. Let him stay." Then her vision cleared and she saw Rendail. She watched, a part of her outside, observing, another part locked inside the mind of her father as he was, a young child no older than herself. Rendail was leaning against the door considering them, smiling the same smile that had so terrified her mother. But now she was where her mother had never been, and where her father would not have let her go if he had known. She felt the arms around Arghel tighten, and his mother whispered in his ear, "I'm here Arghel. I am always with you. We can never be parted, you and I. Don't be afraid of them."

His mother got up and set him down behind her, placing herself between him and his father, glaring at Rendail as if daring him to come closer. Amarisse heard Rendail laugh.

"Come, Sherenne," he said, straightening himself up and taking a pace forward into the room. "It is quite a delightful idea, that you could keep me from my son. You know he is no longer yours, that he is forbidden to come here. Stand aside now, before I grow tired."

He came forward another pace, and Sherenne, in the blink of an eye, darted to the nearby fireplace and took up a heavy poker that was lying there. Holding it with both hands she brandished it in front of her, hissing, "Leave him!"

Meanwhile, another figure – Malim, she realised – came forward from the shadows. Malim seemed to think the entire proceeding a joke and was laughing quietly, watching to see what would happen next. Rendail, however, was no longer smiling. He fixed Sherenne with a contemptuous, stone cold stare, but she stood her ground, gripping the poker, and stared straight back. Everything seemed frozen. There was a silence, in which Amarisse could hear her father's heart, still thumping, his body rigid with fear.

Then, all hell broke loose in the room. Rendail sprang forward, agile as a great cat. Sherenne swung at him with all her strength with the poker, but he caught it effortlessly and knocked it out of her hand. He seized her by the arm and dealt her a savage blow with his fist that sent her flying halfway across the room. Meanwhile, Arghel had exploded into life. All his fear was suddenly transformed into a murderous fury. Seeing Sherenne knocked down and Rendail distracted, he ran forward and grabbed the poker, which was almost as heavy as he was, and with the strength of his rage managed to lift it above his head and hurl himself at his mother's assailant. The speed of his forward momentum and the weight of the metal was enough to bring the poker down with a crack on the side of his father's head. The impact sent it jumping out of his hands, and it skittered along the floor towards the doorway. For a split second he saw surprise, then pain register in Rendail's eyes, but there was not time to see the anger. He jumped, grabbing handfuls of the long black hair and tried to use it to haul himself up, aiming with his nails for the neck, the face, the eyes. Rendail was on his knees, but nevertheless was too big, too strong. He grabbed the child by the hair, tore him off and flung him to the ground, his face pale with fury, his hair matted with blood.

But Arghel did not stop. He tried to get up, and when he was kicked back down he grabbed the foot and pulled, aiming kicks and punches that landed no higher than his father's knees. All of a sudden, Malim came forward, grabbed Arghel by the hair and dragged him into the courtyard, down and out of the women's compound to one of the fires that were kept lit on the settlement boundary to keep away wolves and other scavengers. He had the poker with him, which he thrust into the heart of the fire, and was holding Arghel down with a foot on the back of the child's neck. Arghel kicked and bit and scratched, but it did no good. Malim drew the poker from the fire and raised it. Arghel kept on struggling, and heard the sound it made as Malim swung it through the air. It struck his back, and as he lurched his body round, the tip of it scraped around his side and onto his stomach. The pain was so great he almost fainted, and his head began to swim.

He heard Malim start to swing again, and knew from his brother's thoughts that he would not survive. He stopped struggling and dug his fingers into the ground, waiting. Then, he heard his father's voice.

"Enough, Malim."

He heard Malim curse under his breath and try again. The poker came down, he could feel its heat, but something stopped it. Rendail had taken hold of Malim's wrist, and was holding the thing away from him, just a few inches above his skin. For a moment it was suspended there, and then his father spoke again, this time with anger in his voice.

"I said, enough. I would not have him die."

Malim cursed again, and Arghel felt the heat move away from him. He heard the sound of the poker being thrown and landing with a dull clang on the hard ground some distance away, followed by Malim's footsteps fading into the dusk. Rendail had crouched beside him, and he heard his father speak a third time, quietly, his voice gentle, almost sad.

"Brave little Arghel," he said. "You are worth a hundred of that monster. But perhaps it might have been better for us both if I had let him kill you."

Arghel was not sure whether his father had intended to address him. He did not even know whether Rendail remembered he was there. The pain from the burn was so terrible that he felt light headed, and wondered if he could have imagined the voice, it was so unlike any tone he had heard his father use before. He felt tears start to prick his eyes, and couldn't stop them. It made the pain worse, but even that didn't make them stop. He wrapped his arms around his father's knee and cried and cried, clinging on as though his life depended on it. Between his sobs he asked, over and over, "Why? Why can't you love me, Father? Why do you love Malim? Why not me?"

Rendail did not kick him away. Nor did he stroke his head or make any move to comfort him. He simply squatted, still, staring out into the distance as though the child at his feet did not exist. At length he rose and prised open the arms clamped around his leg, not roughly, but firmly, and left his son on the ground alone, still sobbing as though his heart would break.

Arghel heard his mother's voice inside him, saying, "I am here, my darling. I am with you."

"Liar!" he shouted, through his tears. "You are not here, Mother. I am outside, you are inside. I can't feel you, I can't hold you. I want my Father. I want him to love me. Why doesn't he love me, Mother?"

Every time he took a breath it hurt him, his head swam and his body was drenched in sweat. He heard her silent voice again.

"Use the gift, Arghel. Use it to come to me, and then we will be together."

"Liar!" In his mind he was screaming at her. "I don't want the gift. I don't want you! Don't say you love me Mother. It is not enough."

Abruptly, he shut her out, his mind closed, his sobs becoming weaker and weaker until, despite the pain, exhaustion took him, and he slept.

* * *

At sixteen, Amarisse was already beautiful, a perfect blending of her parents, with her mother's emerald eyes and pale skin, made paler by the mop of dark, unruly curls that bounced and tumbled round her pretty face, and behaved themselves less well than her father's. He told her often how like she was to her mother, and she knew it gave him comfort to see the likeness. She wanted to fill the empty place in him that had been part of Karisse, just for a while, until she came back.

"Amarisse, come!"

"Coming, Father." She raced down the tower steps, across the courtyard and on down towards the lower gate. He was happy, she could tell from the little rush of pleasure that accompanied his silent voice. There was some impatience there too. He had something for her and wanted her to see. She tried to make out a picture of it from his thought, but he resisted her playfully, wanting it to be a surprise. She reached the gate, out of breath, and stopped short, gasping with delight at the gift he had brought for her. It was a young colt, barely weaned and not yet big enough to ride, but already strong, its shining coat completely black except for a little white sock on the right foreleg.

He stood aside and she steadied herself, breathing deeply, making herself quite calm. Then she closed her eyes and carefully began to project her thought towards the animal, seeking its nature. For a moment she was inside its skin, becoming a part of it, understanding the world through its eyes, knowing its needs, what it liked, what frightened it. It was not afraid of her. She withdrew, and as she opened her eyes it flicked its tail, shook its head and trotted up to her, burying its soft nose in her chest.

212

"He's beautiful! Thank you, Father." Again, she felt his happiness, his contentment. She liked these moments, when the shadow passed from him for a while. She wished she could keep it away from him, stop the sadness from coming back.

"When can I tell him?" she asked the Other, again and again, and the Other always answered, "Soon."

He never went to look on the warm, breathing body that lay in a house just a short ride from the fortress. She asked him why and he answered, "Because she is not there. If I wish to see her face, I look at you."

He would take her in his arms and let her hold him, saying over and over with her silent voice, "I love you, Father," wanting desperately to add, "Everything will be all right when Mother comes back."

* * *

From the top of the north tower, the view stretched at least twenty miles in any direction. It was Amarisse's favourite place, and on a clear day she could sit for hours, following the Dance, doing as her mother used to do and finding an interesting creature to be, or just thinking, talking silently to her mother, imagining she could hear. She would relate what she had done that day, or how well her father looked, just all the things that she would say if they were sitting side by side. Often, her thoughts would wander back to that moment, when she had begun to understand the 'why' and saw how it was possible for a person to be too sad. She wondered whether she should tell her mother, when she came back, what she had seen, and decided it would not be right, but that perhaps her father should.

When she looked to the North, towards the place where the Family lived, she felt such a hatred it made her tremble, and it became her ritual, whenever she went onto the tower, to send out the thought with all the power she could muster; "Grandfather, I will kill you."

The Other, reading her thought, knew what she had seen and she felt its anger too.

213

"One day," it said, "we will go together, and he will pay for all that he has done."

The thought gave her a great deal of pleasure. She was not at all afraid, any fear she might have had turning instantly into cold, calculating anger, of the sort that can wait forever, knowing that a day of reckoning will eventually come.

On this late spring morning she had been turning things over in her mind and was sitting on the parapet lost in thought, making one idle pattern after another in the dust with her foot. Suddenly, she heard the voice of the Other, urgent, excited.

"Amarisse! Go and find your father. Bring him to the north gate. Tell him I am coming. Be quick!"

She jumped up and looked out to the north. At first she could see nothing, but then, right on the hillside, maybe five miles away, she saw a speck, moving fast – a rider, coming towards the fortress at full gallop but too far away to make out any detail.

"I'm going," she breathed, talking aloud and in her mind. She shot up and dashed down the tower steps so fast that if she had been in a dress she would have fallen and broken her neck. But she often wore boy's clothes as a habit, as she never walked anywhere and spent almost all of her free time on a horse, when she was not up in the tower, or with her father. She knew he was in the south of the fortress, checking on one of the short lived women who had just given birth, and as she ran she sent out waves of thought, calling to him.

"Come Father, come quickly, the Other is coming!"

She found she was shouting it out loud as well, even though he was not close enough to hear, and she heard his silent voice come back to her.

"What is it? Who is the Other? Can it wait?"

She finally caught up with him as he was leaving the new mother's room and took hold of him, pulling, still shouting as though she were on one side of the fortress and he on the other. He hustled her away down the path and stopped, looking thoroughly alarmed, but she kept on pulling and shouting, eyes wild, breath coming in short gasps as she tried to talk and catch

214

her breath at the same time. He took hold of her shoulders and she heard his voice in her head so loud she almost fell down.

"Amarisse – stop!"

She stopped and fell against him, panting, and realised that she had been gabbling, making no sense, and was frightening him. With a great effort she cleared her thoughts to show him she had not suddenly gone mad and took slow, deep breaths while he held on to her, stroking her head gently to calm her down. Then he sat, right in the middle of the path, and pulled her down next to him.

"Tell me," he said. "Slowly. First, who is the Other?"

She started to gabble again, so he put his hand over her mouth. He kept it there until her breathing was completely calm and slow, then he nodded and took it away. She started again, slower this time, and told him about the Other. She didn't dare to show him, but explained aloud as best she could that the Other had been inside her, ever since the gift came, and that it was a good thing, who knew him and loved him, and was coming to see him, not in his mind but here, now, at the gate, and she had been sent to fetch him. He still looked worried, but got up and said, "Very well. Let us go and see what this 'Other' is, and what it wants, if you think it that important. But," he added, quite severely, "I will not run, and I will not have you shout like that again, disrupting those who need rest. Do you understand me?"

He wasn't angry, but the sadness was with him today, she could feel it, so she didn't argue. She simply nodded and reached up to kiss his cheek, after which she contained herself enough to walk by his side down the path to the gate.

When they reached the gate the rider was no more than half a mile away and had slowed to a sedate trot, coming towards them along the path. They could tell from the slight frame that it was a woman, though dressed in the travelling clothes of a man, her black hair pinned back by a metal slide of the sort a man would use. As she drew closer they could see how beautiful she was, a small and delicate creature, with skin the colour of pale honey and piercing blue eyes.

At around twenty paces from the gate she reined in the horse and, dismounting, stood in the middle of the path, waiting. Her mind was closed, as was Arghel's, so that Amarisse could not tell what either was thinking. She glanced up at her father and gasped when she saw the expression on his face. He knows the Other, she thought with amazement. He knows who she is. Then she realised something else, that their thoughts were together. They were talking to each other and she couldn't hear it.

She looked from one to the other, trying to work out what was happening, what they were saying, and tried to send her own voice to her father asking, "What is it? Who is it? Why can't I hear?" It was as though she wasn't there. For what seemed like an eternity her father did not answer, but continued the silent communication with the Other. Then, just as she was about to burst with frustration and curiosity he turned to her and motioned with his hand for her to stay where she was. He smiled as if to say, 'It's all right. I won't be long,' and began to walk down the path towards the Other.

The Other dropped the reins of her horse and came forward to meet him. They stood together in the middle of the path, still locked in their silent conversation, and Amarisse thought it was as though nothing else in the world existed for them as she watched from where her father had told her to wait. Neither moved for a long time, then the Other reached up and put her arms around Arghel's neck, kissed him lightly on the cheek. He gathered her to him and they embraced, then, hand in hand, they walked back to the gate.

As soon as her father came up to her, Amarisse realised he knew she had seen her mother, had known from her earliest years that Karisse was alive and intended to return, and he knew she had kept it from him. Up until now she hadn't considered the implications of it, how it might seem to him. She had kept silent because the Other had insisted on it. But had that really been a good enough reason to deny him the knowledge that would have given him hope, perhaps helped to fill a part of the emptiness inside him where so much of his sadness lay?

It suddenly seemed a terrible thing to have done, but at the same time like a great weight lifting, not having to hide it from him any more. She managed to say, "I'm so sorry, Father," and burst into tears.

Immediately he caught her up and hugged her, then she heard him whisper in her ear, "My poor darling, how hard it must have been for you," which made her cry more and hold onto him so tightly he could hardly take a breath. He let her recover herself and then said, "Come. Your 'Other' is waiting to meet you."

She had almost forgotten, and looked up to see the woman standing to one side, waiting patiently by the gate. Her father withdrew a little way and the woman came up to her and kissed her on both cheeks. Taking her hands, she said, "You are even braver and more beautiful than your thought has told me. Now it is time to help your mother to end what must be ended, and then she and the others with her will come home."

"Who are you?" asked Amarisse. "And how is it that my father knows you? You spoke to each other in a way that only people who are very close can speak, yet he did not know of you until today. I don't understand how it is possible."

The Other laughed. "Oh, that is a very simple question," she replied. "Do I not remind you of anyone?"

Amarisse looked to her father for help, but he just smiled, and as soon as he did she saw the likeness. At the same time she saw in both of them a face she knew, but was not supposed to have ever seen. The Other nodded, and smiled the exact same smile.

"Between Rendail's children, for good or ill, there is a special bond. Arghel knew of me, although he did not see me until today. Look, I have something to show you."

A vision sprang into Amarisse's mind. She saw her mother, dressed in strange clothes, sitting in a small cosy room in front of a log fire sipping something from a cup. Everything was a little odd – the cups, the cushions and walls did not look quite like anything she knew. Her mother was waiting for someone. Beside her on a rug lay a man, a Dancer with golden hair, asleep, the light from the flickering flames falling on his handsome face.

"She is waiting for my son," Maylie said. "And the other you see is his child, my grandson. Just as we three are together, so are they, on the other side of the Great Emptiness. Together, we can end this, we in our time, they in theirs. If we all succeed then the danger that threatens us will be over, and both my son and your mother will come back."

CHAPTER 22

The cruiser dropped anchor a way out to sea. Paul disappeared briefly down below. while Karisse stood at the stern watching the little speedboat racing towards them, throwing out a huge fountain of spray behind. Paul reappeared wearing a thick waterproof jacket and carrying another. which he gave to her, telling her to put it on so that she wouldn't get wet during the ride to the shore. The fabric fascinated her. She couldn't quite see how it would keep out water, as it felt quite soft and looked full of tiny holes. But once in the speedboat with the wind blowing the spray straight into her face, she found that although it got wet outside, underneath her clothes stayed perfectly dry.

She wondered, not for the first time, what Arghel would make of such things, and she dug her nails into her right palm, whispering, "I love you," hoping he might hear. Paul turned off the motor just a few yards from the sandy beach and as before, hopped out into the water, not caring whether he was wet or dry, and hooked the rope round a big metal ring that was fastened to a rock. He lifted her out onto dry land and they made their way across the sand to a small two-seater car with no roof that was parked on the road just beyond the beach. Although the car was small compared to the only one she had ever been in before, the seats were comfortable, and as she sank into one he reached over and pulled out a restraint across her chest, clicking it into place somewhere at the bottom of the seat.

She had, over the last few days, learned that nothing was to be gained by considering what was and was not 'normal'. She had ceased to be surprised by most things, so she just sat back and watched his easy, confident movements as he dealt with things that were completely natural for him and his world.

The little car travelled at an enormous speed and, unlike on the boat, the sensation really did frighten her. For most of the journey she kept her eyes shut, wishing that there could at least be a roof so that the noise of the engine would not be so loud. She squinted at Paul once or twice and he seemed to be loving it, his eyes shining almost as much as they had during the boat trip. Eventually, the car stopped and he unhooked the seat belt to let her out. She got up, a bit unsteadily, and saw that he was allowing himself a little grin.

"How could you possibly enjoy doing a thing like that?" she asked, still feeling dizzy.

Immediately the grin disappeared. "I'm sorry. I forgot. It's such a good car to drive, you can't really go slowly in it. Are you all right?"

"I will be," she replied, "when the other half of me catches up." He looked so upset that she added, with a smile, "What were you thinking, when you were smiling just now?"

"Oh." He looked even more sheepish, then confessed, "I was just thinking that if you didn't like the Porsche," he pointed at the car, "then I shouldn't offer to show you what it's like to ride on a motor bike."

They had arrived at a large stone cottage set some way back from the road. Taking a key from his pocket, he opened the front door and led her in. They went down a small hallway and she found herself in a lovely, cosy little room with a sofa and rugs arranged round a large fireplace ,which had already been laid and was ready to light. He handed her a small box.

"Matches," he said. "You take one out and rub the head on the side of the box. Do you think you can light the fire while I make tea?" He disappeared into another room, she assumed a kitchen, and she set about using a match to light the fire. It was so simple it made her laugh, and by the time he returned with mugs the fire was blazing. They both sat down on the rugs in front of it, sipping their tea in comfortable silence. After a while he said, "Look, I'm afraid I have to sleep. Will you be all right for a while?"

He was starting to look haggard, and she wondered how long it had been since he slept. Nevertheless, he was clearly worried about leaving her alone, and she thought that if he went to another room he would only stay awake.

"Of course," she said. "But why don't you sleep here, in front of the fire. Then, if anything happens I can wake you and you won't have to worry about me."

She took a cushion from the sofa and gave it to him to put under his head. He stretched himself out on the rug and within seconds his breathing told her he was fast asleep. She sat beside him, watching him and drinking the tea.

He was around forty or so, she guessed, still quite young. He really was most beautiful, of perfect height and build for his kind and a face, she thought, that would have nearly every short lived girl within a hundred miles going to any length to catch his attention. Yet from a Dancer's point of view, there was an innocence about him, almost a total lack of knowledge of his own nature and of the effect, both visible and otherwise, he must have on others around him. She realised then that his encounter with her had been literally the first time he had ever come across a female with the gift. It must have been completely overwhelming for one with so little experience of what to do.

She remembered what Amarisse had said – that the 'Other' loved him very much, and that care should be taken not to harm him. She understood now how easy that would be, for although he was a Dancer of phenomenal strength, his mind was fragile, unused to sharing thoughts, which made him vulnerable to many stray and false impressions. He wrapped his thoughts in an impregnable silence, much more so than Alex. Yet it had been he, not Alex, who had been the doorway back to her past and her memory. Why him? Why not Alex, the stronger of the two? There was something else, something that was eluding her but which was sitting at the back of her mind, frustratingly out of reach. There was a familiarity about the look of him, the way he moved, his expressions. It had struck her particularly on the boat, but try as she might she could not place it, and the more she thought on it the more the answer seemed to slip away. Eventually, she gave up and leaned back against the sofa, turning her gaze to the fire, letting the comforting flicker lull her as it grew brighter in the failing light.

Just after nightfall she heard the soft click of a key turning in the lock. The thought said, "No danger," and she leaned forward to put another log on the fire. Alex came in carrying a bottle and two glasses.

"My mother used to tell me that is not generally recommended for a Dancer to take strong drink," he said, sinking to the floor beside her, "but I often feel the need of it."

He poured himself a large glassful from the bottle and another, just half full, for her. He took a swallow and looked across at Paul, who was still completely lost in a deep, untroubled sleep. He reached forward and stroked his brow affectionately.

"He hasn't slept for several days, not since his encounter with you. It wasn't easy for him. But then, nothing is easy for him." He shook his head and took another sip of the whisky.

"Several days?" She was momentarily confused. She tried to calculate how much time had passed since her awakening, and the return of her memory. She found she could not.

Alex laughed quietly. "When you returned to yourself you didn't move for three days. I carried you to your bed. If you had slept much longer I would have wakened you. I really was quite worried. Allowing Paul to enter your mind was a desperate measure," he added, "but the time grows desperate and you needed to remember why you are here. Thankfully, your memory and your gift were restored. Otherwise we all might be in some difficulty. For Paul, though, it was – shall we say, difficult? It was a painful journey for him, and he is still recovering from it. "

She thought about this for a while, taking a mouthful of the drink he had given her. As soon as the liquid passed her lips she felt a little jolt, and suddenly all her senses seemed heightened, her mind clearer. Physical things, like the crackling of the fire, became sharper and more distinct, and she found that if she let her thoughts range, her gift could detect a great many things that it did not before, such as the quiet currents of the short lived people in the nearest houses some two or three miles away.

"Yes," said Alex. "It does have that effect. Sometimes it can be very useful, but you need to be careful not to take too much. I have to confess that after two glasses I find myself becoming quite mischievous, but then, my mother says it is my nature and there is nothing much I can do about it."

Karisse couldn't suppress a smile. Taking another sip of whisky she found she could sense in him a really quite devilish humour, but one which he tempered, not without effort, with great gentleness and protectiveness towards those he cared about. She found herself liking him immensely and wondered what particular mischiefs he had let loose in this strange, entirely short lived time. She knew, however, that more serious matters needed to be discussed. Who was Alex, and from what time? And how long had he been here, 'waiting' for her, as Paul had put it? If they had both come here for the same reason, then why did they need her? Was the source of the voice so strong that it needed both of them to put an end to it? Or was Alex here to stop her?

Suddenly the truth hit her, sending a shiver of fear down her back. Both Alex and Paul could make their minds silent. Alex had crossed the Great Emptiness to the future. Therefore, both must be of the Family. She stared at his face, scrabbling for the source of the sense of familiarity that tugged at her. The honeyed skin, fine bone structure, the long, blue-black hair – she gasped as recognition came to her and instinctively drew away. Alex gave a slight nod of confirmation.

"Yes," he said. "Rendail is my grandfather, although he doesn't know I exist. I am the son of Arghel's sister."

Swallowing the initial shock, she nodded, and let her eyes stray once again to Paul. He lay there, breathing quietly, his face composed in sleep, a golden haired, golden skinned angel, the very image that the short lived people held in their minds of what was meant by 'goodness' and 'innocence'; a creature completely devoid of evil. When the realisation came it was with a clarity that startled her. She couldn't understand how she had not seen it before. Just one brief glimpse, so many years ago, of that same angelic face, the hair that might have been spun gold. The face of an angel, her grandfather had said.

"Malim," she said quietly. "You are setting a trap for Malim, and I am the bait."

* * *

Wroughton sank back into a window seat in the hotel lounge and sipped her coffee. Her boss had treated her to a most enjoyable dinner accompanied by an even more enjoyable bottle of Rioja, and throughout the course of it they had chatted companionably about all manner of things, carefully avoiding any mention of the events of the morning. Before dinner he had made a call to Inverness and had returned with a glint in his eye.

"Guess what?" he said gleefully. "As of now, we are on holiday – semi-officially of course. As long as there are no complaints we can ask the odd question or two, but if anything important comes up the local lads will want to know about it. Not that anything important has come up, has it Detective Constable?"

He winked, and trotted off to the bar to order aperitifs. After dinner he went out, saying he wouldn't be too long. That had been two hours ago and it was starting to get quite late. She finished her coffee and watched the lights bobbing out in the harbour for a while, then decided it was time for a search party and got up to go and find her coat.

When she got outside she saw him at once, a dark silhouette sitting on the harbour wall opposite the hotel. She went over to join him and sat down, feeling glad that she'd thought to grab her old sheepskin jacket on her way out of her front door, as it was getting decidedly chilly. They sat together in silence for a while watching the lights, listening to the gentle swish of the tide on the rocks below them. Finally he spoke, a quiet satisfaction in his voice.

"In a small place like this," he said, "the local people are bound to know everybody else's business. That's the great thing about being a country policeman. You get to know everybody and everybody gets to know you. Very good for the crime rate, and also very good for getting information when you need it. Take the local fishermen for example. I was chatting to one of them just now, passing the time, enquiring about the boats, how much they

224

cost, what they could do, which were tourist boats and which were locally owned, that sort of thing, you know?"

She was about to answer that she had a pretty good idea, but he went on, "They are amazing things, boats. Sort of conspicuous, especially big, expensive ones. Anyway, I got talking about them and do you know, that big one over there," he pointed to a reasonable sized, snappy cruiser moored just offshore, "would cost around a million brand new? Can you imagine it? That some people have that much money to spend on a boat? That one belongs to a fat cat from Jersey up for his holidays. I said that I bet you wouldn't see a local with a boat like that, and do you know what he said?"

This time he looked at her sideways and saw from her expression that his story was going well.

"He said that you wouldn't think so, but in fact there is a locally owned boat that knocks that one into a cocked hat. A big black cruiser, always kept polished and ready to go, even with its own crew of three on board most of the year keeping her in shape. Must have cost a fortune he said, and bought new just last year. I was quite surprised and asked him who on earth round here would have the cash for something like that. I didn't think there were that many multi-millionaires around, not in a small place like this. Well, he said there were one or two, and some pretty big mansions dotted around, mostly owned by self made businessmen of one sort or another. This particular vessel, he said, is owned by one Paul Quillan, a chap of around forty who lives down the coast a way, and has made his money, it seems, as a dance instructor and choreographer, although he wasn't sure of the details, not knowing much about it himself.

"I must admit I was getting a bit bored with the details, but luckily our fisherman friend was determined to finish his story. This Mr. Quillan is so popular with the ladies that they follow him around in droves trying to get a passage on the boat, but he rarely shows any interest. After all, said my friend, he can afford to be choosy. He could see the attraction though – this Quillan is a good looking chap, very distinctive, tall, with long blonde hair and blue eyes. What's more he's a pretty good sailor himself by all accounts, and has a yacht which he races from time to time. In fact, our man said he had caught sight of the cruiser around midday while he was out at sea, going at a fair pace, heading north towards Durness. He said if we were up that way she was worth seeing if I was interested in boats. If Paul's around, he said, she will be moored offshore and I should look for a big black beast by the name of 'Wave Dancer II.'"

Taylor didn't have to ask his colleague what she thought. Whatever her experience had been in the morning, her eyes were glittering with excitement now.

"So," he said. "Looks like the next stage of our tour of the Highlands is a visit to Durness. Come on, lets get some sleep. I have a feeling that tomorrow will be an interesting day."

CHAPTER 23

"I cannot allow it."

Amarisse had never seen her father look so horrified. He had stopped pacing up and down and was staring out of the window, his restless fingers trying vainly to push the wild strands of hair away from his eyes. His whole body radiated a mixture of anger and frustration that made the air around them vibrate with it. Maylie sat quietly in a corner, not looking at either of them, her face impassive. Finally, Arghel turned to his daughter, fixing her with a stare so withering it almost made her take a step backwards. Slowly, emphasising every word, he said, *"I. will. not. allow it!"*

He had never spoken to her like this and it was beginning to exasperate her. She stood her ground and said, quietly, trying to keep calm, "I am not a child any more, Father."

"Oh, but you are. That is *exactly* what you are." His voice had dropped almost to a whisper and she could feel the tremors running through him as he fought to keep control of his temper. "You are barely sixteen years old – you know nothing of the world or what is in it. You have not the slightest notion of what you are saying. If you did, you would not dare to suggest such a thing, not in my house, and not to me. You have no idea at all what could happen to you. You have not seen that place, you don't know. You are too young to understand, and on account of that perhaps I can forgive your stupidity. But I forbid you ever to speak of it again. Do you understand me Amarisse? I forbid it!"

He had taken her by the arms and pushed her backwards against the wall. He was hurting her and she was suddenly furious, that he should take hold of her, use his greater strength against her like that.

"You think I know nothing?" She was shouting at him, her eyes blazing with indignation. "It is you who knows nothing, Father. I do know. I have seen. I have seen where they live, and what they do, and I have seen *them*!"

His grip tightened as she saw her meaning begin to sink home. She pressed on.

"It is not I who am afraid, Father. It is you. You look at yourself and you fear what you see. You are one of them. You belong to them. You see them in you and that is why you are afraid. Why don't you wish me to go? Is it to protect me, or to preserve my blood?"

He released her suddenly and took a step back. There was a deathly hush and for one awful moment she was sure he was going to hit her.

"And what will you do if I choose to disobey you?" she whispered. "Will you do as your father would do?" She turned on her heel and walked out of the room, slamming the door behind her.

An hour earlier, just over a day since Maylie's arrival, Arghel and Amarisse had joined her in the tower room. When they entered she was still, her eyes closed, her breathing almost imperceptible. They waited quietly for several minutes, until she sighed deeply and slowly uncurled and stretched her limbs, reacquainting herself with time and place.

"All is well," she said softly as they came to sit with her. "Karisse knows what is needed and has agreed to it." She turned to Arghel. "Alex says she thinks constantly of you. She knows the danger, but she knows you will be with her and that the two of you together cannot fail." Arghel nodded, but said nothing. She continued, "We must follow my son's lead now. Although I can see his thought across the void he cannot see mine, so it is for us to ensure that we all act together, at least for the present. He has seen Malim. It seems our brother is not content solely with the destruction of the Dancers, but is quite willing to wreak havoc upon the short lived world he has entered, regardless of the danger or the cost."

"But why?" asked Amarisse. "Surely he realises that by his actions he is destroying his own people? Why does his father not stop him? I don't understand." She looked to Arghel, but he remained silent.

"I don't think Rendail cares," said Maylie. "Since his earliest years Malim has had little to restrain him. Even in childhood he would kill for no reason other than that it gave him pleasure to take life. He sees no consequences to his actions, and seems incapable of any reasoning beyond his own desires. It is a kind of madness, and one that I think has been with him from the moment he was born. Rendail is vicious, yes, and relentless, but all that he does is governed by reason. His actions have a higher purpose, and can be understood, however vile they are." She turned to Arghel. "Malim's sole purpose has been to lure Karisse to a place where he thinks you cannot reach her. Once that is accomplished it is his intention reveal his triumph to you, and thus condemn you to a living death, knowing that she lives and suffers, and that you are powerless to prevent it."

Amarisse was watching her father as Maylie said this. There was no flicker of movement in his face, not even the slightest hint that he was listening. His mind was completely closed to her, so that it might have been a stone statue sitting there between them. She could not even hear him breathe. Maylie reached over and touched his hand briefly, but he did not respond.

"My son has discovered no Dancers on the other side of the Great Emptiness," Maylie went on. "He says there are some short lived people with the smallest vestige of the gift, but most times it is so weak they do not even know it. Even though he has taken great care to leave the people undisturbed, you can understand that there have been times when his very presence has put those around him in danger. Imagine, then, what a man like Malim could do with just a fraction of the power he has inside him. He could rule great cities of millions of souls with almost no effort, destroy thousands with a single thought, and there would be no one to oppose him.

"He has it in his mind to use Karisse to sire a dynasty that will subjugate the whole population from one shore to another, and he will be its cruel and murderous emperor. And that won't stop him from coming back. When Rendail dies, he will rule the Family as well. It is unthinkable. We have to stop it. Malim is from our time and place and, whether we like it or not, he is of our blood. We cannot stand by and let him destroy both present and future."

Amarisse shook her head. "How? If he is as powerful as you say, we have no hope of stopping him. I don't see how your son could make any difference – except to put Mother in even more danger. If he can't stop him ..." She glanced at her father again, but he still said nothing.

Maylie sighed, and said, "We all know that Malim's greatest weakness is his failure to control his passion. Karisse intends to show herself to him, to draw him out. The very sight of her will cause his desire to possess her to blind him to all else. Then Alex and Paul will have the chance to destroy him. For this to be done Karisse must place herself in terrible danger, but she knows the risk, and has agreed to take it.

"Even if they succeed it is unlikely Malim will die. His essence will simply leap back across the Great Emptiness, into the body that is here, in this time, and still lives. That body is hidden somewhere within the settlement, protected by Rendail. We must find it and, at the moment that his mind returns, destroy it. That is the only way to be sure. It takes a short while for mind and body to become accustomed to each other after a journey of such distance, but in the case of Malim it will not be long, and once he and his father are reunited the task becomes almost impossible."

She turned to Arghel and took his hand. "So, we must find out from Rendail where the body is hidden and you, Arghel, must be there when the moment comes. Unfortunately, Rendail has few of Malim's weaknesses. He is hardly likely to simply tell us what we need to know. Although he can't make his thought completely silent as we can, he can hide those things he does not wish others to know and the barriers are, for most, impenetrable. Neither you nor I could take from him a single thing that he does not wish us to see. But there is one who could. There is one whose thoughts can be made completely invisible to him, and whom he will not suspect."

Maylie paused again. Arghel had still given no sign, made no movement. Amarisse felt her heart beat faster and clutched her hands together in her lap, hardly daring to breathe.

Maylie glanced at her and went on, "Amarisse has the ability to cut through his mind to the heart of all his secrets without his ever becoming aware of it. He knows nothing of her gift, and the power she has to close her mind to others surpasses even yours or mine. She is young and can easily present herself as one in whom the gift is new and unformed – I do not think he will question it. It will still not be easy, but I think I can provide a sufficiently worthy distraction to occupy our father's thoughts. After all, I am his daughter – the most magnificent example he could wish for of a female of the blood, don't you think? When I reveal myself to him I believe the shock of my existence will take over his conscious thought, at least for a short time, and he will let down his guard.

"You understand," she took a deep breath and looked across to Amarisse, who nodded for her to finish. "You understand that this cannot be done from a distance. We have to go there. The three of us. Amarisse can do nothing unless she is very close to Rendail. We two must be with him, alone. Until Malim is dead he cannot know that you are with us. After that, no one can know what will happen, but I believe that the three of us together are strong enough to repel Rendail if he stands alone. If not…we must still take the risk, for Karisse, and for all those who are to come."

Maylie was finally silent. She and Amarisse waited for what seemed an age, until at last Arghel rose and walked to the window, where he stood, staring to the north, motionless except for the ripples of his curls, caught in the early afternoon breeze. Then they heard his voice, quiet, but firm, with an air of finality.

"No."

"There is no choice," said Maylie, gently.

He turned back from the window and looked from one to the other, his eyes finally resting on Maylie.

"We have a choice," he said slowly. "You and I will go. We will find a way to do as you propose. But Amarisse will not.

231

What if Karisse fails? What if we fail? Then, must I spend my life knowing that I allowed my mate to fall into the hands of Malim and that I gave my daughter to Rendail? Even if Malim dies we are none of us safe in that place. I cannot do it. I will give my own life to try to bring Karisse home, but I will not give the life of my child. The decision is mine to make, and I have decided. She will not go."

"No, Father." Amarisse's voice was as firm, as determined as his own. "It is not your decision. It is mine. I have made it – and I will go."

And so it had begun. He used every argument he could think of to dissuade her, but her mind was set. Nothing he said seemed to make any difference, until finally he felt his temper rising and could do nothing to stop it. At first he wasn't angry with her, only at the horror of what might happen to her if she had her way. But then she turned on him with such force, such venom, the words so cruel she might as well have stabbed him through the heart. He had almost struck her, and the thought of it sickened him. He stood now, staring at the heavy door through which she had run just a moment before, the noise of its slamming still in his ears. He felt helpless, disorientated. He had no idea at all what to do. He felt Maylie come up behind him, take his hand and squeeze it gently.

"She has too much wisdom for her years," she said softly. "She loves you. Go and talk to her."

"Is it true?" he asked, his eyes still stricken with horror. "What did she see? How? Tell me, Maylie, what does she know?"

"Enough," she replied. "Enough to know that you need her." She deliberately avoided a direct answer. "As for what she has seen, yes, she has seen the faces of both Malim and Rendail, images that you hold in your thought. She has also felt a little of what they are. But you are right. She does not *know*. How could she? For that matter neither do I. No one who has not lived in that place can really know. Perhaps it is better that she does not. But, Arghel, listen to me. Even if she did, she would still choose to go, for her mother's sake and for yours. She knows that we cannot succeed without her, and she could no more bear to lose you than you could bear the thought of losing her. Go and talk to her, Arghel. She knows that her words hurt you and that she can't take them back."

"I don't know what to say."

"Then say nothing until you do."

Amarisse was standing, her back to him, at the head of the winding staircase that led down from the tower. He saw her stiffen as he approached, as though she was afraid of him. It sent another little shaft of pain though him as he remembered how many times he had seen that same involuntary movement in his mother on hearing Rendail's footsteps in the courtyard outside. He made his step very gentle and, walking past her, sat down on the top step. He neither looked at her nor spoke. After a pause, he felt her come forward and sit beside him. They sat together in an agonising silence, until finally she spoke.

"I should not have said those things," she said. It was a nervous declaration, but he could detect no apology in it, just regret. She was standing her ground, her unspoken voice telling him that he would not override her decision, that he would have to physically restrain her to do it. She was so brave, he thought, and so beautiful, and he loved her so very much. He wanted to take her in his arms and tell her that everything was all right, that he was there, would protect her, would love her, no matter what she said or did. But he did none of those things. He just asked, his voice quiet, calm, "Is it what you truly believe, Amarisse? Is that what you think I am?"

He still couldn't look at her. He felt her body start to shake and she began to cry.

"No, no of course not," she said between her sobs. "How could I think it? I love you Father. Please don't hate me. Don't hate me for what I said." But his thoughts were a long way away, in another place, another time, and it was several minutes before he came to himself and realised that he had made no move to comfort her. She was beside herself with anguish and had curled herself into a little ball, her head resting in his lap. He gathered

233

her up and held her, rocking her to and fro the way he had when she was a little child.

After a while she stopped crying and nestled into him, the force of her emotion entirely spent. She should never be afraid, he told her with his thoughts, that he would stop loving her, or that he would ever hurt her.

"A long time ago," he said aloud, "I learned that if I tried to go anywhere without you, you would follow on behind me just the same. As I would rather I knew exactly where you are, perhaps we should go together, as I will worry less if I can see you." The last part was a lie and they both knew it. His fear for her was so great it was impossible for her not to see it. "It is a terrible thing," he went on, "to ask me to accept the danger you wish to draw down upon yourself. Even now I don't know if I can do it. But you and Maylie are right. We must all go together to the last place in the world that any of us would wish to go, or the threat from Malim will never be ended."

Amarisse said nothing, but wrapped her arms tight around his neck and kissed him, and for a while they clung to each other. Finally, he heard her voice, timid, uncertain, in his ear.

"Father?"

"Yes?"

"I'm frightened."

"I know. It is that more than anything else that has convinced me you are no longer a child."

CHAPTER 24

"Oh, come on Mickey, where's your sense of adventure? You could at least look as if you're enjoying yourself. This is a holiday, remember?"

As far as Wroughton was concerned the word 'holiday' had always been defined as a period of consecutive days which did not start until lunchtime, took place in hot countries and usually ended with loud music and the ingestion of copious amounts of alcohol – that is if you were unlucky and ended up going back to the same hotel that you started from. Nowhere in this definition was there any mention of getting up at five in the morning, driving to the top of a deserted cliff and sitting on damp grass in the freezing cold watching someone else looking intently through binoculars for hours on end. It was now almost eight thirty and she was very hungry, very cold and very tired.

She was about to suggest that perhaps they might just have time to get back to the hotel in time for a traditional Scottish breakfast when Taylor leaped up off the grass with an excited shout, nudging her in the ribs on the way.

"Got her," he said triumphantly. "Can't see the name but there's no doubt about it. I can't make out too much detail, but there can't be another boat like it round here – magnificent! Come on, come and have a look. Our fisherman friend was right – must have cost an absolute fortune."

She got up wearily and took the binoculars. She could just make out the cruiser's outline, way out to sea, almost lost in the early mist rising off the water. A faint light flashed on and off every so often to mark its position. Despite herself she felt a little twinge of excitement, the sort she always felt when, after hours of sitting in some old, cramped car drinking cold coffee out of plastic cups, she was able to pick up the radio and announce, "The target has just entered the building."

"I don't know about you," said Taylor, "but I would say it's about time for breakfast. After that, a visit to the harbourmaster I think. Come on, Mickey – we can't sit about here all day enjoying the view."

By ten o'clock Wroughton's spirits had risen considerably, aided by a large plate of bacon and eggs and several cups of very strong, hot coffee. She sat dozing in the car while Taylor struck up a conversation with a solitary local boat owner. After about half an hour he got back into the driver's seat looking glum.

"Its not going to be as easy as I thought," he said. "There's no one specifically in charge of boat movements here and this chap says he's never met the owner, doesn't know much about him. It's always one of the crew that comes into town, and apparently they're a tight lipped bunch – never volunteer more information than is necessary. In fact, he spent quite a while complaining to me about their lack of conversational skills. They must be pretty determined – he could talk into the middle of next week! He reckons that a few of the larger boat owners have the same sort of arrangement, it's not unusual. They get ashore elsewhere and, unfortunately, that could mean just about anywhere along the coast. There are literally dozens of little beaches and coves. Damn!"

He lapsed into silence, except for sucking in a breath through his teeth every so often and staring through the windscreen as though he expected inspiration to come round the corner of the narrow lane. As it happened, it came from a little closer to home.

"The yacht, Sir," exclaimed Wroughton, suddenly sitting up in her seat.

"What?"

"The yacht. Didn't the fisherman say he had a racing yacht somewhere up here? There must be a marina or something, and he doesn't get his crew to race it for him does he? So someone has got to know him haven't they? All we have to do is find the yacht."

"Of course!" Taylor thumped the steering wheel in jubilation. "DC Wroughton, I hereby declare you an honorary sergeant! In fact, if I wasn't a married Detective Inspector I'd kiss you." He had started the engine before the sentence was finished, and set off back towards the town with the eagerness of a bloodhound back on the scent.

* * *

Paul and Karisse watched as Alex paced up and down in front of the cottage, one of the tiny mobile phones pressed to his ear. Every so often Karisse saw him say something into it but mostly he just listened, a slight frown indicating that whatever was being said was not altogether good news. Her eyes drifted to Paul, sitting opposite her at the small kitchen table under the window. He had slept for some fifteen hours and looked completely rested, his hair brushed smooth and held back, in the manner of a Dancer, by an intricately engraved metal clasp. She also noted with some satisfaction that he seemed much more relaxed in her company and had dispensed, for the moment, with the contact lenses, providing her with a pleasing confirmation of his nature.

The clasp, he explained, belonged to Alex – he had pawned it on his arrival from the past and quickly discovered the modern version of the gambling den. After amassing a healthy sum of money at a casino in Inverness he had returned to the trader and used his considerable powers of persuasion to reclaim it, the man returning it to him for far less than the sum of the original transaction. Paul smiled as he told the story and Karisse concluded that perhaps he was not as entirely without humour as she had supposed. She also realised, on thinking about it, that his diffidence must stem largely from the fact that for most of the time he was unable to freely express what he was, living as he did in a world populated by those who would either be horrified or terrified, or probably both, had he revealed himself to them.

"Actually," he said, responding quite comfortably to her thought, "it isn't that difficult. I find I don't seem to need the company of others in quite the way Alex does. In fact, even Jenni and the others at the house crowd my thoughts too much. Then I have to go out on the water, and sail until there is no one and my mind is quiet. I suppose that seems strange to you. Alex tells me that a female of our kind lives her whole life with a head full of noise."

Karisse couldn't help laughing, although she had the feeling that this last remark had been made in seriousness.

"It's not quite the description I would use," she said, still smiling. "Yes, it is true that the Dance is in us in a different way. We can choose to ignore it, we can follow one wave of thought or many, as we wish. But it is always there both in males and females, and even in those who choose to be alone there is no real 'aloneness'. At least," she added, "for me not until now. I feel all manner of creatures as I sit here, and could follow the vision of any one of them, but I am used to the constant presence of many of our kind, and there is an emptiness in this time that I long to fill."

She paused, thinking of the space inside her that had been Arghel's presence, and found herself unable to go on. Paul said nothing, but took her hand, and they sat for a while in silence.

At length they heard the latch of the front door, but Alex did not come back into the kitchen. They heard his light footsteps pass on into the sitting room, then everything went quiet.

"Something is wrong," Paul said softly. "He's worried. And he is hiding it from me. He rarely does that. It's not his way."

He got up and she followed him into the sitting room where they found Alex, sitting on the sofa, staring intently into the dying embers of the fire. His face was pale, without expression. They sat and waited, neither wishing to break in on his thoughts before he was ready to speak.

Finally, without looking up he said, "Malim is here. He has been to the house. Last night – late. There was nothing for him to learn except that the one he sought was not there. I was careful about that. Old Jim saw him coming across the grounds in the dark." He paused, and put his head in his hands. "Malim killed him."

It took a few moments for the implications of the statement became clear. Karisse felt suddenly cold. Until now, the idea of coming face to face with Malim had been simply that

– a distant prospect, the form of which could be kept safely at arms length, out of mind, not a part of the present reality. But now it was in the present and was fast becoming a reality. The encounter might be only hours away and if the others could not destroy him, she knew that he would do nothing quite so simple as deprive her of her life. She began to feel a little sick.

Paul, meanwhile, sat in horrified silence, his eyes not leaving his father's face. It was a while before he could bring himself to ask the question.

"The others? What about the others? Father, you must tell me. Are the others all right?"

Alex looked up. "I sent them away last night, before I left – a precaution, but one that I almost felt was unnecessary." He shook his head. "It was Jenni who rang just now. She went back to check the house this morning and found Old Jim. She rang all the others and told them not to go back there."

He fell silent again. Paul jumped up from his chair and grabbed Alex by both arms. His hands were trembling.

"What else?" he asked, his voice unsteady. "What about Mary? You know she wouldn't leave, not even if you asked her to. Tell me, Father – where is she? Where is Mother?"

"I don't know," Alex said, his eyes filling with tears. "She's gone, Paul. No one knows where she is, and my gift can't reach that far. She is frail, and can't reach out to me like she used to. She is alive, though. I am sure I would feel it if …"

He stopped, and squeezed Paul's hand, then went on, "Young Jim is gone too. There was no sign of them this morning when Jenni got there. There was nothing broken, no sign of a struggle, they were both just gone and Old Jim dead on the lawn. Malim was clever. He made it look quite natural. One of the cars was gone too – the big four by four. He may have taken it. Oh, Paul, if he has taken her…"

He struggled to control himself, without success, and wiped away a tear. Paul wrapped his arms around his father and they held each other for a while, until Alex finally mastered himself and, looking at Karisse, went on grimly, "If Malim has Mary, if he has seen her mind, then he has seen me. He will know who I am and why I am here. He will also know about Paul. Much worse than that, he will know *where* I am, and what our intentions are. The element of surprise was possibly our only advantage. If we have lost it and he is prepared for us, then I do not think we will survive any confrontation."

He paused for a moment, trying to gather his thoughts, then continued, "I thought we would have more time. I didn't expect him to go to the house and it was my plan to lure him here somehow, when we were ready. How did he know? I thought we were safe, at least for the moment. Our minds are silent to him unless we choose for them not to be, at least unless he is very close. I don't understand it. And more to the point, I have no idea what to do. It was dangerous before, but if this is true the situation becomes impossible. Karisse, if he knows you are here he will come, and if I read the situation right we will be unable to protect you."

Paul broke the ensuing silence with just one word.

"David."

Alex stared at him, realisation spreading over his face, and put his head in his hands.

"Oh, dear God, no."

Karisse looked from one to the other, and when no explanation was forthcoming, said, "Well? What is it that you're not telling me?"

Alex shook himself, and sighed. "I made a mistake. A big one. When Malim was last in this time I thought I sensed you, and I was anxious to find you without alerting him. I couldn't risk him being anywhere close if I found you. He was on the east coast at the time and I sent David to follow him. Plus, I wanted more information on how he was living, where he'd set himself up and so on, so I asked David to find out, take photos, etcetera. I thought the information might be useful later, and I couldn't get that close myself. He would have discovered me, without doubt.

"I thought it would be safe – the Family tend to filter out signals from the short lived, find the chaos of those without the gift too painful to live with. I placed a block in David's mind, so that should any Dancer try to access his memory, all reference to me or to Paul would be veiled. It was just a precaution. I believed he would be safe, as long as he didn't draw attention to himself.

"And you were wrong?"

Alex nodded, drawing a hand across his brow.

"I was wrong. David wasn't careful enough, and Malim got hold of him. You have no idea …" He swallowed. "It looks as if Malim wasn't as stupid as I thought. He put his own veil on David's mind, but of a different sort. It's a clever trick – I've seen it done once or twice before. David would have been undetectable as long as he remained close to me, but as soon as he moved far enough away from the house, Malim would be able to track him down. I couldn't see Malim's veil, any more than he could see mine. I sent David off to Edinburgh so that he would be out of the way when we lured Malim here, but all I've done is send an innocent boy to his death. I might as well have put an advert in the paper announcing your address. The result would have been the same, and David might have been spared. And now, if Malim has Mary too, he knows about me. "

Alex shook his head, struggling to come to a decision. He looked at her again and said, "The choice has to be yours. I will not continue with this unless you wish it. If you wish to leave, you can go with Paul – take the boat, find somewhere safe for the time being. Paul has the ability to help you to return to your own time if that is what you want. As for myself, I will stay here. I will go nowhere until I know what has become of Mary. If necessary I will try to fight him alone, but you may be assured that I will not die until I am sure that Mary is either dead, or safe."

In the silence that followed, Karisse felt the air in the room grow thick, and her chest tightened so that her breath came in shallow gasps. She felt dizzy and found herself on her feet, walking towards the door, wanting only to be outside in the fresh air where she could breathe, clear her head. Neither Paul nor Alex made a move to stop her. As soon as she opened the front door a strong, cool breeze swept over her and she drew in a lungful of the sharp air. Her heart was beating like a hammer and she had to lean on the house wall to steady herself. There was only one image in her thoughts – the vision of Malim and Rendail that she had plucked from Arghel's mind on the day of their joining and which had so terrified her despite its being only a reflection of an old memory.

When it came down to it, she honestly had no idea if she could do what she had agreed to do. But if she didn't, what then? Would she let Paul take her away, condemning Alex to die? Of course, if Malim were to find Alex, Paul would not be safe for long, and he could not return with her to a time that was not his. At least, she did not believe it possible. If she did go back, would she return to her own time to find that both her mate and her daughter were gone? No, she thought. I do not have a choice. She walked out onto the track and sat on the bonnet of Alex's yellow jaguar, sending out her unanswered message, "Arghel, I love you," this time adding, "Help me."

The sky was clear and from the position of the sun it must have been nearing midday. She suddenly took in her breath sharply and straightened up. Then she started to laugh. And once she had started she found it almost impossible to stop, and found herself thinking that it was fortunate that the sitting room was on the other side of the house and that neither Alex nor Paul had come outside to look for her. She finally managed to regain control of herself, and with a sigh got up off the bonnet and made her way back to the house.

* * *

For Wroughton and Taylor it had been a frustrating morning. Having found that there was no official marina in the area, they had spent a great deal of time hunting around the town for signs of people who might be yachting enthusiasts. It didn't help that sailing gear seemed to be a current fashion, or at least a practical one given the vagaries of the local weather. At last, to Wroughton's relief, Taylor declared it to be almost lunchtime. Although it was only some three hours since breakfast, the idea of sitting somewhere out of the sea wind with a hot drink and perhaps just a nibble of something to go along with it was very appealing.

Eventually they found a pleasant looking little tea room down one of the side streets with a tempting array of home made cakes and ordered a pot of tea and two large slices of devil's food cake. They seated themselves by the window at a delicate looking table, complete with lace trimmed white cloth, and turned their attention to dissecting their confections using dainty cake forks. Normally, the use of such a utensil would have sent Wroughton into a slight panic, but Taylor had noticed that over the last day or so, since the revelation back in Ullapool of their shared experience with MacIntyre, she had looked visibly more confident, more graceful even, less tentative in her movements. He wondered for a moment whether the two things might be connected, but whether they were or not it pleased him to see it.

It was, unfortunately, often the case that fitting in at the golf club dinner was as important as nicking villains when it came to opening the doors to the upper ranks, and he wanted her to go a long way in the force. He doubted he would ever be promoted beyond his current rank for the very same reason, and Mickey Wroughton was just what the top brass needed – a tenacious little bulldog who would sink her teeth fearlessly into the ankle of any one of them who dared to get in the way of real police work.

He was deep in his reverie and Wroughton had just attained the rank of Detective Chief Inspector in his imagination when he became aware of someone standing at the table, waiting politely to be acknowledged. He looked up to see a fair haired, pleasant looking young man of about twenty-five looking down at him. The chap was tall and lean, dressed casually in a cabled sweater and jeans and he had obviously just introduced himself, an event that had passed Taylor by completely. Wroughton helped him out.

"This is Mr Jensen. He does some yacht racing and he heard that we were looking for Paul Quillan."

The man smiled and held out a hand. Taylor half rose and invited the newcomer to sit. Jensen declined a cup of tea, saying he was on his way to lunch with friends and had just happened to spot them as he walked past the window.

"I race against him sometimes," he explained. "I know he keeps the yacht, Mary's Pride, over in Golspie during the summer. I don't know where he moors her in winter. We all usually go for a drink after the race, although he doesn't join us often. I like him though – a quiet chap, never says much but he's a damned good yachtsman. I don't think I've managed to get ahead of him more than once in the last three years."

Jensen paused for a moment, obviously reminiscing about some race or other, then went on, "Anyway, last spring I was up here visiting and bumped into him in town. We went for a quick drink and I asked him what he was doing up this way, and he said he had a cottage outside town, somewhere near the coast road to the south. I'm afraid I don't know where exactly, but he said it was a couple of miles or so and handy for when he came up in the cruiser because there was a good mooring spot for the speedboat not too far from it. Sorry I can't be more specific. That's all he said about it I'm afraid. But if he's here and you want to get hold of him, that's where he's likely to be. Sorry – must be off or I'll be late. Good luck!"

He shook hands with them both and went on his way. The two detectives looked at each other, drained their cups and, grabbing their coats, ran out to the car.

* * *

When Karisse walked back into the sitting room neither of the men appeared to have moved, but she knew that some unspoken argument had taken place between them and could easily guess what the gist of it had been. She sat and said, clearly and emphatically, "He has not got Mary. I am sure of it." They both looked up, surprised at the firmness in her voice. "How long did it take you to get here?" She directed the question at Alex. He shrugged.

"I suppose two hours, maybe a little less. I was driving quite fast. Why?"

244

"What time did Malim get to the house last night?"

"Jenni says it must have been in the early hours of the morning – not after three, probably earlier."

"It is noon now, Alex – more than nine hours at least since Malim left the house. If he had Mary he would know we were here. From what we know of his nature he wouldn't wait. He would come straight here. He would have been here before dawn, assuming he was not on foot, and probably none of us would still be alive. Is that not so?"

She saw Alex's brow start to furrow, but he didn't reply. Paul, on the other hand, had come back to life.

"Father, Karisse is right. Malim wouldn't wait and he is hardly likely, in this time, to travel on a horse. If he hasn't seen Mary then there is every chance he still doesn't know who we are, or that we are here. All he knows is what knowledge he could gain from Old Jim. That is, that his quarry was staying at the home of a rich businessman until yesterday and that perhaps she has not gone far. Nothing more. He doesn't even know that for certain. Wherever Mary is, she is not with Malim."

They saw Alex's expression slowly change, the possibilities taking shape in his mind. Then he actually laughed, just as Karisse had done outside, when she had seen the sun and with it the same simple fact.

The feeling of relief however, was short lived. Alex rose and went into the kitchen, returning with the habitual whisky bottle and tumblers. He handed them each a generous measure and sat back down, his face now reflecting a different concern. It fell to Karisse, however, to give voice to it.

"We cannot delay," she said quietly. "We don't know how Malim found out that I was at the house, but if it was from David, then that is all he knows. We should assume he may soon discover the rest. If we don't act now we may lose any chance we have of success."

She realised she was trembling and took a mouthful of the whisky, hoping that its calming effect might mask the fear she felt.

Alex moved to her at once and, taking both her hands in his, asked gently, "Are you sure?"

She met his eyes, and nodded. "I have no choice," she said. "We cannot go back. Too much depends on it. But there is something I wish to do first." She looked at Paul. "Before I open my mind to Malim I must speak to Amarisse. No one knows how this will end. I have to see Arghel, to know that he is at my side even if I can't feel him. I have to know that my child is with him and is safe. Will you help me?"

Paul reached across and gently squeezed her arm.

"You know I will," he said.

CHAPTER 25

David thought he would be safe in Edinburgh. It was his town, they were his streets. He could lose himself in an instant in the winding cobbled passages around the castle, the dark alleys behind the nightclubs in the middle of town. He loved the work, too. Paul's dance studio, one of several set up for disadvantaged local kids, was popular, and he frequently acted as a stand-in, so they knew him, looked forward to his occasional visits as much as he enjoyed being with them. For the first time since the horror of Inverness, he felt content.

It was a warm evening, a couple of hours light still left as David made his way out of the studio, just off the Royal Mile. It had been a good session. Two of the youngsters had shown real promise, and he made a mental note to pass the details on to Paul later. For now, though, his main thoughts were of a shower, then maybe a drink at the wine bar a couple of doors down from the flat Paul owned in the shopping area of town. He was smiling, thinking about his last visit, of evenings spent with Paul discussing dance routines and the strengths and weaknesses of various students over pasta and wine at the nearby Italian restaurant.

At first, he didn't notice the shadowy figure at the end of the deserted alley. He carried on walking towards it, still lost in pleasant reminiscence. He was no more than a few feet away when he heard it – the familiar soft laugh, the one that cut off the sun's warmth, made him double over as if his stomach had been pierced by shards of glass. He looked up, met the gaze that dispelled any shred of hope that he might have been mistaken.

"You've been hiding from me, David."

The voice was soft, with just a hint of reproach. David felt sick as Malim placed an arm around his shoulders, leaned forward and kissed his cheek. They were side by side now, walking towards Malim's red Jaguar. Malim opened the passenger door and David got in without a word.

"Tell me, David. Where have you been hiding?" They were moving, away from the centre, out towards the docks.

David felt his heart contract. "Nowhere. I haven't been anywhere ..."

After fifteen minutes or so the car jarred to a halt. Before David could gather himself Malim had yanked open the passenger door, caught him by the hair and dragged him out, up a short flight of steps and through a door into a dark hallway that stank of tobacco and cat's piss. He was pushed down to the end of the hall and through another door into a room that smelled even worse. An old sack at the window blocked most of what light was left. Blinking in the sudden gloom, David could just make out the shape of a motionless figure, stretched out on a bed. It was a woman, painfully thin. As he got used to the darkness he saw an empty syringe on the floor beside her open hand. Malim ignored her and, with a swift movement, pinned David against the wall, a hand around his throat.

"I've missed you, David. Now, I'll ask again. Where have you been?"

David shook his head, mute with fear. A second later a blinding pain exploded in his head. It seemed to go on for hours, but at last it stopped and he was able to focus, through a blur of tears, on Malim's face, just a few inches from his own. It was filled with fury.

"Where is she?" The mocking tone was absent now, the hand tightening on David's neck, cutting off blood and air. "I see her, in your mind," Malim hissed. "You know her. She is shielding the place. You will tell me."

David's head was starting to swim. He realised that Malim had detected Alex's barrier, but for some reason the veil had allowed an image of Karisse to slip through. Malim, however, unable to see the real originator of the block, had made the assumption that Karisse must be the source. David felt consciousness slipping away and, in a last, terror fuelled burst of effort, tried to resist the relentless mental probing. He knew, as darkness finally came, that he had failed.

When David came round, surprise at still being alive was overtaken by pain as he tried to swallow. He could feel the swelling bruises around his neck. The room was pitch dark, but the sound of laboured breathing somewhere off to his right told him he was not alone. He stayed still, afraid to move in case Malim was somewhere in the darkness watching, waiting for him to regain consciousness. As if it made a difference, he thought. Malim was inside his head. He would know. And he also knew where to find Karisse. He knew, now, where Alex lived.

David heard a rustle followed by a low moan – the woman on the bed. He waited, but there was no other sound. He started to crawl, feeling his way round the wall. He half expected to hear the familiar laugh and braced himself against the pain that would inevitably follow. Nothing happened. He continued on until he felt a wooden doorframe under his hand and followed it up, groping the wall for a light switch. He finally found one and, to his relief, when he flicked it, a dull glow illuminated the shabby room. He sank down, exhausted. The woman was awake, staring at him, her eyes filled with a terror he knew only too well. Even in the dim light he could see the dark shadows of bruises on her face. Her wrists were tied to the legs of the iron bed frame. Malim was gone.

David pushed himself upright and moved towards the bed. The woman started to whimper and he put a finger to his lips.

"He's gone," he said, his voice a harsh rasp through his swollen throat. "We have to get out of here."

She stopped whimpering and nodded, although her gaze was still filled with suspicion. David fumbled in the pockets of the light jacket he was still wearing. Just one thing was missing – his mobile phone. He cursed under his breath. But at least neither Paul's nor Alex's number was programmed into it – a precaution taken after Inverness. Mercifully, he still had his wallet and keys and, attached to his keyring, a Swiss Army knife. The woman let out a frightened gasp as he pulled open a blade.

"It's all right," he managed to croak, and leaned down to saw through the ties at her wrists, which turned out to be nylon stockings, probably the ones she had been wearing when Malim

249

picked her up. He shuddered. "We have to get out," he repeated. Can you stand up?"

She pushed herself up on her elbows and peered at him with glazed eyes. "My bag. Can you see my bag?"

With an impatient sigh he looked round the room. A battered leather shoulder bag had been flung into the corner under the window. He fetched it and held it up.

"Is this it? Now come on! We haven't got time to mess about. He may come back any minute."

The threat seemed to sink home and she swung herself into a sitting position, but made no attempt to stand up. "Give it to me."

He handed over the bag and she rummaged in it, drawing out a small foil wrapped packet and a syringe.

"Oh, Jesus Christ!" David snatched them off her and dumped them back in the bag, then hoisted it over his shoulder. "Are you insane?" He grabbed her round the waist and pulled her upright, dragged her to the door as she made feeble attempts to grasp the bag and yank it away from him. To his relief she had some clothes on, a short black skirt and grubby white blouse, and beside the door he found a pair of black patent stilettos. With difficulty he bent and picked them up, and made his way out into the breaking dawn, one hand practically carrying the woman, the shoes in the other.

He didn't dare take to the main streets. The chances of finding a cab for hire at that time in the morning were close to zero, and with what was in the bag he couldn't risk being stopped by the police. It wasn't as if they looked like a couple on a pleasant morning stroll. She was unkempt and uncooperative, and he got the feeling he didn't look a lot better. It was a long and painful walk and he was giddy with relief as, two hours later, he closed the door to Paul's flat and leaned against it, almost tearful. His charge tottered into the living area and he heard a dull creak as she dumped herself onto one of the sofas. He flung the bag into a closet, out of sight, and stumbled into the kitchen.

When he came out, carrying two mugs of strong coffee, the woman had fallen asleep, stretched out on the sofa. He put her mug on a coffee table and sank to the floor, studying his new, unwilling companion. Underneath the thick mask of makeup and grime was the face of a young girl, no more than seventeen or eighteen, he guessed. Her clothes were better suited to a much older woman, and accentuated a form that was almost emaciated. Both her arms and the backs of her hands were dotted with needle marks. She was most likely a prostitute, certainly an addict.

She was also all he had left. He had betrayed Alex and all the people at the house. Whether or not Malim had discovered Alex's true nature, he now knew where Karisse was. Malim would go there, to Alex's house, and he would find out everything. Paul, Mary, Jenni and the others would all die. David could never go back there. His only hope was to lose himself, hope that Malim would never come looking for him again. And he could try to save the girl. At least then, he thought, he might somehow be able to live with the guilt.

* * *

David sat on the edge of a short concrete pier, his feet dangling in the dark water of the loch. The warm night air was swarming with midges, which nibbled mercilessly at every inch of exposed skin. He didn't notice, his mind too occupied seeking the courage to slip off the end of the pier, put an end to his misery and guilt. He knew it was a vain search. He also got the feeling that even if he managed to end it, Malim would find a way to bring him back.

As he sat, staring out over the dark water, David wondered if he had made yet another mistake. He heard the car door slam behind him and the padding of bare feet as the girl, Maggie, she had told him, came and sat down beside him.

"Did you get the stuff?" Her voice was a pleading whine.

"No. I got this, though." He pointed at a bottle of Scotch on the concrete beside him.

"So what fucking use is that to me? About as much use as you are, you stupid bastard! I should kill you, find somebody who can get what I need."

"So what's stopping you?"

He realised, suddenly, that she was crying and when she spoke again she sounded like the child she was, frightened, lonely.

"I'm pregnant. It was *him*. I know it was. I'm never late, you know? It's six weeks now, and there was only *him*. You won't leave me, will you, David? I don't want to be on my own. I don't want *him* to come back and find out."

"Oh, God!" He put his arm round her, drew her close, unscrewed the bottle and took a slug, then handed it to her. "It's all right, Maggie. I'll look after you. I won't let him find you, I promise."

CHAPTER 26

After ten days of riding the strain was beginning to tell on Amarisse. Both her father and his sister were seasoned travellers, used to being on horseback for weeks at a time. They said nothing, deliberately slowing their pace to allow her to keep up without too much discomfort. Even so, they must be covering some forty miles each day, starting at dawn and not stopping for more than a few minutes at a time until it was quite dark. For the last three nights she had been almost too tired to eat, yet clearly too uncomfortable to sleep.

Arghel acted as a silent witness to her struggle but did not intervene, knowing how much she wanted to prove herself to him. He looked on, filled both with pride and admiration for her dogged determination, but at the same time wishing she would bend just a little, enough at least for him to help her get a good night's rest. Their goal was less than two days away now and when they reached it she would need all her strength. There was a difference, he reflected, between independence and stubbornness. Watching her, he tried vainly to remember at what point in his young adulthood he had learned that particular lesson, if indeed he ever had.

The light was already failing and Maylie turned from the track, leading them deep into woodland almost too dense to allow the passage of the horses. It was a place she knew well and at length they came to a small clearing, too far from the track to give any physical sign of their presence, where even the light from a small fire would be swallowed up by the dense undergrowth. Amarisse slid to the ground gratefully, watching as Maylie produced two freshly killed rabbits from a small sack and gave them to Arghel, then went off in search of wood and water.

Arghel drew out the sharp blade that he kept always under his shirt next to his skin and set about preparing them. She wanted to help but was too exhausted to move. Instead she watched him as he worked, skinning the little animals with quick, deft movements, the whole process finished with hardly time to blink an eye. Maylie returned with a small bundle of wood, then went away again, and he started to build the fire. By the time Maylie came back with water and more wood there was a bright little blaze in the middle of the clearing, the rabbits dangling above it on a spit. He came to sit beside Amarisse and began to clean the knife.

It was an exquisite thing, the blade some eight inches long, fine like a needle and deadly sharp. The delicate hilt was fashioned in the image of a snake, its eye a tiny red jewel glinting in the light of the fire. The motif continued along the length of the metal sheath, so realistically engraved that, as a child, she had often run her fingers along it just to make sure it was not alive. When he had finished he put it back in the sheath, but instead of hiding it away, he placed it on the ground in front of them. Then he took the silver clasp from his hair and laid it next to the knife, so that she could see both things together.

"They were made from the same ore," he said, "by a craftsman that no one remembers, so long ago that even the oldest of us can say nothing of where they were made or for whom. Together, they passed to Amala from her mother and, as you know, when she fled the Family the clasp went with her. But this," he pointed to the knife, "she dropped to the ground as she started her long ride away from that place and it was picked up by her brother, Rolan, who kept it and gave it in turn to his son."

Amarisse knew the story of the clasp well, but this part was new to her. She wondered why he chose to speak of it now, but did not interrupt him to ask. He went on, "Rolan's son was very like his father. Like us, they were able to keep their minds hidden, both from Corvan and, later, from Rendail. The son was called Amal, to remind Rolan of his sister. When my mother was about your age Amal came to her and gave her the knife. In past times, the two things had always been given together by a woman to a man at their joining, and from him they were handed to the first female child to be born of the line. However, whereas the clasp was passed on by a father to a daughter at the time of her own joining, the knife was considered a symbol of a father's protection of his child, and was given to her at her coming of age, to keep her from harm in those places where he could no longer watch over her.

"This tradition once acted as a confirmation of one of the most deeply held convictions among Corvan's people, that each life is governed by its owner and that no one, not even a parent or a mate, may control the choices of another, once that person is of age. If a woman did not wish to join she could withhold the token. Likewise, a man could refuse it. A father must, at the proper time, relinquish the power he has over his daughter, for although he has a lifelong duty to protect her, he must not use his greater strength to force her from her own choices. Once there were many such tokens, but most are now destroyed. These two are among the most ancient, and it was Rolan's wish, and Amala's too, that one day they would be reunited and used for the purposes for which they were made.

"As I said, Amal gave the knife to Sherenne, and just before she died she gave it to me. When your mother gave me the clasp, the hopes of Rolan and Amala were fulfilled. To Rendail, we are a constant reminder of all that the Family was before the coming of Corvan and, while they may think themselves more powerful, they still fear us because of what we represent. I believe that there are some who, like Rolan and Amal, would have gone back to the old ways were it not for the threat of almost certain death both for them and their families. As it is, they stayed, did what they could to make the lives of the women and children less harsh, and I do not blame them for it. In fact, sometimes I think they had the greater courage, as they remained there while I ran away."

He paused and took her hand. "You spoke the truth when you said I was afraid to return to that place. I was the same age that you are now when I last saw my father's house. I fled, out into the world, and any that came after me I destroyed. I thought I

255

was free. But that freedom was an illusion. No matter where I go or what I do, I remain Rendail's son. I live because he allowed it. I believe I escaped because he allowed it. We are close to him now, and I feel his presence all around us as though the air were robbing me of breath. I wonder, are we here because my father has allowed it? When I rode away, I thought it would be like waking from a terrible dream, but after all this time, still the dream has not ended. I think it is so for all who go there. A part of them is trapped there and can never leave."

Amarisse was surprised by his openness. It was the first time he had ever willingly revealed to her any sign of weakness. For a moment she was unable to fathom why he should choose to tell her now. Then, suddenly, she understood. He was giving her a way out. He was saying to her that the choice was still hers, whether to go on or to turn back, and that if she chose the latter course he would think no less of her for it, just as she felt no less of him for showing her his own doubt.

She reached down and picked up the clasp, then leaned back against him, studying the fine engraving that flowed across the otherwise smooth and unadorned metal. At length she got up onto her knees and gathered up his hair, snapping the clasp back into place.

"You shouldn't take it off," she said. "You should wear it even when you sleep, especially here. Then, Mother is with you even though you can't hear her."

She looked up to see him smiling. He drew her into a hug and, encouraged, she went on, her voice serious, "It is true that you are the son of Rendail, but do not forget that you are also the son of Sherenne, and that you are a part of her as much as you are a part of him. You should not be afraid, Father. She was much braver than Rendail and so are you. Grandfather may control the lives of many but in his heart he is alone. You have Mother and Maylie, and most of all you have me. What he sees as our weakness is our greatest strength." She stopped, then added, a little less certainly, "All our lives you have looked after Mother and me. Now I think it is time for us all to look after each other."

She looked up at him and found that he was still smiling, then, to her surprise, he started to laugh. She found herself bristling with annoyance and understanding suddenly why it was that her mother had found her first encounters with him so frustrating. She glowered at him and at once he became serious again.

"Amarisse," he said, kissing her, "how can I help but laugh when you fill me with so much light, even when my mind is in a place as dark as this? Sometimes I forget that I am not alone, and you were quite right to remind me of it. I am so proud of you, and I think that if your mother were here she would be too. I miss her, Amarisse. I long for her every moment of every day, and I can't bear the thought of her alone and in such danger, in a place where I can't reach her."

"But she is not alone, Father, any more than you. She has Alex with her, and Paul. I have seen Paul, and I know that they both place her life above their own. She will come back Father, I know it. You will kill Malim and she will come back."

She watched as he helped Maylie take care of the horses, and a little time later he brought her some food, which she ate obediently even though she didn't feel hungry.

"We will rest here," he said, "until noon tomorrow, and then we must ride for the rest of the day and the whole night. That way there is less risk of a chance encounter with one of Rendail's people. Do you think you will be able to manage that?"

"Yes, of course I will," she answered, but wholly unconvincingly, thinking that she had never felt less able to even stand up, let alone ride for some eighteen hours without stopping.

"Then," he said, "I will leave you to sleep. Try to get as much rest as you can."

He rose and walked a little way, but she called him back.

"Father?"

"Yes?"

"My back hurts." He sat down again, smiling. "In fact my arms hurt and my legs hurt, and just about every part of me hurts, and I never want to see a horse ever again, and I can't sleep either!"

Straight away he set about easing the stiffness in her joints, letting her become comfortably drowsy in his arms. This time she didn't mind that he laughed, because it reminded her of the short time before her mother went away.

The next morning dawned bright and clear. They had travelled a long way north and there was a sharpness in the air despite the coming of summer. Amarisse woke sometime in the late morning to find all the aches and pains of the previous few days completely gone, her mind refreshed and clear. Arghel was nowhere to be seen and his horse was gone. For a moment she panicked, but then saw Maylie come into the clearing and beckon for her to follow. Maylie led her down a slope to a small stream where she could wash.

"Don't worry," Maylie said. "Arghel will return soon. He has gone to decide which is the best path for us to take. There are several, but not all are safe to ride and we can't leave the horses."

Amarisse nodded and plunged her head under the water, washing the dust out of her hair. She emerged, dripping, in time to catch Maylie's troubled expression. A second later it was gone, replaced by the calm, impassive look so reminiscent of her father.

"What is it?" she asked at once. "You know something. I saw it in your face and you wish to hide it. You have seen Mother, and something is wrong."

Maylie hesitated, examining the young girl's anxious face, then nodded.

"I have seen my son," she said. "He is worried. Malim is closer to them than they thought and may know who they are, and where. Also, he has a short lived mate and she is missing. He frets over her, but he doesn't think Malim has found her, at least not yet. They have decided they must make their move as soon as possible, perhaps within the next few hours, as there is a chance still that Malim has not learned the truth. The longer they wait, the smaller that chance becomes."

Amarisse stopped drying her hair and came to sit beside Maylie.

"Have you told Father?" she asked, her voice filled with apprehension.

"Yes," Maylie answered, "last night. That is one of the reasons why we must start soon and ride through the coming night. We must reach Rendail's settlement by dawn tomorrow at the very latest or Malim may escape us – that is, if Karisse and the others can indeed force him back into his own time. I know Arghel has already asked you this, but I have not, and I ask you now. Are you certain you wish to go on? Even if Malim dies there is no guarantee that once we have entered Rendail's house we shall ever leave it."

"I don't wish to go on at all," Amarisse replied. "I'm tired and I'm afraid. But so are you, and so is Father, Mother, Alex and Paul. I go on for the same reason you do – because none of us really has a choice. There is only one thing I wish, and that is to speak with Mother again. It's so long since she came to me, and I would like to tell her that I love her, and that Father loves her. I think if she could see him it would give her strength, just to know he was thinking of her and has not forgotten her." She saw sadness in Maylie's eyes and added, "Perhaps if she came to me, Alex could see you too. It must be lonely for you without him."

"Yes, I miss my son," Maylie replied. "I think you would like him, although he can be a little wayward. But he is brave and strong and has a good heart. I think he has fallen a little in love with what he has found on the other side of the Great Emptiness. He always had the excitability of a short lived one and a passion for new things far beyond what is usual for a Dancer. Now he has mated with a short lived woman and has a son, who is really a most extraordinary child. I watched Paul grow and love him dearly, but I fear for him, a Dancer trapped in a time where there is no gift, with no way back to his father's people. Perhaps he will, in time, be strong enough to use his gift of memory to travel to us. It is that which gives him the ability to help your mother to see you. Alex does not have that gift, which is why the connection comes through Paul. But even so, he will find it hard without his father, and if we all survive this I do not know what will come after."

A slight rustle at the top of the slope signalled Arghel's return. By the time the two women had climbed up he had kicked over the ashes of the fire and readied the horses, so that it looked as though they had never been there at all. He kissed them both and lifted Amarisse onto her mount, an act to which she did not object. He made sure she was seated comfortably enough for what was to be a very long, arduous ride. They set off just after noon and rode as quickly as the terrain allowed until just after nightfall, when they stopped briefly to take a little food and let the horses rest. It seemed to Amarisse that no sooner had they stopped than they were on their way again, the horses following narrow paths that she could not even see in the pitch darkness.

After some twelve hours of riding Arghel looked back to see that his daughter was hovering dangerously close to sleep. The third time she fell into a doze he came up beside her, lifted her gently and took her in front of him on his own horse, where she immediately fell asleep leaning against his chest. At long last they stopped. It was still more than an hour before dawn and he lifted her down, still fast asleep, onto a patch of soft grass, wrapping her in a blanket to keep out the chill. He and Maylie moved a little distance off so as not to wake her and sat down together, holding hands but not speaking, the distant glow of watch fires telling them what they would see set out below them when the sun rose.

The blackness of the night was just beginning to lift when Arghel turned to see his daughter sitting upright, staring straight ahead as though she had just seen some terrible apparition coming towards her through the trees. In a single bound he was at her side, Maylie right behind him. He went to take hold of her but Maylie grabbed his arm and shook her head.

"Wait!" she said in an urgent whisper. "I don't think she is in any danger. Quite the opposite in fact. Leave her for a moment. Don't disturb her."

He obeyed, but not without difficulty, and watched anxiously for any sign of distress in Amarisse's face. However, he saw none and realized that there was no tension in her expression, more an attitude of contemplation. He glanced back at Maylie and, seeing that she was also lost to the present, understood that they had joined their thoughts together, sharing the same experience through the Dance. Amarisse remained still for several minutes, and then he saw her eyes close. At the same time he felt her mind reaching for him, her voice inside him, very soft, calling, "Father – come!"

He followed the thread of her thought, letting her guide him into the Dance, through the seemingly infinite number of undulating waves that form the core of the female Dancer's gift. It was a place in which a male, alone, might flounder, losing focus among the myriad visions assaulting the senses, threatening to distract and confuse. But she held on to him, leading him through the maze until the swirl of images began to fade and he sensed the thoughts of Maylie. He saw nothing. There was no image, no sound, only a blackness so enveloping that he might have panicked had he not felt the presence of the two women, holding onto him with their minds as though he were a child who might get lost. He was far into the Dance – disoriented and completely reliant on Amarisse and Maylie to keep his senses steady, his thoughts anchored to his body. He heard Amarisse again, her voice distant, inside but without direction, so that he could not orient himself towards the sound.

"Wait, Father. When I tell you to come back, you must follow me."

He sent his acknowledgement and waited. A moment later he heard another voice, faint, far away, but unmistakeable.

"Arghel."

"Karisse?"

He felt the slight tremor of her thought run through his mind in a tiny whisper. The thought said, "I love you, I long for you, I need you," but without words, as though the distance was too far, the effort too great to make the sound. Using all his strength, he sent back the thought and felt another wave come to him, almost imperceptible, but enough; "soon."

"Father! You must come. It is dangerous now. You must come back."

He remained still, his mind locked on the far distance, searching, but it was empty now. Again, Amarisse sent her voice, insistent.

"Come, Father – you must follow me."

With an effort he pulled his mind away and let her lift him out of the darkness. He saw the visions again, surrounding him, wave upon wave of them, and tried to shut them out, concentrating on his daughter's thought as she led him back with the sureness of a pilot navigating a straight path through a storm.

With a suddenness that made him gasp he found himself thrust out of her mind and back into his own body, just in time to see her sway and fall into Maylie's arms.

"It was a great strain for her," Maylie said. "She took you right to the edge of the Great Emptiness and held you there, just for a moment, but it was long enough. I was able to help a little. You could so easily have become lost, but we considered the reward worth the risk." She smiled. "It was, was it not?"

Amarisse stirred and opened her eyes. With a sigh of relief Arghel took her from Maylie and kissed her.

"Thank you, darling girl," he whispered in her ear. She smiled.

"Mother needed to see you," she said. "I thought if I tried hard enough you might see her too. But she is so far away. I did not have the strength."

"I felt her, Amarisse. Just for a moment we were together and it was enough."

Amarisse was recovering rapidly and the three of them sat in silence, watching as the coming sun chased away the last traces of grey to reveal, in the distance below them, the great sprawling settlement that was the stronghold of the Family.

CHAPTER 27

There had been no sound now for more than an hour. Karisse knew the others were close by, but she had no idea where. There was not the slightest indication of their presence and she could not even tell whether they were inside or outside the house. Both she and Paul had recovered quickly from the effort of their second journey back to her own time. This time they had both been better prepared. Paul had been less afraid of the experience and, by drawing on the strength of his gift, she had quickly found the thread of her daughter's thought.

Amarisse had astonished her. It wasn't just that her daughter had grown up. She had grown into something quite beyond her imaginings, from the physical look of her to the manner of her thought. She could discern both Arghel's nature and her own, combined to form something miraculously beyond the elements that had created it. They had said nothing to each other. Of what was to happen there was nothing to say, so they simply let their minds run together, feeling, affirming.

Karisse marvelled at her daughter's skill. To do such a thing had required an enormous effort of will, but Amarisse had known the importance of it, both for her and for Arghel. Now, as Karisse sat alone, her mind completely open for Malim to find, that brief and distant touch sustained her, giving her both courage and hope.

Paul's Porsche and Alex's Jaguar were tucked away in an already half full tourist parking area a mile or so up the coast from the cottage. The men themselves were hidden, somewhere nearby. It had been agreed that Karisse should not know the exact plan that her protectors had chosen to adopt, nor their whereabouts. It would reduce the risk that Malim might pick up any stray impressions from her. There had, however, been a vigorous debate between the two men before they set off, one which was plainly the continuation of a long standing disagreement between them. Paul was in favour of the use of

263

firearms while Alex fiercely opposed the idea. It was not merely a matter of morality, although Alex found modern weaponry distasteful. His objections were purely practical, on two counts.

Firstly, Malim's reactions were so fast that anything other than a single, instantly fatal shot would result in disaster, and neither were sufficiently practiced to guarantee that eventuality. Secondly and, Karisse sensed, more importantly as far as Alex was concerned, Paul was already guilty of causing one death. To be found responsible for another, particularly one involving the use of a firearm, might lead the relevant authorities to conclude that the first had been more than a simple act of passion. Paul had eventually been forced to concede, and so it was decided to stick to the original plan, using the combined power of their gifts at close range in a surprise attack, whilst Malim was distracted and thus undefended.

"You will neither hear nor feel us," Alex had said, "but we will be close. And, we have one advantage – we are both able to silence our minds, yet still hear others." He smiled. "Traitors to the Family we may be, but not because of any weakness in our blood."

They had embraced and kissed her, then left her alone in the growing silence.

* * *

Paul, secreted in a small barn just to the right of the cottage, felt it first. Just the slightest of tremors in the air, a cold breath that stroked the outer edge of the shield that kept his mind invisible, then passed on. He knew it must have reached Karisse a second later, but she did not waver. The signals flowing from her were perfect, an impression of one entirely confused, lost, searching for an understanding of a strange world. By degrees, the atmosphere was slowly thickening, becoming oppressive. To one without the gift there would have been no perceptible change in the air, but for the Dancers it was as still and heavy as the silence before a great storm. Malim was still some way off, approaching warily, scanning for the presence of others of his kind.

Alex, who had taken up his position some hundred yards to the south, flat on the ground, concealed by a low outcropping of rock, had the best vantage point, able to see Paul's hiding place and both the front and rear entrances to the cottage. The force of Malim's gift was not unfamiliar to him, and he did not doubt his ability to maintain his guard. He was uncertain of the others, but so far they had stood firm and he did not dare to make any attempt to contact either of them. Another thirty minutes or so passed, in which he felt wave upon wave of Malim's thought, directed ever more strongly towards Karisse, pinpointing her exact location and moving steadily towards it. Then he heard the sound of an engine coming towards them, but saw nothing on the road. It took him a moment to gauge the direction, then he saw it – a large four by four, a Range Rover he guessed, off road and approaching from the north, the only side of the cottage out of his line of sight. That was not an undue worry. Unless Malim had learned how to dematerialise, to enter the cottage he would have to go through the door. Smashing windows, he decided, was not really this man's style.

The vehicle stopped some two hundred yards away. Its occupant got out and leaned against the open door, watching for any sign of movement. He was superficially very like Paul, for the two were not far removed by blood. But Malim was a good three inches taller, the hair longer and perhaps a little more lustrous, the body more muscular. His skin had the light golden sheen characteristic of the males of Rendail's line, and Alex had to admit that it would be impossible to find a more beautiful monster, nor one who moved with such elegance and grace, dressed all in black, which showed off the golden hair to perfection.

"Extraordinary vanity," Alex muttered to himself, watching with fascination as Malim pushed himself upright and shut the car door with a soft click, then began to stride towards the cottage, his step relaxed, full of self assurance. But the eyes were still watchful, the mind scanning for any hint of another presence nearby. He came to the low fence behind the barn and stepped across it easily. Just a few yards from the front door he stopped and remained still, eyes running across every inch of the house, grounds and outbuildings. For a few awful seconds, Alex saw Malim seemingly stare straight at him, but the gaze passed on to the road, then back past Paul's hiding place to the door.

Malim appeared to make up his mind and, taking a step towards the door, pushed it open and went inside. Alex counted slowly to ten and saw Paul appear, a little way back from the entrance to the barn, just visible in the shadows. Paul gave a quick signal, and Alex was about to raise himself from the ground when he heard a noise. He signalled rapidly back to Paul to stay still. There was no sound from the cottage, no sign of movement. But from the road he could hear footsteps, two people, hidden from view where the track had been cut out of the uneven hillside, but unmistakeably coming towards them. Paul had heard it too and withdrawn out of sight.

Alex stayed flat and waited. The footsteps stopped and he heard murmured voices, one male, one female. Then they separated, one coming in his direction, the other moving off to the left, away from the road and towards the cottage. He held his breath. They both appeared at the same instant and Alex felt his stomach lurch. He watched, horrified, as Detective Inspector Taylor marched purposefully towards the front door of the cottage, while the woman, DC Wroughton, headed for the back door, passing not five yards in front of his nose.

There was nothing to do but watch. Taylor drew alongside the barn and walked on, his intention to simply knock on the door.

"Fool!" Alex thought, helplessly. "Not even armed, not that it would do any good."

He saw Paul reappear, eyes wide with disbelief. He did not dare to signal in case Wroughton should catch sight of it, but thankfully Paul stayed where he was, and the two of them looked on in appalled fascination as Taylor continued his resolute progress towards the door. He never reached it. The speed of Malim's attack was blinding. Taylor was hurled some twenty yards backwards, landing in a crumpled heap by the entrance to the barn. In the same second Alex saw Paul fall, just a yard or two from the policeman. Then the wave hit him like a sheet of fire, every nerve in his body racked by an almost unendurable pain. The wave passed, leaving him stunned and gasping for breath but, remarkably, still alive.

As Mickey Wroughton's world slowly came back into focus, her first thought was, *Bomb!* She was flat on her back, out in the open some twenty feet from where she had been standing, and felt as if the flesh had been incinerated from her bones. Sinking in a haze of pain and terror, her years of police training took over, responding from habit, her brain visualising the classroom handouts entitled 'What to do in a Major Emergency', and 'First Aid at the Scene of a Disaster'.

One: check yourself for injury. She checked. No burns. She wriggled her fingers and toes. No broken bones. Just pain.

Two: Survey the scene for damage. She blinked at the cottage. It looked just as it had a moment before. No fire. No broken windows. No bomb blast. Just pain.

Three: Look for casualties. She turned her head, looked past the cottage to the barn. There were two bodies in the yard, not moving. One of them was Sam Taylor. She could just see a flash of colour from the distinctive designer sweater he had been wearing under his overcoat when they had set off.

Four: Call the emergency services, give first aid to survivors where possible.

She rolled over and got to her knees, gritting her teeth against the pain. She fumbled in her pocket for her mobile and started to dial. A moment later, her fingers burned as though she had received an electric shock and, horrified, she saw the phone sail out of her hands and land some ten yards away on the grass. At the same time she heard a car engine start, and turned to catch a glimpse of a Range Rover shooting out from behind the house and speeding away across the rocky ground behind.

She turned back to the phone and started to crawl after it, whimpering with fear and pain. It seemed to her that the short distance took forever. She finally closed her fingers around it, panting with exhaustion. But as she pulled it to her a hand grabbed her wrist and the phone was wrenched away. She watched, helpless, as a booted foot came down on it and smashed it into pieces. Then, she was pulled onto her feet and dragged roughly towards the barn. She screamed in pain and tried to kick, but it was no use. She was pushed to the ground next to the body of Sam Taylor, and looked up to find herself staring into the eyes of Alex MacIntyre.

Alex watched the young policewoman, on the ground but moving, struggling to get to her feet. He was momentarily frozen by indecision, whether to make for the rear of the cottage to try to confront Malim alone, or to go to the front, attempt to get Wroughton away before Malim sensed her and attacked a second time. Either way, his chances of survival were slim and any possibility of escape for Karisse practically zero. He made his choice, pushed himself painfully to his feet and made for the back door. He was half way there when he caught sight of Wroughton, fumbling in the pocket of her coat, pulling out a mobile and starting to dial. He stopped dead and with a thought sent the phone flying out of her hand. In the same moment he heard a car engine and saw the Range Rover reverse, turn, and shoot off across the hillside at a dangerous speed. It was over. They had failed.

Alex felt despair start to overtake him, but there was no time. Wroughton was on her hands and knees, unable to stay upright, crawling towards the mobile, some ten feet away. He lunged down the slope after her, almost crying out from the pain that shot through his body, but kept running, catching up with her just as she reached it. He snatched it out of her hand stamped on it until it shattered. He grabbed her roughly by the arm and dragged her towards the barn, to the two motionless bodies lying almost side by side in the yard. He was vaguely aware that she was kicking him, trying to undo his grip with her free hand, shouting at him, but he ignored it. He felt something far more important. He felt life.

Paul was deeply unconscious, a leg broken, a dislocated shoulder but otherwise, by some miracle, unhurt. Then he caught the breath of life in Taylor. It was faint and failing, but it was there. Alex turned to Wroughton, who was screaming at him, still trying to break herself free. He let go of her and, using his gift, held her there, paralysed, unable either to move or make a sound. She looked terrified, but he had no time to worry about it and knelt by Taylor's body. The injuries were extensive and there was internal bleeding. The pulse was barely discernable – the policeman's life was hanging by a thread. He could feel Wroughton struggling against him, using all her effort to try to move. Without looking at her he put the words into her mind with as much clarity and authority as he could manage.

"I can keep you still or I can help your friend. I am too weak to do both. If I do not help him, he will die. If I release you, you must promise to stay still and not speak. If you don't, I will have to use my mind to restrain you, in which case he will die. Do you understand? Think the word, and I will hear it."

He heard her answer, "Yes."

"Do you promise not to move or speak?"

"Yes."

He released her and turned his energy to the injured man. She sat watching him, trembling but quiet, and did not try to move. After perhaps an hour he sighed and, sitting up, turned to her.

"He will live," he announced, "and he will recover in a few hours. You must help me take him inside. Can you do that?"

The look on her face was a mixture of confusion and disbelief, but she nodded and tried to get up. With a little cry of pain she fell back and shook her head. Then he remembered that she had also been in the path of Malim's fire and must be suffering the same residual pain in her joints that he was himself, although she had been a little further away and so was possibly less affected. He moved to touch her and she shrank away.

269

"Don't be afraid," he said, as soothingly as he could. "I won't hurt you."

She acquiesced, letting him move his hands over her body, and he concentrated on lessening the swelling of the tendons enough for her to move more freely. A little of the mistrust left her eyes and together they lifted Taylor and carried him inside, setting him down on the sofa in the sitting room.

"I have to go and see to Paul," Alex said gently. "Will you stay here until I return?" She nodded, still in a state of shock. At the door he turned and said, "I give you my word, you can trust me."

* * *

The two men sat side by side on the ground, leaning against the wall of the barn. Paul had finally regained consciousness, but was still too weak to stand. Alex was drained to the point of exhaustion and in considerable pain. Surveying the wreckage that had been his plan he wanted to bury his head in his hands and weep, but now was not the time. He had to decide what to do with the two officials who had been largely, but innocently, responsible for the fiasco. The fact that they were still alive was nothing short of a miracle, but as a result he was faced with a seemingly insoluble moral and practical dilemma. If he kept them there, others might come to look for them. But to let them go, after all they had witnessed, might make matters even worse. He could attempt to radically change their perceptions of the events of the last few hours, but such a thing might damage them, something he was unwilling to do, even though the circumstances were extreme.

There seemed to be no resolution, and beyond it lay the larger crisis. Malim was gone and Karisse with him. A sense of helplessness threatened to overwhelm him and the more he struggled to fight it off the more hopeless everything became. He closed his eyes and tried not to think of anything.

He heard footsteps and opened his eyes to see Wroughton coming out of the cottage. To his immense relief she didn't try to

270

run, but walked tentatively across to him and stopped a few yards away, as if waiting for his permission to come closer. He gave a slight nod and she came forward, kneeling beside him.

"I thought you would want to know," she said nervously, "that my boss – the Inspector – he's awake. I think he's okay. He – well, he wanted to talk to you, so he asked me to come out and make sure you were still here. I said you would be, because you said you would come back. I hope you don't mind – you did say…"

"I don't mind. I don't mind at all. Thank you for coming to tell me." He tried to give a reassuring smile, but wasn't quite sure how well he managed it.

She paused and then asked, "Your friend – will he be all right? Was he badly hurt?"

She was staring at Paul, and Alex sensed a sudden confusion in her, followed by a realisation. Then it hit him. They had been searching for a man, tall, distinctive blonde hair, good looking. All they had to work from was a black and white photograph. They had caught sight of Malim and, believing him to be Paul, had followed, with catastrophic consequences. Malim had been too intent on guarding against the possible presence of other Dancers to take note of two insignificant short lived people following at a discreet distance, who only became a threat when they practically trod on his toes.

Alex nodded wearily. "He will recover. Thank you."

She got up and turned to go, but then stopped. She crouched down again and said, "Thank you for what you did. I believe you did save his life. An ambulance wouldn't have got here in time. I don't know how… but thank you."

When he said nothing she hesitated, then reached out and timidly put a hand on his shoulder. He saw concern on her face as she said, "You don't look too good yourself. Look, I know this sounds silly, but I could make some tea – strong, with lots of sugar – they say it's good for shock."

Despite everything, he couldn't help but laugh. Not knowing why, he replied, "Unfortunately, the trick only works on others. We have some difficulty healing our own bodies. In a

271

little while Paul will be strong enough to do me that service. And yes, tea is a wonderful idea. I will come in, but Paul won't be able to move for a little while. Would you be kind enough to bring some out here for him? I think I might spill it."

She nodded and managed a smile, then walked off back to the house.

Paul had kept his eyes closed throughout the conversation, but now he opened them and said, "Now you have told them that there are two of us. Was that wise?"

"No, not wise at all," Alex admitted. "But somehow I trust that girl. I trust both of them. At least I have to believe I do. The alternative is unthinkable. There is something about her. But then, I might be wrong. I might have made another mistake. Just another error in a long string of errors that has brought us here. I should have listened to you, Paul. I should have let you use a gun. It could not have made matters worse than they are now."

"I don't think it would have made a difference." Paul raised himself slightly and flexed his arm, testing his shoulder. "Those two inside might have been in greater danger if I had. It wasn't your fault. We are alive, and while we are alive we can search, and we can try again."

There was a short silence in which Alex felt an undercurrent of apprehension behind his son's words.

"And what is it," he asked finally when Paul did not volunteer the cause, "that you have not told me? Whatever it is, it can't make any difference now."

"Oh, I think it can," Paul replied, turning his head away. "Malim saw us. Now he knows who we are and why we are here. I'm sorry, Father. I couldn't let that man die. I had to try to protect him. When Malim sent out his power I tried to deflect it and for just a few seconds I was visible to him. He got inside my head – I felt it – only for a moment, before I lost consciousness, but it was enough. I think that's why he ran. It was my fault Father, not yours. Now he is gone, and when we find him he will be waiting for us."

Alex let out his breath in a long sigh.

"What else was there to do?" he said gently. "You saved their lives and perhaps you saved ours. It is not their cause, at least not yet, and we could not let them die for it."

The door opened and Wroughton came across the yard carrying a mug of tea for Paul. He took it gratefully, nodding his thanks, and Alex tried to get up. He had been still too long and the joints were now so stiff and swollen he could hardly stand. Wroughton saw him sway and immediately took his arm. He was forced to lean on her heavily but she took his weight, and with her help he made it to the cottage door and disappeared inside.

* * *

It was another hour before Paul's leg had mended enough for him to walk. He found Alex with the others in the sitting room. The Inspector was laid out on the sofa propped up on two cushions, the girl sat cross legged on the floor leaning back against one of the armchairs. Alex was slumped in the other, ashen faced, plainly losing his struggle against pain and exhaustion. Ignoring Taylor's curious stare, Paul went straight to him. The others watched as he performed the now almost familiar miracle and Alex's breathing became easier, the colour returning to his skin. Paul went out into the kitchen, coming back with a large measure of whisky which his father downed in a single gulp. Alex stretched his limbs and, shifting himself upright in the chair, gave a sigh of relief followed by a reassuring smile to the assembled company. Wroughton moved over to allow Paul to sit in the vacant chair. Taylor was still staring at him, eyes alert, face alive with curiosity. The policeman glanced briefly at Alex, who gestured for him to speak.

"Mr. MacIntyre here," he said, clearing his throat with a little cough, "has told us a most fantastical tale. Now, were we in a police station late on a Friday night I might hear such a tale and not pay too much attention to it – I'm sure you understand my meaning." Taylor paused and Paul looked across at Alex, whose face was completely impassive. "But," he went on, "we are not in a police station and this is not Friday night – at least, I don't think

273

it is. Also, neither DC Wroughton here nor I can dismiss certain things we have seen and experienced over the last two days. Therefore," he coughed again. "Therefore, I think we have both agreed that we are inclined to believe what Mr. MacIntyre has told us, however far fetched the story appears to be.

"Your name is Paul Quillan, is that correct?" Paul nodded cautiously. "And you are normally resident at the home of Mr. MacIntyre here?" Paul nodded again. "So perhaps you can tell me, Mr. Quillan, where you were between midnight and six am on the fifteenth of May?"

Paul hesitated and looked again at Alex, who gave no sign, either outwardly or in his thought. Finally, Paul answered, "I think you know where I was Inspector, and what I was doing."

Taylor nodded. "Thank you, Mr. Quillan." Paul opened his mouth, but Taylor held up a hand. "I have no doubt that both you and Mr. MacIntyre here are quite capable of disposing of we two troublesome police officers if you so wished. However, if either of you had such an intention you would not have acted as you did earlier in our defence. Not to be too dramatic, you saved my life, and in doing so you almost lost your own, and allowed a friend of yours to be abducted by a very dangerous man. There is no doubt in my mind, Mr. Quillan, that you are not a danger to society. The man that you are pursuing, however, most certainly is, and if I understand Mr. MacIntyre correctly, he intends to unleash himself on an innocent populace. If that happened we would be helpless, and the consequences too horrible to imagine. We need you. We need you to get rid of this menace, and you need to get your friend back before she or anyone else gets hurt. Therefore, I am going to break every rule in the book and pretend, for the moment, that certain parts of this conversation have not taken place. I'm sure DC Wroughton will concur."

He looked at Wroughton, who immediately nodded in agreement.

"There are two more things," he went on. "Firstly, you know that a murder investigation will not stop simply because I am not pursuing it. If not I, then others will keep looking and although to you a lifetime, in our terms, is not so long, there will always be the chance that someone, somewhere will find you. Secondly – well – I owe my life to you, and I'm grateful."

Taylor fell silent, watching Paul intently. There was a long silence. Finally, Paul said softly, "When this is over, if we succeed and I survive, I will come to you. I give you my word."

Taylor nodded gravely in acknowledgement. Then, to the surprise of both of them he said, "May I make a suggestion?"

"Please do," Alex responded, curious.

"This man, Malim – he has been to your house you say?"

"Yes – last night. Why?"

"Well, in my experience of the workings of the criminal mind, a villain will always try to find the last place that we will think of looking for him. That place is usually somewhere he has been already, as he believes we will not expect him to return and so not look a second time."

Paul and Alex looked at each other, then back at Taylor.

"Inspector," said Alex, "I get the impression you are a very clever man. I think it is time for us to leave. Will you both be all right here?"

"Of course," Taylor answered. "You need to go as quickly as you can. I'll be fine in a few hours, and Mickey here can go and fetch the car shortly. Just make sure you find this monster and get rid of him." They rose and Wroughton moved with them to the door. "Good luck!" Taylor waved, and they stepped out into the hallway.

"I'll go and get the Porsche," Paul said, already on his way out of the front door. "You are not fully recovered and it's too far for you to walk down to the car park."

Alex nodded and was left alone with Wroughton, who seemed, for the first time in several hours, to be unsure of herself.

"I'm sorry," he said, "if I upset you."

"I understand," she answered. "I didn't know what was going on. I was going to phone for backup – you had to stop me."

"No," he said. "I mean the other time. I'm sorry. I should not have done what I did. It was unfair. Will you forgive me?"

She blushed and looked at the ground. "Do you see what's in people's minds all the time?"

275

"No – only when I wish to."

"Are you looking into mine now?"

"No."

"Thank you. For telling me I mean. What do you think will happen?"

"I may not come back. Malim is stronger than either of us. He may kill us. If that happens you must try to make people understand. He cannot be confronted. Perhaps you will find some way to destroy him, but you will never do it directly. You must think of some other way. Promise me, if anything happens to me you will not put yourself in danger."

In a rush he found her wrapped round him, hugging him fiercely.

"You will come back?" she whispered unsteadily. He returned her hug.

"I promise, I will try."

CHAPTER 28

Maylie and Amarisse reached the foot of the slope and stood looking out over the mile or so of flat exposed heath and riverbed that separated them from the eastern boundary of the settlement. The river that ran across the valley bottom, cutting the heath land in two, was wide, but shallow where the path ran up to the east gate. It was a natural ford, passable in summer as the streams coming off the crags slowed to a trickle. To the south, a large part of the distance was under cover of woodland, the remainder fenced off, used mainly for grazing.

Maylie knew the southern approach well and many times had kept watch on the comings and goings of the Family from the cover of the trees. But for their present purpose concealment might work against them. An open approach, she hoped, would signal that they were not a threat, and so reduce the risk of a challenge before they reached the gate. Word of two lone women in the valley would reach Rendail in seconds, she was sure, and she was counting on his curiosity to see them safely though to the inner pavements.

Maylie went in front, Amarisse following as they made their way slowly along narrow paths bordered on each side by gorse and brambles, in places waist high. Amarisse wished with all her soul that she was still standing on the top of the rise, her father's protective arms around her, shielding her from her own doubt. He had not spoken, but at their parting had pressed the snake's head dagger into her hand and closed her fingers around it. Then he had kissed her and silently walked away into the trees, leaving behind him not the slightest trace. It was as though he had vanished from the earth. It was really only then that she had absorbed the enormity of the task before her, and had been so numbed by it that Maylie had been forced to take her by the hand and lead her down the slope as though steering one who was blind.

On reaching the valley floor she recovered herself a little and, looking down, she realised she was still clutching the knife. She opened her right hand to look at it, and with the fingers of the left she traced the engraved snake image from the tip of the tail right up to the glinting red eye in the perfectly formed head. On one side of the sheath was a small clip and she found that being dressed more or less in a man's clothes, she could slip the knife under them and clip it at her waist, secure and invisible next to her skin. It was as though Arghel had put a spell on the thing, for as soon as it was in place she felt his presence there with her, an echo of his strength surrounding her, giving her the courage she needed to go on. Maylie had been watching her, and seeing her find her resolve squeezed her hand gently. Then, together, they started the long trek across the heath towards the heart of Rendail's power.

The outer boundary of the settlement was marked by a low wooden fence no more than five or six feet in height, sufficient to deter casual wanderers and scavenging animals, but clearly not intended to provide any other form of defence. Given the nature of the inhabitants, any greater form of protection was unnecessary. Beyond the fence a scattering of dwellings, some stone, but mostly of wood, had been constructed on the wide tract of no mans land that separated the outer fence from the massive inner complex. This inner structure was built entirely of stone and accessible only by passing through one of three gates, either to the East, West or South. The heart of the settlement was laid out in a great square, completely enclosed by stone buildings, all three stories high.

A wide pavement separated these from the largest building of all. It formed three sides of a square with a large courtyard in the centre, the eastern boundary of which was formed by a low iron fence running from the north side of the building to the south, access provided by a great iron gate. All the doors and windows faced the courtyard, the outer walls composed of smooth, solid stone. Both Maylie and Amarisse had absorbed the images of the layout that Arghel had shown them from his own mcmory. As they drew closer they saw that it had changed little over the centuries, apart from an increase in the number of buildings inside the outer fence. He had made them repeat several times the locations of all the gates, the paths that were most closely watched, the places where it was possible to evade detection, at least for a short time, should they need to hide themselves. Maylie had pointed out the unlikelihood of an opportunity for any sort of concealment, given the nature of their mission, but he had insisted nonetheless. So, they were armed with a fairly complete map of their destination as they made their way slowly towards the east gate.

Maylie became increasingly anxious as they approached the outer fence, but said nothing to Amarisse. She had expected to gain some sense of being observed, for although they had both made their minds silent they were clearly visible now to any watcher within the settlement. But she detected nothing. The oppressiveness that both she and Arghel had felt in the preceding two nights had lifted. It was as though a path was being made clear for them, inviting them closer, drawing them in.

The soft undercurrent of the Dance was there, as always, in the background of her consciousness, but no thought was directed towards them, not even in curiosity. The path on which they were travelling had grown wider and they were now able to walk side by side. Together, they reached the fence, followed its line until they came to the wide gap that gave access to the east gate. She sensed the unease in her young companion. The long road leading up to the gate was deserted, but there were people all around. She could feel them – a host of signatures, running through her mind but outwardly silent and still. There were no voices, no footsteps, not even the sound of a child, although she could sense the presence of many throughout the settlement. Still the air around them was light, bearing no trace of hostility. She felt Amarisse reach out for her, and hand in hand they began the long shallow climb towards the gate.

They had gone about half way when Maylie felt a tug on her arm. She looked up and followed Amarisse's stare, back the way they had come. The tall figure of a male, arms folded across his chest, was leaning against the boundary fence, watching their progress. They stopped. Maylie took a step towards the figure and immediately felt resistance – no more than a gentle push backwards. She took a second step and this time the pressure was stronger, a warning. Amarisse had gone white and tightened her grip on Maylie's hand. There was no option but to go forward. Maylie turned, and giving Amarisse's hand a tight squeeze they continued on to the gate.

When they reached it they found it open and apparently unguarded. They passed under the great archway and found themselves on the wide pavement of the square, facing the iron fence on the east side of the central compound building, some two hundred paces in front of them. Like everywhere else, the place looked deserted, but the presence of many women, hidden behind the walls, made both of them shudder. On either side the pavement stretched away to the far distant corners of the square, completely empty, no sign of life.

The two women had taken perhaps a dozen paces when they felt, rather than heard, a slight movement. Looking back, they saw that two more tall, powerful males had appeared on either side of the archway behind them. Like the first, these two made no attempt to approach them, but leaned lazily against the stone, regarding them without curiosity. However, the intent was clear, that it would be useless to try to go back the way they had come.

Maylie stood still, unsure whether to turn to the left or the right. She put an arm round Amarisse, who had begun to tremble although she kept her head up, a look of grim determination on her face. Then, once again, she felt a gentle pressure, this time in the middle of her back, pushing her to the right. Without looking back she obeyed the silent command and they both set off towards the right hand corner of the square.

Under the gaze of the two watchers at the arch, they finally covered the seemingly endless distance to the edge of the east side and turned left along the north pavement. They walked on until they reached half way, then Maylie suddenly stopped. She felt the pressure again, all around her, preventing her from moving either forward or back. She looked at Amarisse, who was clearly restrained by the same force, her eyes wide with fear. To their right there was a thick arched wooden door, standing open. Maylie took a tentative step towards it. No resistance. Stepping across the threshold they found themselves in a wide flagged chamber, the height of which extended to the roof. On their right, a staircase was set into the wall leading up to brightly lit corridors that stretched back as far as they could see. On the ground floor there were no other doorways apart from the one through which they had entered. The only sound was the echo of their footsteps on the stone.

They advanced to the centre of the chamber and waited. As they came to a halt there was a soft click behind them as the outer door closed. For the first time, Maylie sensed a slight heaviness in the air. The next moment she felt momentarily dizzy, and realised that they had both been subjected to a swift but thorough interrogation. The source seemed without direction, the trace of it lingering all around them, a nebulous, detached presence colouring the air, remaining just outside her grasp. She didn't need to reach out to recognise it.

Her voice clear and firm, and with an air of authority she didn't feel, she said aloud, "Come, Rendail. Or are you afraid to show yourself to us?"

There was a faint shimmer of anger, immediately restrained, followed by a hint of amusement. A silence followed in which the air around them became even more oppressive. Then, they heard soft, unhurried footsteps above, and looked up to see the unmistakeable figure of Rendail standing at the top of the staircase, regarding them calmly, the shadow of a smile on his lips.

Maylie met his gaze as he slowly descended the stair, his eyes locked on her, completely ignoring Amarisse. He came to a halt not two feet from her and let his eyes wander over her in a casual inspection. Then he reached out and very gently took her chin in his hand, turning her face first to the left, then the right. Apparently satisfied, he let his hand drop and inclined his head in appreciation. Finally he spoke, his voice dripping into the air like warm honey.

"Welcome, Maylie. I am pleased you have decided to visit me at last."

Maylie felt her heart sinking and tried as hard as she could to keep her mind blank, impassive. But she saw a slight nod and another flicker of a smile.

"I understand," he said, a touch of sympathy in his tone. "You had hoped to surprise me and I have disappointed you. However, I can assure you that I suffer no disappointment. I am delighted to see you, even more so as you have brought me a gift."

He turned to Amarisse, who seemed rooted to the spot, her eyes fixed on the ground, refusing to look at him.

"My son did well," he said, "to sire such a charming child. Come, your courage has brought you this far. Are you so afraid now that you will not look at me?"

He put out a hand and caught up one of her long curls, let it run across his fingers. Maylie sensed a change come over Amarisse. Until now she had been frozen with terror, but at Rendail's touch she passed beyond fear and into a realm far more dangerous. Slowly, she lifted an arm, and taking Rendail's wrist pushed his hand away from her. Without letting go she raised her eyes and, looking straight at him, said quietly, "I have not come to see you, Grandfather. I have come to kill you."

Maylie stopped breathing. From where she was standing she could feel the weight of Rendail's thought bear down on Amarisse as though to crush her, but Amarisse held firm, her eyes fixed unwaveringly on him. As suddenly as it had fallen the weight lifted and he laughed quietly, bowing his head in acknowledgement. She let go of his wrist and he stepped away.

"Perhaps," he said, his tone still soft, "we should find somewhere more comfortable in which to continue this fascinating conversation."

He gestured for them to ascend the staircase, following on a few paces behind. When they reached the top he directed them through the first door to the right off the long corridor. They

282

found themselves in a large room with a high arched window, sparsely furnished with simple matting covering the floor, a plain, low table in the centre. He seated himself comfortably on the floor and indicated that they should do the same on the opposite side of the table. At once a young boy appeared, seemingly out of nowhere, carrying food and drink. They heard him take in his breath sharply as he caught sight of them, but he recovered himself and with a nervous glance towards Rendail, set down the tray and disappeared, closing the door behind him.

"You must forgive the boy," Rendail said, his tone conversational. "His surprise is understandable. Women are not permitted to enter these buildings and so your presence here, although delightful, is somewhat unusual. As you are visitors, an exception to our Rule has been made in your case."

He paused to pour three cups of wine from a large jug on the table and pushed one towards each of them. Taking the third he leaned back against the wall. Maylie took hers with a cautious nod, but Amarisse remained still, glaring at Rendail with a look of pure hatred. He ignored it and, addressing Maylie, continued, "Now that we are settled, I think it is time you told me why you have come."

Again, Maylie felt the cold humour brush across her senses, seeking to sap her resolve. She replied, as evenly as she could manage, "Perhaps it is simply that I wished to meet my father. After all, you sired me. Is that not a natural thing?"

He closed his eyes and appeared to think about this for a moment then, without opening them, said, "An interesting notion, but I think not. If you have no objection I would be pleased to give you some assistance. You came here believing that I had no knowledge of you. In that," he opened his eyes and fixed them on Maylie, "you were mistaken. Your purpose was to distract me and thus allow this child," he gestured towards Amarisse, "whose gift is already considerable, to hunt through my mind seeking the resting place of my heir. You thought me unaware of her quite remarkable talent. In that you were also mistaken. Her father is waiting for this information and intends to dispose of his brother at the earliest suitable opportunity. Oh, and of course, the child

283

has a most extraordinary desire to dispose of me. I believe those to be the main facts – unless you have anything to add?"

Maylie struggled to keep her expression calm, her mind still, but she knew it was a vain effort. Rendail was reading the surface emotions easily and she felt his satisfaction coming back at her, restrained, polite, almost tinged with regret at being the cause of her discomfort. Denial was pointless. After a long silence she found her voice and, fighting to keep it even, asked, "How long have you known this?"

"If you mean," he replied, at the same time sending a silent acknowledgement of her admission, "how long have I known of your existence, I have known from the very beginning. Or do you think me so blind that I cannot distinguish my own child from a dead gutter rat? However, it pleased your mother to believe she had deceived me and so I did not disillusion her."

Maylie was unable to prevent herself from betraying her confusion. He waited until she had composed herself, then went on, "As for the child, she is clever, but young, and she could not help but show herself to me just now, having, as she does, her father's impetuous nature. Now, regarding the rest, I regret that I have information that may cause you some pain. I have to tell you that your son has failed in his somewhat clumsy attempt to drive Malim back to this time. Unfortunately, I do not know whether he and his half breed child still live. It is, however, certain that they were harmed. You must be aware that Malim does not act with a great deal of restraint."

Maylie lowered her eyes, utterly defeated. She heard Amarisse stifle a cry, which Rendail appeared not to notice.

"Do not be too distressed," he said, his voice gentle, filled with sympathy, still directing his words only at Maylie. "You can be assured that Malim will take great care of his property."

There was no mistaking his meaning. It was too much for Amarisse. Before Maylie could stop her she leapt to her feet and with a cry of desperation launched herself at Rendail. She never reached him. She found herself thrown backwards, slamming painfully into the wall behind her. She hit the ground, stunned, and stayed still. Rendail did not move or even turn his head.

284

Maylie started up, but he touched her arm gently and shook his head.

Maylie sat back down as Rendail continued, "I have to say that I have enjoyed our conversation very much. However, you have come a long way and I would fail in my duty as a host if I did not allow you to rest. A room has been prepared for you. I look forward to our next meeting."

He rose and, at the same moment, the door opened and a man appeared. He nodded respectfully to Rendail and gestured for Maylie to follow. She looked back at Amarisse, who was once more alert but had not moved from where she had fallen.

"Do not be concerned," said Rendail, following her glance. "I will take good care of her." He smiled in a manner that Maylie found far from reassuring, but she had no choice and so allowed herself to be ushered from the room.

Rendail waited until the sound of Maylie's footsteps had faded, then finally turned his attention to Amarisse. He walked over to her and held out a hand to help her up. She shrank away from it and struggled to her feet.

"As you wish," he said softly. "Come, I have something to show you."

He walked out into the corridor and, when she did not move, beckoned for her to follow. Warily, staying several paces behind, she followed him down the stairs and out onto the pavement. The place still appeared deserted even though it was still broad daylight, sometime just after noon. Walking swiftly, so that she almost had to run to keep up, he led her back the way they had come until she stood once again by the arch of the east gate. But then he turned inwards, taking her up to the great central building. They passed through the open iron gate in the centre, across the courtyard and through a side door into a large room. Once inside, he closed the door and leaned back against it, watching her closely.

She did not need to ask him why he had brought her here. She recognised her father's former home at once. The room was large, with just one window opening out onto the courtyard. It was entirely barren of furniture of any sort, the floors and walls of smooth, polished stone. She walked slowly from one end to the other, past the great stone fireplace in the middle of the far wall and back to the centre, her heart pounding as hard as her father's had done when, as a child, he had stood in that very spot. Her hatred, like his, rose up, threatening to supplant her fear.

She felt Rendail come up behind her and turned to face him. He nodded and said, "I understand." Without taking his eyes off her he reached down and unsheathed the long curved knife that hung at his side. She shuddered at the sight of it and was suddenly convinced he meant to kill her. But instead he held it out on his open palm, the hilt towards her, and said, "If you desire my death, take it. It is sharp enough. I will not hinder you."

He was holding it less than a foot from her. For an instant her senses deserted her. She could not even hear her own breathing, which had seemed so loud a moment before. The world faded around her so that all she could see was the knife on his outstretched hand. She had but to lift her arm to take it and she, her father and Maylie would be free of him forever. But her body had turned to stone, and no matter how desperately she willed it, her arm would not move.

She heard his quiet, mocking laughter and the spell broke. She tried to seize the knife from him, but not fast enough. In a swift movement he snatched it away, grabbing her wrist with his free hand. He gave it a sharp twist, forcing her onto her back, and she screamed as he brought his knee heavily down onto her chest, pinning her to the stone floor. Weeping with terror, she felt him take hold of her hair and bring down the knife, hacking away handful after handful of it, the blade passing just a fraction of an inch from her scalp. He did not stop until there was nothing left.

Finally she felt the pressure on her chest lift, saw him sit back and carefully replace the knife in its sheath. He leaned forward and lifted her head until her face was just an inch from his own. In a low voice, he said, "We have a saying here. If you wish to pull a wolf's tail, be sure that you are ready for its bite." He stroked her tear stained cheek gently with a finger, then set her down and walked away. As the door closed behind him she heard the sound of a sliding bolt, followed by his footsteps fading away across the courtyard.

CHAPTER 29

Karisse opened her eyes to pitch darkness. She was lying on her side on what felt like wet earth, the cold moisture from the air clinging to her skin. Her nostrils were thick with the combined smell of damp and congealed blood. There was something sharp, perhaps a stone, digging into her cheek and she tried to shift her position slightly. The tiny movement sent a spasm of pain through her, forcing her to remain still. She closed her eyes again, trying to piece together a sequence of events from the jumble of disjointed images fading in and out of her memory. The effort made her head ache and she felt a slow trickle of blood run across her forehead, down the side of her face to join the sticky pool that had formed on the ground by the corner of her mouth. Shivering with cold, she forced herself to concentrate, to take her mind back to the start of it all, to the moment when everything had started to go so badly wrong.

* * *

The waiting seemed to go on forever. She felt Malim's approach like a great tide rolling in on her, and it took every particle of her strength to keep her mind receptive without giving her companions away. When she finally heard the sound of the latch and soft footsteps in the hallway, she was all but exhausted. She sat still as stone, cross legged on the sofa with her hands in her lap and her eyes closed, trying to think of nothing. A second later he was standing right in front of her, so close she could feel the heat from his body, the movement of the air from his breath.

She looked up and saw for the first time with her own eyes a face that might have been breathtaking in its beauty had it not been so clear a mirror of his thought. The expression was one of complete triumph and uncontrollable lust, and beneath the surface she felt his utter contempt washing over her, turning her blood to ice. He reached for her, and as his hand closed on her wrist she

288

heard a sound outside, a scraping on the gravel just beyond the front door. She realised that this was a stranger, one without the gift, coming to the door with no knowledge of the danger that lay inside. Malim had heard it too and was still, listening, his other hand tight around her neck.

There was a second crunch of a foot on the gravel and, without letting go of her, he let loose a dreadful force in the direction of the intruder. In her mind's eye she saw the man crumple to the ground, but just before he fell she felt Paul's mind open, reaching out to protect the stranger from Malim's fire. Then Paul's thought went silent, like a candle flame snuffed out. She looked at Malim in dismay. There was no way he could not have seen it. He was quite still, staring questioningly towards the door. Then he turned his gaze on her, and the look on his face left no room for doubt.

A split second had been all he needed to lay the trap open, to see what they were attempting to do. With startling swiftness he fell on her, not with his mind but with his fists. In a savage rage he rained down blow after blow until she ceased to feel them and her eyes lost focus. Then he dragged her out of the cottage, flung her into the back of the four by four and drove off like a madman over the bumpy turf.

She remembered trying to crawl to the rear door. He saw the movement and, slamming the car to a halt, leapt onto her and bound her hands behind her with some sort of metal wire, so tightly that it bit into her wrists and she felt blood running down into her palms. The last thing she heard before drifting down into peaceful darkness was a sharp splintering sound as he brought his boot down onto her ankle.

* * *

She had no idea how long she had been lying there. Her head ached from a deep cut that was more recent than the others. She felt the stiffness of drying blood on her clothes. Her wrists were still bleeding, encased in the sharp wire, and her ankle too, although mercifully she could not feel it if she stayed still. There was a sharp pain in her chest and taking even shallow breaths was painful. He was close by, somewhere up above, watchful, alert for any sign of pursuers. But her own scan told her there were none. In all likelihood Paul and Alex were already dead, together with the unfortunate stranger who had so innocently crossed Malim's path.

Soon she would die too, unless he decided to keep her alive. Every so often, his thought rested on her and she strove to stay silent, willing him to believe she was still unconscious. Apart from his presence there was total silence and complete darkness. Only the lack of air movement told her she was not outside. She began to drift again. She imagined Arghel was with her, holding onto her. She heard him say, "You must stay. What shall I do if you are gone?" Then her daughter, pleading with her; "Wait, Mother. You cannot come back yet. I will die. Father will die. You must wait."

"No time," she heard herself say. "No time left. Stay with me. Stay with me until I go to sleep."

She thought she felt Arghel's kiss, his touch on her forehead, and all the pain stopped. His body was warm and she snuggled into him, feeling the chill recede from the air. She wanted to talk to him but was too tired, so she closed her eyes and let herself float down into a dreamless sleep.

It might have been the noise of the door slamming open that woke her, or the blinding light that hit her face, ripping past her closed eyelids and dashing against the back of her head like a hammer. She heard Malim's footsteps, above her at first, then coming down what must have been a staircase, getting closer. She didn't try to move and the pain in her head prevented her from opening her eyes.

"Leave me," she thought. "Let me go back to sleep."

He was standing over her and she felt him nudge her body with his foot, but it didn't hurt. Nothing hurt any more except her head. Then her head was yanked back so that she was forced to open her eyes, look straight into his face.

She summoned her last ounce of strength and through the blood that was coming up into her mouth whispered, "Your passion has betrayed you. You have destroyed what you most desire and can take nothing now from my blood. Arghel has beaten you. Always, he has beaten you." She watched, calm, without fear as he drew back his fist to deliver the final blow. It never fell.

There was a noise like thunder coming from somewhere behind him and she saw his eyes widen in surprise. His fist still raised, he slowly twisted his body in the direction of the sound. There was a faint smell of burning that made no sense to her. Malim was motionless. It was as though time had stopped, leaving him frozen in space, his head turned away from her, his arm suspended in the air ready to continue its downward arc the moment the clock began to tick again.

Suddenly, in a ferocious outpouring of power, she felt his whole being rise up and out of his body, whipping the air into a violent storm. She heard the loud thud of something hitting the floor on the other side of the room, then a heavy pressure across her chest. It took her a moment to realise that Malim's body was on top of her, crushing out what little remained of her breath. As her sight faded she found herself staring at what had once been the back of his head, but which was now just a splintered mass of hair and bone, his blood pouring onto her face and mingling with her own.

* * *

The voice was calm, soothing. It was in her mind, a Dancer's silent voice. There was a hand too, warm beneath her sweater, stroking her stomach gently, and a light tingling in the touch that sent a heat right through her body. A moment later she felt the hurt again underneath the hand, growing every time it moved. The voice said, "Hold on, Grandmother. Hold on. They are here now. They are coming. Not long. Hold on."

She didn't understand the words and didn't want the pain. But the voice was insistent, making her listen, pressing her to answer, to give some sign that she had heard. It spoke again, concerned. "Grandmother, you must hear me. Hang on. Don't die, Grandmother. You must not die." She thought, tried to make a question, failed and settled for a single word.

"Who?"

The whisper in her mind said, "Michael."

She repeated the word; "Michael."

"Hush," said the voice. "They are here. Live." Then the hand and the voice were gone.

There were footsteps, two people, coming to the door, down the steps, their low voices in the air. Two Dancers, their minds numbed by the horror of what they saw. She heard one of them start to weep, the other thinking, "Dead, all dead."

"No." She tried to make the thought carry to them. "Alive. Not dead."

They did not hear. One of them came to her, kneeled beside her, stroking her hair. She tried again, this time making her lips move.

"Alive."

She felt a recoil, realisation following close behind. Then they were both there, hands all around her, taking the wire off her wrists, lifting her, carrying her away to somewhere warm, cutting away the bloodstained clothes. One of them ordered her mind to sleep and she didn't resist. When she opened her eyes again she was in a warm bath of sweetly scented water, supported by a strong arm, the other gently sponging away the blood and dirt from her face and hair.

"Alex," she whispered, trying to look up into his face.

"Hush," he said softly. "Yes, I am here. Don't try to talk. We are here now."

"That's what Michael said. 'Hush' he said. 'Live'."

Alex looked concerned for a moment, then said, "Don't talk. You are not strong enough. You will have to stay quiet for a while yet. You are still half in dreams. We will talk later, when you are feeling well again."

He lifted her out of the bath into a nest of warm towels, then carried her into the next room and laid her on a soft bed, propping her head comfortably with thick pillows. He poured her a glass of warm milk and helped her to take a few small swallows, then took the glass away.

"It is best that you don't take too much into your stomach," he explained. "But a little at a time will do you good. Just a few sips when you are thirsty."

He sat on the bed next to her and she was able to see his face properly. He was drawn and tired and, beneath that, she could see that his eyes were filled with grief. He saw her studying him and said, "Not now. Later."

It was still an effort to talk, easier to use her mind as she asked, "Paul?"

"Alive. Don't be concerned for him. We are all tired and we are all hurting in one way or another. But he is well. He has been here while you were sleeping, and will come back soon so that you can see him."

She sighed with relief and reached out for the glass. He gave her another sip of the milk. She began to feel sleepy and relaxed back into the pillows, but as she did so the image came thudding back into her mind of Malim, face down beside her in the dirt, the blood pouring onto her from his shattered skull. The hideousness of it overwhelmed her and she began to cry.

Alex lay back on the bed beside her and took her in his arms.

"Don't worry," he said. "I won't leave you alone. None of us should be alone tonight."

As she closed her eyes she heard the door open and felt Paul come to lie on the other side of her. Together, the three of them sank into the dreamless sleep of exhaustion.

* * *

When she woke the sun was streaming in through the great window opposite the end of her bed. She recognised the room at once as the one she had occupied in Alex's house. She wondered briefly how she had come there, but did not dwell on it. She was warm and comfortable, and all seemed so still and quiet after a night filled with such terrible dreams. She caught sight of her arm resting on top of the thick quilt, the deep cuts forming a crisscross pattern across the back of her wrist. They had been cleaned and were beginning to heal slowly. A part of the dream. There was a movement by the window and she saw Alex sitting in an armchair at the end of the bed, watching her. Seeing her awake he got up and came to sit beside her.

"The healing will take some time," he said, feeling her forehead and examining the cuts gently. "We were a long time getting to you, so the injuries were not all fresh. In two, maybe three days, we will see."

She nodded, not ready to talk just yet, and found that her head no longer ached when she tried to move it.

"There is a man," he continued, "who would like to meet you. He has been waiting since early morning and I told him I would ask you as soon as you were awake. We can wait a little while, until you are strong enough, but if you can, it would help if you would talk to him."

She nodded again and with an effort said, "If you wish it." She felt that all decisions were beyond her, but heard the urgency behind his voice. It was important, but he didn't want to put pressure on her. "Tea," she said, remembering the sharp, invigorating taste of it from her day in the kitchen with Mary, what seemed a lifetime ago. "Tea, and then I will meet this man."

Alex smiled his thanks. "I will fetch tea immediately," he said, and added lightly, "and perhaps clothes?" She realised she was completely naked under the cover and, for the first time in what seemed like forever, smiled, then closed her eyes while he went to see to her request.

* * *

Inspector Taylor was in the lower cellar, trying to make a decision of his own. He surveyed the grisly scene with a furrowed brow; the body of Malim, lying just beyond the foot of the staircase, death resulting from a single rifle shot at close range. The assailant had not been an expert. Even at a distance of a few

294

feet the aim had been wild, slicing horizontally across the back of the head. Nevertheless, it had been efficient enough, taking away half the skull and a good portion of the brain. It was a mess.

The second body was on the other side of the cellar, the Winchester rifle, one shot fired, lying next to it. This body belonged to an elderly woman in her seventies, perhaps early eighties, Taylor estimated, cause of death a fall of some twenty feet from the top of the stairs to the floor beneath, resulting in a broken neck. And then there was the other victim, the kidnapped woman. A new bulb had been fitted so that the cellar was now brightly illuminated, and he could see the dark patches next to the man's body that were not his blood but hers. He walked carefully around them and, fishing a ballpoint out of his pocket, used it to pick up a length of bloodstained barbed wire which he examined carefully, his face wrinkling in disgust.

"He used this to tie her hands?" His tone was one of disbelief.

"Yes." Paul was sitting halfway down the steps, watching Taylor's examination of the scene. "It was the sort of thing he'd do," he added, his voice unsteady. Taylor grunted and carefully replaced the wire, then came up the steps to join the other man and they sat together staring out across the cellar, each wrapped in his own thoughts.

Eventually, Taylor spoke. "Given what I know of the two of you which, granted, is very little indeed, I find it hard to believe that a creature with skills – if that's the right word – such as yours could be capable of such things."

"Thankfully," Paul replied, "there are very few like him – none quite like him, except perhaps his father, and had he been here I doubt he would have made such a mess of things." He paused, and met Taylor's eye. "Of course, that doesn't mean we are not capable of acts of great violence. Sometimes, if we become angry, we do things we regret, as all men do. I …"

Taylor quickly interrupted him.

"Please – do not give me any sort of confession. I am quite happy in my own mind about the course of events, and any additional information might …well, muddy the waters of my mind, you might say. Best to leave things as they are for now, wouldn't you say?"

Paul stopped, puzzled. He found he could read nothing of what was in the Inspector's mind, but caught a definite warning in his eyes to say nothing further. Taylor continued, in a softer tone, "I'm sorry. About your mother." Paul gave a slight nod. "She was a brave woman," Taylor said, "but I can't understand how she managed to get so close to this character. From what I was told it was almost impossible for anyone to get anywhere near him. Yet she was able to get within a few feet and fire at him. It was the fall afterwards that was fatal. I can't explain it."

"Her mind was practically invisible, even to us," Paul replied, his voice strained with grief. "Only my father could hear her thoughts without an effort, as she could hear his, and then only over short distances. I doubt any one of us could have detected her, even Malim. And he was completely distracted. All the weight of his mind was on Karisse and he didn't expect to be disturbed."

Paul paused, then went on, "I know it is hard for you to understand Inspector, but my father loved Mary. Even though she changed and he didn't, he loved her with all his heart. He knew of her death before we entered the house. The part of his thought that he gave to her, to join them until her death, came back to him as we waited for Malim's watchfulness to waver. First we felt Malim fall, and then my father felt the end of my mother's life. You should be glad you do not have our gifts, Inspector, and can't feel his grief."

Taylor put a hand on Paul's shoulder. "Believe it or not," he said, "I understand, possibly better than you think." He hoisted himself to his feet and walked slowly back up the stairs, leaving Paul to grieve alone.

* * *

Karisse felt an immediate liking for the gentle, diffident man sitting at her bedside. Alex had been reluctant to leave her alone with him, but she had reassured him that she would call him if

296

she felt tired, and the policeman, standing quietly at the door, had convinced him that he would take care not to distress her. Alex had acquiesced finally, and left them alone. Taylor listened without interrupting or trying to hurry her as she related all she could remember of events since Malim's arrival at the cottage. Several times she faltered, finding it difficult to relive the memory, but he waited patiently, pouring her more tea and patting her hand encouragingly.

When she had finished he said nothing for a while, then asked her what she could remember about her time in the hospital. He seemed particularly interested in the director, Gerald Flynn, and the activities of the nursing assistants. He asked nothing about her journey from the hospital, or about Paul. Again, she answered as best she could and he seemed satisfied. Alex had told her that the Inspector knew, in basic terms, where she was from and why she had come, but she could feel the confusion in his mind. He had no doubt as to the truth of it, but to him it seemed so impossible, was so beyond his experience that his normal assumptions, that the rules by which he acted in his role as an upholder of the law no longer helped him. He had no idea what to do.

"I have to go back," she said. "As soon as I am well enough I must go back to Arghel, away from here. I have done what I came to do and I should not stay here any longer. My mate and my child will be waiting for me. You understand that, don't you?"

Taylor nodded. The situation was impossible. He had the dead body of a man who should not exist, shot by an elderly woman in the defence of a woman that was about to disappear, in the home of two men who were not, in his view, whatever they claimed to the contrary, entirely human. It would be a very tricky court case to say the least. Already he had broken two rules that gave his professional life meaning, and he was about to break another. He had said nothing to the authorities about Paul. According to his duty he should have called in the murder scene the moment it was discovered. Now he was on the verge of standing by while a victim and principal witness became

297

invisible. He sighed and scratched his head. Thanking her for her patience and cooperation he left her and found Alex waiting outside in the hallway, ready to go back to her side as soon as the interview was over. He motioned for Alex to wait.

"She's fine," he said. "Resting. I need to speak to you for a few minutes if you can spare them."

Alex conducted him down the hall and into the sitting room, where they seated themselves opposite each other. Taylor came straight out with what was on his mind.

"I have to report this in a few moments," he said, apologetically. "I don't really have a choice."

Alex nodded. "Of course, Inspector, I understand. None of us here will try to stop you."

"I didn't think for a moment that you would," Taylor replied. "Tell me, what would happen if our forensics team analysed the blood down there, or Malim's body? Would there be any indication that anything was not – normal, if you see what I mean?"

Alex thought for a moment, then said, "I have no idea. I am sure there are differences in that respect, but what they are or whether modern science could detect them I simply don't know. My instinct says not. After all, Karisse must have been examined during her time at the hospital, and nothing untoward was noticed then. I see your problem though. If something is found that couldn't be explained away, it might be – awkward."

Taylor mulled this over, then nodded and went on, "I have a theory. My theory is that a violent criminal, very probably under the influence of some kind of drug, took prisoner a young woman and brought her to this house, knowing it to be empty. However, his arrival was observed by the housekeeper who, in a state of great agitation, grabbed a rifle that just happened to be handy, you understand, for her own protection against this dangerous intruder. She followed him to the cellar where she saw him abusing his captive. She must have made a noise because he turned and saw her, and was about to attack her when she let off a warning shot to frighten him. But being unused to firearms it turned out that her warning shot missed – if you see what I mean

– because it actually hit him and was the unfortunate cause of his death. The poor lady stepped backwards in shock and fell." Taylor stopped, seeing Alex's eyes cloud with pain. "I'm sorry. This must be very painful for you, I know."

Alex acknowledged the policeman's sympathy and waved a hand for him to continue.

"Well," Taylor went on, "as I said, she fell and, during the confusion, the captive woman was able to crawl away from the scene. After a while, she recovered enough to make her way from the house and may never be found. We have the evidence in the cellar to prove she was there of course, and we can show that the person who dispatched the intruder is also beyond our justice. I am sure the authorities will be very sorry that such a terrible event took place in your house. Well, that's my theory, and regardless of any forensic evidence I would think it is a fairly reasonable one. I could stretch a point and make my call in, say, two hours. That young lady should be as far away from the scene of her trauma as possible, don't you think?"

Alex rose and held out his hand. Taylor took it and shook it warmly.

"You don't have to do this," Alex said. "We never expected to survive, and we don't wish to create any difficulties for you."

Taylor nodded. "I think that if your friend stayed it might create even more difficulties. Best to keep things simple, yes?" The two men walked together downstairs to the front door. "I suppose I had better let my colleague know I'm all right. I left her at the hotel, you know. She was a little tired. But she will be delighted you are well. I hope I can convey your good wishes to her?"

"Yes, of course," Alex answered. "Tell her…" He stopped and sighed. "Tell her we are all grateful for what she has done to help us. And say goodbye to her for me. Will you do that?"

"I understand," Taylor said softly. "I'll tell her."

They shook hands again and Taylor made his way out into the late morning sunshine to find a nice warm spot in the garden where he could doze for the next couple of hours.

CHAPTER 30

It was past midnight now. Torches had been lit in the courtyard, sending dim fingers of light through the high window that were swallowed by the darkness long before they reached the ground. Amarisse had been left alone for more than twelve hours in the barren room. No one had brought her any food or drink and she had eaten nothing since early morning. She was filthy and desperately wanted to wash, but there was no water. Outside, the settlement had come to life and she could hear movement and voices, the opening and closing of doors, women out in the courtyard speaking together softly. Occasionally, footsteps came close to the bolted door, but they never stopped and the door did not open. She sat huddled against the far wall, her head resting on her knees, her hands clasped tightly together to stop herself from reaching up to feel the ugly little tufts that were all that remained of her long, glossy curls.

She was desperate to know what had become of Maylie. Ever since night had fallen, plunging her into almost total darkness, the need for her companion had done battle with the fear of Rendail, who, she was sure, would know the moment she opened her mind. Eventually, the darkness and her thirst persuaded her, and she resolved to search with her mind for Maylie. Even if Rendail were to detect it and come to stop her, he might at least give her something to drink. She let her thoughts sink down into the Dance, hoping that Maylie had opened her own mind enough to allow them to find each other.

There was a crackling somewhere across to her right and she felt suddenly warm. Opening her eyes, she found she had not moved – she was still hunched in a corner of the room, in the shadows, away from where the fire was casting its flickering light. But the room had changed. It was no longer bare stone. There were large square mats scattered on the floor and the walls had bright woven hangings. The room was divided into areas, in one place a long low table and in another, piles of rugs and furs for sleeping. Candles burned in little holders all around the walls and the door was propped open with a stone. The effect was one of sparse comfort. There was bread on the table and cold meat, and she swallowed hard to keep back her hunger.

Footsteps echoed out in the courtyard and a woman came in carrying wood. She kicked away the stone and swung the door closed with her foot. Amarisse recognised her at once. She watched as her grandmother, Sherenne, crossed to the fireplace and heaved the logs onto the hearth, then went over to a large barrel just inside the door and scooped out a pitcher of water, pouring some into a small bowl to clean her hands. She hadn't noticed Amarisse, hidden in the shadows.

Taking a deep breath, not sure whether or not she would be heard, Amarisse called out softly, "Grandmother?"

Sherenne took in her breath and turned round, peering into the corner. "Who is it? Who is there?"

"Amarisse, Grandmother. Amarisse, daughter of Arghel." She shifted slightly so that Sherenne would see her, but found she could not move from her place in the corner. Bringing a candle, Sherenne crossed the room and held it up to examine the intruder more closely.

She stared at Amarisse in disbelief, taking in every detail. Then she reached out to touch the shaven head, but Amarisse pulled away and felt a tear roll down her cheek.

Sherenne's expression softened and she said, her voice full of compassion, "Oh, you poor child. Rendail has done this, I know it. Why are you here? Did he steal you from your father, just as he stole me from mine? Or is Arghel dead? Please tell me that he lives and that Malim did not destroy him."

"My father is alive," replied Amarisse, "and he is here. He has come to kill Malim, but we don't know how to find him and Rendail has imprisoned me here. I was trying to find Maylie but I came here instead. I don't know how or why."

"Maylie? Maylie is here?" Sherenne looked horrified. Quickly, Amarisse explained, and Sherenne listened, her face composed and thoughtful. When Amarisse finished her tale

Sherenne got up and paced the floor, her brow furrowed in concentration.

Suddenly, she stopped in her tracks, took in a breath and said, "I think I know where Malim hides himself. I am not certain, but of all the places, it is the safest. Do you remember the chamber below Rendail's rooms? You must have entered it to reach the rooms above."

Amarisse nodded. "There was nothing there but stairs and only one door, the one by which we entered."

"There is another door," said Sherenne. "It is cleverly hidden and leads to a chamber beneath the floor. It is behind the stones on the wall opposite the entrance door. I don't know how it opens. But Arghel will never reach the chamber without Rendail knowing of it. Always, he has his eye on that house. Even if Arghel reached the place he would need time to open the door. It is impossible. He will only go to his death if he attempts it."

Amarisse thought, then said with conviction, "I will find a way. Father must find Malim. I will help somehow."

Sherenne was about to say something else when they both heard a soft tread coming towards the door.

"Rendail," said Sherenne in a whisper. "Go. If you give this information to Arghel, tell him to be careful – and tell him he has a very brave and beautiful daughter." She kissed Amarisse and moved away to see to the fire.

Amarisse opened her eyes once more to the semi-darkness. Without hesitation she began her message to her father, concentrating only on him so that her thought would be heard by no one else. Although she felt no trace of him she knew he would hear her and, as if to reinforce the bond, she slipped her hand under her clothes and clutched the hilt of her dagger. By some miracle Rendail had not noticed it or, if he had, he had paid it no heed. As soon as she touched it she felt a little thrill run through her hand and up into her mind, like a tiny spark thrown from a fire. It was her answer. Arghel had heard and understood. At the same moment the door was flung open and she saw the unmistakeable outline of Rendail.

She crouched back into the furthest corner, afraid of what he might have heard. He seemed unconcerned, however, and stayed for a moment in the doorway, watching her. Then he came in carrying two torches and, closing the door behind him, placed them in niches in the walls, bathing the room in a comfortable glow. In his other hand he had a basket and placed it on the ground, taking care not to come too close to her. She could see bread inside, cheese and apples, and a jug of water.

"I hope I did not disturb your rest," he said, his tone light, his manner calm. Lowering himself to the floor, he helped himself to an apple from the basket and took a bite, regarding her all the while with a look of amused interest. When she didn't move, he took another apple and held it out to her. "Come, you must be hungry. I will not harm you. We have reached an understanding have we not? You still wish to kill me, I understand that. You, on the other hand, now understand that it would be unwise to threaten me again in my own house. I really suggest you eat. You will be of no help either to your father or to me if you starve."

He leaned forward and set the apple down, then sat back and waited. Amarisse tried to fight the hunger, not wishing to be any closer to Rendail than she was already, but in the end the sight of the food got the better of her fear and she came forward until she was within reach of the apple, grabbed it, and retreated just out of his reach. He smiled his approval and reached back into the basket, took out a cup and poured her some water, which he again placed on the ground but a little nearer to him. It was as though he was training a timid animal. He let her take the cup and drink, then refilled it for her. He shifted back slightly to allow her to come to the basket, and she sat there for a while, helping herself to bread and cheese. He didn't hinder her or speak to her while she ate, but kept his eyes on her, studying her, his chin resting on his hands.

Amarisse avoided his gaze, letting her eyes rest on the ground. When she had finished eating she looked up. She could read nothing from his expression, and found herself unable to decide whether his coming had been in response to the detection of her thought, or simply a coincidence. Somehow, the idea of its being a coincidence was not very convincing. He seemed to be taking great pains to put her at ease, sitting back, making no sudden moves. But the dangerous half smile that hovered constantly behind his eyes left her in no doubt that every word and action should be chosen with great care.

Keeping her voice as steady as she could she asked, "What have you done with Maylie?"

He raised an eyebrow slightly. "I am surprised," he said, "that one of your resourcefulness needs to ask that question."

Amarisse suppressed a tiny sliver of excitement. One of her questions had been answered. He knew she had entered the Dance, but not precisely what she had gained from it. He had assumed that her search had taken her to Maylie. He was perhaps unaware that she possessed the gift of memory, possibly because until a few moments ago she had been unaware of it herself. She realised something else. Although Rendail could easily scan any surface thoughts or strong emotions, it was possible that he was unable to break through the wall of silence with which she, her father and Maylie could surround themselves. It did not explain how he had known of Maylie since the beginning, but perhaps he had learned of that by other means. Assumptions, however, were dangerous, and she knew that any deviation in her thoughts from what he expected to see could only bring disaster.

She locked her hope away and said, with a look of confused sadness, "I tried to find her and couldn't. I fear for her. Please, won't you tell me what you have done with her?"

She felt the pressure of his thought on her for a moment, his eyes examining her closely, then, apparently satisfied, he answered, "Do not trouble yourself. Maylie has been given rooms every bit as comfortable as your own." He smiled pleasantly. "I promise you, she will not be harmed. She is, after all, my daughter, and so is very precious to me." He paused, then added with another smile, "You are both very precious to me."

"And what of my father?" asked Amarisse, just a touch of anger creeping into her voice. "Is he also very precious to you?"

For a moment she thought she had gone too far, as she felt his warning hang briefly in the air. But the threat receded and he said, very quietly, "My dear child, your father is the most precious to me of all. I grieved when he left me, and I desire nothing more than to see my son again after all these years. Now that you are here and, of course, his sister also, I have no doubt that my wish will be fulfilled. I am sure we will have a great deal to say to each other, and our reunion will be a most joyful event."

"Then," Amarisse persisted, disregarding the likelihood that she was now on very dangerous ground, "if my father means so much to you, why did you drive him away?"

She continued to look him in the eye with an expression of innocent enquiry. Incredibly, he did not seem to mind this interrogation, and replied quite calmly, "A fair question. However, I regret it is not one that I am prepared to answer. Suffice it to say…"

He stopped. Amarisse saw his eyes suddenly widen in surprise, and he turned his head towards the door as though listening intently. When he turned back to her the mask was gone, a look of pure horror in his eyes, the intensity of his emotion rushing through her like a storm. She knew the reason, it was plain in his thought – the image of Arghel, in the chamber, carefully seeking a method by which he could reveal the door that led to the hidden chamber below.

Rendail controlled himself with an effort, and with a slight inclination of the head whispered, almost respectfully, "What a clever child you are. I shall remember not to underestimate you in the future. However, I hope you will excuse me for the present. As you know, I have an urgent matter to attend to."

He rose, and Amarisse found herself frantically trying to think of some way to prevent him from reaching her father before he found a way to open the door. It seemed hopeless. She knew that Arghel could not withstand Rendail and Malim together, and so his only chance of success lay in her somehow delaying Rendail. He was on his feet and turning away from her. In desperation she sprang up and with a cry hurled herself at him, catching him full in the chest, knocking him a pace backwards.

He caught hold of her left arm, and she expected him to simply thrust her away, but to her amazement, nothing happened. He simply stood still, staring at her, his hand locked around her arm. Her body was pressed to his, so close she could feel the rise and fall of his chest as he breathed. She waited for a reaction to come, but still he stood as though he had, in the space of a second, been turned to stone. Then, very slowly, he took pace back and then another, pulling her with him until his back was against the wall, a yard or so from the door. His eyes held her, and in them she saw a new sentiment. The cold humour was gone and with it all trace of anger. In its place she saw an unmistakeable glow of pride.

Her right hand felt warm, sticky. She looked down and saw her fingers wrapped round the hilt of the snake's head dagger. The blade was entirely buried in Rendail's side and blood was flowing out over the hilt, spreading across her hand, soaking into the front of her shirt. With his left hand he held her right hand fast, so that she could neither withdraw the blade nor let it go, and he slowly slid down, pulling her with him until they were both sitting on the stone floor.

She tried to pull away, but he did not loose his grip on her for an instant. However, he prised her fingers from the hilt of the knife and held her hand fast in his so that she would not attempt to pull it out of the wound. His breathing was shallow but strong, and he spoke quietly and clearly.

"No," he said. "You cannot serve any purpose by going to him now. It is between Arghel and his brother. We can no longer interfere." He paused, as though using his voice was causing him some pain, then recovered himself and continued, "You really are a remarkable child. There is even a possibility that you may have achieved your ambition. I should tell you that I have no desire for your death. For your sake, I hope your father survives this encounter. If he does not we may both find ourselves in some difficulty."

She tried to pull away from him again, but his grip was far too strong, and he held her fast beside him.

"Not yet," he whispered. "First there are things you must see. Surely you owe me that courtesy? If Arghel lives I would speak to him, for there are things he must know. Meanwhile, you cannot help him, and I will not allow you to destroy yourself for no purpose."

She knew he was speaking the truth, and that to go to her father now would be madness. She stopped trying to loose his hold and sat still. The effort of speech was draining him. He fell silent and, speaking only with his thought, he began to tell her those things he wanted her to know, show her what he wanted her to see. She opened her mind to him, and listened, and watched.

CHAPTER 31

"He has gone too far this time!" Karim paced the floor of his room, his face twisted with disgust. "Women! In his house! Intolerable!"

Thalis was getting tired of Karim's protestations. He helped himself to more wine, despite Karim's glare, and shrugged.

"So why don't you do something about it? Or are you all talk, Karim? It seems so from where I'm sitting. And who are they, anyway? Just a couple of strays who got lost on the way home from somewhere, or something more? Maybe he wanted a little fun before he put them with the rest of the brood mares. At least they are in the compound now, so they must be of adequate blood. Otherwise they would be dead."

Karims stare was withering. "Our Lord, Thalis, does not 'have fun'. Tell me – in all the years you have been in his service, have you ever seen him laugh? The day Rendail finds anything funny will be the day you stop being a half wit. And I don't see that happening for at least the next two hundred years. Tell me this. If they are strays, why did he confine the entire settlement to their houses? Why did he have Sevrian and his brood patrolling the gates to make sure nobody went outside? He's up to something, but what?"

He stopped pacing long enough to grab his cup and drain it noisily. Thalis winced. The man had no manners.

"I can't say I have found you to have much of a sense of humour either, Karim," he commented, then instantly regretted it as Karim threw his cup at the wall with enough force to dent the metal.

"And who would, if they had to rely on you for information? The heir has been gone for how long this time? Years! And you still haven't managed to find out where Rendail keeps his body. You were supposed to be Malim's keeper, his confidant. You are useless, Thalis, and if it weren't for the fact that Rendail would notice, I would break your limbs and drag you out for the wolves. Our Lord only knows why he hasn't done it himself!"

"It is impossible," Thalis complained. You know how tight minded Rendail is. Sevrian knows, I am sure, but he's almost as bad as our Lord. I've tried to threaten Nyran, but he knows as well as anyone else that all he has to do is call for his precious master. Rendail would be on me before I twisted the boy's little finger. Malim must be away from the settlement somewhere, and that's a lot of country. I've been out hunting, but the heir could be anywhere. I tell you, Karim, if you are so quick to criticise, you try it. You won't do any better, I guarantee it."

Karim flushed, then waved a hand and sat down.

"I know, Thalis. You do your best with what you have, little as it is. I can't take the risk, not yet. Rendail's spies have their eyes on me every minute of the day. I can't so much as cough without him hearing of it. It's infuriating!"

Karim shot up suddenly as a young boy burst into the room after a cursory knock on the door.

"How many times have I told you to wait until I invite you in?" Karim snapped, treating the servant to a hefty blow on the ear.

The boy cringed. "Forgive me, my Lord, but Estil is here. He says he has news about the women – the ones who ..."

"Yes, yes. I know which ones. Well, don't just stand there, tell him to come up. It's about time somebody had information about something!" he glared meaningfully at Thalis, who felt himself colour, and the boy shot from the room like a rabbit.

A moment later the gangly blonde figure of Estil appeared in the doorway. He was almost as uncomely as Karim, a little too thin for his height, shifty eyed and with a long hooked nose that made it difficult for Thalis to concentrate on anything else when he looked at his face. His solution was to look at it as little as possible. Estil did, however, have one attractive quality that made his shortcomings tolerable. He was of the line of Rolan, and thus was possessed of the gift to make his mind silent. It was much weaker than that of his illustrious grandfather, but nevertheless useful, especially given Estil's ability to lurk about in dark corners and overhear conversations without being seen.

Thalis nodded a greeting and sat up straight. This was going to be interesting.

"They are related," Estil announced, and grinned as Karim's eyebrows shot up to his hairline.

"What?" Thalis exclaimed, equally surprised.

Estil's grin grew wider. "One of them is his daughter. I managed to overhear Sevrian talking to Nyran in the reception hall, just before the guard closed the door. A woman of his blood, Karim – can you imagine? And she isn't that young. Didn't he have a daughter once? Do you think it's the same one?"

"Don't be stupid." Karim sat down, thoughtful. "It died. Before Malim was born. We all saw it. It's not that one, so where has it come from?" His brows knotted for a moment, then he laughed. "The old goat! Rendail must have found himself a stray. It happens. But he must have known he'd sired a brat. So why didn't he bring the woman back? He knows how valuable a child of the blood is – especially breeding stock. It doesn't make sense."

"It might," Thalis said, and to his satisfaction both pairs of eyes turned to him. "I know Malim's habits. He's taken a stray or two out in the woods, when his father gets tired of dead stock in the compound. Thing is, they never survive, or at least none have, to my knowledge. He uses them and leaves them for the crows. Like father, like son? It's possible Rendail left the woman wherever he found her and thought her long dead. Now, the daughter turns up and proclaims her blood. Actually, the mother must have died when the child was very young, else she would have warned the girl away from here. I can't imagine any woman *wanting* to join the Family, can you?"

Karim nodded his appreciation. "Finally, I remember why you are so useful, Thalis. I think you may have the root of it there. But what about the other? Who is she?"

"Her daughter?" Estil suggested. "She is much younger. Perhaps she is Rendail's grandchild. That would explain why she is currently languishing in Sherenne's old room. He wants to keep

310

her to himself, obviously – breed from her. He went in just now, and hasn't come out yet. Maybe she's not too keen on the idea." He frowned. "I don't think I would be either."

The comment drew a chuckle from Karim, but then he grew serious.

"Ah well. I suppose our Lord must have his pleasures. But I still think it was a strange way to go about things. To entertain women outside the compound is an outrage. Had they not come from outside the settlement it would have been a definite breach of the Rule. And I am still not entirely satisfied. I think, Thalis, that tomorrow we must redouble our efforts to find the resting place of the heir. Perhaps the time for action is closer than we think."

Thalis sighed and got up to take his leave. Tomorrow, he thought, was going to be a very long day.

CHAPTER 32

As dusk fell, Arghel emerged from the trees on the south side of the settlement and began to make his way across the fields towards the south gate. He made no attempt to conceal himself. His walk was casual, his mind entirely hidden save for a veneer of non committal anonymity. He had wetted his hair and scraped it back into a long leather thread with which he had bound its entire length to make the tell tale curls lie flat. In the growing dark it worked well enough. Over his shoulder he carried a large bundle of logs. There were men out in the fields tending the horses and others coming and going on the path to the gate, but no one paid him any heed. His stature and bearing were unmistakeably those of one of Rendail's people, and in the busy time just before nightfall the only challenge he might meet would be at the gate itself.

He was still not altogether happy with his strategy for getting past the gate. He had chosen this time as it was normally the busiest of the day, and he was resting his hope on a certain amount of complacency on the part of the two gatekeepers, who might not enquire further than a superficial scan. It was not a good plan, but there was no other way to reach the central square and so there was no alternative. The gates had not always been guarded. The innovation was, Maylie had told him, Malim's idea, not to guard against attempts to escape from inside, but to prevent those that were considered to be of inferior blood from entering. However, the new rule was effective both ways, regardless of its original intention.

He kept his pace steady and moved on, through the outer fence and up towards the gate arch. The timing was bad. A group had just passed through and there was no one between him and the gate. Another group was coming up behind, but too far back. and he dared not slow his pace. He could see the two guards now, one on either side of the arch, both watching his approach. He forced his mind to project an air of total placidity and kept walking. He felt a growing suspicion coming from one of them. He had made his mind too still, too calm, and this one was clever enough to realise that it was unnatural. He gathered himself to meet the challenge, outwardly appearing unconcerned. The guard started to walk towards him and he could feel the thought, questioning, unsure.

The man had covered about half the distance between them when he heard another voice, unspoken, urgent.

"Wait! Follow my lead. Do as I do. Turn round!"

He heard footsteps coming up quickly behind him and he turned to see a young blonde man running towards him, his face fixed in a cheery smile. He stopped to let the youth catch up, and the stranger clapped him fiercely on the back, holding up a string on the end of which dangled at least half a dozen large fish.

"What did I tell you, Uncle?" he demanded, putting on a triumphant expression and waving the fish in front of Arghel's nose. "Didn't I say that there was a good catch in the west stream? At least," he eyed Arghel's bundle, "It looks as though you haven't been completely idle. But should one of your advanced years be carrying such a burden? Here, I'll take the wood and you take the fish – they aren't quite so heavy."

Arghel gathered himself and set his face into an expression of indulgent humour.

"Indeed," he said, as cheerily as he could manage, "you are quite right. I am getting rather tired, and it's good for the young to develop their strength." He shrugged the bundle off his shoulder and pushed it so forcefully into his new companion's arms that the youth fell over backwards, while Arghel neatly caught the fish. As the boy scrambled to his feet, laughing, Arghel saw, in the corner of his eye, that the guard had stopped, uncertain.

"Come then, Uncle," the boy said loudly, "You may be able to live on twigs, but a growing boy needs frequent feeding."

He threw an arm round Arghel's shoulder and propelled him swiftly to the arch. The guard continued to eye the pair for a few seconds, then shrugged and turned away. Together, Arghel and his accomplice went on through the gate and into the great inner square.

"Keep smiling, keep walking," the boy conveyed, but Arghel needed no telling and let the boy lead him along the south pavement and in through the door of one of the large perimeter houses. They carried on along a corridor, up a flight of stairs, and finally into a large comfortable room with windows overlooking the outer fence. The boy set the bundle of logs in the fireplace and quickly returned to relieve Arghel of the string of fish, which he put in a pot on the other side of the hearth. That done, he turned to Arghel and heaved a huge sigh of relief. "My apologies," he said. "I hope I did rightly. You looked as though you were in need of assistance."

Arghel stared at the youth in amazement. He could not have been more than twenty years old, a handsome, fair haired boy with bright inquisitive eyes and a mouth that seemed to want to smile given the slightest excuse. He also had the gift of silence and was still keeping his mind veiled, speaking now only with his voice. He looked pale and there was a touch of strain in his face. His actions had obviously been quite spontaneous and had frightened him.

Arghel gave a shallow bow and replied, "I am indebted to you. You have done me a great service, although why you should risk yourself for me, I don't understand."

The boy shrugged. "I was curious. Only descendants of my grandfather, Rolan, possess the silent gift. I recognised it in you and had to find out where you had come from. When the guard came forward I thought you might be in difficulty and had to act quickly. I regret to say, I didn't think first, which is as well for you, as now I am shaking all over with fear and I don't think I would dare to do it again." Arghel smiled, and the youth responded with a sheepish grin. "But come," he continued. "We are quite safe here, and I would like to know who it is that I have saved from Malim's guards – that is," he added quickly, "if you are willing to tell me. My name is Rassim, son of Amal, son of Rolan. Welcome to my house."

"I am honoured to meet you," replied Arghel. "I knew your father well. I am Arghel, son of Rendail, son of Corvan."

Arghel saw Rassim's jaw drop in astonishment. The boy recovered himself and, with a shy smile, said, "I am most grateful you didn't tell me that before we walked through the gate," to which Arghel found himself laughing despite the gravity of the situation and took Rassim's hand.

There was nothing now to do except wait for word from either Amarisse or Maylie, and it seemed there was no better hiding place than where he was, so Arghel helped Rassim to build a fire and prepare and cook the fish. They talked little until their hunger was satisfied, then sat together by the fire.

"It is a strange day," Rassim commented. "First, the two women that came to Rendail, and now you." He looked at Arghel questioningly. "It would be a stranger thing if the two events were not in some way connected."

The reaction in Arghel's face answered his question. "You know of it?" Arghel asked. "How? Do you know what happened to them?"

Rassim nodded. "I know what I saw in the minds of those who knew something of it, but that is not a great deal. Except for four or five of those closest to Rendail, all of us were ordered to stay inside from dawn until just after noon. Two women came, one grown, one still very young. They spent some time with him – in his own house, which is a very unusual thing. I don't think it has ever happened before. Then they were taken into the compound and are still there, as far as I know."

"They were taken together?" asked Arghel, and Rassim caught the anxiety in his voice.

"You do know them then? No, not together. The older one was taken first, to one of the upper rooms I think. Then, a while later, the child was taken by Rendail himself, and locked in the room that had once belonged to his mate. They say..." He stopped, seeing the look on Arghel's face. Arghel nodded for him to continue. "They say that before he left her Rendail cut off all her hair. I'm sorry. That is all I know. I don't think he harmed her in any other way."

Rassim saw Arghel stiffen, but his expression revealed nothing, except perhaps for a slight narrowing of his eyes.

"I will understand," Rassim said "if you don't wish to tell me what your purpose is in coming here, you and these two women. But if I can be of any use to you, you need only ask. My father spoke often of you, always with great affection, and with great sadness too. He said that when you left us you took the future of our people with you, and it was his belief that you would one day return and take your brother's place as Rendail's heir."

"You have already been of great use to me," replied Arghel, "and I am grateful. But apart from allowing me to stay here for a short while longer, I would not ask anything more of you. I have come here to find my brother, and to destroy him. But I have no desire to take his place as Rendail's heir. In that, Amal was mistaken. Neither, I think, does my father have any wish that I should succeed him. If I accomplish my task and take Malim from him, it is unlikely Rendail will allow me to live. He will, by now, have other, more pleasing sons from which to choose."

Rassim glanced at Arghel in surprise.

"But that is not so. Since Sherenne's death Rendail has taken no other woman. My father was sure of it. When you left he ordered that her room be swept clean and all the contents burned. Then he went himself and closed it up, forbidding anyone to enter. In all those years the door has never been opened – at least, not until today. This child must be of great significance to him, to cause him to set his foot once more inside that room."

Arghel nodded, his face still without expression. "Of great significance indeed. She is my daughter. And the other, the elder of the two, is his firstborn, my sister."

This time, Rassim's look was one of shock.

"You let your child come here, to walk straight into Rendail's arms? Surely that was madness. She can't be more than eighteen years old at most." Then, seeing Arghel's lips tighten a fraction, he said quickly, "Forgive me. I know you would not place her in such danger without good reason."

"There was good reason, and not simply my own," Arghel replied, his face softening a little as he looked at the boy. "It was her choice to come with us and I could not dissuade her. She was afraid, but she knew we needed her and so she would not be left behind. If my father has hurt her…" He trailed off for a moment, staring into the fire. Then he said, "Rassim, I do not wish to put you in any more danger than you are already. But there is something you can do for me if you are willing."

"Of course," Rassim answered at once. "Tell me what you wish me to do."

"Will you try to see them, make sure they are not hurt? And if I am unsuccessful, will you watch over them, perhaps even try to help them to leave this place? It is a lot to ask, I know, but…"

"You know I will. But you will not fail, I know it. You are stronger than Malim, my father told me that, and you will defeat him. But if it makes you feel better, I promise to care for your sister and your daughter and to take them away from Rendail. I will go with them, and protect them with my life."

This he said with such youthful confidence that Arghel was moved once again to smile.

"I am honoured," he said, clasping Rassim's hand. Then the two fell silent, gazing together into the embers of the fire.

It was late, past midnight. Rassim had fallen asleep where he sat and Arghel had not moved, his eyes still fixed on the dying glow, his mind alert for even the smallest sign from either Amarisse or Maylie. When it came he was almost unprepared for it. The message was no more than the softest whisper, first only words, the image crystallising more slowly. And the words were not his daughter's, but those she had overheard. The voice belonged to his mother. He sucked in his breath and sat upright, concentrating hard. With effort he could just make out the images, seen through Sherenne's eyes. The room was as he remembered it, the

317

colourful hangings that adorned the walls making it seem less like a prison, adding comfort to the sparse surroundings.

He caught sight of one picture in particular that hung above the fireplace, of a leaping white horse on a background of deep green. It had been his favourite as a small child, sitting before the fire, dreaming that he was on its back, riding away so fast that not even his father could catch him. He remembered Rendail coming to find him, seeing him engrossed in the picture. Without a word his father had torn it down and thrown it into the fire, then taken him by the hand and led him out while his mother looked on, helpless to interfere. He had been little more than four years old then. Yet in the vision the leaping horse was in its place, neither it nor his dream yet burned away.

He had no time to dwell on it, for Sherenne was speaking and his daughter was acting as the conduit through which the key to finding Malim was being given to him. He listened and learned what he needed to know. Then the communication stopped abruptly. Amarisse was afraid that Rendail would hear and could not risk a longer message. Digging deep and using all his skill he sent a brief signal back to her, no words, no vision, just the essence of his love for her, as powerful as he dared.

"Oh, Sherenne," he whispered softly into the dying light. "You knew what was to come. Perhaps even before the gift came to me, you knew. And you gave your life to bring me here, to end the life of another of your own children."

He became aware that Rassim was awake, and watching him.

"I understand now," Rassim said. "Your child was the only means by which you would find your brother. I will do as you ask. As soon as you are gone I will seek out your sister and your daughter and try to release them. I might even provide something of a diversion for Rendail and his servants."

He attempted a smile, but his face was full of apprehension. They both got up and Arghel embraced the boy. "wait until after moonrise," he said. "Then keep watch at the compound gates. If you have not heard from me by dawn, do

318

what you can for them." He didn't wait for a response, but stepped out into the corridor, closing the door behind him.

As Arghel entered the ground floor chamber of his father's house he felt Rendail's thought bear down on him with terrifying speed. He crossed quickly to the rear wall, trying to close his mind to the invisible eyes that were on him and began to search the stones for gaps or flaws – anything that might reveal a hidden catch or opening behind. He had examined about half of the stonework when suddenly he felt the pressure lift. He was no longer being watched. He took no time to ponder on it, but continued his rapid, yet painstaking investigation, pressing lightly on each stone, his ear to the wall listening for any audible cue. Suddenly, he felt a slab give under his hand, and sprang back just in time to see an opening appear, some four feet high by two feet wide, formed by two large slabs that moved inwards without a sound.

Cautiously he went forward and found himself at the head of a steep, low spiralling stairway. He started down, descending in a series of narrow circles that seemed to plunge down into the centre of the earth. There was no light and no way of knowing how far down the staircase went, so he felt his way slowly and carefully, one hand firm against the side wall. After what seemed like minutes he saw a light far below. The stairs ceased to spiral and went down straight, but steep. The light grew brighter until finally he found himself in an arched entrance opening onto to a great circular chamber, well lit by torches placed in tall iron sconces around the walls.

He stopped in the archway and took in the detail of the room. There were three large fireplaces, all lit and burning. Around the circumference there were more arches similar to the one in which he stood. He counted at least four, darkness behind them. In the centre lay a great stone slab at least four feet high with a broad, flat surface covered in skins and furs – Malim's resting place, he supposed. But of Malim there was no sign. Warily he took a pace into the chamber, alert for any change in the atmosphere, however slight. The only thing that came back to him was the echo of his footsteps.

He stepped up to the stone slab. The furs were heaped to one side as though recently tossed there, and in places the pile was flattened. Someone had lain on them. He reached out to touch them and as he did so he felt the air begin to thicken. Malim's presence was all around him like a great weight, becoming heavier with every passing second. There was no sense of weakness, disorientation. Malim was in possession of his full strength. How long he had been back in his own time there was no way to tell, but it was clearly long enough. Arghel's heart sank. Whether or not the return had been an involuntary one was immaterial – he had lost an important advantage. At least, he thought, there was no hint of his father's presence anywhere, not since the brief scan in the upper chamber.

He had no time for puzzlement, as the tension in the room gathered itself like a giant intake of breath. Stillness hung in the air for several heartbeats, then, with a great rush, Malim's force bore down on him like a tidal wave. The impact knocked him off his feet, but the few seconds warning had been enough and he was able to shield himself against the attack. Grabbing the corner of the slab he pulled himself upright, winded and momentarily disoriented, but otherwise unhurt. He heard laughter behind him and turned to see Malim leaning against an arch, his lip curled in a satisfied sneer.

"Welcome, Brother," he said. "I do believe you have grown a little since we last met. Not a great deal it is true, since you were always destined to be the runt of the litter. I really can't imagine why our father didn't have you drowned at birth. I suppose, if nothing else, you provide a good example of the disastrous effects of impurity in the blood. I see that at least," he gestured casually towards Arghel's flattened curls, "you have had the decency to hide the evidence of our mother's tainted ancestry."

Arghel said nothing, his face impassive, and watched as Malim straightened up and took a pace towards him. Of the two, Malim was the taller by a hand's span, his build slightly broader, his features less delicate, less refined than those of his younger brother.

"You are surprised to see me." Malim cocked his head to one side, his eyes intent on Arghel's face, watching for any change in expression. "I am pleased to say that your former mate and her accomplices were most forthcoming as to the nature of your plans. So, I was able to inform our father of your impending arrival, so that he could provide a suitable welcome for our sister and, of course, for that detestable insult to our family that you had the effrontery to sire. He has plans for her, you know. I wanted her, but he refused me. But then, he is no longer young and I can wait." He smiled sweetly and added, "At least he had the good sense to relieve the creature of those abominable curls, or so I hear."

Arghel still did not move and made no sign. He simply stared back at Malim, his eyes blank, his face still. Malim, on the other hand, was having difficulty hiding his frustration at his brother's lack of response. The smile faded and Arghel felt the irritation start to turn into a smouldering anger, ready to ignite at the slightest provocation. At any moment Malim would lose his composure, give in to his ungovernable passion and that, Arghel knew, might be his only chance.

Malim's voice dropped a little, real satisfaction in it now.

"As for your mate, I must thank you for the great pleasure she gave me in the short time that we were together. It is a pity she was not of stronger blood, for in the end I believe my attentions were too much for her. When I last saw her she was no longer in a position to send you her good wishes, and so I feel obliged to do so in her place."

The image that Malim gave him filled Arghel's mind with an irresistible fury and his heart with an unendurable grief. But he did not falter, his expression as still as a mill pond as he stared his brother down. It was finally too much for Malim. His rage and frustration broke like a storm, and he lunged at Arghel, his eyes on fire with pure hatred. But Arghel was ready and was quicker, more agile. He sidestepped, flung his whole weight on Malim from behind sending him crashing into the stone slab. Malim's head struck the corner of the stone and he folded to the ground, blood streaming from his forehead. But he was only dazed for a second, and before Arghel could move in on him he was back on his feet, crouched to spring, his eyes alert for any unwise movement.

Arghel moved back and readied himself for a second attack. He felt Malim's gift stretching out towards him like a finger of fire and prepared to repel it but realised, too late, that he had not been the target. Malim had loosened a great stone from the roof and it plummeted down on top of him. He sprang away, but not fast enough and the stone fell with all its weight onto his left leg, pinning him to the ground. His defence had been enough to stop the bones from breaking, but he could not move the stone. He watched, helpless, as Malim got to his feet, wiping the blood out of his eyes. Going to the wall, Malim took one of the flaming torches in both hands and ripped it out of its cone shaped sconce, which came loose from its bolts and clattered to the ground. All the while, Malim's thought was on Arghel, a venomous stream designed to leech Arghel's strength. Using his own mind, Arghel pushed Malim back, but he knew that as long as he was pinned down it was only a matter of time before his strength was drained. Malim had the greater endurance. He simply had to stand and wait.

For an interminable time the standoff continued, but finally Arghel felt exhaustion take over and saw Malim start towards him, a look of triumph spreading slowly across his face. Defeat was inevitable now, so he withdrew what remained of the shield that protected him and, directing his thought as guardedly as he could, called out with his mind, "Rassim, take care of Amarisse." Then he looked up and saw his brother standing over him. Malim was breathing heavily, his mouth forming the familiar contemptuous sneer.

"As I said, little brother – you have always been the runt of the litter. At last Rendail has seen fit not to interfere and I am free to rid this Family of the taint of your blood."

Arghel said nothing, but met his brother's eyes as Malim took up the flaming torch and prepared to bring it down into his face. But at that moment there came a shrill scream and a figure leaped in from the entrance archway. Arghel saw the figure stoop, take something from the ground, then rush at Malim with a terrifying shriek. Malim, taken by surprise, wheeled round and swung the torch in the direction of the intruder, but at the wrong height. The figure dived under his outstretched arms, nimble as a goat, and with a cry drove the point of the iron sconce up under his ribs, burying half its length into Malim's chest. He was dead before he fell. The point had gone straight through the heart and his body crashed to the ground, the sightless eyes seeming to reflect an attitude of complete astonishment. He had not even had time to make a sound. A second later the figure was on Arghel, kissing him, stroking his face, weeping, asking, "Are you hurt? Speak to me, Arghel, say something!"

"Maylie," he whispered, managing to put an arm round her, kiss her face. He heard her sigh with relief. She got up and tried to move the stone that trapped his leg, but it was heavy, and even together they couldn't move it. After several efforts she went to one of the fireplaces, which were stacked with logs. After a search she found one the right width and length. Using it as a fulcrum she was finally able to lift the stone just a fraction, enough for him to roll out from beneath it. The leg was badly bruised and bleeding, but nothing was broken. He managed to get to his feet and the two of them stood for a moment, locked in a tight embrace. He glanced back once at Malim's body, then turned to the archway leading up out of the chamber.

"Amarisse," he said. "I must go to her."

Maylie nodded. "Rassim has gone to find her. He came and let me out, then said he was going to find Amarisse. But he thinks Rendail may be with her. If that is true it is too dangerous for you to go to her now."

He simply looked at her and said, "I will go. Now."

Knowing it was useless to argue, she put his arm round her shoulder and they set off towards the steps. As they began to climb Arghel heard Rassim, his thought urgent.

"Come quickly!"

He gritted his teeth and, with Maylie's help, started up the stairway.

After what seemed an age they emerged once more into the upper chamber. As he walked, Arghel removed the ties from his hair and shook out his curls. Then, from a pocket he took the silver clasp and fastened it in place. They continued on, out of the chamber and onto the square. No one hindered them. As they rounded the corner onto the east pavement they could see Rassim, standing at the iron gate of the central compound. When he saw Arghel, Rassim began to run. Arghel could feel his agitation, the confusion spilling out from him in a jumble of chaotic thoughts.

Rassim reached the pair, out of breath, and immediately took over from Maylie as Arghel's support. There was near panic in his eyes.

"You must hurry," he said quickly between his gasps for breath. "There is not much time. I have done all I can but I have not the skill. Amarisse will let no one near him. She says he asked for you, and only you. She says he felt Malim's death – we all did – and then he commanded everyone to wait until you came."

"Amarisse?" Arghel stopped and looked at Rassim, his face filled with concern.

"Unhurt," replied Rassim. "But behaving strangely. She says she will not move until you come and won't let me touch her. I fear for her, Arghel. Perhaps, when she sees you, she will calm herself. But you must hurry."

They set off, Arghel leaning on Rassim, Maylie on his other side. Everyone they passed stepped aside to let them through, and finally they reached the gate. For a moment Arghel stopped, staring at the open door, then, taking a deep breath, walked through the courtyard and across the threshold of the room in which he had been born.

The moment Amarisse saw him she leapt to her feet with a squeal and raced into his waiting arms. He clutched her fiercely to him as she wrapped her arms around his neck, crying, babbling. He tried to hush her and, looking past her, his eyes rested on the figure of Rendail. His father was slumped against the wall, the snake's head dagger still buried deep in his side. The face was peaceful, like one asleep, but pale, the thread of life barely discernable and becoming weaker with every passing second. Arghel stared, unbelieving, his eyes taking in the scene, his mind refusing to acknowledge it. Suddenly he became aware of his daughter's words, only just intelligible through her tears.

"Help him, Father. You must help him!"

"Hush," he replied soothingly. "No one can help now. It's over, Amarisse. He is gone."

"No!" His words caused her to become even more agitated. "No, Father. You must help him. You can save him. You must – you have to." She was screaming in his ear. "Please, you have to. He can't die. He must not die."

He set her back from him and looked at her. She was dirty, covered in Rendail's blood, her eyes bright and frantic, almost feverish. She was exhausted from crying. When she met his eye she seemed to calm a little and he stroked her face and head gently. Her breathing quieted and she fell silent, looking expectantly up into his face.

"You can't ask me to do this," he said, his eyes imploring her. "I will not do it. You don't know what you are asking. In a few moments, the threat to us all will be ended. What is done is done. I cannot change it."

"No, Father!" She started to cry again, grabbing on to him, trying to shake him as if to make him understand. "You are wrong. You have to help him. Now, before it is too late!" She was once again overcome by her distress and buried her head in his shirt, her fists beating feebly on his chest.

"Maylie," he said, turning to his sister. "Take her away from here. Take Rassim with you. Go to his house and wait there until I come."

Maylie silently took Amarisse in her arms and led her away. He heard Rassim follow them out across the courtyard and onto the pavement. He waited until their footsteps had faded, his eyes never leaving Rendail. There was not much time now – perhaps only minutes. He could feel his father's strength failing with every heartbeat, and for at least a minute stood transfixed, unable to move or look away. Then, as if against his will, he lowered himself beside the body and slowly, with great care removed the knife and began to work. When he had finished he sat back, beyond weariness. With a sigh he buried his head in his hands and whispered, "Why?"

CHAPTER 33

The fuss was all but over. Five days after the event the various official bodies finally packed up and went away, taking their cameras and plastic bags full of trophies with them. The cellar was still cordoned off with lengths of tape. It was watched over by a solitary uniformed constable, whose task it was to ward off the remaining trickle of media representatives, still turning up on the off chance of an exclusive photograph of the crime scene or an impromptu interview with one of the residents of the house.

Everyone was considerate, sympathetic, almost apologetic. The police interviews were conducted quickly on the first day, and after that great pains were taken not to further disturb the household, the officers almost tiptoeing round the house, their voices hushed, deferential. It was concluded early on that Old Jim's heart attack had most likely been caused by threatening behaviour on the part of the intruder while trying to gain access to the house. The rest was as Inspector Taylor anticipated and, in his quiet way, encouraged, by pointing out a theory here, an explanation there.

Alex relied on him totally for the first two days and the policeman went out of his way to help keep the contact and questioning to a minimum, allowing Alex to remain largely undisturbed with his grief. The latter was grateful beyond expression for that, and found his liking for the Inspector developing into a deep affection. When Taylor finally left for home they exchanged private phone numbers and addresses, promising to keep in touch.

"I would be most relieved," Taylor said as he left, "to know that the young lady had got home safely. You will keep me informed of her progress. I trust." Alex promised he would and stayed at the front door gazing out towards the road long after the Inspector had driven away.

Alex sat alone now in the empty kitchen. Someone had lit a fire and he sat in front of it hugging a cup of cold coffee, lost in memory. There was a light rustle behind him and for a moment his heart leapt, but in the next instant he was back in the present, looking across at the vacant armchair by the hearth, the stacks of books still piled haphazardly all around it. He felt a hand on his shoulder, and without looking up reached out and patted it gently. Jenni drew up a chair beside him.

"You look as though you need a hug," she said, her voice quiet, uncharacteristically subdued. Without waiting for a reply she took the cup out of his hands and put her arms round him. He leaned against her for a while, then sighed and straightened up to look at her.

"I'm all right Jenni. Really. But it's good to have you here. I don't know what I would do without you. You even lit the fire. There should always be a fire in here, don't you think?"

She gave him a squeeze and kissed his cheek, then got up and went over to the counter to get more hot coffee from the filter machine. She poured them each a cup and they both moved to the table, sitting opposite each other. Apart from the policeman outside the front door they were alone in the house, and an eerie quiet had settled over the place, making the crackling of the fire seem overly loud.

At last, Jenni broke the silence. "I came down to give you some good news. Susan called. She says that Young Jim turned up on her doorstep last night. He was the one who took the car, you know. He left just before it all happened, and when Susan told him he was devastated of course. They are coming back tomorrow, and Grace, too. It will make things seem a bit more – well – normal, if you know what I mean."

Alex smiled and took her hand across the table.

"Yes, the place is very empty without them. I'm glad." He knew he sounded anything but glad, but appreciated her effort. "And I'm glad about Young Jim. I was worried about him. Although," he added sadly, "I suppose it's just 'Jim' now."

Jenni nodded. "I suppose it is. But perhaps not for too long. I haven't told you the best part. Jim said he went away because he needed to sort a few things out in his mind. And he came straight out and said he loved Susan and wanted to marry

328

her. She said she nearly fell over with shock. But guess what? She said yes. They asked me to talk to you because they wanted to know if they could have the wedding here. Not right away of course – they understand you might not want to think about things like that just yet, but they would like to do it quite soon, I think. And Susan said that as she doesn't have a father she wanted to ask you to give her away, but she was afraid to ask, things being as they are. I think it's wonderful news – it sort of gives you hope doesn't it, after everything?"

He looked at her and smiled, unable to prevent a glimmer of warmth from pushing its way into the chill of his grief.

"It is wonderful, Jenni. The best possible news. And I see no reason for them to wait. Call Susan would you, and tell her to come with Jim to see me as soon as they get back. We must arrange it properly, just as they would like. And of course I will give her away. I will be honoured. It's what Mary would have wanted, I'm sure. Life must go on and there is no better way than this." He paused, then asked quietly, "And you, Jenni? What about you? Paul will be back in a few days. He loves you. You know that – he just hasn't realised it yet. You should talk to him."

Jenni blushed and said, laughing, "Alex! I mention a wedding and the next thing I know you want to marry us all off! Thank you for the advice, but I think I'll wait. After all, he will realise it eventually and I don't have any plans to go anywhere else just yet."

"Nevertheless," Alex responded, "It has been a difficult time for all of us. I think I might suggest that he take you away on the boat for a while. You could both do with a holiday."

"Stop scheming!" Jenni chided, still smiling. "Sometimes you really can be impossible. It's clear you're getting back to normal, so I think I'll go back to bed before you tell me any more of your grand designs."

She got up and left, giving him another hug and a kiss on the way, and he was left alone again. With a sigh, he sat back and stared at the flames through the open door of the range. There was one name Jenni hadn't mentioned. "David," he whispered. "Forgive me."

Karisse was recovering rapidly from her ordeal. The wounds on her wrists and head were now little more than rapidly fading scars. The healing of the internal injuries was taking more time but she was eating well, becoming fitter with each passing day. She had learned from Alex that both he and Paul had waited, helpless, outside the house for two days and nights, hoping Malim would let down his guard. But it had been hopeless. She had been on the point of death when they finally reached her. It had taken Alex and Paul almost twelve hours working together to bring her back. Even now, Paul insisted on carefully checking her progress each day, helping to speed the recovery.

The second night after Malim's death she spent alone in a hotel. Paul stayed with her all evening, showing her how such establishments worked, how to use the telephone to ask for room service, and many other small things that she knew about theoretically but had not had the opportunity to try for herself. Even in her own time she had never stayed away from either her own home or those of other Dancers, so the experience of exchanging money for bed and board was entirely new to her. When she awoke the next day she found herself alone, but with the help of his precise instructions managed to order breakfast on the telephone and have it brought to her in her room. Then she slept again.

At around lunchtime Paul returned and the pair left for Inverness, booking into rooms in one of the city's most prestigious hotels. What followed was one of the most extraordinary weeks of her life. No expense was spared. Paul took her to the very best restaurants, where the food bore no resemblance, either in appearance or taste, to anything she had ever encountered before. They went to department stores, Paul looking on as she gasped with delight at the rows of furs on one floor, kitchen utensils on another, children's toys in the huge basement.

The electronics department was particularly astounding. Paul made her put two tiny, round sponge covered balls in her ears, attached to little wires that plugged into a box so small she could hold it in the palm of her hand. Then, telling her not to be afraid, he pressed a button on the box. Despite his warning she screamed in terror as she heard, for the first time, a full symphony orchestra in the throes of the final movement of Beethoven's Ninth. Once the initial shock had passed, however, she was transported and left the store with the little box in her pocket, the earphones firmly in her ears.

They even went to the cinema, after which she emerged, blinking, into the evening light speechless with wonder. Even in the hotel there was no end to the marvels. The place had a large ballroom with live music in the evenings and Paul, a skilled dancer of the conventional type, taught her the basics of two or three classic dances, which, much to his appreciation, she picked up with ease. Finally, over breakfast one morning, he told her it was time to return to the house. Reading between the lines he was telling her that she was now strong enough to make the journey back to her own time.

Since Malim's death she had managed to keep the thoughts buried, but now that the time was close all her longing and dread came flooding back to her, a reminder that only half the battle had been won. If Arghel failed she might return to find her mate and daughter gone, and Malim resurrected in his own time, waiting. He saw the disquiet rising in her and took her hand.

"Arghel is strong," he said, "much stronger even than Alex. If anyone can confront Malim and win, he can. You must trust him. We have done what we set out to do and what happens now is out of our hands. He will do his part, I am sure of it."

She relaxed a little. He squeezed her shoulder and said, "Before we go back there is one more thing I would like to show you. It's a little out of the way, but I've spoken to Alex and he thinks it's a good idea. Another day or so will make little difference, and it will take that long for you to regain your full strength."

She nodded, and managed a smile. Three hours later, racing across the water, watching Paul set the sails from her safe position by the tiller, she began to believe that all things were possible, and that one day soon she would feel Arghel's arms around her, the part of his mind that was hers where it should be, in the space that had seemed so empty for so long.

* * *

Back at the house the atmosphere was lighter, beginning to fill with the familiar buzz of activity as people returned from their enforced absence. The only former resident missing was David, and no one seemed to have heard from him since the night before Malim's first visit. Alex said nothing, keeping his counsel, but it was plain that what he thought he did not wish to share. For most, the initial shock of the deaths of Mary and Old Jim had subsided, and there was an unspoken agreement to keep the kitchen as the centre of social contact. Mary, they all said, would not have wanted anything else.

Alex found himself comforted by their presence and buried his own sadness by becoming absorbed in helping Jim and Susan plan for their wedding, determined that it should signal a new beginning, for him and for everyone in the house. As if to confirm his new found optimism the newspaper headlines were already proclaiming that a man fitting the description of the dead intruder had also been wanted by the police in connection with the suspicious death of a mental health auxiliary just outside Bristol. Yet again, he sent his silent thanks for the fortuitous meeting with Inspector Taylor.

At first, he worried that Karisse might find returning to the house difficult, but within hours she had relaxed, and with her new found knowledge of modern life was able to contribute several suggestions for menus and music. Alex laughed with delight at her suggestion that the entire Berlin Philharmonic Orchestra come to play for the couple before the ceremony. Her collection of recordings had become immense, and she confessed to Paul that apart from Alex and himself the only thing she would really miss when she went home was the little player with its thunderous noise and tiny headphones.

332

She spent another week in the house before finally making the decision to leave. She was completely well now, and strong, and with each passing day her longing for Arghel and Amarisse grew until she could not put it off any longer. The thought still haunted her that they might not be there to welcome her home, and she silently confessed to herself that fear was the main reason for her delay. But for good or ill she had to know, so one night, after the household had retired, she resolved to wake Alex and Paul and go back to her own people.

As she passed the kitchen door she was drawn to go inside. It was high summer now, and the veranda doors had been left open. She walked through onto the veranda and found herself tracing a path down to the lake that took up a large part of the grounds to the rear of the house. She carried on to the edge of the water and sat down, watching the surface ripples catching reflections from the lights on the upper landings. She was startled by a noise and, looking up, saw the shadow of a figure coming towards her across the lawn. The figure was tall and graceful, long hair tied back in the familiar way, but she couldn't make out any detail in the darkness. Her heart pounding with dread, she opened her mouth to scream, but immediately a silent voice said, "Hush – no danger."

She stifled the cry and watched as the Dancer came towards her. He passed under the light from a window and she caught a glimpse of a face half familiar, fine delicate features and skin like honey, but hair the colour of bronze, falling down in loose curls behind the shoulders. She held her breath in fascination as the stranger came up and sat down beside her, stretching out his long legs towards the water's edge.

"You are well again, Grandmother," he said. "I am glad."

"Michael?"

"Yes. I should not have come, but I felt your concern. You are afraid to go back because you don't know what you will find. You don't need to be afraid. You have done all you can. You should go back now. Arghel will be waiting for you."

"I don't understand," she said. "Are you from a past time? If so, what time? And why do you call me 'Grandmother'? You

333

kept me alive, I remember. Alex said I was dreaming, that there were no other Dancers here. But I knew you weren't a dream, and that you came to me before the others. I owe you my life."

"I am from this time," he replied. "Alex and his son know nothing of us. There are many of us here, although for the most part we live alone or with our mates, and travel a great deal from one side of the world to the other. In this age we do not have cities or towns of our own, and those without the gift know little of us. It is better that way. We intervene in their affairs from time to time as Alex does, but the less they know of what we are the better for all concerned. That is the way of things now, and we are content. I am your grandson, the continuation of your line. I would have left things to run their course, but I had no choice. I could not let you die, and Alex was too far away to stop it, so I intervened. I had to go, before they came and saw me. The gift of silence in your line has grown stronger over the centuries, and we can hide ourselves easily, even from one as strong as Alex. Perhaps I should have let him persuade you that I was only a part of your imaginings, but I wanted to see you once more before you leave, to tell you not to fear your return."

He sighed and pulled his legs up under him, turning so that she could see him more clearly.

"You are the son of Amarisse?" Karisse asked, her eyes wide with wonder. She realised now why he had looked familiar. The shape of the face, the colour of the skin were all signs of Arghel's blood, but more than that, the unmistakeable curls made him without doubt one of Derlan's people.

"Oh, no," he answered, smiling. "I am Michael, son of Devren, son of Arghel. That is, Devren who was named after your grandfather."

"But I have no son," she said, confused. "My daughter is my only child."

"You have no son *yet*," he laughed. "Now do you see why you have no need to fear. I am here, am I not?"

At last his meaning became obvious and she laughed with him.

"And when am I to have this child, your father?"

"I believe he told me that you crossed the Great Emptiness and went back to those you loved. Less than a year later my father was born. He also told me to look out for your coming at around this time and to watch, to make sure all went as our history has it written. When you have gone I will stay. Sooner or later Alex must go back, although it will be some time yet. But when he is ready I will tell him of us and take his son to meet the Dancers of his own time. Then he will know that Paul won't be alone. Until then, it is best that we do not interfere. Now it is time for you to go. It has been an honour to meet you, Grandmother."

He got up and she followed. They embraced briefly and then he turned and walked away without another word. For a while she stood alone by the lake, her eyes wet with tears. Then she raced back across the lawn and in through the veranda door. She was finally ready to go home.

CHAPTER 34

The sunlight, streaming through the window and beating down on Arghel's face, caused him at last to open his eyes. His head was on something soft – a cushion, and someone had lain a blanket over him while he slept. He lay still on the stone floor, disoriented, struggling to get his bearings, remember where he was. There was a movement behind him and he twisted his head in the direction of the sound. Rendail was leaning against the fireplace watching him intently, still pale but clearly returning to his full strength. He had bathed, and changed out of the bloodstained clothes. He stood alert, composed, regarding his son with an air of curiosity.

The flood of memory rushed back to Arghel and with it utter dread. Tossing aside the blanket he sprang to his feet, so quickly that his head began to spin and he was forced to put out a hand to steady himself against the wall. Rendail made no move, but simply waited. Arghel closed his eyes and forced his breathing to slow. How long had he slept? Judging by the position of the sun, long enough. He heard his father speak in answer to his unspoken question.

"Your child is where you sent her. No one has interfered. She, also, has slept and is at this moment taking refreshment. She knows you are here. Communicate with her if you wish."

Arghel straightened, and turned slowly to look Rendail in the eye.

"There is no need," he said quietly. "If you say it is so, then it is so."

Rendail nodded and, coming forward, sat in the centre of the room, motioning for Arghel to do the same. Warily he complied, lowering himself just more than an arm's length away, noticing that his injured leg was now completely healed and free from pain.

"Forgive me," said Rendail. "I thought it my obligation to return the courtesy. I trust you have no objection." When Arghel said nothing he continued, "You surprise me. I can imagine no man with a greater desire to seek my death, and yet you gave me back my life. I was not at all certain that you would accede to your child's wish. However, I am relieved that you placed her desire above your hatred of me. The decision must have been a difficult one, considering the possible consequences of my recovery."

"It was difficult." Arghel's voice was as level, its tone as smooth as his father's. "And you are right. You owe your life to Amarisse and not to me. But for her, I would have let you drown in your own blood."

He paused, sensing no anger in Rendail's thought, only acknowledgement and perhaps, strangely, a touch of regret. The encounter had begun to take on the quality of a dream. In the bright sunlight the room seemed smaller than he remembered it. He found himself rising to his feet, walking its length, running his fingers along the smooth stone walls. His mind sketched the positions of the rugs, hangings and other small adornments with which his mother had skilfully transformed her barren prison into a home. He came to the fireplace and, lost in memory, could almost feel her presence, her scent all around him, the soft rustle of her clothes as she came to kneel beside him on the warm hearth. But then came the fear and, with a shudder, he came awake to see that Rendail had also risen and was standing quietly behind him, watching.

For a brief second his childhood helplessness threatened to overcome him, but he forced his mind to be still and, once more meeting Rendail's eye, continued, "But perhaps I am wrong, Father, and simply found myself without the courage to do nothing, as I should have done. Neither could I match my brother's strength. It was left to your daughter to rob you of your successor. It was she who ended Malim's life, not me."

On hearing this Rendail's eyes widened slightly and then, to Arghel's complete confusion, he began to laugh. It took him a full minute to recover himself, then with a sigh he shook his head and said sadly, "Poor Malim. He always had some difficulty with women. I don't think he ever truly recognised their value. Don't you think it a cruel irony that he was twice dispatched by the creatures he most despised? But then, his capacity to reason was never among his greatest strengths."

Arghel found himself speechless, his face reflecting his incomprehension. His father paced to the window and stood for a moment looking out over the courtyard. When he turned all trace of amusement was gone and he said softly, "Brave little Arghel. Didn't tell you, long ago, that you were worth a hundred of his kind? It was not lack of courage that prevented you from allowing me to bleed to death. It was your reason – that, and your trust in your child. Malim would not have done so. Neither would he ever have succeeded me, and in his heart he knew it. He was a tainted creature, unfit to lead this Family anywhere except to its destruction. Just as some of our children are born with twisted limbs, he came into the world with his mind deformed. He was like a lesser animal, controlled entirely by his passions – cunning, yes, and with a powerful gift, but with the mind of a beast nonetheless. The only thing he ever feared was my anger, but even so he would try to defy me if his rage grew great enough. Even if those reasons were not enough, there were others."

Rendail paused and sat down again, leaning his back against the wall.

"Forgive me. The wound is not yet entirely healed and I am a little weary."

Arghel remained standing, staring at his father in disbelief. Finally he found the words and said, his voice trembling with anger, "You knew all this and you let him live? You, whose only ambition it has been to further the purity of the blood? If you knew his blood was defiled, why did you not destroy him as you have destroyed so many others for much lesser faults than his? You call him a beast, a creature of twisted mind, having no power to reason. What of your reason, Father? Was it your reason that caused you to beat my mother, to force her to lie with you, so that she lived in fear of your footstep for all the time I remember? What reason did you have to hurt my daughter unless it was for your own pleasure? Are those not the actions of a lesser animal? I don't know what you said to her that caused her to forgive you, but for my part, I would still kill you for what you did to her and to my mother."

"But not for what I did to you?" Rendail's voice was little more than a whisper. "Don't let your temper get the better of you, Arghel. I admit I was a little harsh with your child, but I did her no real harm. In fact, I think she avenged herself upon me quite adequately – don't you agree? She is an extraordinary child my son, and one quite worthy of her sire. As for what I said to her, she simply asked me the question that has always been in your mind. I answered her, and in time she may pass the answer on to you. Concerning your mother, what passed between us is for us alone. But I will tell you that I never took her by force, not from the day she was given to me until she died. You may accept the truth of it or not, as you wish. Now, will you sit? It tires me to be constantly looking up."

He sighed as though trying to explain something to a petulant child. Arghel reluctantly sank back down onto the stone floor, controlling his anger with an effort.

"These things are unimportant," Rendail continued, once Arghel was seated. "You ask why I did not destroy Malim? The answer is a simple one. It was too dangerous. As soon as his gift became known my hands were tied. There are those here whose only ambition is to take control of time, to use it to further their own blood, shape the path of the future. They are every bit as mad as your brother was, and if they are ever given power, they could destroy us all. You think I am a monster, that I have absolute power? It is true, but only for as long as I maintain the Rule. If I am seen to go against it, they will use the Rule against me and, strong as I am, I am not strong enough to oppose them all. No, I could not kill Malim without risking a bloodbath – one that might destroy not only the Family, but signal chaos in the wider world. For that danger to be averted, I needed you.

"There is something else you should know. Malim was able to cross vast distances at will, and saw many things. Unfortunately, as a result, he also learned that what he craved most he would never have – my position and my power. That discovery began the chain of events that has led us here. He put himself out of my reach, thinking to create his own empire in the far future. Against my will he lured your mate there, the only living female with the power to cross the Great Emptiness. Always, he coveted Karisse, not for her gift, but simply because she was yours, and I refused him. His envy of you overwhelmed him. From the moment you were born he was consumed by it. He even sought to kill his own mother to prevent your conception. But that is of no importance now.

"I watched and waited, and finally learned of Alex, and of your plan, when Malim drew it from the mind of Paul, Alex's child. That is how I was ready when you came. I felt Malim's mind return to his body and knew that he had been forced there. Shortly after, I saw you searching for the way to his hiding place. I would have come to your aid, but was prevented by your child, who believed it was my intention to do you harm. In the event, help came from another, most unexpected source, and the outcome, thankfully, was as I hoped. At least, almost as I hoped. Malim should not have taken what was yours. Her gift was beyond price, and she would have provided you with young of great power, even greater, perhaps, than that which your daughter possesses."

"Karisse is dead then." Arghel felt the deadening grief rising in him, mingling with his simmering anger, and fought to keep it away.

"I have seen only what you have seen," Rendail replied quietly, "the vision that Malim gave you. Whatever the truth of it, that is what he believed."

There was a silence, in which Arghel struggled to understand his father's words. He could feel the emptiness that had been Karisse, seeming to swallow him up so that even his vision was becoming dulled. Rendail looked away as though extending a courtesy, allowing a moment for his son to recover himself.

Finally, Arghel pulled himself away from the spiralling numbness and asked, his voice unsteady, "What was it that

Malim learned that made him so certain he would not take your power? Surely in the end he could have seized it after your death? He was strong enough, and none could have prevented it."

"Again," Rendail replied, turning his gaze back on Arghel, "the answer is simple. He learned that he would not survive me. And not through any misfortune other than the nature of the gift. It is a strange thing, the working of the blood. In each the gift is different, even in those of the same line. All of my offspring inherited my strength. It was for the power of my thought that my father chose me to succeed him. Malim took from Amala the gift to cross the Great Emptiness, but he had no gift of memory, neither could he silence his mind as can you and your sister. It may interest you to know that while I do not have that skill, I could always reach through the veil a little way. That is how I knew of Maylie and how her mother took and hid her. It was an admirable act and I let it pass, knowing I could retrieve the child if I so wished. Meanwhile, your mother was content. I was angry, yes, and I beat her. I will not ask you to believe how much I regretted my weakness. That you also had the silent gift was not a secret from me.

"But there was one part of my gift of which I was not aware until Malim went into the Great Emptiness and discovered it. That the potency of the gift extends the span of life is well known. Malim's natural life might have reached four hundred years. However, what the gift has given to me is a life of unnatural length. Had he lived his entire span, he would never have outlived me."

Rendail paused, studying his son closely, as if considering how to proceed. Arghel avoided the gaze, tried to look as though he were not listening. All at once Rendail seemed to make up his mind and continued, "Malim came across this truth before you were born. And before you were born he knew I would have a second son, and that this son would inherit the same gift from me. That was the seed of his hatred of you and his consuming envy. Your life will far exceed mine, Arghel, and from the beginning it was clear that you would be my heir, and not Malim."

For a long while Arghel made no response, but continued to stare at the stone floor as though he had heard nothing. Then, without looking up, he spoke.

"Malim I can understand," he said slowly, as though speech was a great effort. "You are right, Father. It is indeed a cruel irony, that he should think himself robbed of all he desired by one who never wanted it. But you, Father? What planted the seed of your hatred of me? You refused me your love. You denied to me all that you gave to Malim, and yet now you say I am your heir, that it was always in your mind that I would succeed you. Do you truly believe I will accept this? That I will continue this horror that you have perpetuated in my Grandfather's name? If so, it is you who have lost your reason and not my brother."

Rendail gave a quiet laugh. "Oh, yes," he said. "You will accept it. You are thinking with your heart, my son, and not with your head. I have long yet to live, but when I am gone all choices will be yours. I have commanded it and all here have acknowledged it. Will you not choose to come back, to throw open all the locked doors of this place and set your people free? Will you not raze the entire compound to the ground and tear the settlement apart stone by stone? Any who oppose you, you will destroy, and so remove the threat that is posed to all our kind by those who, like Malim, would rid the world of all but their own unfit blood. When the time comes your strength will be greater than mine, as your power will continue to increase with your age. If all those with Malim's lust for power were set free now, even you and I together could not destroy them all. The threat would remain. As it is, all I can do for the present is contain it.

"The ambitions of Corvan, my father, were admirable, but they were flawed. The purity of the blood leads to great power, it is true, but also to great disaster, something he did not take into account. Already, after only three or so generations, more than half our children are so deformed they do not survive. Of those who do the coming of the gift in the males leads too often to the same madness and lack of reason that afflicted Malim. If this

342

isolation continues, all that has been gained will be lost, the Family will destroy itself, and perhaps all of our kind with it.

"No, Arghel. You will not refuse. In time you will return, and you will tear down all that I and my father made and so ensure the continuation of all of our kind, at least for a little while. As to your other question, you must ask it of your child. There is no answer I can give you that you will accept. You must take your child now, and your sister, and leave here. We may not meet again, and the next time you come to the place of your birth it will be as head of this Family, and you will do what you were born to do."

Rendail got up and walked to the door. As he reached the threshold, he turned and said, "Take Rassim with you. He is in danger now. Not from me, but from others. He has no father and no mate to keep him here. You will need him in the years to come. And I ask a favour. Arvan is your friend. When you were a child he saved you from Malim's madness more times than I can count. If he ever comes back to you, I ask you, not for my sake but for yours, to treat him well."

So saying, he walked away, his soft footsteps fading across the courtyard and out onto the pavement beyond. Arghel did not look up. For a long time he remained, his eyes fixed blankly on the floor. Finally he rose and, with a last long look at the room that had once been his home, he went out into the sunlit courtyard and made his way along the pavement to Rassim's house.

CHAPTER 35

Thalis fancied he heard Karim's teeth grinding as they stood at Karim's window, watching the small party make its way down the path from the south gate arch. It was something he could not have foreseen in his worst nightmares.

"Why?" he whispered, half to himself.

He heard Karim grunt. "If you mean, why didn't the traitor just let him die, I'm asking myself the same question." In a sudden movement, Karim brought his fist down on the stone sill with enough force to take the skin off his knuckles, making Thalis jump. "I swear our leader was born covered in grease," he muttered, with feeling. "Rendail should never have survived his father's rule. Now he slides away from death yet again and there is absolutely nothing we can do about it, Thalis. Nothing!"

Karim spat out of the window onto the pavement cobbles, a habit Thalis had always found disgusting. He was so stunned by the by the horror still unfolding before him, however, that he hardly noticed.

"The traitor has murdered the heir," he murmured, still disbelieving, "and Rendail has let him go. And the women – they are both of the blood, and guilty of the worst crime that exists under the Rule. Even if they had not conspired against the head of the Family, to allow such valuable breeding stock to simply walk out of here is an outrage. The heir is dead, and Rendail has gone against the Rule. Surely it is time to move against him?"

"The heir is dead, long live the heir!" Karim snapped. "It is a wonder you still have your head, Thalis. I can't imagine why Rendail hasn't removed it purely because he is tired of your stupidity! The fact that Malim was under our noses all the time, probably on an upper floor of Rendail's house, is proof enough of your idiocy! Rendail has not gone against the Rule, he has used it. The people are saying his actions are a fine demonstration of justice. Not everyone wished to see Malim inherit his father's title, despite his gift. Not only is the traitor Rendail's only remaining son, he is the carrier of that gift and he saved his father's life. A life for a life, that is the Rule. In this case, three lives – a favour from the head of the Family. He has the right to bestow such gifts as he chooses. As for Malim, it was a matter between brothers, a fight over blood. Arghel has simply proved his superior strength, or at least that is how it seems. How he did it escapes me, but the fact is, he succeeded. Now, he not only has his freedom, he has breeding stock as well."

Karim sighed at Thalis's still puzzled look. "Rendail has named Arghel heir. The entire Family is in agreement. No, Thalis, we cannot move against him now. If we did, enough of the settlement would rise against us to pose a danger to our success. The future is closed to us, for the present at least. We must wait, be patient. Our time will come, when Rendail dies and Arghel tries to take control. He has not lived inside these walls since he was a boy. He will soon find that leadership of the Family is no simple task. He will fail, and our time will come." He turned to Thalis with a thin smile. "Until that time, Thalis, you are Rendail's second advisor. I suggest you go and advise."

* * *

Arghel knew he could not put it off forever. The four travellers had been riding now for fourteen days, moving at a leisurely pace. There was no need now for haste and they made their way for the most part in subdued silence. That is, with exception of Rassim, who seemed to think it his duty to care for Amarisse, riding by her side, talking to her quietly all the while, telling her stories to keep her mind away from all that had happened and trying to make her smile. Arghel was thankful for his presence and his irrepressible humour which was the only thing, he thought, that kept his daughter from feeling his own grief and despair.

Maylie, riding beside him, reached out and took his hand.

"There is still hope," she said. "Malim's mind was full of deception. He may have lied both to his father and to you. He sought to weaken your resolve with a falsehood, that is all."

345

Arghel shook his head. "It was the truth. The vision he showed me came from his own memory. I would have known it otherwise. There can be no doubt, Maylie. You yourself have said that your own son's vision is clouded, that you cannot see beyond his grief. You don't even know if his child still lives. Amarisse has not seen her mother since she was a tiny creature Karisse carried in her arms. How do I tell her she will never see or touch Karisse again, except in memory. I can't. She is tired and her mind still bears the scars of Rendail's treatment of her. I will not burden her with this, not yet. When she is stronger, then I will tell her."

"As you wish," replied Maylie. "But she will find out for herself soon enough. She has only to look into your thoughts deeply enough and she will see. It is better that you talk to her, Arghel, before that happens. In less than a day we will be home and she will start to look for her mother, to wait and hope for her return. If it is a false hope it would be better for her if you didn't let it grow. Tell her, and let her share your grief. It is what she would wish."

The dusk was growing and the last evening meal of their journey was over. Maylie had gone to see to the horses. Rassim and Amarisse had wandered down to the nearby stream leaving Arghel sitting alone by the little fire. He sat gazing into the flames as though they might lend him the resolve that he needed. Finally he sat upright and, with a sigh, started to his feet, his mind made up. But as he got up he heard his daughter cry out, the sound piercing the growing peace of evening. For a moment he stood frozen with dread, then sensed that the cry had not been from fear. Nevertheless, he set off at a run in the direction of the noise. Ducking under the branches he ran through the trees to the edge of the clearing that led down to the stream.

At the sight that met his eyes he stopped short and, withdrawing a pace back into the shadow of the wood, looked on in amazement at the scene that played out before him. Rassim had tried to make Amarisse a little hat with which to cover her rapidly growing but still short, uneven locks. It was a crinkled, grotesque thing, displaying quite clearly his lack of skill at the craft of

346

weaving. As if to demonstrate its practical value Rassim had perched it on top of his own head. This had evidently caused the cry that Arghel had heard as Amarisse had shrieked in mock horror at the sight. Admittedly the effect was quite comical and as Arghel watched she tried to grab the hat back off Rassim's head. The procedure became quite a game as Rassim tried to prevent her, an easy thing given his height, and she jumped up, laughing as he dangled it just out of her reach. Finally he managed to catch her unawares and jam it down onto her head, which caused even more hilarity, making her laugh so much that she had to sit down.

Rassim flopped down beside her and, from his position leaning against a tree trunk a little way inside the wood, Arghel saw Rassim reach across, gently remove the hat and toss it aside. A silence fell in the clearing and Rassim put out a hand and stroked Amarisse's cheek tenderly. Then he pulled her to him and placed his lips on hers. Open mouthed, Arghel saw his daughter return the kiss and in consternation started towards them, but found a hand on his arm holding him back.

"Leave them," Maylie said quietly. "She makes her own choices now, remember? She will be safe with Rassim. You know, it is the first time I have seen her smile since the day we left for Rendail's house. Doesn't it do your heart good to see her?"

He let Maylie lead him away, back to the little camp fire.

"You are right," he said as they sat down together. "It gives me joy to see her happy. But I can't help but think it was not me that made her laugh. Perhaps she is so grown up she doesn't need a father any longer. I have lost Karisse and now I will lose our child, for if not to Rassim, there will be another. She will leave and go to another man's house and I will be forgotten."

"Arghel," said Maylie, smiling, "for one so wise you display the most extraordinary lack of understanding. How could she not need you? As for her joining, that is a long way in the future, but somehow I believe she has already made her choice, and that the effect will be rather the opposite of what you expect."

Arghel looked across at Maylie and, seeing her smile, kissed her cheek.

347

"In the matter of rearing daughters," he said ruefully, "I am truly in need of education. I have decided that what I have to say can wait a little longer, until we come to our own house. Until then she should have her happiness with Rassim, and I would not take it away from her."

After a short silence Maylie said, "You know we have a shadow?"

Arghel nodded. "Since we left home. He followed us here, and it seems he does not wish to leave us."

Maylie's eyes narrowed. "You knew about him? Why didn't you say anything? Who is he?"

Arghel gave a wry smile. "A man who saved my life many times, although I barely remember it. Do you know of Arvan, son of Orlim, Rendail's horse master?"

Maylie took in a breath. "Malim's keeper? What does he want with us? To avenge his master's death? Why do you allow him to follow us? There is enough danger from the wild beasts without the risk of being murdered as we sleep."

Arghel shook his head. "I don't think you need be concerned on that score. My father's last words to me were to request that I treat Arvan well – for my sake, he said, not his. I think Rendail cast him out knowing he would come to me. If anything, I would say Arvan is trying to be more a protector than a threat. He must realise I know of his presence. I think he is waiting for an invitation."

Maylie looked dubious. "So, what are you going to do?"

Arghel smiled again. "Invite him, I suppose."

* * *

It was early afternoon when they reached the top of the rise and saw the walls of the fortress rising dark on the horizon in front of them, just two hours or so away at a gentle pace. Amarisse rode in front, with Rassim, Maylie just behind. Arghel guarded the rear, keeping a close eye on the newcomer to the group. Arvan had said little since joining them. He had responded to Arghel's summons, falling to his knees in the clearing and bowing low, first to Arghel, then, to everyone's surprise, to Maylie. For a male of the Family to even acknowledge a woman's presence was almost unheard of. Arghel took the gesture as a sign of good faith. Maylie was less generous. Since then, Arvan had done his best to prove himself both useful and trustworthy, finding and carrying wood and water, bringing them small game. He rode now in silence, enduring both Arghel's watchfulness and Maylie's antagonism with calm acceptance. Amarisse and Rassim had both greeted Arvan with a warmth that had, at first, disturbed Arghel. Rassim was clearly an old friend. Amarisse behaved in a way that suggested she knew something her father did not. Arghel had learned, however, that there were depths to his daughter's gift he didn't fully understand and so, despite his wariness, he trusted her judgement and made Arvan as welcome as he felt able.

The group halted at the top of the rise, watching the sun arc down towards the distant towers. Amarisse rode to Arghel's side and leaned over to take his hand. Her eyes were shining with anticipation, so much that he could hardly look at her.

"We are almost home, Father," she said, her voice full of excitement. "And when we are there it can't be long before Mother comes home."

She squeezed his hand and without waiting for a reply started down the slope at a brisk trot, Rassim at her side. Maylie drew alongside him and said nothing, but brushed his arm, and together they followed the pair down into the wide valley that lay between them and the fortress.

They were close enough to see the faint outline of the gate when Amarisse suddenly reined in her horse and stopped dead, still as stone in the saddle. Rassim turned to Arghel, who had fallen a little way behind, his face clouding with apprehension. Immediately Arghel rode to his daughter's side. She sat upright, her eyes closed, her brow furrowed in concentration. He reached out to touch her, but without opening her eyes she put out an arm and pushed his hand away. Filled with apprehension he watched and waited.

After what seemed an age she took in her breath and her eyes snapped open. She turned to Arghel and whispered, her voice trembling with excitement, "Wait, Father. Listen."

He waited, trying to concentrate his mind on her, but could feel nothing. He opened his mouth to speak but she held up her hand.

"No, Father!" she hissed. "Wait!"

Then he felt it. Faint at first, just a trickle of warmth spreading slowly through his mind, almost imperceptible, but there and growing with each passing second until it became a flood, filling up the empty space in his thought like a bursting dam. He closed his eyes against the dizziness and clung to his saddle as though he might be washed away. When he opened them he saw the exhilaration on his daughter's face.

"I told you, Father!" she said, breathless with excitement. "I told you it would not be long. Mother has come back. Can you feel it, Father? She is here, waiting for you. You must go quickly. She is coming to the gate!"

Arghel nodded, speechless, put out a trembling hand and touched her arm. He felt rooted to the spot, unable to move.

Amarisse laughed. "Go, Father," she urged. "We will follow – just go!"

He looked at her once more and finally came to life. He turned, spurring his horse to a full gallop, and raced away like the wind towards the tiny figure that could be seen now, waiting at the gate.

* * *

For the hundredth time Karisse was trying to show him what a music player was, calling up the little snatches that she remembered of the symphonies and songs that came through the little earphones.

"It was like having a hundred Dancers in your head at once," she said, "and all the music coming through your ears but being right in your mind, just like the thoughts we give each other, only louder."

350

Again she tried to show him but it was no good – the music she was trying to convey was too complex and her memory wasn't accurate enough. Finally, when he wouldn't stop laughing, she gave up and snuggled into him, drinking in the warmth and the feel of him, the gentle rhythm of his thoughts. After a while he spoke softly, a hint of anxiety in his voice.

"Now that you are back, will you miss all those things? Cars and boats and – what was it – telephones, that let you hear people speak over greater distances than our minds can travel? It must be strange for you to be without them and have to make fire with sticks, and use candles for light. Life must be so much easier, so much better in the far future."

She raised her head to look at him and seeing the seriousness of his expression took his face in her hands and kissed him.

"Yes, in some ways it is easier," she replied, matching his gravity, "but in others it is so much more complicated. And it is lonely there, Arghel. There was not a moment I did not long for you in my thoughts. I felt so empty I thought I would die of it. There is nothing I would wish to have other than you and Amarisse – except …" She bit his ear playfully. "Except a music player, of course."

With a sudden movement he rolled over, tipping her off his chest onto her back. Propping himself up on one elbow he said, "Aside from your longing for a music player, there is one more very serious matter that we should discuss. What exactly was it that our grandson told you concerning the birth of his father?"

"If I remember correctly," she replied, "he said that I crossed the Great Emptiness, and less than a year later his father was born."

"In that case …" He struggled to retain a grave expression, "I think we should give some thought to the future of little Devren, as our instructions on the matter have been so precise."

"Thought?" Karisse furrowed her brow in puzzlement. "We have great gifts my love, but in this case I somehow think that thought will be insufficient to bring about the desired result. Have you no more practical suggestions?"

Later that evening, the matter of little Devren having been satisfactorily addressed, Arghel made his way to the north tower. It had been almost a full cycle of the moon since the joy of his reunion with Karisse had put out of his mind the events that led to his homecoming, and released him from the need to confront the consequences of his extraordinary meeting with his father. Now, sitting on the high tower looking out over the road that led to his former home, he felt the shadow once more bearing down on him, the pain of the old unanswered question made sharper by Rendail's refusal to give him the understanding he had so often vainly sought.

He heard light footsteps coming up the steep stairway and Amarisse came to sit beside him. Her pretty black curls were growing fast, already springing down over her ears, resisting any attempt to pin them up out of her eyes, so that she had developed her father's habit of idly and ineffectually brushing them away. He put his arms around her and she nestled comfortably into him, resting her head on his shoulder.

"The sadness is with you, Father," she said quietly, not questioning, her voice matter of fact. He said nothing, but held her closer, running his fingers through her new grown curls. "You shouldn't be sad," she went on. "Grandfather gave me a gift. He said if the sadness ever came I should come to you and show you what he gave me, so that you would understand and be content."

Arghel looked down into the clear emerald eyes that eagerly awaited his consent.

"Show me," he said.

The night had become damp and chill and the fires were burning low. The child still lay on the ground, deeply unconscious now, in the grip of a burning fever. The moisture streamed off his shaking body and his breathing came in fitful rasps as his lungs protested the chill in the air. Rendail wrapped the boy in a blanket, gently picked him up and carried him to a nearby barn, where he made a nest in the straw and carefully laid him down. First he checked the fever, sending him into a deep sleep. Then he ran his fingers along the livid burn Malim had inflicted with the poker, so that when the child woke the pain would be gone. He sat for a while watching, listening until the breathing became calm and regular, the body still. He reached out and stroked the curly head, then, on an impulse, he lifted the boy again and cradled him in his arms. Quietly, in the stillness of the night, he began to speak.

"Arghel, my beloved son." His voice was a whisper. "The words I say now, you may never hear. Aside from your mother you are the only thing in my life that I have ever truly loved. I could say but one word and you would come to me, stand beside me, be your father's son. But I will not. For you to know this would mean your death, and that is something I cannot allow. Your only chance of life is your hatred of me. Learn to hate, my son. Let your hatred carry you away from this place, away from your brother and those like him.

"I must place myself beyond your forgiveness, and I expect none, neither for what I have done, nor for what I will do. But know that each day of my life you will be avenged, for the wound I inflict upon myself will never heal, and the pain of it will be with me until I draw my last breath. You must live, as only you will have the strength to take my place and do what is right for this Family and for the blood. The price I pay for your life is almost beyond my endurance, but I pay it willingly for the sake of your future and mine.

"Perhaps, in the far future, when the threat from Malim and his kind is over and you have grown strong, we will talk. I will be forced once again to look on the hatred in your eyes. I will not profess my love for you then, because you will not believe it, but know that my heart will be filled with joy at the sight of you, and that your rejection of me will be my greatest suffering."

Rendail gathered the sleeping child to him and kissed him tenderly, then laid him down on the bed of straw, gathering the blanket round him so that he would not be cold. Without looking back he left the barn and walked away.

After the vision had faded Arghel sat silent, staring out over the high parapet like one in a dream, his chin resting lightly on Amarisse's head. For a long time he didn't move, then suddenly he drew his daughter to him and hugged her close. He could feel the tears spring into his eyes and could not hold them back. He clung to her and wept.

He heard her whisper in his ear, "Oh, Father, it is so wonderful!"

The statement was so startling that he found himself laughing through his tears.

"What is, my darling? What could be so wonderful?"

"That you are no longer too sad to cry," she said, and buried her head once more contentedly in his chest.

* * *

Detective Sergeant Michelle Wroughton slammed the front door and leaned wearily against it for a moment before reaching across and flicking the light switch, at the same time kicking off the wretched heels that had been pinching her feet since breakfast. It had been one hell of a day. The lads had insisted on a lunchtime party at the station local to celebrate her new found status and it had been a good turnout, swollen to excessive proportions by the presence of the recently retired Inspector Taylor, who had let it be known that he would be there to wish her good luck, and catch up with a few old mates.

He caught up with her towards the end of the party and they slipped off together to talk over old times. Naturally the subject of the Scottish trip, almost exactly a year ago to the day, came up, and they reminisced pleasantly in a quiet corner over half a pint of bitter and ham sandwiches. Taylor had heard once from Alex, in the form of an invitation to the wedding of Jim and Susan, but regrettably work had prevented his attendance. Since then he had lost touch and assumed that Alex had returned to wherever it was he had come from, leaving Paul in charge of the house. Wroughton privately admitted to feeling a little put out but said nothing. She asked Taylor to let her know if he ever received any news, and he in turn made her promise to keep in touch.

They parted, and it seemed as though a whole chapter of her life had suddenly come to an abrupt and unsatisfactory end. Life was moving on and she was moving up. Well, she thought, as the chief constable had told her several times that morning, she was a rising star in the force, on the fast track, and it wasn't as if there was nothing to occupy her mind or her time.

She pushed herself upright and made for the bedroom, starting to peel off the dreadful regulation pencil skirt on the way. By the time she reached the en suite shower she had divested herself of all but her underwear and with a final sigh of relief she turned on the shower and set the dial to hot. She had just stepped out, her hair dripping, and thrown on a towelling robe, when the doorbell rang.

"Bugger!" she muttered and, ignoring it, started to delve in the airing cupboard for a warm towel. It rang a second time and she said, under her breath, "I'm not in," but she had the distinct feeling that the caller wasn't going to be put off. For one thing she had flicked on all the lights, and whoever it was had probably seen her cross to the airing cupboard through the glass sections in the front door. Cursing again, she stomped to the front door, clicked the chain into place, opened it a fraction and peered out into the gathering gloom.

"My apologies," said Alex with a small bow, "if I have called at an inconvenient time…"

"Er…no – no, not at all. Please, come in." Wroughton unhooked the chain and opened the door, realising as she did so that she was naked except for the bathrobe and dripping water all over the carpet. Alex appeared not to notice and walked into the hall, a small paper bag in one hand, a bottle in the other.

"I felt," Alex continued, "that I owed you something of an apology. I was a little – shall we say indisposed, for a while, and didn't have the opportunity to thank you in person for all the help you gave us last year. So, as I was passing I have come to apologise, and to extend my gratitude once again. I hope you don't mind? If I am disturbing you …"

355

He looked her up and down, a tiny smile playing about his lips. Instinctively she clutched the neck of her robe, pulling it tighter, and managed an embarrassed smile.

"No – no you aren't disturbing me at all. It's very nice to see you. But you say you were just passing? Are you sure you didn't take a wrong turn somewhere? It's rather a long way from Sutherland isn't it?"

He laughed. "Well, actually, I confess. I went to visit my friend the Inspector and he just happened to give me your address. I was hoping you might have dinner with me. That is, if you would like to?"

She smiled nervously and gestured to her hair and the sodden bathrobe.

"I would love to," she said, "but as you see..." She paused, feeling herself starting to blush. "But I could make us something here – that is, if you would like. If you could just give me a minute to change ..."

"Oh, please don't trouble yourself." He cast an appraising eye over her. "I think you look just perfect as you are. And I rather hoped you might prefer an evening at home." He opened the bag and took out a small jar of caviar and a box of crackers. "What do you think?" he asked, and at the same moment she felt a little thrill run through her and gave an involuntary gasp. Holding her with his eyes he held up the bottle. "Strathisla," he said. "You never know what you will like until you try it."

Cast of Characters and exclusive extract from the third book in the series follow ...

Cast of Characters

The Family

Alex   Son of Maylie, grandson of Rendail, father unknown

Arghel   Second son of Rendail, known within the Family as 'The Traitor'

Amal   Son of Rolan, protector of Sherenne during her imprisonment within the Family

Amala   Rendail's elder sister, also his aunt. First of the Family to cross the barrier of time. Escaped to the tribe of Derlan before Rendail's birth

Arvan   Son of Orlim, servant and companion to Malim, known as 'Malim's Keeper'

Corvan   Founder of the Family and its first ruler

Estil   First son of Amal, co-conspirator with Karim and Thalis

Karim   Son of Selim, Rendail's cousin. Leader in the conspiracy to overthrow Rendail

Malim   First son of Rendail, heir to the leadership of the Family

Maylie   Daughter and eldest child of Rendail, believed to have died at birth

Nyran   Rendail's servant and principal bed partner

Orlim   Son of Ilvan, Rendail's brother, and Rendail's Horse Master. Disinherited following the execution of Ilvan early in Rendail's rule

Paul   Son of Alex and short lived mate, Mary. Great grandson of Rendail

Rassim   Second son of Amal, later the mate of Arghel's daughter

Rendail   Son of Corvan, 2nd ruler of the Family

Rolan	Rendail's elder brother, also his uncle. Assisted in the escape of Amala during the rule of Corvan
Sevrian	Rendail's first advisor and illegitimate son by Rysha, Ilvan's mate
Thalis	Son of Thorlan. Rendail's second advisor and great nephew, later Malim's servant. Conspirator against Rendail

Derlan's tribe

Alisse	Mate of Rolan
Derlan	Founder of Derlan's line. Rescued Amala following her escape from the Family
Devren	Son of Rolan, Karisse's grandfather
Feylan	Son of Devren, father of Karisse
Karisse	Daughter of Feylan. The first female since Amala to travel forward in time. Intended mate of Malim
Mirielle	Mate of Devren
Rolan	Son of Derlan and Amala, named after Amala's brother
Sherenne	Daughter of Devren, his first child. Taken by the Family in revenge for the escape of Amala. Mother of Maylie, Malim and Arghel
Vail	Karisse's uncle and close confidant of Arghel

The Short Lived

David	An Edinburgh street boy, taken in and raised by Alex. Works as a dance teacher with Paul
Gerald Flynn	Director of the Moordown psychiatric hospital, Somerset
Grace	Alex's bookkeeper
Jenni	Taken in by Alex as a child, works as Alex's receptionist
Mary	Alex's wife, Paul's mother

Old Jim   Alex's Gardener

Susan   Alex's Secretary

Sam Taylor   A Detective Inspector with the Somerset
                      police force

Michelle (Mickey) Wroughton A Detective Constable with the
                      Somerset Police Force

Young Jim   A street boy taken in by Alex. Works as Old
                      Jim's assistant

Exclusive extract from the third book in the series ...

MALIM'S LEGACY

CHAPTER 1

Lord Rendail sat motionless in the saddle, eyes fixed on the distant watchtowers silhouetted in the growing dusk. They reminded him of the fingers of a great hand, held up in warning to any who approached. He had not moved for more than an hour, and every so often his horse stamped restlessly, snorting in protest. His face betrayed neither impatience nor discomfort. He paid no heed to the coming dark, nor to the fine drizzle glistening on his skin, the rivulets of water running into his eyes.

The drizzle turned to heavy rain, but he made no attempt to seek shelter despite the fact that his cloak was stowed in his pack. He remained perfectly still, waiting, long dark hair plastered to his body as weed clings to the surface of a rock; the earth turning to mud under the horse's hooves.

When it came, the acknowledgement was brief and cold – less, even, than a word. But it was a sanction nonetheless, the equivalent, in thought, of a curt nod. Rendail responded by starting down the slope into the valley, moving without haste, keeping his mount to a steady trot.

It took a little under two hours to reach the gate, which had been opened to allow him passage into the fortress. He dismounted and walked through, the horse following him into a rough, cobbled yard. The gate swung closed. A groom, deliberately avoiding his eye, took the reins and led his mount away, leaving him standing alone on the steep path that led up to the inner wall. The rain had stopped, but water still cascaded down the path, turning it into a narrow torrent that spilled over the tops of his boots. Not that it mattered, as he was already soaked to the skin.

He followed the path to a stairway cut into the inner wall, running up some six feet to a gap wide enough to allow the passage of a man. On the other side, the path descended, continuing past a large number of dwellings both of wood and stone. It came to an end in front of a set of wide steps leading up to the entrance of the stone building that lay at the heart of the fortress. The doors stood open, and again he felt the wordless inner voice give its terse consent. He walked up the steps, and went inside.

The only source of light in the vast entrance hall came from two small torches on the wall above a great arched fireplace. They cast no more than a dim glow into the centre of the room, leaving the rest in almost total darkness. Rendail moved forward until he was standing in the light and waited, the water running off him and forming a large puddle around his feet. There was a scuffling somewhere in the shadows, off to his right, and he heard a suppressed giggle. He followed the sound with his eyes, but could see nothing in the gloom.

After another minute or so, the hidden observer's curiosity got the better of the desire for concealment and another rustle was followed by the sudden appearance of a boy, perhaps nine or ten years old, staring from beneath a tangle of black curls, a hand over his mouth in an attempt to stop himself from laughing.

The youngster mastered himself and, looking the guest up and down, declared loudly, "You're wet!"

Rendail allowed himself the faintest flicker of a smile, but said nothing.

"My father says you're dangerous," the boy went on. "But you don't look dangerous to me," and he continued to stare, full of curiosity, but despite his pronouncement stayed well out of reach.

Finally, Rendail spoke.

"Tell me," he said quietly, "what does someone who is dangerous look like?"

The boy's eyes narrowed as he pondered the question.

"I suppose you're right," he said. "My father says I shouldn't judge things by their appearance. But you do look very wet."

"What else does your father say, I wonder?" Rendail muttered, half to himself. Then, to the boy, "And did your father send you here simply to see what I look like? Or did he send you to greet me, in his place?"

The boy flushed a little and lowered his eyes.

"Ah." Rendail nodded, and again showed the faint hint of a smile. "Then I suggest that at this moment you are in more danger from your father than from me."

As he spoke, the atmosphere in the room grew tense, and at the sound of approaching footsteps the boy paled slightly. He scurried across to Rendail, who placed a protective arm about his shoulder, and together they awaited the arrival of the owner of the footsteps.

The newcomer strode into the room, stopping a few feet from them, and fixed the boy with a withering look. The child began to tremble, and Rendail squeezed his shoulder for reassurance.

"Come here, Devren," commanded the other, and Devren reluctantly obeyed, although Rendail noted a slight softening of the father's expression as the boy slipped under the waiting arm. He felt the attention shift back to him but said nothing, letting his eyes drift over his host in an unhurried appraisal. His first thought was that physically there was little difference between them. The man before him matched him in height and build. It was not always so, he reflected, his mind framing the picture of a young boy, a child no more than four years old, clutching fearfully to his mothers skirts, black eyes flashing hatred. The fear was still there, but buried now. Not so the hate.

He pulled a veil across the memories and continued his perusal of the man in front of him. To a casual eye they might have been brothers. Both had hair as black as their eyes. However, whereas his fell completely straight, almost to his waist, held back from his face by a small, carved wooden slide, the other's formed a mass of long unruly curls, most of which were trapped in place by a silver clasp.

At last Rendail sighed, and broke the silence.

"Your son," he inclined his head towards Devren, who pressed himself against his father, holding his breath, "has been a most delightful host. Please don't be angry with him. He has entertained me well while I waited for you." The boy exhaled, and shot him a grateful little smile. Rendail bowed in the boy's direction and continued, deliberately adopting the mode of speech reserved for formal exchanges among high ranking Family members. "Thank you, Devren, son of Arghel, for your welcome. I am honoured to be admitted to your father's house."

It was clear from his expression that the opening step in the ritual dance of courtesies was not lost on Arghel. He said nothing, however. Instead, he nodded to his son, who took a nervous pace forward and returned the bow, adding the correct response, "The honour is mine," then, after a pause and a glance backwards, "and my father's."

Arghel stroked the boy's head gently and whispered, "Go to your mother now, and wait with her until I come."

He waited until Devren's footsteps faded along the corridor before addressing his visitor for the first time, his tone distant, his voice even.

"You must realise, Lord Rendail, that you are not welcome here. May I remind you that you are a long way from your own house, and that your usual bullying tactics will be quite ineffective here. The reason must be pressing indeed, to force you from your stronghold – you have not dared to cross your border for more than two hundred years."

Rendail lowered his eyes. "Lord Rendail?" he murmured to himself. Then, looking up, he said aloud, "You still refuse to call me 'Father', then?"

When Arghel didn't respond, he sighed and went on, "As you rightly say, the reason is pressing, and as you have been watching my approach for some time, you also know that I have come alone. It should be quite clear to you by now that I would harm neither you nor your family. There is a threat, certainly, and a grave one, but it is not from me. Now," he gestured towards his sodden clothing, "I would prefer to be dry, and perhaps rested, before we discuss the matter fully. That is, if you are prepared to extend your hospitality as far as a fire and somewhere to sleep."

Arghel hesitated, then sent out a silent command, and a moment later a young man appeared at the doorway. The youth was one of the many short lived people who had their homes within the walls of the fortress, one without the 'gift', as it was known. Seeing the guest was another mind reader he gave Arghel a nervous glance. Arghel gave him a reassuring smile, then turned back to Rendail.

"I forbid you to use your gift in my house. You will communicate by speech, and speech alone. Neither will you influence anyone using thought. If you cannot submit to these conditions, leave now."

Rendail raised his shoulders in a slight shrug.

"As you say, it is your house. I give my word that unless directly threatened, I will influence no one, except through speech. This meeting is difficult enough as it is – for both of us. I have no more desire than you to make things any worse. Are you satisfied?"

Arghel's eyes narrowed, but he gave a curt nod. "Until morning, then," he said, and turning on his heel swept out, leaving the youth to lead Rendail away down the corridor.

* * *

The quiet hours before dawn seemed, to Arghel, to accentuate the uneasiness that hovered about the whole household. Even at this time of night the house was not normally so silent. It was as though the fortress itself was holding its breath, dreading what the presence of Rendail within its walls might mean. Karisse, his mate, slept fitfully in the next room, and he sat alone in the outer chamber, every so often reaching forward to throw another log onto the fire. His face was wholly devoid of expression, like one whose entire spirit rested in another place, another time. Nevertheless, a faint rustle behind him drew an immediate response.

"What is it, Devren?"

There was a patter of bare feet across the stones, and he held out his arm to accommodate the boy, who said nothing, but curled up against him, shivering with cold. His feet were half frozen.

"How long have you been waiting outside?" his father asked, reaching over for a blanket and wrapping it around the boy's shoulders.

"A long time, I think," Devren replied through chattering teeth. "I was afraid to come in. I thought you might send me away again."

Arghel admitted to himself that his fury at Devren's earlier disobedience had been a little disproportionate. He had forbidden the boy to leave the upper rooms, and had placed him in the care of Sasha, the ageing nurse. Naturally, Devren had sneaked away at the first opportunity, eager to see the cause of all the fuss, and so had found himself concealed in the entrance hall at the very moment of Rendail's arrival. Arghel had been unable to bring himself to thrash the boy. In the end, he had simply ordered that Devren spend the following day confined with Sasha, helping to wash blankets. At least, then, his son would be out of Rendail's way. He had also forcefully reiterated his original command – that Devren have no contact with the visitor whatever.

He pressed the boy close to him and said, "You know I would do no such thing. I am not angry with you any more. Tell me, what's the matter? Can't you sleep?"

Devren didn't answer straight away, but pursed his lips and stared thoughtfully into the fire for a while, before taking a breath and venturing, "I've never seen you look at anyone the way you looked at Grandfather. And I know Mother was upset. Her hands were shaking when she put me to bed. When I asked her about it, all she said was that I wasn't to call him 'Grandfather'. But he is my grandfather, so why can't I call him that?"

Arghel tensed, but was helpless to deny the boy's logic. He offered what he hoped was an adequate reply.

"Yes, he is your grandfather. But that doesn't give him the right to be a part of our family. I don't know why he is here, but I

366

will tell you that the sooner he leaves, the better. It is likely that when he goes, we won't ever see him again, and you are not to try to see him while he is here – do you understand?"

He looked down to see a resentful pair of eyes staring back up at him. Things, he thought, were not going to be that easy. Devren was too inquisitive to be put off without any explanation. He sighed, resigned to the fact that he would have no peace until he at least tried to satisfy the boy's curiosity.

"Rendail once did your mother's family a great deal of harm, and she holds him responsible for it. Also, he did other, terrible things, for which she will never forgive him. There are many things for which I can't forgive him either. One day, perhaps, when you know the whole story, you will be able to decide for yourself. But come." He hugged the boy again and smiled, hoping to ward off the inevitable questions. "At last you have met your grandfather. What do you think of him?"

Devren weighed his words for a moment, then said, "He was very kind to me. But he doesn't always tell the truth."

His answer took Arghel by surprise. "How was he kind to you, and when did he lie?"

Devren hesitated, then said nervously, "He told you that I greeted him well. I didn't. I laughed at him."

With an effort, Arghel suppressed a smile. "What else?"

"He is in great pain, Father, but he pretends he isn't. He hides it from you and the others. He forgot about me, but when he realised I felt it, he closed his mind to me. There was something strange, too, that I didn't understand."

"Go on – what was strange?"

"I can't explain. But sometimes his thoughts weren't connected to his words – at least not entirely. I am sorry I was rude to him. I shouldn't have laughed as I did."

"You shouldn't have been there at all," Arghel replied sternly, but at the same time drew the boy a little closer to him and stroked his head gently.

"Do I have to spend the whole day tomorrow with Sasha?" Devren asked, pouting.

"Of course – the whole day. How else will you learn not to disobey me?"

There was another pause, after which Devren said, a little sheepish, "I didn't tell you the truth either, Father."

"Oh?" Again, Arghel managed with difficulty not to smile. "It seems this is a night for confessions. Tell me then, what is so serious that you felt the need to lie to me?"

"I told you I hate to wash blankets."

"And you don't?"

"No. Washing blankets is one of my favourite things. Sasha lets me go into the water and jump on them. It's great fun."

"Thank you for telling me Devren. I will bear it in mind. Now, perhaps you should go to bed. Otherwise you might be too tired to enjoy your day."

"If I must – but will you tell me if anything important happens while I am asleep? I wouldn't want to miss anything."

"I promise." He kissed the boy's forehead. "Goodnight, Devren."

No sooner had Devren closed the door than he heard soft laughter, and Karisse came up behind him, folding her arms around his waist. He closed his eyes, feeling her nakedness as she nestled into his back, visualising the smooth, pale skin, the teasing look in her eye, the long, raven locks that tickled his neck as she leaned forward to kiss his cheek. He smiled, despite his mood, and tipped his head back to return the kiss.

"You are not firm enough with him," she said, still laughing. "He defeats you at every turn."

"I know." He sighed in despair, but could not help but finally break into laughter himself. "But he makes me smile, and it's so difficult to be angry when I am trying not to smile. I confess, my children leave me helpless, and I am a complete failure as a father."

"You are the most wonderful father," she replied, kissing him gently, "and I love you for it. But I am afraid for Devren. From the moment she was born, his sister had a wariness that Devren does not yet possess. He might have come to harm, alone with Rendail. I shudder to think of it, even though you say he was quite safe. You let him disobey you too often, and he has become too fearless and too fond of following his own inclinations."

Arghel sighed again, leaning back against her.

"Very well," he said with an air of resignation. "I promise that if he disobeys me again I will beat him, but only because you wish it, and I do not think it will have the slightest effect on his insatiable inquisitiveness."

They sat together in silence for a while, then Karisse said, "What does he want? He knows he is not welcome here, and yet he appears not to care. I want him gone, Arghel – out of this house and away from my children. Preferably by dusk tomorrow, even if he has to ride all the way back in the snow."

Arghel took her hand and pulled her round to face him. "Tomorrow," he said firmly. "As soon as it is light, we will find out what brings him here. Meanwhile, there is no point worrying about things we can do nothing about." He kissed her cheek, and then let his lips stray idly to her neck. "Until tomorrow," he whispered, "we will have to find another diversion that will help us both to sleep."

COMING SOON ...

BIOGRAPHY

Following first degrees in psychology and pure science, Jo went on to gain a PhD by research at the University of Bristol, specialising in behavioural psychology and brain physiology. She worked for seven years as a research associate/lecturer, working on the interaction of genetic and environmental factors. Jo has twenty research publications in academic journals from that period. She still lectures for the Open University, and works part time as a freelance educational consultant.

Jo was winner of the Daily Telegraph Travel writing award 2008, and has had short stories published in a number of national magazines, including Mslexia.

Her novels, *The Tyranny of the Blood* and *A Child of the Blood* were both finalists in the Arts Council supported YWO book of the year awards.

Jo went on to win an 'Apprenticeship in Fiction' award (www.adventuresinfiction.co.uk) supported by the Arts Council and a grant from the Oppenheimer John-Downes Memorial Trust.

Lightning Source UK Ltd.
Milton Keynes UK
03 December 2010

163792UK00001B/151/P